*Irresistible millionaires have chosen their
brides! They won't take 'No' for an answer*

# His Chosen Wife

Three exciting romances from
favourite authors

D1099200

# His Chosen Wife

ANNE McALLISTER

CHRISTINA HOLLIS

SUSANNE JAMES

MILLS & BOON

First published in Great Britain 2012
by Mills & Boon, an imprint of Harlequin (UK) Limited,
Eton House, 18-24 Paradise Road, Richmond, Surrey TW9 1SR

HIS CHOSEN WIFE © by Harlequin Enterprises II B.V./S.à.r.l 2012

*Antonides' Forbidden Wife*, *The Ruthless Italian's Inexperienced Wife* and *The Millionaire's Chosen Bride* were published in Great Britain by Harlequin (UK) Limited.

*Antonides' Forbidden Wife* © Anne McAllister 2008
*The Ruthless Italian's Inexperienced Wife* © Christina Hollis 2008
*The Millionaire's Chosen Bride* © Susanne James 2008

ISBN: 978 0 263 89709 8
ebook ISBN: 978 1 408 97078 2

05-1212

Printed and bound in Spain
by Blackprint CPI, Barcelona

# ANTONIDES'
# FORBIDDEN WIFE

BY
ANNE McALLISTER

Award-winning author **Anne McAllister** was once given a blueprint for happiness that included a nice, literate husband, a ramshackle Victorian house, a horde of mischievous children, a bunch of big, friendly dogs, and a life spent writing stories about tall, dark and handsome heroes. 'Where do I sign up?' she asked, and promptly did. Lots of years later, she's happy to report the blueprint was a success. She's always happy to share the latest news with readers at her website, www.annemcallister.com, and welcomes their letters there, or at PO Box 3904, Bozeman, Montana 59772, USA, (SASE appreciated).

# For Janet

# CHAPTER ONE

"Mrs. Antonides is here to see you."

PJ Antonides's head jerked up at the sound of his assistant, Rosie's, voice coming from the open doorway. He leaned his elbows on his desk and pinched the bridge of his nose in an attempt to hold off the headache that had been threatening all afternoon.

It had been a hellish day. Murphy's Law had been written expressly for days like this. It was only two in the afternoon, but as far as he could see, anything that could go wrong, already had.

As the head of Antonides Marine since his brother Elias had, literally and figuratively, jumped ship two years ago, PJ was no stranger to bad days. He'd stepped into the job willingly enough, could never complain that he hadn't known what he was getting into. He had known. And oddly he relished it.

But there were days—like today—when memories of his carefree years of Hawaiian sand and surf were all too appealing.

Mostly the good days outweighed the bad. For every disaster there was usually a bright spot. When something fell apart, something else worked out. Not today.

The supplier of sail fabric for his own design of windsurfers had rung this morning to regret that they couldn't fulfill the order. A Japanese hardware firm who had been trying to track down a missing shipment reported cheerfully that it had never left Yokohama. And his father, Aeolus, had called to say he was flying in from Athens tonight and bringing house guests for the week.

"Ari and Sophia Cristopolous—and their daughter, Constantina. More beautiful than ever. Single. Smart. She's dying to meet you. We are expecting you out at the house for the weekend."

Subtle, Aeolus was not. And he never stopped trying even though he knew—PJ had told him often enough!—that there was no point.

A trickle of perspiration slid down the back of PJ's neck.

Not that he wasn't sweating anyway. The air-conditioning in the building hadn't been working when they'd arrived this morning. The repairmen had left for lunch two hours ago and no one had seen them since. Everyone was sweltering in the July heat and humidity. The latest temp girl had gone home sick because she couldn't stand the heat. An hour ago, PJ's computer had stopped typing the letter *A*. Half an hour ago it had flat-out died. He was back to calculating requisitions with a pencil and paper.

The last thing he needed right now was a visit from his mother.

"Tell her I'm busy," he said gruffly. "Wait. Tell her I'm busy but that I'll be there Friday for dinner."

Agreeing ahead of time to the inevitable dinner invitation— even though it meant meeting Ari and Sophia and their beautiful daughter—was a surefire way to prevent Helena Antonides from demanding to see him this afternoon.

"I don't believe she asked," Rosie said doubtfully.

"She will. My mother always asks." In his thirty-two years on the planet, PJ couldn't remember a weekend that Helena Antonides hadn't demanded the presence of all of her children within a hundred miles. It was why he'd headed for Hawaii right after high school and hadn't come back until two years ago.

"This isn't your mother."

He blinked at Rosie. "Not—?" He brightened and took a deep relieved breath. "Oh, well, if it's Tallie—"

PJ had no problem with seeing his sister-in-law whenever she chose to drop in. His older brother Elias's wife was still on the governing board of Antonides Marine and, as far as PJ was concerned, she was always welcome. She had good ideas, and she didn't meddle.

She didn't have time. While she had once been a hardworking full-time CEO, now she was a hardworking full-time mother. She and Elias had year-and-a-half-old twins: Nicholas and Garrett.

PJ brightened further at the idea that she might have brought his nephews to visit. They were a handful and a half, but he was always delighted to see them. But, he reflected, he didn't hear the sound of anything breaking in the outer office, so he supposed she must have come alone.

No matter. He was always glad to have a visit from Tallie.

But Rosie was shaking her head. "Did you forget? Tallie and Elias and the boys are in Santorini."

Oh, hell, yes. He'd forgotten.

Good grief! Surely it wasn't his grandmother! *Yiayia* was ninety-three, for heaven's sake.

She was hale and hearty, but she didn't travel to Brooklyn on a momentary whim. On the contrary, since her ninetieth birthday, she had expected the world to come to her.

"Don't tell me *Yiayia* is out there," PJ muttered. But stranger things had happened. And she had been on his case recently.

"You're old," she'd said, shaking a disapproving finger at him last month when he'd seen her at his parents' house on Long Island.

"I'm not old," PJ had protested. "You're the one who's old!"

*Yiayia* had sniffed. "I already had my children. I want babies around. You will need to give me great-grandchildren."

"You have great-grandchildren," PJ told her firmly. "Four of them." Besides Elias's twins, there was Cristina's Alex and Martha's Edward. And Martha had another one on the way.

*Yiayia* had sniffed. "They are good," she admitted. "But I want handsome babies like yourself, Petros, *mou*. It's time."

PJ knew what she meant, but resolutely he had shaken his head. "Forget it, *Yiayia*. Not going to happen." Or the chances were a million to one that it would. "Forget it," he said again.

But he could tell from her narrowed gaze and pursed lips that his grandmother hadn't forgotten what he'd told her last year. And he began to regret sharing his plan with her. Surely she hadn't decided to bring the battle to Brooklyn.

"Not your grandmother," Rosie confirmed.

"I don't know any other Mrs. Antonideses," PJ told her irritably.

"That's interesting," Rosie said, looking at him speculatively, her dark eyes wide as her gaze flicked from him back through the open door toward the outer office beyond. "This one says that she's your wife."

"Mrs....Antonides?"

For an instant Ally didn't react to the name, just sat staring blindly at the magazine in her hand and tried to think of what she was going to say.

"Mrs. Antonides?" The voice was firmer, louder and made her jump.

She jerked up straight in the chair as she realized the secretary was speaking to her. "Sorry. I was just—" *praying this would go well* "—woolgathering," she said, raising her brows hopefully.

The secretary was impassive. "Mr. Antonides will see you now." But Ally thought she detected a hint of challenge in the woman's voice.

Ally wet her lips. "Thank you." She set down the magazine she hadn't read a word of, gave the other woman her best hard-won cool professional smile and headed toward the open door.

Six feet of hard lean whipcord male stood behind a broad teak desk waiting for her. And not just male—a man.

The man she'd married, all grown up.

Ally took a surreptitious, careful, steadying breath. Then she swallowed, shut the door and pasted on her most cheerful smile. "Hello, PJ."

Even though he was looking straight at her, his name on her lips seemed to startle him. He took a single step toward her, then stopped abruptly, instead shoving his hands into the pockets of navy dress-suit trousers. He dipped his head in acknowl-edgment. "Al." The nickname he'd always called her by. His voice was gruff.

"Alice," she corrected firmly. "Or Ally, I guess, if you prefer."

He didn't respond, left the ball in her court.

Right. So be it. "Bet you're surprised to see me," she added with all the brightness she could muster.

One brow lifted. "Well, let's just say, you didn't make the short list of any Mrs. Antonideses I might have been expect-ing." His tone was cool, edged with irony.

And while a part of Ally wanted to throw her arms around him, she knew better. And any hope she'd entertained that they might be able to go back to being pals was well on its way to a quick and permanent death.

"I shouldn't have done that," she apologized quickly. "Shouldn't have used your name, I mean. I don't ordinarily use your name."

"I didn't imagine you did." The edge again.

She let out a nervous breath. "I just…well, I didn't know how busy you were. President. CEO." She glanced back toward the main door where she'd seen a plaque with his name and title on it. "I thought you might not see me otherwise."

His brows lifted. "I'm not the pope. You don't need to request an audience."

"Well, I didn't know, did I?" she said with asperity, dislik-ing being put on the defensive. "This—" she waved her hand around his elegant office with its solid teak furnishings and vast view across the East River toward Manhattan's famous skyline "—is not exactly the 'you' I remember."

It might not have been the Vatican, but it wasn't a tiny studio apartment above Mrs. Chang's garage, either.

PJ shrugged. "It's been years, Al. Things change. You've changed. Grown up. Made a name for yourself, haven't you?"

There was challenge in his words, and they set Ally's teeth on edge, but she had to acknowledge the truth of them. "Yes."

And she made herself stand still under the long, assessing gaze that took a leisurely lingering stroll up from her toes to her head, even as it made her tingle with unwanted awareness.

"Very nice." A corner of his mouth quirked in a cool deliberate smile. "I've changed, too," he added, as if she needed it pointed out.

"You own a tie."

"Two of them."

"And a suit."

"For my sins."

"You've done well."

"I always did well, Al," he said easily, coming around the desk now, letting her feel the force of his presence at even closer hand, "even when I was a beach bum."

It was hard to imagine this man as a "beach bum," but she knew what he meant. When she had known Peter Antonides, he had never been about the fast track, never cared about wealth and ambition. He'd only cared about living life the way he wanted—a life on the beach, doing what interested him.

"Yes," she nodded. "I thought…I mean, I'm surprised you left it. It was what you liked. What you wanted."

But PJ shook his head and shoved a lock of hair off his forehead as he propped a hip against the corner of his desk. "What I wanted was the freedom to be me. To get away from everyone else's expectations but my own. I did on the beach. And I'm still free now. This is my choice. No one pushed me. I'm here because I want to be. And it doesn't define me." He paused, then fixed his gaze intently on her. "But I'm not the point. What about you? No, wait." He shoved away from the desk. "Sit down." He nodded to the armchairs by the window overlooking the East River. "I'll get Rosie to bring us some coffee. Or would you rather have iced tea?"

She hadn't come to sit down and be social. "I don't need anything," she said quickly. "I can't stay."

"After ten years? Well, five since I last saw you. But don't tell me you just 'dropped in'?" He arched a skeptical brow. "No, you didn't, Al. You came specifically to see me. You said so. Sit down." It wasn't an invitation this time. It was an order. He punched the intercom. "Rosie. Can we have some iced tea, please? Thanks."

Ally took a deep breath. He even sounded like a CEO. Brisk, no nonsense. In command. Of course he had always had those qualities, Ally realized. But he'd never been in charge of anyone but himself when she'd known him.

Reluctantly she sat. He was right, of course, she had come to see him. But she'd expected the visit to be perfunctory. And the fact that he was making it into something else—something social, something extended even by a few minutes—was undermining her plans.

It wasn't personal, she assured herself. At least not very. And PJ didn't care. She was sure about that. This was simply a hurdle to be jumped. One she should have jumped a long time ago.

She needed to do this, make her peace with PJ, put the past behind her. Move on.

And if doing so meant sitting down and conversing with him for a few minutes first, fine. She could do that.

It would be good for her, actually. It would prove to her that she was doing the right thing.

So she sat down, perched on the edge of one of the armchairs overlooking the East River and downtown Manhattan and tried to muster the easy casual charm she was known for.

But it was hard to be casual and polite and basically indifferent when all she really wanted to do was just feast her eyes on him.

PJ Antonides had always been drop-dead handsome in a rugged, windblown, seaswept sort of way. Not a man she'd ever imagined in a suit.

He hadn't even worn one to their wedding. Not that it had been a formal occasion. It had been five minutes in a courthouse office, paid fees, repeated vows, scrawled signatures, after which they'd come blinking out into the sunlight—married.

Now she looked at him and tried to find the carefree young man he'd been inside this older, harder, sharper version.

His lean face wasn't as tanned as she remembered, and the lines around his eyes were deeper. But those eyes were still the deep intense green of the jade dragon that had been her grandmother's favorite piece. His formerly tangled dark hair was now cut reasonably short and definitely neat with very little length to tangle, though it was ruffled a bit, as if he'd recently run his fingers through it. His shoulders were broader. And though jacketless at the moment, apparently PJ really did own a suit. She could see its navy jacket tossed over the back of his chair.

He obviously owned a dress shirt, too—a narrow-striped, pale-gray-and-white one. He had its long sleeves shoved halfway up his forearms, as if, even in running a corporation, he was still willing to get down and dirty with whatever had to be done. Beneath his unbuttoned collar dangled a loosened subdued burgundy-and-gray-patterned silk tie.

Ally wondered idly if his other tie was equally conservative.

It wouldn't matter. At twenty-two PJ Antonides had been a sexy son of a gun in board shorts with a towel slung around his neck, but at thirty-two in tropical-weight wool, an open-necked dress shirt and a half-mast tie, he was devastating.

And he made her want things she knew were not for her.

She shut her eyes against the sight.

When she opened them again it was to watch as PJ dropped easily into the chair opposite her and sat regarding her steadily from beneath hooded lids. "So, wife, where have you been?"

*Wife?* Well, she was his wife, of course, but she didn't expect him to simply toss it into the conversation.

Her spine stiffened. "All over the place," she said quickly before any tempting thoughts could lead her into disaster. "You must know that."

He cocked his head. "Fill me in."

She ground her teeth. "Fine. Prepare yourself to be bored. As you know, I started out in California."

"You mean after you walked out?"

"You make it sound like I dumped you! I didn't, and you know it! It was your idea…getting married. And you knew the reason! You offered—"

"—to marry you. Yeah, I know." He shifted in the chair, then recited, "So you could get your grandmother's legacy, foil your evil father and live your own life. I remember, Al."

She pressed her lips together. "It wasn't exactly like that."

"It was exactly like that."

"He wasn't evil. Isn't evil," she corrected herself.

PJ shrugged. "Not what you were saying then."

"I didn't think he was evil then! I just…I just didn't want him controlling my life! I told you what he was like. All 'traditional Japanese father.' He who must be obeyed. He thought he knew best—what I should take at university, what I should do with my life, who I should marry!"

"And you didn't." PJ shrugged. "So, what are you saying, that you were wrong?"

"No. Of course not. I was right. You know that. You saw me when—" But she didn't want to go there particularly. So she started again. "I just…I understand him better now. I'm older. Wiser. And I'm back in Hawaii. I've been seeing him again."

PJ raised his eyebrows, but said nothing.

So Ally explained. "He had a heart attack a couple of months ago. I've always kept in touch with my mother's cousin Grace. She knew. She rang me in Seattle, told me he was ill. It was serious. He could have died. And I knew I couldn't leave things the way they were. I wanted to make peace. So I went back to Honolulu. It was the first time I'd seen him since…since…"

"Since he said you were no daughter of his?" PJ's tone was harsh.

And Ally remembered how incensed he'd been when she'd told him what her father had said.

Now she had some perspective, understood her father better. But at the time she'd turned her back and walked away. *Run* away. And even now she tried not to think about the rift between them that had lasted so many years.

"Yes." Because her father *had* said that. Her fingers twisted in her lap. "When I went back, I…I thought he might still act that way. Might just turn away from me. But he didn't." She lifted her head and smiled at the recollection. "He was glad to see me. He reached out to me. Held my hand. Asked…asked me to stay." She blinked back the tears that always threatened when she reflected again on how close she'd come to losing her father without ever having made her peace with him. "And I have."

"Stayed? With him?" PJ was scowling.

"Not at his house. I think he would like that, but no—" Ally shook her head "—it wouldn't be a good idea. I'm an adult. I'm not a child anymore. I have my own apartment in downtown Honolulu. I've been back there since May. I did…go back to the beach and…look for you."

His mouth twisted. "To see if I was still waiting for the perfect wave?"

"I didn't know you'd left Hawaii altogether."

"I can't imagine you cared."

Her jaw tightened, but she didn't rise to the bait. "I went to your place, too."

His brows rose a bit at that, but then he shrugged. "Did you?" His tone was indifferent. Clearly he didn't care if she had or not. "There's a high-rise there now."

"Yes, I saw. And Mrs. Chang…?" She'd wondered about his elderly landlady.

"…went to live with her daughter before I left the island."

"Which was a couple of years ago?"

He raised a curious brow. "I left Honolulu earlier than that. Oahu isn't the only place with surf, you know." He paused, and she thought he might explain where he'd been. But he only shrugged, then added, "I came back here two years ago if that's what you mean. You've been doing your homework."

"I saw an article in the *Star* about some former local turned billionaire—"

PJ snorted and rolled his eyes. "Blah, blah, blah. Newspaper writers like that sort of thing. Gives them a reason for living."

"Everyone has to have a purpose."

"Some people have better purposes than others." He shifted in his chair. "We were launching a new windsurfer in a new venue on the island and—" he shrugged negligently "—my sister-in-law said we should promote it. Suggested I give them a local angle."

The PJ she had known wouldn't have done anything anyone else suggested. Apparently her surprise was evident.

"It was my choice," he said sharply. "And look at its unforeseen consequence. I not only may have sold a few windsurfers, but my wife turns up on my doorstep."

Back to the "wife" bit again. "Er, yes. Something we need to talk about."

But before she could take advantage of the opening, there was a quick tap on the door and his assistant came in carrying a tray with glasses of iced tea and a plate of delectable-looking cookies.

She was completely professional and efficient, but her eyes kept darting between PJ and Ally as if she were in a minefield and either one of them might explode at any moment.

PJ didn't seem to notice. "Thanks, Rosie." He paused, then said, "I don't believe you've met my wife. Not officially. Ally, this is Rosie. Rosie, this is Alice."

Rosie's eyes grew round as dinner plates. "You mean, she really is? You haven't been joking? I mean…"

Rosie didn't look like a woman who would be at a loss for words, but she seemed to be now. And Ally was at a bit of a loss, too, at the notion that Rosie's surprise didn't simply stem from her saying she was PJ's wife.

He'd told his secretary he was married? Ally was sure she had misunderstood.

But then Rosie mustered a polite, slightly amazed smile and held out her hand. "I'm glad to meet you," she said. "At last."

Ally blinked. At last? So PJ had spoken of her? She turned confused eyes his way.

"Rosie runs the show here," PJ said, not addressing her confusion at all. He smiled easily at his assistant. "Hold all my calls, please. And get Ryne Murray to reschedule."

"He's already on his way."

Ally began to get up. "You're busy," she said quickly. "I don't want to disturb you. I can just leave—"

"Not a problem," PJ went on, still talking to Rosie as if Ally weren't objecting at all. "When he gets here, tell him we'll need to get together another time. My wife and I have things to discuss."

"We don't, really," Ally protested.

"And then set up a time early next week."

"Are you listening to me? I don't want to upset your schedule. I don't want to upset your life. The opposite in fact! I should have called first. I don't want—" She started toward the door, but PJ caught her arm.

"It's all right," he said firmly. Then he smiled at Rosie. "That will be all, thanks." And he waited until she'd shut the door behind her before he let go of Ally's arm and settled back into his chair again. "Sit down," he said. "And tell all."

But she shook her head. "What did you do that for? Why do you keep saying that?"

"Do what? Say what?" He handed her a glass of iced tea, then nodded toward the cookies. "My sister-in-law bakes them. They're fantastic. Try one."

"I'm not here for a tea party, PJ! Why did you introduce me as your wife? Why do you keep saying I'm your wife?"

He took a bite of one of the cookies and swallowed before he answered. "You're the one who told her that. I just confirmed it."

"But *why*? And she already knew that you were married!" It was the last thing she'd expected. She'd imagined he'd be keeping it quiet. Instead every other word out of his mouth seemed to be the *W* word.

"Yes. You're my wife, so I'm married," he said simply, and punctuated the reality by taking another bite out of a cookie.

"Yes, but—"

He wiped powdered sugar off his mouth. "You'd rather I'd call you a liar?"

"No. Of course not." Ally sighed and shook her head. "I didn't imagine you shouted it from the rooftops. You didn't say anything in the article about being married," she reminded him. "On the contrary, the article said you were dating hordes of eligible women." She could have quoted word for word exactly what it had said, but she didn't.

"Hordes." PJ gave a bark of laughter. "Not quite. I escort women to business functions. Acquaintances. Friends. It's expected."

"But they don't know you're married."

"Hell, Al, most of the time, I barely even know I'm married!"

His exasperation relieved her and swamped her with guilt at the same time. "I know,' she said, clutching the glass tightly in both hands. "I'm sorry. It was selfish of me, marrying you. We never should have. *I*—" she corrected herself "—never should have let you do it."

"You didn't 'let' me," PJ retorted. "I offered. You just said yes. Anyway—" he shrugged it off "—it was no big deal."

"It was to me."

Marrying PJ had given her access to her grandmother's legacy. It had allowed her the freedom to make her own choices instead of doing what her father prescribed. It had been the making of her. She owed PJ for her life as she knew it.

"Well, good," he said gruffly. "So tell me all about it. We didn't have much of a chance to talk…last time."

Last time. Five years ago when she'd come back to Honolulu for an art opening, when he'd showed up with a gorgeous woman on his arm. Ally gave herself a little shake, determined not to think about that. "It was a busy time," she said dismissively.

"So it was. You're a household word now, I gather."

"I've done all right." She'd worked very hard, and she was proud of what she'd accomplished. But she didn't want him to think she was bragging.

"Better than, I'd say." PJ leaned back in his chair and ticked off her accomplishments. "World renowned fabric artist. Clothing designer. International entrepreneur. Business owner. How many boutiques is it now?"

Clearly he'd done some homework, too.

"Seven," Ally said shortly. "I just opened one in Honolulu last month."

She had gone to California to art school after leaving Hawaii—after their marriage—and to supplement the money from her grandmother's legacy, she'd worked in a fabric store. Always interested in art, she'd managed to put the two together rather quickly and had begun to design quilts and wall hangings that had caught the public's eye.

From there she had branched out into clothing design and creating one-of-a-kind outfits. "Art you can wear," she'd called it.

Now her work was featured not only in her own shops, but in galleries and even a few textile museums all over the world.

"Impressive," PJ said now. He balanced one ankle on the opposite knee.

"I worked hard," she said firmly. " You knew I would. You saw that I had." Five years ago, she meant.

"I did," he agreed, lounging back in his chair, and regarding her intently as he drawled, "And you didn't need any more favors from me."

Ally stiffened. But she knew that from his perspective she was the one who had been out of line. "I was rude to you that night."

It had been the last time—the *only* time—she had seen PJ since the day of their marriage.

She'd come back to Honolulu for her first local public art show. It had been in the heady scary early days of her career when she certainly hadn't been a "household name" or anything close. In fact the show itself had doubtless been premature, but she'd wanted desperately to do it, to prove to her father that she was on her way to making something of herself, and—though she'd barely admitted to herself—she'd hoped to see PJ, too, to show him that his faith in her had not been misplaced. So she'd jumped at the chance to be part of the show when another artist backed out.

She'd sent her father an invitation to the opening and had waited with nervous pride and anticipation for his arrival.

He'd never come.

But PJ had.

Looking up all of a sudden to see him there across the room, big as life and twice as gorgeous as she remembered, had knocked Ally for a loop.

She hadn't expected to see him at all.

When she'd known she was coming back, she'd casually asked a friend who had gone to the same beach with them about where PJ was now.

May had shaken her head. "PJ? No idea. Haven't seen him in ages. But you know surfers—they never stay. They're always following the waves."

So the sight of him had been a shock. As had the sight of the woman on his arm.

She was, in a blonde bombshell way, every bit as gorgeous as PJ himself. With his dark hair and tan and her platinum tresses and fair skin, the contrast between the two was eye-catching and arresting. The artist in Ally had certainly appreciated that.

The woman in her didn't appreciate him striding up to her, all smiles, hugging her and saying cheerfully, "Hey. Look at you! You look great. And your stuff—" he let go of her to wave an arm around the gallery "—looks great, too. Amazing. I brought you a reviewer." He'd introduced the blonde then, took her arm and pulled her forward. "This is Annie Cannavaro. She writes art reviews for the *Star.*"

He had not said, "This is Ally, my wife."

In fact, he hadn't mentioned any relationship to her at all. Not that Ally had expected him to. She knew their marriage had been for her convenience, not a lifelong commitment. He'd done her a favor.

But standing there, being introduced to the *Star*'s art critic, made her realize that PJ thought she needed another favor now. The very thought had made her see red. She was not still the needy girl she'd been when he married her!

He'd been perplexed at her brusqueness. But Ally had been too insecure still to accept his freely offered help.

And—a truth she acknowledged to no one, barely even to herself—seeing PJ with another woman, a far more suitable woman for him than she was, had made it a thousand times worse.

She'd been stiff and tense and had determinedly feigned indifference all the time they were there. And she'd only breathed a sigh of relief when she'd seen them go out the door. Her relief, though, had been short-lived.

Right before closing, PJ had returned. Alone.

He'd cornered her in one of the gallery rooms, demanding, "What the hell is wrong with you?" His normally easygoing smile was nowhere to be found.

"I don't know what you're talking about," she'd replied frostily, trying to sidestep and get around him, but he moved to block her exit.

"You know damned well what I'm talking about. So you don't want to know me, okay. Maybe you're too much of a hotshot now. Fine, but that's no reason to be rude to Annie."

"I wasn't! I'm not—a hotshot." Her face had burned furiously. She'd been mortified at his accusation. "I just…I didn't mean to be rude. I just don't need your help. You don't need to keep rescuing me!"

"I'm not bloody rescuing you," he'd snapped. "I thought you'd like the exposure. But if that's the way you see it, fine. I'll tell her not to write anything!"

"You can tell her what to write?" So it was true!

He'd said a rude word. "Forget it. Sorry I bothered." He spun away and started out of the room.

But she couldn't let him go without calling after him, "Is that all?"

He looked over his shoulder. "All? What else could there be?"

Ally's mouth was dry. She had to force the words out. "I thought…I thought you'd be bringing the divorce papers." She'd feared there was a quaver in her voice, but she tried not to betray it.

PJ stared at her. She met his gaze even though it was the hardest thing she'd ever done.

"No," he said at last, his voice flat. "I don't have any divorce papers."

"Oh." And there was no accounting for the foolish shiver of relief she'd felt.

Still they'd stared at each other, and then she'd dragged in a breath and shrugged. "Fine. Well, I just thought…whenever you want one, just let me know." She'd tried to sound blasé and indifferent.

"Yeah," PJ said. "I'll do that." And he'd turned and walked away.

She hadn't seen him again, hadn't heard from him, hadn't contacted him—until today.

Now she said carefully, "I apologize for that. I was still trying to find my own way. I'd depended on you enough. I didn't want another handout."

"Is that what it was?" There was a rough edge to his voice. The cool irony of his earlier words was past.

Their gazes locked—and held—and something seemed to arc between them like an electric current.

Or rather, Ally assured herself, more like a sparkler on the Fourth of July—bright and fizzing, ultimately insubstantial—and definitely best ignored.

Determinedly she gave her head a little shake. "I'm sure that's what it was," she said firmly. "I shouldn't have done it, though. Anyway, I've found out who I am and what I can do. And I owe it to you. So I came to say thank you belatedly and—" she reached down and picked up the portfolio she had set by her chair and opened it just as she'd rehearsed doing "—to bring you these."

She slid a file of papers out of the portfolio and held it out to him.

He took the file, looked at it, but didn't open it. "What are they?"

"Divorce papers. About time, huh?" She said it quickly, then shrugged and grinned as brightly as she could, willing him to grin back at her.

He didn't. His gaze fixed on the file in his hand, weighing it, but he didn't say a word.

"I know I should have done it sooner," she went on, papering over the awkward silence. "I'm sorry it took so long. I thought you'd do it. You could have had one at any time, you know. Well, almost anytime. After I turned twenty-one anyway. I told you so, remember?"

He still didn't speak. He didn't even blink. His face was stony, his expression unreadable. And so she babbled on, unable to help herself. "I know it's past time. I should have taken care of it ages ago. It's a formality really—just confirming what we already know. I don't want anything from you, of course. No settlement, naturally. But," she added because she'd already decided this, "if you want a share of my business, it's yours. You're entitled."

"I don't." The words cut across hers, harsh and louder than she expected.

"Well, I wanted to offer." She took a breath. "Okay, then it will be even easier." She reached inside her portfolio for a pen. "In that case, all you really need to do is sign them. I can take care of the rest."

"I don't think so."

The rough edge was gone now. PJ's voice was smooth and cool, like an ocean breeze. Ally looked up, startled.

He was sitting up straight in the chair and was regarding her steadily.

"Well, of course I'll understand if you want a lawyer to look them over...." Still she fumbled for the pen.

"I don't." Still cool. Very cool.

She frowned, rattled. "Well then—" Her fingers fastened on the pen at last. She jerked it out and thrust it at him, giving him one more quick smile. "Here you go."

He didn't move. Didn't take it.

And of course, she realized then, he didn't need one. He already had a pen in his shirt pocket. She felt like an idiot as she gestured toward it. "Of course you have your own."

But he didn't get it out. Instead PJ dropped the papers on the table, then looked up and met her gaze squarely. "No divorce."

# CHAPTER TWO

"WHAT? What do you mean, no divorce?"

"Seems pretty clear to me. Which word didn't you understand?" He raised an eyebrow.

Ally stared at him, unable to believe her ears. "Ha-ha. Very funny. Come on, PJ. You've had your joke. You made your point. I was rude. I'm sorry. I've grown up, changed. Now just sign the papers and I'll be on my way."

"I don't think so."

"Why not?" She was rattled now. "It doesn't make any sense."

"Sure it does." He shrugged. "We're married. We took vows."

"Oh, yes, right. And we've certainly kept them, haven't we?"

The brow lifted again and he said mildly, "Speak for yourself, Al."

She gaped at him. "What are you saying?"

"Never mind." He looked away out the window, stared out at Manhattan across the river for a long moment while Ally stewed, waiting for him to enlighten her. Finally he looked her way again. "I'm just saying we've been married for ten years. That's a long time. Lots of marriages don't last that long," he added.

"Are you suggesting that more people shouldn't see each other for ten years? Or five," she added, forcing herself to add that one disastrous meeting.

He shook his head, smiling slightly. "No. I'm saying we should give it a shot."

"What?" She couldn't believe her ears. "Give what a shot?"

"Marriage. Living together. Seeing if it will work." Deep green eyes bored into hers.

Ally opened her mouth, then closed it again. She couldn't believe this was happening. Not now! Not ever, for that matter. That had never been the plan. Not for her, and certainly not for PJ.

"We don't know each other," she pointed out.

"We were friends once."

"You were a beach bum and I was the counter girl where you bought plate lunches and hamburgers."

"We met there," he agreed. "And we became friends. You're not trying to say we weren't friends."

"No." She couldn't say that. They had been friends. "But that's the point. We were *friends*, PJ. Buddies. We never even went out! You certainly didn't love me then! And you can't possibly love me now."

"So? I like what I see. And a lot of marriages start with less."

He made it sound eminently sensible and reasonable—as if it were perfectly logical for two people to go their separate ways for ten years and then suddenly, without warning, pick up where they left off.

Maybe to him it was. After all, he'd married her with no real forethought at all. It had been useful to her, so he had done it.

She shook her head. "That's ridiculous."

"No, it's not."

"Of course it is. We don't live anywhere near each other. We have entirely different lives."

"I'm adaptable."

"Well, I'm not! I've got a life in Hawaii now. I've come home, settled down. I like it there. I've worked hard to get where I am, to do what I'm doing. It's time to take the next step."

"Which is?"

"Get a divorce!"

"No."

"Yes! I've got to," she said. "I…I'm getting a life!"

"Finally?" His tone was mocking.

She wrapped her arms across her chest. "I had other things to do first. You know that."

"And now you've done them, so you want a divorce." A brow lifted. "Why now?"

"Because I've found you, for one thing," she said with a touch of annoyance. "And why wait? It's not as if we've got a relationship. On the contrary, we have nothing."

"We have memories."

"Ten-year-old memories," she scoffed.

"And one five-year-old one," PJ reminded her.

Ally's face burned. "I've apologized for that!"

"So you have. Thank you," he said formally. "Anyway, it's not my fault we didn't keep in touch," he pointed out. "You're the one who didn't leave a forwarding address."

"Mea culpa," Ally muttered. But then she added, "Maybe I should have kept in touch, but—"

But doing so would have been a temptation she didn't want to have to deal with. Marrying PJ had been one thing—it had been a few words recited, a couple of signatures scrawled. It had been a legal document, but it hadn't been personal. Not really.

That night, though—that one night with PJ—had destroyed all her notions of their marriage being no more than an impersonal business proposition. It had made her want things she knew she had no business wanting, things she was sure PJ definitely didn't want. She knew he'd married her to help her out. To change the rules after the fact wouldn't have been fair.

She shook her head. "I just thought it was better if I didn't."

"No distractions," PJ translated flatly.

"Yes," Ally lied. "But times change. People change as you said." She gave him the brightest smile she could manage under the circumstances, but she couldn't quite meet his eyes.

"So what's the real reason, Al?"

The question cut across the jumble of her thoughts exactly

the way his suggestion that he marry her had cut across the morass of worries she'd wallowed in all those years ago.

She hadn't counted on that, any more than she'd counted on this.

She'd assured herself that seeing PJ again would be a good thing. That it was the right thing to do—the polite thing to do— come and ask him face-to-face to sign the divorce papers rather than simply mail the papers to him.

She'd been convinced that seeing him again would bring closure.

She'd convinced herself that she would walk into PJ's office and have changed enough to feel nothing more than gratitude to the man she had married ten years before.

And even if she'd still felt a twinge of regret, she'd been sure he would be delighted to comply with her request. After all, being married to her was holding up his life, too. With the papers signed, they would go their own ways and that would be that.

Now she watched as PJ took a sip of tea and cocked his head, waiting for her answer.

"I'm getting married," she said at last.

PJ choked. "What?"

"I said, I'm getting married. Not everyone considers me a charity case," she said sharply. His eyes narrowed, but she plunged on. "I'm…engaged. Sort of."

"Isn't that a little…precipitous? You already have one husband."

"It's not official," she said. "It's just…going to happen. After. Which is why I brought the divorce papers. So you could sign them. It's a formality really. I could have sent them by mail. I just thought it was more polite to bring them in person."

"Polite," he echoed. His tone disputed her assertion.

"I am polite," she defended herself. "I didn't imagine you'd have any interest in…keeping things going. It's not as if we've ever had a real marriage."

"We did for one night."

Her teeth came together with a snap. "That wasn't…real."

"Felt pretty real to me."

"Stop it! You know what I mean!"

He sighed. "Tell me what you mean, Al."

"I mean it's time to move on. I should have done something sooner. Contacted you sooner. But I thought you would…and then five years ago, I was sure you would…and then I just…got busy. And after I came back to Honolulu, I wasn't sure where you were and I didn't think it mattered and then things got…serious. Jon…proposed and…"

"He didn't know you were married?"

"He knew I *was*. I guess he thought it was in the past," she added awkwardly. How did you tell someone you were seeing that you still had a husband, you just didn't know where?

"And you didn't bother to set him straight?"

"It never came up."

PJ's eyes widened. "Really?" Patent disbelief.

"We didn't spend a lot of time talking about it!" she snapped. "What was there to say? He said he'd heard about my marriage from his brother and I said yes. There was nothing else. He, well, he assumed it was over. And I…said it was."

PJ raised an eyebrow.

"Well, it has been—in everything but the formalities. It never even really got started!"

"Oh, I think you could say it got started, Al." The look he gave her reminded her all too well of the night that had been anything but platonic.

"It was one night!"

But what a night. Especially for a wedding night that wasn't supposed to have happened at all.

Making love with PJ hadn't been part of the deal—the original deal. She'd never intended to consummate their marriage. And PJ had never mentioned it, either.

But after the ceremony, when she'd gone home to tell her father she was married, he had just stared at her and, after what seemed an eternity, he said, "You're married?" Even longer pause. "Really?"

And long after he'd walked away from her, those two words had still echoed in her head.

Was it a marriage? Was saying words and scrawling signatures enough to make it a marriage? Or was there more to it than that?

Of course there was. Ally had always known that.

She'd seen the deep love of her parents. She'd witnessed the shattering pain her father had felt at her mother's death. Her marriage to PJ, in that light, was a sham indeed.

And while she knew ultimately why they had married, she felt compelled by her father's doubt and, even more, by her own convictions, to want a "real marriage" with PJ Antonides.

And so that night she had gone to PJ's apartment.

She could still remember the incredulity on his face when he had opened the door and found her standing there. "Ally? What's up?"

"I…" She'd swallowed hard. "I need another favor."

"Yeah, sure, name it." He'd shrugged, still looking at her strangely because, of course, he hadn't expected to see her at all.

Her fingers had twisted together, strangled each other, as she looked up into his eyes. "Could you, um, please make love to me?"

He'd looked at her, stunned. And for so long, that she'd been tempted to turn tail and run. She'd tried to explain. "I know why you married me. I know you're doing me a favor, putting your name on a piece of paper, But I…I just want it to be real!"

He didn't move. Didn't blink. Just stared.

"I know making love doesn't make it 'real'—not like other marriages," she said hastily. "And I know it won't happen again. I just thought—if you wanted…" Her voice trailed off. "Maybe you don't find me attractive. I understand. I—"

"Don't be stupid," PJ said harshly. He grasped her hand and drew her in.

And Ally's breath caught in her throat. "I don't expect—"

"Shh," PJ's voice was a whisper, a breath—that began on his lips and ended on hers.

The touch of his mouth, warm and persuasive against hers, made Ally's legs weak, made her mind spin, made her clutch his arms, then wrap hers around his back and hang on for dear life as he pushed the door shut behind her and steered her to his bed without ever breaking their kiss.

And then he made love to her.

Ally had expected it to be quick and uncomfortable and perfunctory—one coupling to make their marriage "real." And, because she supposed that PJ would enjoy sex, she'd considered that to be the one small thing she could give him.

As far as she went, as a virgin, Ally had no real experience to draw on. And everything she'd heard had made "first times" sound something to be endured rather than enjoyed.

On the contrary, PJ had made it the most amazing night of her life.

Making love with PJ, sharing intimacies with PJ she'd never shared with anyone, had been such an incredible experience that she had never been able to forget it. She hadn't wanted to.

There had been nothing quick or perfunctory about it. PJ had been gentle and thorough, touching and caressing her in ways that made her ache with longing for him. His gentleness had made her want to weep at the same time it had made her exult with the joy of finding out what her body was all about.

And if there had been a bit of discomfort the first time, it was nothing in the face of the concern PJ expressed, his determination to make it good for her, too. And he had. All night he had.

If she hadn't been already half in love with PJ Antonides, she certainly would have been by the next morning. Not that she could tell him so. That, too, would have been changing the rules.

But it didn't stop her thinking about him. Didn't stop her loving him from afar. Didn't stop her reliving those memories. They were memories she'd lived on for years.

For a long time those memories had made her doubt that she would ever be able to look at another man.

The fact was, she hadn't really looked at another man until she'd met Jon.

And she still had no idea if it would be the same with Jon as it had been with PJ. She hadn't wanted to find out. She hadn't made love with Jon.

"I can't," she'd told him firmly when she'd also told him that she was legally still PJ's wife. "I can't make love with one man when I'm still married to another."

"I admire your scruples," Jon had muttered. "Get the damn divorce so we can get married, then."

And so she was.

She loved Jon. In his way he was exactly what she wanted and needed—a kind man, a caring man. A man who wanted a wife and a family. A man who was tired of being a workaholic, just as she was.

"We're good for each other," Jon had said not long ago. "We want the same things."

They did. Something she and PJ had never done. Would never do. They wanted different things. As soon as the divorce was final, she was going to marry Jon, make a life with him. And she was going to have children with him. She was going to give her father the grandchild he longed for.

And she would make new memories, wonderful ones that would supercede those of one night in PJ's arms.

"It was a deal we made," she told PJ firmly now. "It was never a real marriage."

"It was," he said. "And you know it."

She'd thought so then, but now she shook her head. "I was immature. Marriage is a lot more than one night in bed."

"Of course it is. But it's all we had. You left."

"Would you have wanted me to stay?" she challenged. "I don't think so! You didn't want a marriage then, PJ, and don't pretend you did! You wanted to surf and cut class and hang around on the beach. You know that." She glared at him, defying him to contradict her.

His lips pressed together. And he didn't speak for such a long time that Ally found herself sitting on the edge of her chair, wondering if he might actually do that.

But then he shrugged lightly. "You're right."

She let out a harsh breath, deflated and relieved at the same time. "Of course I'm right."

But even knowing that, her gaze locked with his. And Ally couldn't help it. She found herself once more remembering the night, the tenderness, the passion, the emotion, the unexpected intimacy—and how very real it had felt.

PJ cleared his throat and looked away. He took a long swallow of his iced tea and said briskly, "So who's the lucky guy?"

"You remember Ken? That guy my dad wanted me to marry…"

"Oh, for God's sake, Ally." The words exploded from him. "You're not going to marry him!"

"No, of course not! I'm not going to marry him! He's already married. He has three kids. But he also has a younger brother. Jon's a doctor."

"A doctor." The words dropped like stones into a pond.

"A cardiologist," Ally clarified. "Very well respected. Not my dad's doctor, but in the same practice. I met him when he was filling in on rounds and came to see my dad. We hit it off. We like the same things. We want the same things."

"And so you're going to marry him? Just like that?" PJ's tone was scathing.

"I married you 'just like that'! A whole lot faster, in fact."

His mouth twisted. "For ulterior motives," he reminded her. "Do you have ulterior motives this time, Al?"

"No!"

"So you're in love with him?"

"Of course I'm in love with him!" she said quickly. "He's a wonderful man. Hardworking. Intelligent. Clever. He cares about people. Tries to heal them. To give them a new lease on life. He respects me and what I've accomplished. I respect him. It's a good match. And it's the right time for both of us. We both want a home, a family, children. I don't want my family to be just Dad and me. Neither does my father. He's over the moon about Jon."

"I'll bet."

She bristled at his tone. "I'd marry him even if Dad didn't like him. Jon is a great guy."

"Which doesn't change the fact that you're still married to me."

And there they were—back at the divorce papers again. The divorce papers PJ wasn't signing. The divorce papers that were sitting on the table between them. The divorce papers that even now he refused to look at. And Ally knew from the stubborn jut of his jaw—the same one she'd seen when he'd been determined to ride waves in surf sane men back away from—that he wasn't going to change his mind now.

She let out a breath and stood up. "Fine. You don't have to sign them." She picked up her portfolio. "I can do it without your consent."

A muscle ticked in his cheek, but he didn't answer, just looked at her.

She plucked her business card out of the portfolio and tossed it on top of the divorce papers. "Really, PJ, I—"

But his expression was entirely shuttered. Okay, so she'd been wrong to come. Jon had been right when she'd told him where she was going. If he'd been taken aback that she was still married, he'd been even more upset at her notion of coming to see PJ and giving him the papers in person.

"Don't open a can of worms," he'd said. "You could get hurt."

But she'd insisted it was the right thing to do. PJ had done her a favor once. The least she could do was say thank you when they ended their marriage.

At least, that had been the plan.

Now she said to PJ, "Call me if you change your mind. I'll be in the city until Friday. Otherwise, I'll see you in court."

\* \* \*

"You do have a wife."

"I said I did," PJ replied sharply.

It wasn't news. He'd never said otherwise. It wasn't his fault no one believed him. They'd always treated his assertion as if it were a joke.

It wasn't a joke.

Or if it was, the joke was on him.

Sometimes he thought that his marriage to Ally was more like a dream—a distant recollection of one moment out of his life that seemed to have no connection to the rest of his life, except for one, which had ended badly.

He should have left it there. Or filed for divorce himself after their set-to at the gallery five years ago.

But he hadn't. Why bother?

He'd certainly had no intention of marrying at the time. In fact having a wife in absentia had actually been convenient. He'd had a built-in reason for never getting serious. It had stood him in good stead in Hawaii back in his beach-bum days. But it had been even more of a godsend since he'd come back to New York and his parents had begun dragging out every available woman they knew.

"Don't bother," he'd said straight off. "I'm married."

They hadn't believed him, of course.

Where was his wife? *Who* was his wife? They'd dismissed it as a joke, too, until he'd shown them the marriage license.

Then they'd had a thousand questions, each nosier and more personal than the last. He'd only answered the ones he wanted to. He'd told them her name, where he'd met her, why he'd married her.

"A favor?" his father had sputtered. "You married her for a favor?"

"Why not?" PJ had said flatly, folding his arms across his chest. "She was between a rock and a hard place. She needed a way out. You'd have done the same," he said bluntly. His father, for all his bombast, was a far bigger softie than any of his children. "Wouldn't you?" he'd challenged the old man.

Aeolus had grunted.

"So when is she coming back?" he and Helena had both wanted to know.

"When she finds herself," PJ had replied. That was probably the closest he'd come to telling a lie.

How the hell did he know when or what Ally would do? He'd have thought she'd be glad to see him when he'd turned up at her gallery opening. Instead she'd been stiff and remote and defensive.

She hadn't even seemed like Ally. She'd been dismissive of Annie, completely misunderstanding his reason for bringing the other woman along. She hadn't seemed at all like the girl he'd married. He'd told himself it didn't matter, that he should just forget her.

But he couldn't. She was always there—Ally and the one night they'd shared.

"You should go get her," *Yiayia* told him. *Yiayia* was always full of ideas. The minute word of PJ's marriage had come to her ears, she'd been busy figuring out how to bring them together again.

"No." PJ was adamant. "Things are fine just the way they are."

If he'd hoped they would be different, if now and then he had even begun to think about how to make them different, it wasn't something he'd spent a lot of time dwelling on. Nor was he going to discuss it with *Yiayia*.

"Pah," *Yiayia* had said. "What good is a wife when she is not here? It is not good for a man to be alone, Petros. And it is not good for a great-grandmother to be denied her rightful great-grandchildren, either."

He'd glowered at her. "That's what this is all about really," he'd grumbled.

"Do you think so?" *Yiayia* said. Then she'd shaken her head in dismay. "You are hiding behind her skirts."

"I am not! How the hell can I hide behind the skirts of someone who isn't even here."

"You use her not to deal with the women your father brings you."

PJ shrugged. "I don't want them."

"Because you want her."

"That's not true!"

"So prove it. Not to me." *Yiayia* cut off his protest before he could open his mouth. "For yourself. Go find her. See what she is like now. Bring her home. Or get a divorce."

He ground his teeth, but *Yiayia* just looked at him serenely. Finally he'd shrugged. "Maybe I will."

"'Maybe' builds no fires to keep me warm. 'Maybe' gives me no great-grandbabies."

"Fine, damn it," he said, goaded. "It's our tenth anniversary in August. I'll track her down. Take her out to dinner to celebrate."

And sort things out once and for all.

*Yiayia* smiled and patted his knee. "Bring her home to meet us. It is good she meets your family, *ne*, Petros?"

PJ hadn't answered that. But he knew she was right about one thing.

He was thirty-two years old now. Not twenty-two, or even twenty-seven. He was ready to be married to someone who was actually present in his life. And though some of the women his father turned up with were actually quite nice, he still hadn't forgotten Ally.

And now Ally was back.

"She's gorgeous," Rosie said now.

"Yeah."

In fact, gorgeous didn't cover the half of it. Ally had always been amazing looking. He'd been struck by that the first time he'd seen her behind the counter at Benny's taking orders.

The combined genes of her Japanese father and her Chinese-Hawaiian-Anglo mother had come together to make Alice

Maruyama an absolute beauty with a porcelain complexion, high cheekbones beneath wide slightly tilted dark eyes, with the longest eyelashes he'd ever seen.

Her shining black hair had always been neatly tamed, nicely brushed, pinned down or pulled up.

Except for the night he'd made love to her. And then it had been a lavish black silk curtain, loose and lush, that begged him to thread it through his fingers, bury his face in it, rub his cheek against it.

The second she'd walked through the door this afternoon, his fingers had itched to undo that sleek librarian's knot at the back of head, let down her hair and do all those things again.

Good thing he had a well-honed sense of self-preservation. Good thing he'd learned something from going to see her at her gallery opening wearing his heart on his sleeve. He'd been a fool for her once. He wasn't doing it again.

But he wasn't letting her walk blithely away, either.

There was still something between them. Electricity. Attraction. Unfinished business.

Had she ever spent a night like their wedding night with bloody Jon? His fingers balled into fists at the thought.

How could she just walk in here and toss divorce papers at him? Why should she want to marry another man?

*What the hell was wrong with the one she had?*

And how could she be sure their marriage wouldn't work if they'd never even tried?

"—wants you to call her." Rosie's voice cut through his irritated thoughts. "She called while your, um, wife was with you."

PJ's thoughts jerked back to the present. "Who? What?"

Rosie gave him a long-suffering look. "Cristina," she repeated patiently. "Your sister?" she added when he didn't respond. "She said Mark just got back from San Diego and wants to discuss that new powerboat line he's been looking at so she wondered if you'd like to come to dinner."

Dinner. Cristina. Mark.

PJ dragged his brain back to business, determinedly putting Ally on a sidebar long enough to make sense of what Rosie was telling him.

His twin sister Cristina's husband, Mark, worked for Antonides Marine as well. They had a brownstone not far from his place in Park Slope and sometimes it was easier to talk business over the dinner table than in the office. It was, after all, a family business.

Ally wanted family. She'd said so. She didn't just want it to be her and her father anymore. She'd said that, too.

Well, hell, PJ thought, cracking his knuckles. If Ally wanted family, he had more than enough to go around.

"Call Cristina back and tell her I can't make it," he instructed Rosie. "Tell her I'll catch Mark in the office tomorrow." He smiled a cat-who'd-eaten-the-canary smile. "Tell her I'm busy tonight. I'm fixing dinner for my wife."

"So, did you get it?" Jon asked.

"Not yet," Ally said, pacing around her hotel room. She hadn't wanted to call without things being settled, but when they didn't she knew she had to call anyway. She just hoped she didn't have to listen to Jon say, I told you so. "I will," she promised, but it didn't forestall the discussion.

"Didn't you go see him? I thought you knew where he was."

"I do know where he is," she said. "I saw him. And I will get it. I just didn't…think it was right to waltz back into his life and fling divorce papers at him first thing."

"I knew this was a bad idea."

"It was not a bad idea," Ally retorted. "He was surprised."

"To see you or to get the papers?"

"Well, both, I guess. Don't worry. I'm sure he'll sign them. PJ doesn't react well to pressure."

She should have remembered that. Should have recalled

why he'd said he'd come to Hawaii in the first place: to get his family off his back.

She should have been less…pushy. She should have simply chatted with him, got him to talk, acted interested in what he was doing now, what had happened to him in the past ten years, how he'd come to be where he was and doing what he was doing.

The trouble was—and the very reason she didn't do it was—that it wouldn't have been an act.

She had gone to PJ's office hoping that their encounter would be polite and perfunctory. In a best-case scenario she would have felt no more connection to him than she had to Jon's brother, Ken.

She would certainly *not* have felt an instant stab of lust and longing. Her eyes would not have fastened on PJ's well-dressed body and lingered, cataloguing every inch of it. And they would definitely not have mentally undressed that body while her brain wondered as they did so how the man in the suit would compare with the naked twenty-two-year-old she had spent her wedding night with.

Not something she should be contemplating now, either.

"So when?" Jon asked. "I'll be having dinner with your dad tonight. He'll want to know. I was hoping to be able to tell him it was a done deal and you were on your way home."

"I won't be home until the weekend. You both know that. I'm going to be visiting a gallery here, too, talking to Gabriela, the owner. This trip wasn't all about PJ."

"No. It's about *us*," Jon reminded her. "It's about you finally putting the past behind you and moving on. You are moving on, aren't you, Ally?"

"Of course I am."

"Well, I'm only saying…your dad's heart isn't strong. It's not going to hold out forever. And I know you—and I—wanted him to be at our wedding."

Ally swallowed against the lump in her throat. Yes, she did know her father's condition was delicate. And she knew how happy seeing her married to Jon would make him. And she did want him to be happy. She wanted them all to be happy.

"I'm working on it."

"Good. I'll tell him that. Then hurry up and get home. I miss you. I work twenty hours a day when you're not here."

Ally knew the feeling. "I'll do my best," she promised. "I'm getting another call. It might be Gabriela. I'd better take it."

"Forget Gabriela. Forget the gallery. They aren't that important. Not now. Get the papers signed."

"Yes. Maybe this is PJ," Ally suggested hopefully. "Maybe he's already signed them and is telling me when to pick them up."

"Let's hope." Jon sounded encouraged. "Talk to you tomorrow. I'll tell your dad you've got everything under control."

Ally hoped it was true. She punched the connect button on her phone. "This is Alice Maruyama."

"Have dinner with me." The voice was gruff and male and needed no identification.

She'd heard it only an hour before, but if she hadn't heard PJ Antonides's voice for ten years, she would have recognized it. There was a sort of soft, lazy, sexy edge to it that made her toes curl.

"Who is this?" she said with all the starch she could muster.

He laughed. "Check your caller ID. Come on, Al. Don't be a bad sport. You never used to be a bad sport."

"This has nothing to do with sports. It has to do with you signing the divorce papers."

"So convince me over dinner."

"PJ..."

"Are you chicken, Al? Afraid?" It was the same old taunt he'd used years ago. In the same teasing tone.

When she had met him she'd never surfed in her life, and he'd been appalled.

"Never surfed? And you live where?" He'd stared at her, stunned. She'd just handed him his order from the lunch counter and expected him to move along, but he stayed right where he was, ignoring the line behind him.

"Not everyone who lives in Hawaii surfs," she'd said haughtily.

He'd shrugged. "Guess not," he'd agreed. Then he'd slanted her a grin. "And why should you if you're chicken?"

"I'm not chicken!"

"Then come out with me," he'd suggested. "I'll teach you."

"I have work to do." She'd waved her arm around, pointing out the fact that she had responsibilities, even if he didn't. "I can't just walk out and go play with you."

"So come tomorrow morning. Better surf then anyway. I'll meet you here at seven." He'd tipped his head, the slow grin still lingering, green eyes dancing. "Unless you're—"

"I am *not* chicken!" Ally said it then. She said it again now. "Fine. I'll have dinner with you. We can catch up on 'old times.' And you can sign the papers. Where shall I meet you?"

"I'll pick you up."

"I'd rather meet you there."

He paused, then said, "Fine. Suit yourself." He gave her a street corner in Brooklyn. "You can take a cab or the subway. Either way, I'll meet you at the Seventh Avenue subway stop."

"I'll go to the restaurant."

"I'll be at the subway stop. We can walk from there. Seven o'clock. It's a date."

# CHAPTER THREE

IT WAS *not* a date.

Ally had never been on a date with PJ Antonides in her life—unless you counted their date to meet at the courthouse where they got married, which she wasn't, she thought irritably, jerking clothes out of her suitcase, trying to find something suitable to wear.

Not that it mattered. It wasn't a date, despite what he had said. And they weren't a couple!

She was annoyed. With PJ. But even more with herself. And even more that she was annoyed and had let him get to her.

She was kicking herself now for having done the polite thing and come to give him the papers in person. Jon was right. She hadn't needed to. She could have sent them through the mail. And if he hadn't signed them, oh, well. She'd have proceeded with the divorce anyway.

Of course, she still could. But it was worse now, having stirred the pot, so to speak. And she couldn't understand why he was being obstinate. She'd thought her task would be simple.

She'd expected that PJ would be delighted to see her, that he would tease her a bit—as he always had done—then, still joking with her, he'd sign the papers, maybe buy her a cup of coffee, then give her a wink and a wave as she walked out the door.

Her only qualm about seeing him again had been wondering what her own reaction would be.

PJ had turned her world upside down the night he'd made love to her. He had made her want things she hadn't suspected existed—things that she'd tried to put out of her mind ever since.

Worse, he had made her want him.

And, on a physical level, her body still did.

Which was why she was putting on a tailored black pantsuit and knotting her hair up on top of her head—tamping down and buttoning up—to remind herself that this was not about physical desire.

It was about commitment and family and eternity.

It was about ending their sham of a marriage so that she could move on and make a real one with Jon.

"Just remember that," she told her reflection, staring intently into her dark eyes and willing herself to be strong. "PJ doesn't love you. He's just getting his own back."

She was fairly sure that was what this reluctance was all about. He was making her pay, no doubt, for having been rude and distant the night he'd come to her opening.

"He doesn't love you," she repeated once more for good measure, then added severely, "and you don't love him, either."

The subway ride from her midtown Manhattan hotel to the Seventh Avenue stop in Brooklyn wilted her pantsuit. A strap-hanger's charm bracelet snagged her hair. She was disheveled, unkempt and perspiring by the time she emerged onto the street. She wished he'd told her what restaurant they were going to so she could have gone there and repaired the damage before she met him again.

But he was already there waiting when she appeared. He was still wearing the trousers and shirt he'd worn at work. His jacket was slung over his shoulder. His tie was gone. The power was still there. It was like seeing the wild animal let out of his cage.

Ally caught her breath.

"Right on time," he said approvingly. "No trouble getting here? You look great."

That was so patently a lie that Ally laughed.

He grinned. "Ah, a real smile at last."

"It's just that I'm so delighted to be here," she said sarcastically.

He laughed. And before she realized—or prepared, or dodged—he swooped around, ducked his head down and kissed her.

It was a quick kiss—a street-corner kiss. A smack of lips, an instant's worth of the taste of enticing sexy male and nothing more. It was the sort of kiss that happened every day on thousands of street corners around the world. Nothing earth-shattering about it.

At least, no one else's world shattered.

Only hers.

Because that one brief touch of PJ's lips brought everything back. The memories she'd wallowed in at first, then spent years sublimating or suppressing, crashed back in on her as if the years of constructing defenses had never even happened.

That one instant, that one taste—his lips on hers, his scent filling her nostrils—and for a split second she was back in Hawaii, back in PJ's apartment, back in his arms.

She swayed, stumbled.

He caught her before she could fall on her face. "Are you okay?"

Of course she was, but he kept his arm around her as she wobbled on knees of jelly. And she gripped his shirtfront as she righted herself, then let go as she straightened and pulled away. "I'm fine. It's the heat. And…and I just t-tripped, that's all."

"You sure?" He was so close. She could see each individual eyelash. They were long and thick and wasted on a man. He bent close again, looking worried and solicitous.

Ally stepped back quickly, out of kissing range. Definitely out of kissing range!

"It was hot in the subway. The air-conditioning wasn't working on the train. Where are we going? Is it far? I need to splash some water on my face."

"Not far." He still had his arm around her as he steered her along Flatbush Avenue and into a grocery store.

She frowned. "Where are you going?"

"Just have to get a few things. Come on." He came back and snagged her wrist to take her with him. She pulled out of his grasp, but followed as he picked some steaks, salad vegetables, a loaf of country bread and fresh olives. Then he hesitated a moment, as if weighing his options, and grabbed a couple of ears of corn on the cob.

Suspicion began to dawn. "Why are you shopping now?"

"Because until an hour ago, I didn't know I was having company for dinner."

"We're not…I mean…*you're cooking?*"

"No end to my talents." He slanted her a grin as he grabbed a fresh pineapple off the display and tossed it to her.

Instinctively Ally caught it but protested as she did so. "You don't have to cook for me," she said quickly. "Let's go out. I'll buy dinner."

"No. You won't. Come on. No trouble at all. I like to cook."

"But—"

But he was already leading the way toward the checkout. "Hey, Manny. How's it going?" he said to the teenager who began to ring up the groceries.

"Ain't. Too hot," the boy said. "Dyin' in here. Better outside. Don't forget. Softball tonight."

"Not me. Other plans."

The boy's gaze lit on Ally and he looked her up and down assessingly. "Nice," he said with an approving grin.

"My wife," PJ said.

Ally stiffened beside him. He didn't have to keep telling everyone.

The boy was clearly surprised. His eyes widened. "No joke?"

"Yep."

"No," Ally said at the same instant.

Manny blinked. PJ's scowl was disapproving.

"Only officially," she muttered.

PJ's jaw tightened. "Officially counts." He pulled out his wallet and paid for the groceries. "Hit a homer for me."

Manny grinned and winked. "Hit one yourself."

Ally's cheeks burned as she followed PJ out of the store. "Why do you keep telling people I'm your wife?"

"Because it's the truth?" he suggested.

"But not for long." She practically had to lope to keep up with him.

"You're here now."

"Just for the night. I'm leaving Friday."

"Stop thinking so damn far ahead, Al." PJ shifted the grocery bag into his other arm and took her by the elbow as they turned the corner onto one of the side streets. His touch through the thin fabric of her jacket made her far too aware of him. And she jumped when his lips came close to her ear and said, "Interesting things can happen in a night if you let them."

"Nothing's going to happen tonight," she said firmly, "or any other," in case he had any more ideas.

PJ didn't reply. He led the way with long strides. And keeping up with them reminded her of those bright mornings on the beach when he'd been determined to teach her how to surf and she'd practically had to run to match his strides across the sand.

Just when she was about to say, Slow down, he veered over midblock and steered her up the stairs to a very elegant-looking town house.

"Here?" Ally didn't know what she'd expected, but it wasn't this.

One in a row of late nineteenth-century four-story brownstone-and-brick homes, all of which were as attractive and appealing now as she was sure they had been then. The building PJ was leading her into was a far cry from the grim studio apartment over the garage of Mrs. Chang's old stucco house.

"My brother Elias lived upstairs from the office where you were today," he told her. "Antonides Marine owns the building

and he fixed up the top floor for himself. It's pretty spectacular—great view—and when he left he said I could have it. But
I didn't want to. I like being away from the office. I wanted a
place I felt comfortable. So I found this."

He pushed open the ornate oak-and-glass double front door.
"I've got the garden floor-through—that's the ground floor
front to back—not exactly wide-open spaces, but I've got a
garden. There's a hint of green." He was unlocking the door to
his apartment as he spoke. "And, of course, the park is just over
there." He jerked his head to the west. "Coney Island Beach is
at the end of the subway line. And, as you can see," he said as
he turned the knob and ushered her in, "I brought a little of
Hawaii back with me."

She stood, stunned, at the sight of a floor-to-ceiling mural
that covered one entire wall of PJ's living room. Even more
stunning was that she recognized the scene at once.

It was the beach where she'd met him viewed from above
on the highway. There was Benny's Place where she had
worked behind the counter. There was the surfboard shop.
There were the rocks, the swimmers and sunbathers, the
runners in motion at the water's edge, the surfers catching the
wave of the day.

She was pulled straight across the room to look at it more
closely.

"How did you— Did you paint it? It's amazing."

"Not me. Not an artistic bone in my body. But my sisters
are. Martha, the younger one, did this. It's what she does.
Paints murals."

Ally was enchanted. "It's…captivating. I can almost feel the
breeze off the sea, smell the surf and the board wax and—"

"—and Benny's plate lunch," PJ finished with a grin.

Ally laughed because it was true. "And Benny's plate lunch,"
she agreed, shaking her head. "It's fantastic."

PJ nodded. "I think so. It's a good reminder. Sometimes."

Ally cocked her head. "Sometimes?"

He shrugged. "Things were simpler then. Hopes, dreams. That sort of thing." His mouth twisted wryly for a moment, but then he shrugged. "But the memories are worth it, I guess. At least, most of them."

There was a moment's silence as Ally stared at the mural and reflected on her own memories of those days.

Abruptly PJ said, "I'll get started on dinner."

He vanished before she could say another word, not that she could think of anything to say. She was too captivated by the mural—and by his house.

The furniture here was all spare dark wood and leather. Bold geometric-designed rugs dotted polished wooden floors. The walls, except for the one his sister had painted, were either exposed brick or floor-to-ceiling bookshelves.

When she'd known PJ his bookshelf had been four boards and two stacks of milk crates. And the titles, as she recalled, had run to mechanical engineering texts and the latest thrillers.

His library now was much more eclectic. The texts and thrillers were still there. But there were books on woodworking and history, some art tomes and thick historical biographies. She would have liked to explore more, but the mural drew her back. She crossed the room and studied it more closely, noticing that there were people she recognized.

"That's Tuba," she said, surprised at recognizing the small figure of an island boy carrying his board on his head as he walked toward the surf. "And Benny!" she exclaimed as she found her boss sitting, as he often did, in the shade of a tree away from the bustle of his lunch shop.

"Lots of people you know," PJ agreed.

He had shed the suit and had reappeared barefoot, wearing a pair of khaki shorts and dragging a faded red shirt over his head, then tugging it down over a hard flat midriff.

This PJ she remembered—and he could still make her catch her breath. The view of his tanned muscular belly vanished in an instant, but a single glimpse was all it took. Once Ally had seen it, she could still see it in her mind. And once again she remembered things she didn't want to remember at all.

So she swallowed and dragged her gaze back up to his face, trying to remember what she had been talking about. The mural. Right.

"Am I in it?" She was avidly curious, but didn't want to appear as if it mattered.

"Of course."

She squinted at the beach, at Benny's. "I am?" She frowned briefly and squinted more closely at it. "Where?"

He shrugged. "Doesn't matter. Come on. I'll get dinner started. Want a beer? Glass of wine?"

"Um, wine, I think."

Ally wasn't sure she should be drinking anything. She needed her brain sharp and her wits all under control. But a glass of wine might help her relax. She didn't want to feel as uptight as she felt right now. She wanted to settle down, take a deep breath, stop making such a big deal out of this.

It wasn't a big deal, she assured herself. Just a minor bump in the road on her way to marital bliss.

She should know that there were going to be bumps in the road. It was just that in the last few years she had become accustomed to things going her way. In her work, in her life. She'd made them go her way.

But PJ wasn't quite as easy to steer in the direction she wanted him to go.

She left the mural for later, tempted but at the same time unwilling to explore it further. It spoke too much of the past and she didn't need to be thinking about the past. She needed to think about the future. So she followed PJ into the kitchen.

He was every bit as intriguing as the mural. Probably more so because he was the same, yet different. In part, he was still the man she remembered—casual, easygoing, barefoot here at home—on some level taking life as it came.

But there were obviously parts of this PJ Antonides that she didn't know at all. The man who had worn the suit and stood behind the solid teak desk wasn't a man she'd had any experience with. But he was the man who had said, "No divorce."

So that was the man she would have to deal with now.

"Right," he said. "You want some wine." He removed the cork from a bottle on the counter and poured a glass of red wine, then handed it to her.

"Thank you. You're very civil."

He raised a brow. "Why shouldn't I be?"

"You weren't exactly falling all over yourself to be civil this afternoon."

"You were a bit of a surprise this afternoon."

"And now I'm not?"

"Now…we'll see. Won't we?" There was a wealth of speculation in his tone. But he didn't challenge her, just reached in the refrigerator and snagged a beer, then popped off the top.

Ally, though, thought she needed to challenge him. "Why won't you sign the divorce papers?"

"You've got a one-track mind."

"It's what I came for."

"Not to see me?"

She flushed at the accusation. "Well, of course I'm glad to see you, but…you're right. That was my priority."

"You didn't think maybe you should get to know me a little better before you decided I wouldn't suit?"

She opened her mouth, then closed it again before she said something she'd regret.

But if she'd expected him to go on, she was out of luck. He just stared at her, waiting for an answer.

"It wasn't like that, PJ," she said finally. "I met Jon when I was at the hospital with my dad. I got to know him there. Got to see how hard he worked. How much he cared. I fell in love with him there."

He didn't say a word.

She couldn't tell what he was thinking, and not knowing made her nervous. PJ had always been open and sunny, a "what you see is what you get" sort of guy.

Not now.

She was reminded again of how little she knew of him—of why he wanted her here.

"So we'll have dinner and get to know each other again, and that will do?" she asked.

"Will it?" He took the steaks out of the butcher paper and set them on a plate, then began husking the corn.

"Stop being cryptic," she said, annoyed. "What do you want?"

"What do you think I want?"

"I don't have any idea.

"It should be obvious," he said. "Time to think. I don't move fast. I weigh all my options. And I never sign anything I haven't thought over."

"Except our marriage license."

He blinked, startled, then he laughed. "Yeah. Except that."

"It's not funny. And if you think it is, you can undo it the same way," she said impatiently.

"Too soon."

"It's been ten years! Since when is there a timetable?"

He shrugged. "I don't have one." He finished preparing the corn and, wrapping it in foil, added it to the plate, then carried it out the door to the back garden. "You're the one who has the timetable."

"Because I have a fiancé," she reminded him, dogging his footsteps.

"And a husband," he reminded her over his shoulder before lighting the grill.

It all came back to that.

Ally sighed. "Yes, all right. I know. I should have done it the other way around. My bad. Honest. But think about it, PJ. I didn't even know where you were until the article came out. Was I supposed to put my life on hold until I found you?"

"Did you look?"

"I looked there. At the beach."

"Not very eager to find me."

She'd been very eager, in fact. And disappointed that he was gone. But she'd been philosophical, too. She'd never really expected him to wait around for her. They'd made no promises.

And she wasn't admitting anything now. "I would have been happy to find you," she said politely.

He turned his back to her and put the steaks on the grill. "Oh, right."

She stared at the hard shoulders, the firm muscles beneath his shirt and felt as rejected as he'd been accusing her of doing.

"Did you?" she asked.

"Did I what?"

"Come looking for me?" Two could play that game.

He turned back to face her. "You mean after you were so glad to see me at the opening? Hell, no." The word was firm, forceful. No hesitation there.

And that hurt more, even though she'd known what the answer would be. "So you should be glad to get rid of me now."

"Guess we'll see, won't we?" He tipped his beer and took a long swallow.

"Is that why you invited me to dinner?"

"Yep."

"And what can I do to convince you?"

"Give it your best shot." A corner of his mouth lifted. "Tell me about yourself now. I know what you do. I've seen your work. I didn't have to track you down to do that," he said flatly, she supposed in case she thought he'd been interested enough to do so. "But I don't know why this sudden shift."

"What shift?"

"From fiber artist and international businesswoman to little lady in search of a family." His tone was almost sarcastic but not quite. And she thought maybe if she explained, it would help, that he'd understand.

"I was in Seattle when my dad had his heart attack. I hadn't seen him in ten years."

"Your opening—"

"He didn't come."

PJ swore. "What the hell was the matter with him?"

Ally shrugged. "He wasn't ready to let go of his views, still wasn't ready to believe I could be someone other than the woman he thought I should be then. But he was actually glad to see me when I came home."

She'd been afraid he wouldn't be. Afraid he would turn away from her and shut her out in the cold. "We talked," she told PJ, "for the first time. Not a lot. But it was a start. And I…couldn't leave after that. He was all I had. I realized how much I'd missed him. How much I missed family. Even when it was just the two of us."

PJ opened his mouth, then closed it again. He leaned back against the fence and waited for her to go on.

"It was the first time I'd stopped moving, planning, 'achieving' in years." She sipped her wine reflectively and recalled those days and weeks vividly. "Being there with him for days at a time, first at the hospital, then at home, I was forced to stop and think about what I had achieved and what was missing, and—" she shrugged "—I discovered that I wanted to be more than Alice Maruyama, fiber artist and businesswoman."

It was true. All of it. But Ally stopped, astonished that she had revealed so much. She shot a quick glance at PJ to see his reaction. He hadn't moved. His eyes were hooded but focused directly on her. He nodded, listening.

That was always the way it had been with PJ. He was also focused, always intent, always listening.

"The steaks," she said abruptly, seeing the smoke from the grill.

He turned toward them. "I'll deal with 'em. Go on."

"And we talked—my dad and I—about family. About our relationship." That had been difficult. Neither she nor her father were good at that sort of thing. "And it made me realize how much I'd missed. How much I would continue to miss if I didn't— Anyway," she said briskly, "that's when I met Jon."

"And fell in love?" PJ said. The edge was back in his voice again.

"And fell in love," Ally confirmed. "Why wouldn't I? Jon is great."

PJ flipped the steaks. He didn't reply, just concentrated on the steaks, moved the foil-wrapped corn, totally absorbed in what he was doing. So absorbed that Ally wondered if he had even heard her.

Or maybe he had no comment. That was more likely the case.

And really, beyond "Where do I sign?" what did she want him to say?

"Can I help?" she asked. "Make the salad? Set the table?"

"Why don't you make the salad. Use what I bought and whatever you want from the refrigerator. Stick the bread in the oven, too, will you? Then it will be ready when the steaks are."

Grateful for something to keep herself occupied, Ally hurried back into the kitchen. Like the living room and the dining area she'd passed through on the way, it had walls of exposed brick, too. The cabinets were a light oak, the appliances stainless steel. They were all a far cry from the apartment-size stove and bar-size fridge he'd had on Oahu, and despite her insistence that she just wanted his signature and then she would be out of his life, she found that she was curious about how he lived, who he'd become.

She set about making the salad, periodically glancing back at PJ, who stood silently watching over the steaks. On one level it seemed so natural, so mundane—a husband and wife making supper at the end of a day.

On the other, to be casually cooking dinner with PJ Antonides, as if they were a simple married couple, seemed almost surreal.

She finished the salad and put it on the table, then opened the cupboards looking for plates. His kitchen was rather spare but reasonably well equipped. Obviously he was no stranger to cooking. Did he do it often? Did he have girlfriends who came and cooked for him?

A vision of Annie Cannavaro flashed through her head.

She'd told him about Jon, but he hadn't said a word about the women in his life. The newspaper article had made it clear that there were plenty of them. No one special, though?

Would he tell her if she asked?

She didn't get a chance. When he came back with the steaks a few minutes later, he said, "So tell me about how you got started with the fabric art. I remember you made some funky stuff back in the 'old days,' but I was surprised when you turned it into your profession."

She wondered if he was going to have another dig at her for her behavior at the opening in Honolulu. But he seemed actually interested, and so she explained. "When I was in California and I got a job in a fabric store while I was going to school, it seemed like something to explore further. I had access to stuff I didn't ordinarily have. So I got to try things. Experiment, you know."

He put a steak on her plate and one on his, then unwrapped the corn from the foil and added an ear to each of their plates. She dished up the salad, then cut the bread. He refilled her wineglass and got himself another beer. They sat down. "Right. Experimenting. I did that with the windsurfer. I know what you mean. Go on. I'm listening," he prompted.

She hesitated, torn between wanting to tell him how she'd gone from being a mere girl with dreams to a woman who had realized them and wanting to know more about his windsurfer, which had ultimately brought him here. And of course at the same time she realized that neither one was the reason she'd agreed to have dinner with him.

He gave her a patient smile across the table. "We've got ten years to catch up on, Al, minus one night. We're going to be here a while. So talk. Or are you—"

"—chicken?" she finished for him with a knowing smile.

He gave her an unrepentant grin.

"Fine. Here it is in a nutshell."

And she began to talk again. Maybe she could bore him into signing the divorce papers. While they ate, she began the canned account of how she got into her business, the one she hauled out whenever she was interviewed.

But PJ wasn't content with that. He asked questions, drew her out. "Were you scared?" he asked her when she was describing the start-up of her first shop.

"Chicken?" she asked wryly.

"No, really nervous."

She understood the difference. And she nodded. "Felt like I was stepping off into space," she agreed, and recounted the scary times she'd spent on her own, learning what she was capable of, learning what she liked and what she didn't, learning who she was, apart from her father's not-so-dutiful daughter.

It wasn't something she usually did. Ally had learned early that too much reflection meant that she wouldn't get anything done at all. She'd think about things too much, worry about them too much, and so she'd taught herself to weigh her options just long enough to see a clear direction. Then she moved ahead.

She didn't spend a lot of time looking back or analyzing what she'd done. She'd just done it and gone on.

And while she was busy doing, no one was close enough to her or interested enough to ask.

Even when she'd come home, the questions had been few. Her aunt Grace had been impressed. Her father had been too ill to care, and too glad she was home to do more than give thanks that she was there.

Jon thought anything she did was wonderful. He was proud of her. But he was always busy himself. And Ally knew that saving lives was far more important than her "sewing projects" even though he'd never actually said so. He never said much at all about them.

PJ, on the other hand, kept tossing out questions.

And Ally kept answering.

Maybe she answered so expansively because she was proud of what she'd done. Maybe it was to make sure he understood that she had truly taken advantage of the opportunity he'd given her by marrying her, that she'd built something to be proud of, not merely escaped. Maybe it was to show him that she really wasn't the immature rude person she'd been five years ago.

And maybe, she admitted to herself, it was what happened when she found someone interested enough to really listen.

By the time they had finished dinner, she was aware that she had talked more than she'd talked in ages—and PJ had said very little. He sat there, nursing his beer, tipped back in his chair, watching her from beneath hooded lids.

Her awareness of his scrutiny had made Ally keep talking. But finally she stopped and said firmly, "Enough about me. Tell me about you."

It could be opening a Pandora's box.

She might well be better off not knowing anything more about the man who was her husband. But she couldn't not ask. Besides, she really wanted to know.

"You read the newspaper article." He stood up and began to clear the table.

"As you said, blah, blah, blah."

He paused, his hands full of plates. "They got the basics right. More wine?"

Ally shook her head. "No, thanks." She was mellow enough. She needed to move things along. At the back of her mind she could imagine talking to Jon in the morning, facing again the question about whether she'd got things settled.

"So you don't want to talk about what you've been up to?" she pressed. "I thought this was 'catching up' time."

"I work. I play a little softball. When I have a free weekend I go out to Long Island and surf."

"You're living a completely monkish existence, then?"

He grinned. "Doing my best."

Ally rolled her eyes. That certainly wasn't what the article had indicated. But before she could question him further, the doorbell rang.

"Wonder who that could be," PJ murmured as he rinsed the plates and stuck them in the dishwasher.

"Probably your friend Manny from the grocery store, wanting you to make it to the game." Ally stood up, figuring it was time to go anyway.

But PJ shook his head. "He knows better. Sit down," he said. "I'll see who it is. Get rid of them."

She hesitated. But he was already heading toward the front of the apartment.

Ally knew she really should be going. There was no point in staying here any longer. PJ wasn't going to let her use the opportunity to convince him to sign the divorce papers. And as pleasant as it had turned out to be, just sitting around shooting the breeze with him, it was a bad idea.

It was diverting her from her objective. It was making her fall back into the easy familiarity she'd always felt with PJ. Worst of all, it was making her remember the night she'd spent making love with him.

That was past, she reminded herself. Jon was her future.

From the living room she heard voices. PJ's and others'. He wasn't, apparently, "getting rid of them" because as she listened the voices grew closer.

"...don't believe a word of it, for heaven's sake!" a woman's voice said as she came through the doorway and found herself staring straight at Ally.

And Ally found herself staring back at a pixieish woman around thirty with spiky black hair and the most beautifully expressive dark eyes she'd ever seen.

The eyes gaped at her, then flashed accusingly at PJ.

"You mean," the woman demanded, "it's *true?* You really do have a *wife?*"

## CHAPTER FOUR

PJ APPEARED in the doorway behind her. "I told you—"

But the woman cut him off. "As if you ever told me the truth." She dismissed him with a briskness that made Ally blink. Then the other woman's hard level gaze swiveled back again to zero in on her. "So," she said, "you're PJ's wife?"

The wealth of doubt and the hard edge of challenge in her voice brought Ally to her feet. They also made her do the one thing she never expected to do.

"Yes," she said, "I am." And she met the woman's gaze with a frank, firm stare of her own. "And who are you?"

Because if this short-haired brunette with her chiseled cheekbones, scarlet lips and tough-girl attitude was one of the women in PJ's life, Ally knew one thing for sure: she was obviously going to have to rescue him from this female's possessive talons before she moved on.

The woman blinked, as if surprised by the question, then drew herself up straight. "I? I'm Cristina."

"My sister, God help me," PJ put in.

"And me," Cristina retorted.

Before Ally could do more than gape, another voice said dryly, "God should really have had mercy on their mother." And a thirtyish man carrying a preschool-aged boy followed PJ and his sister into the room. "Imagine having those two as twins."

*Twins?*

But even as she heard the word, Ally remembered PJ once remarking that he had a twin. She'd envisioned a cookie-cutter PJ. A less likely looking twin than Cristina was hard to imagine.

PJ's sister was as short as he was tall. Her eyes were brown; his were green. Admittedly they had the same dark hair. But that was the only similarity Ally could see.

"I'm Mark, Cris's husband." The man holding the child offered his hand to Ally with the easy acceptance that his wife completely lacked. "And this is Alex." He jiggled the little boy in his arms. "And your name is…?"

"Ally." Ally shook his hand, smiled at him, winked at Alex who hid his face in his father's shoulder, then peeked at her when he thought she wouldn't notice. He did resemble his uncle, and she had a fleeting sense of what PJ must have looked like as a little boy. Too cute for his own good. She shoved the thought away. "Alice Maruyama…Antonides."

PJ's sister snorted at that. "Where'd you come from?"

"Play nice, Cristina," PJ said gruffly, stepping between them. "Ally came from Hawaii." He gave his sister a hard look that shut her mouth long enough for him to add, "How about some wine? Beer? You're just in time for dessert. We've got pineapple."

"Don't change the subject, PJ." Cristina was still eyeing Ally like an eagle sizing up its prey. "If she's your wife—"

"She is my wife."

"Then I want to know all about her. We didn't believe him when he said he was married," she told Ally as if he weren't standing right there. "We thought he was just trying to avoid all the women Ma and Pa were trying to shove down his throat."

"Cristina—" PJ said sharply.

"I'll take a beer," Mark cut in. "Sit down," he said to his wife while PJ went to the refrigerator to get one. "You're making Ally nervous."

"Good," Cristina said frankly. "If she doesn't have anything to hide she'll be fine."

"What could she have to hide?" Mark looked intrigued.

"Who knows? Where's she been. What's she been doing. Why she's here now." Cristina ticked off plenty of possibilities. All the while studying Ally as if she had her under a microscope. "Maybe she's after his money."

"Well, she certainly isn't after his well-behaved relatives," Mark grinned. "Cristina can be a little, um, protective."

"She thinks I can't fight my own battles," PJ said dryly, coming back to hand his brother-in-law a beer.

"Because I'm older than you," Cristina said loftily.

PJ rolled his eyes. "Four minutes."

"And I'm married—"

"So am I—"

"Which, amazingly, seems to be true. At least, you seem to have produced a wife."

"I didn't produce her. I married her."

"But you don't live with her, either. *I*, on the other hand, live with *my* spouse. Always have. And I have a child. So I have a wealth of domestic experience you don't have," she said to her brother with a smug grin. "And I'm looking out for your best interests. So go out in the garden and talk to Mark about his trip. Or baseball. Or boats. And let me do my sisterly duty. Go!" she said again when neither man moved.

Mark looked at PJ. "Your fault."

"I didn't invite her over," PJ protested.

"As if you could have kept her away once she found out Ally was here." Mark laughed and shook his head. "You know what Cristina is like when she's got the bit between her teeth. Might as well let her get on with it."

How had they found out she was here? Ally wondered. But she didn't ask. She just turned to PJ and said stoutly, "Go on. I'm perfectly happy to talk to your sister. I don't need you."

PJ's brows lifted. But Ally met his gaze squarely. And after a long moment he turned to face his sister.

"Do not alienate my wife," he instructed.

Cristina looked indignant. "As if I would!"

"You would," he said with conviction, "if you thought it was a good idea. I'm telling you it's not."

Brother and sister stared at each other. It was like watching mortal combat—death by eye contact.

Clearly his sister brought out a side of PJ that Ally had never seen before. He didn't look particularly upset to have his sister here, but he still looked a little wary—as if he didn't entirely trust her.

Ally wasn't wary or worried. She found herself almost eager to confront PJ's sister. Once she understood who the other woman was, the tension inside her eased. This was no floozy she had to warn off. No woman trying to worm her way into PJ's life.

Warn off? Ally jerked herself up short. What was she thinking? She had no interest in PJ's love life! She was only a wife on paper. His women were nothing to do with her.

Besides, it looked as if Cristina was determined to vet any woman who crossed his path. Ally smiled at the thought, feeling instantly calmer and far more in control.

Also she was curious.

She hadn't expected PJ to tell his family anything about their marriage. Yet apparently he had. So, what had he told them? And when? And why?

She also found herself intrigued by Cristina.

She'd never met any of PJ's family. He had talked about them occasionally. She knew he had grown up in the middle of a boisterous, noisy, demanding Greek-American family.

"I was never alone," he said. "Ever. God, I even had to share the womb. I never had silence. Cristina never shut up. I always had to share a room with my brothers. I never had space."

Ally, who had had far too much loneliness, silence and space in her life, frankly thought PJ's childhood sounded appealing. She'd asked questions, but except for a few comments, whenever he had talked about them it had been mostly about how glad he was they were practically on the other side of the world.

Now, face-to-face with the woman he'd "shared a womb with," Ally couldn't pretend indifference.

Neither apparently could Cristina. The men had barely gone out through the door and slid it shut behind them when PJ's sister sat down at the table opposite Ally and jumped straight in.

If Cristina had ever heard of circumspection or tact, she'd determinedly forgotten everything she'd ever heard. She wanted to know where PJ and Ally had met, when they'd married. And why?

"I wouldn't ask why," she said bluntly, "because ordinarily it would be obvious. You're gorgeous and PJ has always had an eye for a gorgeous woman. But if it were for that reason, he wouldn't have let you walk out of his life again. So…why?"

She regarded Ally intently, and in the face of Cristina's clear concern, Ally found herself answering.

She'd never told anyone else. Besides her father and, recently, Jon, she'd never told a soul she was married.

But this was PJ's sister. Ally didn't have siblings. She had never experienced the bonds that could exist between them. But it was clearly there—and just as much in PJ's words to Cristina as in her attempted defense of him. It bespoke a loyalty and love she could only envy.

And in response, she couldn't deny the kindness he'd done her. Nor could she minimize it or pretend it had been some frivolous or foolish thing they had done.

And so she began to talk.

She spoke haltingly at first about her father's demands on her—about what she should take in university, about what job she would hold when she finished, about the man he expected her to marry. It sounded medieval and melodramatic to her ears as she told it, and she fully expected Cristina would roll her eyes.

Instead the other woman listened raptly and nodded more and more vigorously.

"Fathers!" she muttered, eyes flashing in indignation. "Mine is just as bad. They always think they know what's best. And they can be so clueless!"

But her indignation vanished and she beamed gleefully when Ally told her about her grandmother's legacy and how she could use it to avoid having to fall in with her father's demands.

"I couldn't be the person he wanted me to be. I needed to be me. To get away and find out who I was. But I couldn't get away without the legacy. And I couldn't have the legacy without being married—"

"So PJ married you!" Cristina clapped her hands together delightedly, her eyes were alight with satisfaction. And all her original skepticism and animosity toward Ally seemed to evaporate.

"That is such a great story." She cheered Ally's determination—and her brother's part in it. "I should have known he wouldn't do anything stupid."

She didn't even blame Ally for "using" him to get what she needed.

"Blame you?" she'd said, affronted, when Ally suggested it. "Of course not! What else could you have done?"

Ally shook her head, surprised at Cristina's approbation.

"So what did you do? Where did you go?" PJ's sister asked.

And Ally told her that as well. And in telling her the truth about how she had used PJ to get her legacy, to get her education, to travel and learn and work and become the person she'd become, far from putting Cristina off, actually brought her around to Ally's side.

"I think it's absolutely marvelous. What a hero!" And for an instant Ally thought Cristina might jump up and go outside and throw her arms around her brother. Instead she just shook her head and aimed a smile and a fond glance his way.

Ally, following her gaze, knew that what Cristina said was true. "He was, actually," she admitted quietly as much to herself as to his sister.

"And of course you couldn't stay. You had to leave," Cristina went on, telling the story herself now, and believing every word she said. "To find yourself. And PJ was probably distraught, but knew he had to let you go."

"I don't think he was distraught," Ally said.

"Of course he was. How could he not be? You're everything he'd want in a woman." Cristina looked her over with frank admiration. "He's not blind."

Ally felt her cheeks warm. "It wasn't quite like that. Besides, he wasn't ready to be married then. Not *really* married."

"You mean, adult and responsible and all? Yes, I can see that." Cristina's tone grew thoughtful, as if she were remembering, too, what he'd been like ten years ago. "He was a kid. I remember what he was like when he left—moody, distant, could hardly wait to be on his own. Independent to a fault. Yes, he would have needed time and space to find himself, too. But now—" Cristina's voice brightened visibly "—he has. You both have."

"Yes." Ally nodded, glad PJ's sister understood. Now she could explain about why she'd come, why it was time for them to go their separate ways.

"And so you've come back to him." Cristina sighed in pure appreciation. She smiled broadly. "That is soooo romantic. Who'd ever think PJ would be romantic?"

"He's not!" Ally blurted, and this time, at least, she managed to get the words out before Cristina could cut her off.

Cristina looked startled at her vehemence. But then she laughed and gestured toward the living room. "Maybe not. But if he's not a romantic, why did he have Martha paint that mural?"

Ally stared, uncomprehending.

Cristina shook her head. "We didn't understand what he was up to. But it makes sense now." She glanced back toward the living room and its resident mural. "Trust me, under all that cool, PJ's a romantic. And so are you."

There was only one time in her life Ally thought she'd behaved romantically—and that had been the night she'd spent in PJ's arms.

Before and after, she'd been a realist. She'd done what she

needed to do. She was still doing it. She was being a realist now, asking for the divorce, not asking for the impossible.

She was being a realist in choosing to marry Jon, who wanted the same things she did, who felt about her the way she felt about him. She was, she realized, the daughter her father had wanted her to be, after all.

"I'm not a romantic, either," she told Cristina.

But PJ's sister disagreed. Her eyes widened. Her hands fluttered. "Just turning up on his doorstep isn't romantic?" She laughed and shook her head. "It's the most romantic thing I can imagine."

"I didn't mean—"

But Cristina leaned toward Ally across the table and lowered her voice, as if the men outside might be able to overhear. "I know. You don't want to scare him to death. Men can be panicky that way. But, honestly, you picked the perfect time. No matter what he thinks. PJ is ready to be married now. He's settled. Centered. And he dotes on the kids. You should see him with the nephews."

In fact Ally could see PJ with Alex right now.

Other than when he'd tossed a ball or a Frisbee to a kid on the beach, it was the first time she'd seen him interacting with a child. She'd imagined he might be awkward. Lots of men were.

For that matter, she was. She'd simply had no experience with them. But PJ had apparently had plenty. Or dealing with them came naturally to him.

Ally had expected to see Alex cling to his father and duck his head when PJ talked to him, just as the little boy had with her. But the minute they'd gone outside, Alex had flung himself into his uncle's arms. And PJ had accepted him willingly, flipping him up and over his shoulders, then whipping him around his side and tossing the boy into the air.

Ally had watched in almost horrified amazement. But PJ seemed perfectly comfortable, and Alex, shrieking with laughter, clearly loved it.

After that PJ had hung Alex upside down, let the boy climb his legs like a logger going up a ponderosa pine, then somersault to the ground. He was like a human climbing frame and Alex was having the time of his life. Even when they stopped, Alex remained sitting on his shoulders while PJ stood there, listening to Mark.

"PJ will be a great dad." Cristina stated the obvious. "Are you going to have kids soon?"

Ally colored fiercely. "No! I mean—we're not…!"

"Sorry," Cristina said quickly. "That really is none of my business. It's enough that you're back. Whatever happens, happens, right?"

"Y-yes," Ally managed. She needed to say it—to tell this woman why she'd really come. But somehow the words wouldn't form. Because they shouldn't come from her, Ally told herself. They should come from PJ. He was the one who had told his sister he was married. He needed to be the one to tell her they were getting a divorce.

And when he had kids someday—when he was some child's wonderful father—that child would not be hers. And if the thought caused pain, Ally didn't let herself think about it.

"Mom and Dad will be so pleased," Cristina went on. "Mom can hardly wait to meet you."

"*What?*" Ally's brain jerked back to the moment. "Oh, no!"

Cristina made a face. "You aren't going to be able to keep her away. She was so excited to hear you'd finally turned up. She said she'd always believed PJ—about being married. Dad thought he was stonewalling. Dad thought he might have even faked the marriage certificate. But Ma said no. So did *Yiayia*—our grandmother. *Yiayia* said he wouldn't lie about a thing like that."

He'd told them all? He actually showed them their marriage certificate? Ally's brain spun.

Cristina didn't notice. She shook her head. "She was right. Mother's intuition, you think? Before I had Alex, I'd have laughed at that. Now sometimes I think I know what he'll do before he does it. So she may be right."

"No, she's not right!"

At Ally's outburst, Cristina's eyes fastened on her. "What do you mean? You said you were married."

"We are." She chewed on her lip briefly, torn. What could she say? Talk about opening a can of worms. "For the moment," she said at last.

Cristina's gaze snapped up and she frowned. Then her expression lightened. "Oh, are you worried that you might not suit now, after all this time? Don't be. You're soul mates, it will work out."

Ally opened her mouth to deny it, but again the words wouldn't come out. And she couldn't tell Cristina about coming here to get him to sign divorce papers. If he'd kept their marriage a secret, it wouldn't really have mattered. Everyone would know he didn't care. But he'd told them he was married to her.

Word of the divorce would have to be his to tell.

Cristina patted her hand. "Don't worry. It will be fine. The only one who's going to be upset is Dad."

"What does your father have to do with it?" Just what she needed. One more person's opinion to matter.

"Oh, he's a 'never say die' sort. He's still trying to hook PJ up with Connie Cristopolous. Her whole family is coming from Greece this weekend. It's a huge affair. Sort of a family reunion for us, too. Complete with fatted calf or, in this case, sacrificial lamb. At least, it was. That was going to be PJ." Cristina laughed. "But not now, obviously. With a wife in tow, he won't have to worry."

"But I'm not—"

"Poor Dad," Cristina said with relish. "Well, it serves him right. He should have believed." She shrugged. "It doesn't matter. It might be a little awkward at first, but he'll be thrilled to have a son married off and no wedding to have to go to. Dad much prefers sailing and golf."

Before Ally could even begin to think of how to respond to that, Mark opened the sliding door.

"Someone needs to go home to bed," he said. Alex was back in his arms, head against his father's shoulder, looking weepy and out of sorts.

"Yes. And we should let these two enjoy each other's company." Cristina smiled warmly at Ally and then at PJ who, seeing the smile, raised his brows quizzically.

Cristina stood up and went over to him, going up on her toes to kiss his cheek. "I like your wife," she said. "A lot."

The vehemence of her declaration seemed to surprise him. But then he just looked bemused. "She checks out okay, then?"

Cristina swatted his arm. "You knew she would. You married her. You are such a dark horse."

"Me?"

"Such a romantic. Riding in to save her like a knight on a charger."

PJ reddened. "I never—"

"A knight? PJ?" Mark's brows rose. He regarded his brother-in-law with wonder.

"A knight," Cristina said firmly. "Who'd a thunk it? Come on. Let's go home." She linked her arm in Mark's. "And I'll tell you all about it."

At the door, she turned back and looked at Ally. "I want to hear more about your art. And the clothes. They sound fantastic. We didn't even get into that," she said to her brother. "But we will. There's plenty of time now." She went out, then turned to back Ally. "You can fill me in on the weekend."

"The weekend?" Ally stared.

"Oh, I know everyone else will want a piece of you, too. But we're going to talk."

"I'm not—"

"Are you going up Friday?" Cristina asked her brother.

"Yes."

"No!" Ally blurted.

"We're still discussing it," PJ said smoothly.

Cristina laughed and patted his cheek. "Enjoy the discussion.

And the making up after." She winked. "We'll be there Saturday. See you then."

"Yes," PJ said.

"No!" Ally said.

"Oh, this is going to be fun," Cristina said happily. Then as PJ began to close the door, impulsively his sister darted back in to plant a quick kiss on Ally's cheek.

Her eyes were shining and she squeezed Ally's hand as she said, "I just want to say how happy I am for both of you. And…welcome to the family."

# CHAPTER FIVE

"No!" THE door had barely shut behind Cristina and Mark before Ally had the word out of her mouth. "I am *not* going to your parents' house."

"Al—"

"No!" She whirled away from where she'd been standing beside him near the door, stalking across the room, needing to put as much space between them as possible.

Only when she was as far as she could get did she turn and glare at him. "You did this on purpose!"

"Did what?" How could he look so innocent? So completely guileless.

"You set me up! You invited your sister here so she would jump to all the wrong conclusions and then back me into a corner where you think I'll be forced to go to your parents' house with you! Well, I won't!"

"I didn't invite my sister here."

Ally snorted. "Then how did she know to come? She knew I was here."

"They invited me for dinner tonight. I had to decline."

"And you just happened to mention—"

"I didn't even talk to her. I asked Rosie to call her."

"And Rosie just happened to mention—"

He shrugged. "If she did, you can blame yourself as much as me. Who came in and announced she was my wife?"

Ally's teeth came together with a snap. "In my office we prize confidentiality."

"In mine we prize people," he said mildly, putting her back up even further. At the same time she knew he was right. She'd told his assistant who she was. She'd used the relationship first.

"Besides, it doesn't make any difference. You weren't a complete surprise. They knew about you."

Ally couldn't even imagine how that conversation must have gone. "So it seems. And what did you say, 'Oh, by the way, I'm married, but I seem to have mislaid my wife'?"

His lips pressed into a thin line. "The first part, yes. The second didn't come into it. It just…happened. When I came back and decided to stick around, Dad and Mom started throwing women my way. I said I wasn't interested. They said, 'Oh, God, he's gay.'" His mouth twisted. "I suppose I could have let them think that, but it seemed smarter to tell them the truth. So I said, 'No, I'm married.'"

"And they didn't say, 'Show us your wife'?"

"Of course they did. But I couldn't, could I?"

"So what did you do?"

"Told them a shortened version of what happened. Said I'd met you in Hawaii. That we were friends. That you needed to get married. That I married you."

"You said I *needed* to get married? Oh, for God's sake, do they think I was *pregnant?*"

"It did occur to my mother," he admitted. "She asked, rather hopefully, as I recall, if she was going to have another grandchild. Cristina had just had Alex. I said no. I said you needed to stop your father meddling in your life, and marrying me was how you'd done it. No big deal."

Ally's eyes widened. "And they were okay with that?"

"Well, it wasn't their idea of a best-case scenario. They like their children to marry people they can meet and who will have loads of little Antonides babies." He gave her a wry smile and a shrug. "That's the way they are. But what were they going to say?"

Ally couldn't imagine. She knew what her father would have said. It wouldn't have been pretty. She shook her head. She prowled restlessly around PJ's living room, feeling off balanced. Awkward. Guilty.

She'd never really considered how their whole marriage scene would play out for PJ. It had always been about her. Her needs. Her hopes.

"Of course they wanted to meet you," PJ went on. "They wanted to know where you were. What you were doing. When we were going to get back together."

Ally cocked her head. "And you said…?"

"I said I didn't know." He lifted his shoulders, spread his hands. "I didn't, did I? The truth."

Ally grimaced. The truth was supposed to set you free, wasn't it? She didn't feel free at all. She felt trapped, hemmed in.

She picked up the softball on the bookcase and slapped it against her palm. "And now Cristina assumes I'm going to the family reunion with you."

"It's a natural assumption."

"And what will they think when we get a divorce? They'll have expectations," Ally went on. "Cristina certainly has expectations!"

"She likes you." He still sounded almost surprised at that.

Unaccountably, the thought made Ally bristle. "You thought she wouldn't?"

"Nothing Cristina does surprises me. But I didn't know if she'd shut up long enough to find out anything about you. Cristina generally goes into every situation with both guns firing. My sister shoots first and asks questions later. I figured she would like you a lot if she gave you a chance. And apparently she did." He paused. "What did you tell her?"

"The truth."

"That you came for a divorce?" The edge was back in his voice, but he looked perplexed as he said it. "But she didn't—"

"I told her the truth about why we got married. About my meddling father. About needing to find myself. About not marrying Ken. About the legacy. I told her why you married me. She thinks you're a hero."

A grin lit PJ's face. "She said that? I wish you'd got it on tape. It won't happen again in my lifetime."

"She's very devoted. And far fonder of you than you might imagine. She was definitely protective."

"Bossy," PJ corrected.

"She loves you." Ally envied him that familial closeness. She'd never had it. "What you did—she thinks it's the most romantic thing she's ever heard."

PJ laughed. "You put a spell on her!"

"No. She put one on herself. I told her the truth—and she embroidered it to fit her view of the world."

"That's pretty much Cristina in a nutshell. Still, you apparently handled her very well."

"If I had, she wouldn't have assumed I was staying."

"Why didn't you tell her that you weren't?"

"I thought it was your place to do that."

"Mine?"

"Because you said we were married. I felt you should be the one to tell them we're getting a divorce."

"I'm not. You are."

And they were back to that again, damn it. "All right, fine. That *I'm* getting a divorce! Anyway, I didn't think you'd appreciate me announcing first thing that *I'd* come to get a divorce. And Cristina didn't ask why I was there. She just assumed…and then she assumed some more. And more. And finally she just leaped to the conclusion that I'd be coming with you on the weekend."

"Imagine that," PJ murmured.

"You could have told her I wasn't!"

"But I want you to come."

*"What?"* She stared at him. "Oh, come on, PJ."

"Why not? It's a family reunion among other things. You're family."

"I am not!"

"Legally, you are. And of course you should come. Let my folks meet you. See that you're real. That I didn't make you up." He grinned.

"Raise their expectations," Ally muttered.

The grin widened. "Save me from the clutches of Connie Cristopolous."

"Oh, please." She rolled her eyes. "You can save yourself."

"I did you a favor once."

The words dropped quietly between them. An observation. A statement of fact. A reproach. All of the above.

Ally wanted to rake her hands through her hair. Her fingers tightened on the ball, as if she would squeeze it to death.

PJ didn't say a word, just stood there, watched her. Looked expectant.

Ally ground her teeth. "Damn you. I never should have come. I should have mailed you the damn papers." She spun away and paced around the room, furious at having been trapped, knowing she had no choice.

She sighed and tried one last time. "It's a bad idea. Going out to your folks' place will just make things worse."

"For who?"

"For you! If I show up with you, they'll expect us to be a couple after that. And they'll be appalled when you tell them we're getting a divorce."

He propped an arm on the mantel of the fireplace. "Why would I tell them that?"

"Because we are! *I* am!" she said before he could correct her pronoun.

"But I don't want a divorce."

"Damn it!" She wanted to wring his neck. "Why not? And don't tell me you're so afraid of Connie Cristopolous that you want to stay married so your parents don't try shoving her down your throat."

"Well, it is a consideration."

"I'm sure it is," Ally said bitterly. "You're just trying to be difficult."

He gave her a lopsided grin. "Not really."

"Yes, you are! I shouldn't have come here. Not to New York. Not to dinner! And now I need to leave." She grabbed her purse off the bookcase and headed for the door.

PJ stepped in front of it. "Don't be in such a hurry."

"What point is there in staying? We're not getting anywhere."

"We might be."

Her gaze narrowed. "What's that supposed to mean?"

"We're getting to know each other again."

"Just what we want," Ally said acerbically. "PJ, enough! I realize I've handled things badly. I know I should have got the divorce out of the way before I ever let things go so far with Jon. But I had no idea where you were. And I didn't realize things were going so fast. My dad's illness just sort of…accelerated things, and it just seemed like it was meant to be—between Jon and me."

"Jon and me. Jon and me." His tone was mocking. "If he's your dear true love, where is he? Why didn't he come with you?"

"Because he's busy. He's a doctor, for heaven's sake! He doesn't have time to run around chasing down my soon-to-be-ex-husband."

"Does he have time for you?"

"Of course he does! He takes time when I'm there. I give him a reason to take time," she said. And that was the truth. Without her Jon was consumed only by his work. "He loves me. I love him. And we want to get married, have a family, give my dad a grandchild. He wants a chance to meet his grandchild. And his health is poor. Time is of the essence."

"So stick with me. We're further down the road."

"What?" She stared at him.

He spread his hands. "We're already married. We wouldn't have to waste time. No waiting for a divorce. We could have a family," PJ said. "Give him a grandchild. What do you say?"

She wanted to scream.

And worse—in some tiny deranged part of her brain—she wanted to say, *Yes!*

Because Ally knew that if PJ had said those words ten years ago, after one night in his arms, no matter that they had planned it to be purely a marriage of convenience, she would have flung good sense and caution to the winds and believed they could make a marriage work.

Because right then—on that one night—PJ had touched her with such a mixture of passion and reverence, eagerness and gentleness that she'd actually dared to think he might really love her.

But *this* PJ?

This PJ was toying with her.

Oh, she had no doubt he was perversely serious about wanting her to come to his parents' place. It would doubtless suit him to make sure his father and Connie Whosits knew he really was married.

In fact, he might simply want to stay married to her as a way of avoiding all future entanglements.

But there was no love involved.

As for wanting a child, well, maybe he did. Cristina seemed to think he was ready to settle down and have children. And of course, to his mind she would be convenient for that, too.

"I have half a mind to come with you," she snapped. "Then go back home to Hawaii and leave you to sort things out. It would serve you right. Your mother knows I'm here. Did you know that?"

PJ shook his head. "No. But I can't say I'm surprised. Cristina never could keep a secret."

"Did you expect her to?"

"Not really."

It was the last straw. He'd planned this whole thing, had been manipulating her all evening.

He'd set her up to deal with Cristina, had known his sister would pressure her into coming. He'd fully expected his sister to tell his mother. She supposed she was lucky that Mrs. Antonides hadn't turned up on the doorstep, as well.

*Well, be careful what you wish for, buster,* she thought grimly.

"Fine. I'll do it! You want me to meet your parents, I'll come with you and meet your parents. I'll be your wife for the weekend. I'll be sweet and charming and wonderful. But after that you are on your own. The scales are balanced. You did me a favor. I'm doing you one. We'll be even. And then, damn it, PJ Antonides, I'm filing for divorce!"

That went well, PJ thought grimly with more than a little self-mockery.

He stood outside the hotel in midtown Manhattan where he'd just left Ally and stuffed his hands in his pockets, shaking his head.

She'd insisted on leaving once she'd agreed to come to his parents' on Friday. He'd invited her to stay at his place.

"Why not? We might as well begin as we mean to go on," he'd said.

And Ally's black eyes had flashed. "We don't mean to go on. At least I don't. One weekend, PJ. That's all."

And he might not have seen Ally for ten years, but he knew her limits. And the look on her face said that he'd pushed her far enough. He'd shrugged.

"I'll see you back to your hotel."

She'd argued about that. But he wasn't taking no for an answer when it came to seeing her safely back to her room. She might have taken care of herself for ten years, but it was his turn now. At least for tonight. So they'd taken a cab across the river to the big midtown Manhattan hotel where she was staying.

She'd thanked him politely for "the lovely evening" as the cab had drawn up outside the main entrance. He knew she didn't mean it. He also knew she'd mean it less by the time he really said good-night.

"Put your money away," he'd said sharply. "And don't say good-night yet. I'm not leaving."

He'd followed her out of the taxi, paid the driver, then hurried to catch up with her as she was already inside the lobby. It was all polished marble and crystal chandeliers.

"This is totally unnecessary," Ally insisted. "You can go home now. You never felt compelled to see me to my door before."

"That was then. This is now. That was Hawaii. This is New York City. Humor me."

She just looked at him and shook her head. But when he persisted, she shrugged. "Suit yourself." And she turned and marched to the elevator. "But don't expect me to invite you in."

He didn't expect she would.

If there was one thing he'd learned from his years on the beach, it was how to bide his time. You couldn't rush the ocean. When you went out on the water, surfing or windsurfing, success didn't come from pushing or trying to control.

You got into position and you watched and you waited. You learned patience and awareness. And timing.

When the time was right—when you and the wave were in sync—then and only then did you move.

And just like he couldn't push a wave, PJ knew he couldn't push Ally Maruyama.

So he simply accompanied her up in the elevator and down the corridor to her room. He waited silently until she opened the door of her room. He didn't press. Didn't invite himself in or suggest that she should.

"I'll see you Friday at noon," he said. "I'll pick you up."

"I still think this is insane, PJ. How are you going to explain later to your family? You don't know what you're asking."

PJ knew exactly what he was asking. But he didn't think she did. "If you get bored tomorrow, call me."

"I won't be bored," Ally said. "I have an appointment with a gallery owner."

He paused. "Who?"

"Gabriela del Castillo. She's shown some of my work at her gallery in Santa Fe."

PJ knew the name. His sister Martha had mentioned her. Said glowing things. "She going to show your stuff here?"

"I'll know more tomorrow. Thank you again for dinner," she said, once more sounding like the proper well-brought-up girl he remembered. "And for the introduction to your sister," she added a bit grimly.

He grinned. "My pleasure."

"Good night."

"Good night," he said equally politely. But then as she started to close the door, he stopped her. "Ally."

She narrowed her gaze. "What? I told you I'm not inviting you in, PJ. I've got work to do, Jon to call, things to think about. What do you want?"

"Just—" he hesitated, but only for a split second "—this."

And he took one step forward, swept his arms around her, hauled her close and set his lips on hers.

It wasn't planned. PJ didn't plan.

He was an "act now, revise later" sort of guy. He believed in a spur-of-the-moment, caution-be-damned, full-speed-ahead approach to life. Always had. Probably always would.

It had got him into some scrapes. It had got him into a marriage. It had got him where he was today—kissing Ally.

Dear God, yes, he was kissing Ally.

The quick peck he'd managed when she'd come out of the subway had barely given him a taste. But it had whetted his appetite, made him remember the last time he'd kissed Ally.

For ten years he'd wanted more.

And now he had it. Had her lips under his, warm and soft. Resisting at first, pressed together, unyielding. He touched them with his tongue, teased them, and rejoiced when they parted to draw a breath.

It came as a gasp almost. "P—"

But he didn't let her speak. Didn't want to hear what she'd say. So he pressed his advantage, moved in, took more.

And the more he took, the more he wanted. The more the

memories crowded in, the more the woman in his arms seemed to melt against him. His body hardened in response. His heart pounded.

He wanted—! He needed—!

And he knew she did, too. He could feel her softening against him, could feel her whole body now, pressed against his, molding itself to his. Oh, yes! He deepened the kiss.

And the instant that he did, she jerked out of his embrace, pulled back, her eyes wide, her cheeks flushed, mouth a perfect O. He could see the pulse hammer at her throat. She gripped the door so tightly her knuckles were white.

"That," she said icily, "was totally unnecessary."

Slowly PJ shook his head. "Was it?" he said, his own heart hammering so hard he could barely talk. "I don't think so." He managed a lopsided grin. "Tell that to Jon when you talk to him."

And he turned and walked away.

His body would much rather have been doing something else.

"The message you left on my machine was garbled," Jon said. "It sounded like you said you were staying longer."

Ally, who had grabbed her mobile phone when it rang, even though she was still asleep, barely made sense of what he was saying. She pushed herself up in bed and squinted at the clock—9:30 a.m.?

She never slept that late!

But then, as a rule, she didn't lie awake half the night wondering if she'd lost her mind, either.

Last night clearly she had.

She'd shut the door on PJ, bolted it, then leaned against it, breathing as hard as if she'd run a marathon. A marathon would have made more sense!

She would have prepared herself, she would have trained for a marathon.

She hadn't been prepared for PJ. Or for his refusal to sign

the divorce papers. Or for his sister. Or for her agreement to go
to his parents' for the weekend.

Or most especially for his kiss.

Dear God, that kiss.

She'd just been congratulating herself on having made it back
to her room, if not emotionally totally intact, at least unscathed.

And then he'd kissed her. And ten years of carefully papered-
over need had come spilling out of her. Ten years of memories
locked down and shut away had swamped her, and she had been
powerless against the force of them.

Of course, she'd had only a split second's warning.

She had seen something in his eyes at that last second when
she'd started to close the door, something that looked hard and
dangerous and tempting. But she'd discounted it. Had thought
she was safe. Home free.

Wrong.

Very *very* wrong.

Every time she'd closed her eyes all night long, she'd been
swept back to that kiss. The way his mouth had awakened her,
the way the press of his body had made her feel. She'd felt
branded, possessed. And unthinking, she'd responded with a
hunger of her own. It was a feeling she'd only experienced once
before in her life. That night…

Their wedding night.

She had relived it all—that night and this for hours. It was no
wonder she hadn't slept much. It was a wonder she'd slept at all.

"Did you say that or was I hearing things?" Jon said, jerking
her back to something else she wasn't prepared for.

She had called him last night as she'd promised. She'd
waited until she thought she could put together a coherent
sentence or two, had hoped Jon would be there to say sensible
things, to remind her about her father, about her life in
Honolulu, and the world beyond PJ's kiss.

But she'd only got his answering machine, so she'd left a

message. Now she said, "Um, yes. That's what I said. You got it right."

She sat up straighter in the bed, pushed herself back against the headboard and willed herself to sound brisk and in control—not to mention "awake"—though God knew she wasn't at all. She hadn't fallen asleep until dawn. "I'm staying over the weekend," she said.

"What about the hospital benefit on Saturday? You didn't forget."

She had actually. But she also remembered something else. "You said you couldn't go to the benefit," she reminded him. "When I was planning the trip I asked you about it, and you said it wasn't a problem, that you couldn't go, you were too busy."

"I am busy. But I need to go. Fogarty says I'm expected to show my face."

Fogarty was the head honcho in Jon's practice, the senior doctor whose lead everyone else followed. "Then I guess you'll have to show your face. But you'll have to do it alone because I can't be there."

"Ally, what's going on?"

"Something's come up. Something important."

"What could possibly be more important? The benefit is important, Alice."

But it hadn't been until Fogarty had decided it was. "I know. And I did ask," she said again. "But I've made a commitment here now. I have some…unfinished business."

"I know you want that Castillo woman to take you on, but really, Ally, you have plenty of exposure elsewhere. And when we're married, how are you going to keep all the shops supplied? When we have kids…?"

They'd had this discussion before. And after they had children, Ally was certainly willing to put her career on hold and be a full-time mother. She had made up her mind some time ago that if she were ever fortunate enough to have children, she didn't want someone else to raise them. If it were an economic necessity, she would certainly work to support them. But it wasn't. Jon could provide the economic security for the family while the children were young.

Until then, however, she wanted to work, to draw, to paint, to design, to sew.

"When we have kids, I will put them first," she said firmly. "But now I have to stay here until Monday."

And she wasn't entirely averse to taking advantage of the fact that he had assumed it had to do with her art. After all, if she told him why she was really staying, he would like it even less.

"Your dad is going to be disappointed. He was looking forward to seeing you tomorrow."

"I know." Ally felt guilty, but she didn't see any other option. "Well, I'll see him Monday. And if you stop in to see him today, give him my love."

"I doubt if I'll have time to stop by. I have a full day."

"I'll give him a ring, then," Ally said. "And I'll call you as soon as I know what flight on Monday I'll get in on."

"Right. I'll try to be there to pick you up. But I have to go now. I have surgery in less than an hour."

"Right. Of course. Thanks for calling back. And I really am sorry about the weekend. I'll talk to you later. Love you."

But Jon had already hung up.

Ally sat there holding the phone in her hand, feeling sick.

She knew she was letting him down. She knew he counted on her. Depended on her. Loved her. And she knew he didn't understand about PJ. Probably he never would. She wished she'd been able to talk to him. It would have helped so much to have felt able to confide in him about what had happened, to admit that PJ's refusal to sign the papers had unnerved her, that the meal he'd cooked had baffled her, that his sister had charmed her, that going to meet his parents was seriously rattling her.

And then there was his kiss.

Her senses still spun, her brain still whirled every time she thought about that kiss. But of course Jon was the last person she could talk to about any of that.

Would PJ kiss her again this weekend?

Did she want him to?

If he did, how would she react a second time? Why was he doing it? What did he want? He didn't love her.

Did she still, somewhere deep inside, love him?

And if she did, what then?

# CHAPTER SIX

EVERYONE in the office knew about Ally's arrival.

PJ knew Rosie had told his sister. Hell, he'd *wanted* her to tell Cristina. But had she had to tell everyone?

Not that anyone said anything. It was in the way they looked at him and in what they didn't say that told him they all knew.

The minute he'd opened the office door Thursday morning, the conversation had stopped. Rosie and the rest of them had been in deep discussion, and at the sight of him, the room went from full babble to total silence.

They all turned and stared. No one said a word.

"High-level top-secret meeting?" he asked blandly. "Or are you all speechless in admiration of my tie?" He flapped his silver-and-black-striped tie at them and raised a sardonic brow.

One of the architects grinned, flashing his gold tooth, then shook his dreads and headed for his office. "Sorry, boss. Not my style."

The others turned red and mumbled something before vanishing, as well, leaving only Rosie to meet his hard stare unflinchingly.

"Did you put out a bulletin?" he asked acidly.

"Mark was already here this morning," she said. No further explanation was needed.

"Ah. Sorry." He grimaced and headed for his office. He hadn't slept most of the night. He'd prowled and paced and remembered. Lay down. Got up. Relived. And this morning he was edgy and he knew it.

"Ryne Murray will be here at nine," Rosie said to his back.

"Let me know when he gets here." He spoke without turning around, happy to close the door behind him before Rosie could decide that, even though it was business as usual, she was still entitled to ask questions.

He wouldn't mind the questions, PJ thought, tossing his jacket over the back of his chair, then going to stare out the window, provided he knew the answers.

But whatever she might ask about Ally—and he knew that all of Rosie's questions would deal with Ally—PJ didn't have any answers at all.

No, not true.

He had one: he still wanted her.

When he'd married her, PJ had expected nothing. And that was pretty much exactly what he'd got.

After the ceremony—if you could even call it that—where they'd said their vows at the courthouse, when they'd come back outside into the bright Honolulu sunlight, he'd suggested a celebratory dinner.

"After all," he'd told her, grinning, "it's not every day we get married."

But the smile Ally returned had been tremulous at best. "I don't think so. I just—well, I really need to tell my father I'm married."

As that had been the point of the whole exercise, PJ hadn't argued. "Okay. I'll come with you. Moral support."

He'd thought she'd jump at the chance. But she'd declined that, too, shaking her head and saying gravely, "Thanks, but you'd better not. I don't think it would be a good idea. This is between him and me. It wouldn't be fair to bring you into it."

He was already in it. He'd married her, hadn't he? How much more "in it" could he get? But he knew that hadn't even occurred to her. He wasn't sure that it ever would.

But he hadn't argued. He'd married her for her sake.

To his way of thinking she deserved the same freedom to find herself that he'd got by moving away from his family. The fact that he didn't have to marry anyone to achieve it was lucky for him. If she didn't want it to be his business, well then, it wouldn't be his business, he'd decided.

It wasn't as if this was some love match. It was just the sort of thing one spur-of-the-moment impulsive friend would do for another.

"Okay. Suit yourself," he'd said.

But for a long moment neither had moved. Their gazes had locked, and perhaps a faint notion of what they'd just done inside the courthouse occurred to Ally then.

If it had, though, she thrust it away, saying, "I probably won't see you again. I'll be leaving in the morning."

He'd nodded. "Yeah, sure." Then he'd cracked a grin. "Well, good luck. Have a good life."

She'd smiled, too. And they'd both laughed a little awkwardly. She'd said something about he should feel free to get a divorce whenever. And then she'd stuck out her hand to say farewell.

He could still remember that. She'd married him—then shaken his hand. He remembered her touch. Her grasp had been soft and gentle. Just the slightest pressure. Her palm was cold and clammy even though the temperature had been hot that day. He'd wanted to warm it as he'd squeezed her fingers in his big rough callused hand.

He'd wanted to warm *her.* And so as soon as she moved to ease her fingers out of his grasp, he let them go, only to reach out an instant later and wrap his arms around her, draw her slender body against his and touched his lips to hers.

It wasn't intended to be a moment of erotic passion.

It was supposed to comfort, encourage, sustain. And yet, the taste of her, the feel of her soft lips under the hard pressure of his awoke something wholly unintended.

"Warm" didn't even begin to cover what he had felt. And

which of them was more shaken when at last he broke it off, he could not have said.

Ally had stared at him, her eyes wide and astonished. She looked stunned, which was no more than he felt.

And then she said, "I have to go," and turned and ran down the sidewalk as if all the demons in hell were after her.

And PJ had stood there wondering what had hit him.

He had still been wondering when he'd gone to bed that night—his wedding night.

The very notion seemed like some sort of perverse joke. He'd avoided going home for hours. He had gone surfing at dusk, then out drinking with a couple of buddies, doing his best to put it out of his mind.

But he'd still been thinking about it—about *her*—when he'd heard a light knock on the door.

His landlady, Mrs. Chang, was usually in bed before now. But sometimes she came to get him when she needed something on a high shelf or wanted him to open the lid on a jar.

He wasn't much in the mood for Mrs. Chang tonight. He'd been "useful" already once today: he'd married Ally.

But when the knocking continued and grew even more persistent, he got up and opened the door, then stood stock-still and stared at Ally standing there looking at him with wide unreadable eyes.

"What's wrong? Did your old man—"

She swallowed again and gave her head a little shake. "No. I just thought that, um, it's our wedding night and—could you make love with me?"

You could have knocked him over with a breath. He stared at her in astonishment, knowing he should ask her to repeat it, but not wanting to have his dearest dream snatched away when she repeated whatever it was she'd actually said.

But then she went on, "I just…it's a marriage, PJ—and I don't know, it doesn't seem like a marriage. But I thought it might if…I just want it to be real."

A slow smile had dawned. He'd shaken his head, dazed and delighted, astonished at the strange turns of fate, and not about to question his good luck.

"It will be my pleasure," he'd assured her.

And his responsibility. Loving Ally was no problem at all. Being responsible for making her first time—and he was sure it was her first time—good was something else. He was young. Eager. Not untried, of course. But definitely not the most skilled of lovers.

But this was Ally, and she was depending on him. She was trusting him. And he was determined to love her the way she deserved.

He did ask, "Are you sure, Al? Are you sure this is what you want?" because he didn't want there to be any misunderstanding.

She'd nodded jerkily, gulping again, looking terrified. "It is," she insisted. Then, at his look of skepticism, she'd said it again. "I mean it, PJ. I want to."

And then, as if she were determined to convince him, she'd put her hands on his bare chest and leaned in to press a tentative kiss against his lips.

And he'd been lost.

PJ had made love with a few women in his life. It was enjoyable tactile exercise—and nothing felt better. But he learned very quickly that making love with Ally went far beyond that. It wasn't just exercise. It didn't just feel good.

It felt right.

As he unbuttoned her shirt, he found his own fingers trembling. And when he pressed kisses along her jawline and licked the edge of her ear, her tiny gasps sent his heart into overdrive. He almost couldn't get her shirt off. They might have been tangled in it forever if she hadn't finished unfastening the buttons and skimmed it away, then pressed closer to him.

Her skin was petal soft. And warm. Not cold and clammy as her hand had been when she'd offered it outside the courthouse. Now her skin was hot satin beneath his fingers. He stroked and kissed, nibbled and laved. Her small breasts were perfect in the scrap of rose-colored lace that was her bra. But they were even more enticing when he freed them.

And when she arched beneath the touch of his lips on first one nipple and then the other, his own desire almost betrayed him right there.

He backed off, pulled away to take deep harsh breaths, to regain control. He dropped his head so that his hair brushed against her breasts, so that his mouth was barely more than an inch from her navel.

He felt her fingers in his hair, gripping, tugging. "What?" he muttered.

"Y-you're breathing."

An anguished laugh made it past his lips. "Barely."

"On me," she whispered, as if the feel of his hot breath shocked her.

He pressed a kiss to her abdomen. Trailed his tongue down lower. And even lower.

"PJ!" Her whole body was quivering. Her fingers felt as if they were about to snatch him bald.

"Mmm." He gritted his teeth, nuzzled her with his nose.

"You can't! I'm not—I've never—"

"Of course you haven't." He raised his head, pressed one more quick kiss on her belly, then stretched out beside her, cradling her into his chest. "Next time."

"N-next?" Her voice was practically a squeak.

He smiled. "Oh, I think so. Yes."

But this time—her first time—he would take her there slowly and gently with all the care he was capable of, and he'd make every stop along the way.

He kissed her again, feathered light kisses over her shoulders, then up her neck to her face. He kissed her cheeks, her eyelids, the tip of her nose, her mouth.

And the kiss they'd shared that afternoon, startling though it had been, paled in the face of the kisses they shared now.

And the operative word was *sharing*. He wasn't the actor and she the "acted upon." Awkwardly but eagerly she kissed him back. Her hands roved over him, running down his back, tracing the line of his spine, sliding just for an instant beneath the waistband of the shorts he wore.

Shorts that were confining. Annoying. Shorts that he needed to shed. He sat up and made quick work of the skirt she had on, tugging it down over her hips and tossing it aside, then doing the same to his shorts.

As his erection lifted, eager and unconfined, he saw Ally's eyes widen. Her hand reached out as if she would touch him, then pulled back.

He settled back onto the bed again and stretched out next to her. "Go ahead."

She looked at him doubtfully. But then she lifted her hand and ran a single finger down the length of him.

It was his turn to arch and suck in a sharp breath.

Ally snatched her hand back. "Did I hurt you?"

"You didn't hurt me. It feels—" he shook his head, making a sound that wasn't quite a laugh "—wonderful."

Though it might kill him if he let her do it again.

"So, it's all right if I—" and she did it again, then circled him lightly with her fingers.

His breath came quick. His heart pounded. He bit his lip. "Maybe you'd better hold off a bit," he managed.

"I'm sorry. I didn't mean—" She looked stricken.

"It's okay," he assured her. "I like it. Too much. Let me…show you."

He might—possibly—be able to manage that. Giving Ally pleasure was just as exciting as having her touching him. More so, really. It was wondrous to watch her face as he stroked down her sides, as he circled her knees and trailed his fingers back up the insides of her thighs.

She moved restlessly, and he slid a thigh between her legs, opening her to his exploration. Ally's fingers gripped the sheets.

Her tongue slid between her lips as he slowly stroked closer and closer to the center of her.

He closed his eyes at the wet warmth he found there. He drew in a slow careful breath, smiling as he heard her suck in a much sharper one. He stroked deeper.

Her hips lifted. Her breath came fast. She gritted her teeth. "PJ! Oh, dear heavens!"

And he drew her into his arms as she shattered, too stunned to speak. He could feel her heart slamming against his, which had a serious staccato beat of its own. She was trembling as he kissed her, and then, still shaky, she pulled back.

"You," she whispered. "What about you?"

"Don't worry about me. I'm fine. Besides, we've got all night," PJ said. "That was for you."

He so much wanted to give Ally something. And, truthfully, the giving was the most amazing reward in itself.

But Ally wasn't content with that. She wanted to give to him, as well. Insisted on it. Soft hands stroked his body, learned his lines, his angles, his muscles even as he was learning hers.

And when he thought he might die for the mere pleasure of her fingers on him, she said, "Now, I think," and shifted her body, opened her thighs and urged him down between them.

PJ wanted to go slow, wanted to make it last. But the softness he eased into was heaven. The heat consumed him, raised him up, then burned him down at the same time.

"I can't—" he muttered. But he managed. Just. Eased in carefully. Held himself rigid. Excruciatingly still. Allowed Ally to adjust, to accommodate. To open to him, welcome him.

"Is this…all?" she whispered after a moment.

"All?" He almost laughed.

She moved experimentally, drew him deeper. A breath hissed between her teeth.

"Are you all right?" He could barely get the words out.

"I will be," Ally promised. She moved again. And again.

His own breath caught in his throat. "Ally!"

"Love me," she whispered and rocked her hips so that he felt again the tightness of her body around his.

That was all it took. Lose control? He had no control. Had nothing to lose but himself. And he did—in her.

He loved her eagerly, desperately, giving and taking simultaneously. They both did—caressing, stroking, touching, moving together until he had no idea where one of them ended and the other began.

It was only when Ally tumbled to sleep in his arms and he pulled back just enough to look at her sleeping face in the moonlight that spilled through the window that he felt the coolness of separation where the breeze touched his heated skin.

Ally didn't stir. Her black hair drifted against his pillow. He lifted a strand and touched it to his lips.

Then he'd just lain there, shattered, unable to tear his eyes from her, drinking in the sight, dazed and confused at having had a wedding night after all.

And wondering what the hell he had just done.

The intercom's buzz jolted him abruptly, and he realized he was standing at the window of his office, staring unseeing out at the Manhattan skyline.

There was no moonlight, no bed, no Ally.

He reached over and punched the button on the intercom. "What?"

"Ryne Murray is here."

"Give me a minute."

But a minute wasn't going to do it. He took a breath. Then another. Steadied himself. Or tried to. But his brain—and his body—were still focused on Ally.

Ally who was back.

Ally who was still his wife; who said she was in love with someone else.

But who kissed like she loved him.

* * *

Where was he?

Ally paced the length of the lobby for what seemed the hundredth time. It very well might have been.

She'd come downstairs at just past ten, having already paced around her room enough to wear a path in the carpet. Even though PJ wouldn't be there until noon, she'd needed to check out before eleven, and being around a lot of people and watching the passersby, she hoped would distract her, settle her down.

It didn't. A three ring circus underfoot wouldn't have distracted her. A herd of elephants tapdancing on Forty-second Street probably wouldn't have distracted her. She only thought about PJ—about spending the weekend with PJ—and grew more and more apprehensive.

She got a cup of coffee from the hospitality center. Having something in her hands would help. It would keep her from biting her fingernails, if nothing else. She sipped it and burned her tongue, muttered under her breath, paced some more.

She should have said she would meet him in the Hamptons. There were jitneys that traveled back and forth between the city and the Hamptons. She needn't have committed herself to a full afternoon in the car, just she and PJ.

But it was too late now.

She would have needed to make a reservation. And she would have had to tell him. And calling PJ was not on her list of things she wanted to do.

She knew he'd say, "Chicken, Al?"

And she wasn't. Really. She wasn't. Just…wary. Edgy. Nervous.

She would go through with it. Of course she would. But it would help if he would get here so she could stop fretting about it and start resisting.

"Ready?"

The sound of his voice right behind her made her jerk. Coffee splattered on the floor, on her shoes, on her shirt, on her hand.

"Oh!" She spun around and sloshed it on his shoes, too. "Stop sneaking up on me."

"I wasn't sneaking. You were walking away. I couldn't run around in front of you and say, 'Here I am,' could I? Are you okay?" He took the coffee out of her hand and set it down on a table while she tried ineffectually to mop herself up.

"I'm fine. Terrific. Never been better." She was muttering while she scrubbed at her shirt, then sighed and gave it up for a lost cause. "I need to change." She gave her still-stinging hand a shake.

"Let me see." PJ caught her fingers in his and examined her hand. It was red where the coffee had burned. But somehow the stinging from the burn was less intense than her awareness of his touch.

Abruptly Ally tried to pull her fingers away. But PJ held them fast and grimaced. "You should have some ice." He lifted his gaze, meeting hers. "And a kiss to make it better?" He grinned lopsidedly.

Ally snatched her hand out of his. "Ice, yes. A kiss, no."

"Don't want a repeat of last night, Al?" His tone was teasing.

But Ally had spent the night in far too deep a funk where kissing PJ was concerned. She compressed her lips. "I'll just get some ice and change my shirt and we can go."

Before he could reply, she took a fresh coral-colored pullover top from her suitcase, then, leaving the case with PJ, hurried to the ladies' room where she changed quickly, glared at her reflection in the mirror, exhorted herself to shape up, stay calm, cool and collected and, above all, resist PJ Antonides's charm.

Then she got a plastic bag of ice from the ice machine in the refreshment center, put it on her face before she put it on her hand. And then she made her way back to the lobby.

PJ had put her suitcase in his car—a late-model midsize SUV with a surfboard on the roof.

She stared at it. "I'll bet you're the only person in New York City with a surfboard on his car."

"I'm probably not," he said. "You'd be amazed at what you see in the city. How's your hand?" He opened the door for her and she climbed in, glad it was a good-size car and that she would be able to keep her distance.

"It'll be fine." She fastened her seat belt. He fastened his, then slid the car out into the crush of midtown noontime traffic.

Ally loved the city, but she never ever considered driving there. Honolulu was stress enough. But PJ maneuvered through the traffic as easily as he picked out and rode the waves he surfed.

"I become the wave," he'd told her once.

"Do you become the traffic?" she asked him now.

He slanted her a quick grin. "How'd you know?"

She resisted the grin and silently congratulated herself. "You make it look easy."

"I manage." He made a wry face. "It's not the most relaxing way to spend a Friday afternoon."

"You should have let me take one of the jitneys. I could have met you out there."

"No. I don't mind. Besides, it will give us a chance to spend some time together."

Precisely what Ally would have preferred not to have. But she said, "Yes. Are there going to be lots of people there?"

"Enough," PJ said grimly. "All the immediate family. The grandkids. My grandmother. A couple of my mother's sisters. One of my dad's crazy aunts. She's a widow, but her husband was the cousin of Ari Cristopolous, which is why my dad decided he could justify inviting them that weekend."

"But he really invited them because of…you…and the daughter?"

"Not that he'd ever admit it," PJ said cheerfully.

"Won't he be upset?"

PJ shrugged. "He knows now. Ma has to have told him. And he never stays upset long. He's pretty easygoing."

"But what about the Cristopolouses? And their daughter? Won't they be expecting…?"

"An unattached son?" PJ did a rapid tattoo with his fingers on the steering wheel, grinning. "Yep. Poor ol' Lukas."

Ally stared. "Lukas?"

"My little brother." PJ rolled his shoulders and sighed expansively. "Bless his heart."

Ally gave him a long skeptical look.

He just laughed. "Lukas won't mind. He never minds when people throw beautiful women at him."

"Do people often throw beautiful women at him?"

"Mostly beautiful women throw themselves at him. It's a little annoying." PJ shrugged. "They think he's good-looking. No accounting for taste. Tell me," he went on, "what happened yesterday at the gallery? With Gabriela del Castillo?"

Ally was curious about this brother whom women threw themselves at. It was hard to imagine anyone better looking than PJ. But then, maybe women threw themselves at him, too. She wanted to ask. But she didn't want to know. So she focused on the question he'd asked her.

"We had a really good meeting. I took half a dozen pieces—fabric art, quilted pieces, collages—and she accepted them all."

"Like what?"

"Oh, a couple of Thai beaches—very stylized. A couple of New Zealand ones. A bit of Polynesian Maori influence. And some landscape collage type things—a New York skyline at night."

One she didn't tell him about, was a much more personal piece—and one of the earliest she'd done. It had been her memories of the morning after the night they'd spent together, the view from his window toward the sea, the sand, the sunrise, the lone surfer on his board riding toward shore.

All the longing she'd felt that morning had gone into that piece. It had accompanied her everywhere. She'd shown it in several galleries, had had offers to buy it, had never sold. Couldn't bring herself to do it.

But she'd offered it for sale at Gaby's. She'd carried it with her too long. Like the marriage she was ending, it was time to part with it. So she'd told Gaby all the pieces she'd brought were for sale.

"I'm sending her more when I get home, and she's going to do a whole show—we're calling it Fabric of Our Lives."

PJ whistled. "That's fantastic." He seemed genuinely pleased. "Where is the gallery? What's it called?"

"Sol y Sombra Downtown. To distinguish it from another called Uptown she has on Madison Ave. Downtown is in Tribeca. The original is in Santa Fe."

Once she got talking about it, she couldn't seem to stop. And PJ encouraged her. He asked questions, listened to her replies, drew her out, seeming genuinely interested. And maybe because he was the only person to have shown any interest at all, she kept on going.

She told him about the other artists whose work she'd seen there. Gabriela del Castillo represented artists in a variety of mediums.

"I know what I like," she'd told Ally, "so that's what I represent."

She represented all sorts of oil and watercolor and acrylic artists as well as several photographers and a couple of sculptors.

"And she's just hung one room with work by a very talented muralist named Martha Antonides." It was her turn to flash a grin at him now. "I recognized your sister's work right away."

She had been as astonished to turn the corner in the gallery and find herself staring at an eight-foot-by-eight-foot painting that essentially took up a whole wall, a painting that captured summer in Central Park.

It was as if the artist had distilled the essence of New York's famous park—its zoo, its boats, its ball diamonds, fields, walkways and bike paths. The detail was incredible. Every person—and there were hundreds—was unique, special. Real.

And studying it while Gabriela went on at length about its

talented creator, Ally wished she'd gone back to look at the mural in PJ's apartment to find herself in it.

"Have you ever seen anything like it?" Gaby had asked eagerly.

"I have, actually," Ally had said. "I saw a couple of her murals earlier this week. She's amazingly talented."

"You can tell her so," PJ said when Ally repeated her comment to him. "She'll be delighted to hear it. I'm glad she's painting on something smaller than buildings these days. Easier for her, now that she's staying home with a kid."

It was easy to talk to PJ about her work and about his. And since his family figured largely in the company, she found that it was easy to ask about them. He talked readily, telling stories about growing up in a large boisterous family that made her laugh at the same time that she felt twinges of envy for the childhood he had known. It was so different from her own.

And while the thought of meeting a host of Antonideses was unnerving under the circumstances—she felt like a fraud—she found that the more she heard, the more eager she was to meet them.

More than once she said, "You're making that up," when PJ related some particularly outrageous anecdote, many of them having to do with things he and his brothers did or pranks he played on his sisters.

And every time he shook his head. "If you don't believe me, ask them."

"I will," she vowed.

The stories he told surprised her because PJ had always seemed distant from his family in Hawaii, determinedly so. But now he seemed to actually relish the time he spent with them.

"I thought you wanted to get away from your family," she remarked as they headed east through one suburb after another until finally they got far enough beyond the city that there were actually cultivated fields and open spaces here and there.

The sun was shining. A breeze lifted her hair. The summer heat that had been oppressive in the city was appealing out here.

"I did," PJ said. The wind was tousling his hair, too. "They're great in small doses. Like this weekend. But I needed to be on my own. So I left. To find myself. Like you did," he added, glancing her way.

She hadn't thought about that before. She'd been so consumed by her own life in those days that she hadn't really thought about what motivated anyone else. PJ's proposal had been a favor, but had always seemed more of a casual, "Oh well, I'm not marrying anyone else this week," sort of thing.

She hadn't realized that he'd equated her situation with his own.

"Did you realize that then?" she asked.

"It occurred to me." He kept his eyes on the road.

Ally turned her eyes on him, understanding a bit better what had motivated him. Which should, she reminded herself, make it easier to resist the attraction she felt.

She'd been a "cause" for him then. Nothing more, nothing less. And this weekend her chance to pay him back. On Sunday he would take her back to the city. Monday she would catch a plane back to her real life.

And what PJ told his family afterward was not her problem. But the weekend could be a problem unless they discussed it ahead of time.

She turned to PJ. "Before we arrive, we need to get a few things straight."

# CHAPTER SEVEN

"WHAT sort of things?" PJ slanted her a wary glance.

She had seen signs for various Hamptons—West Hampton, Bridgehampton, East Hampton—so she knew they were getting near now. She didn't know which PJ's parents lived in, but the knowledge that she'd be meeting them soon banished her pleasure at the surprising ease of the journey and was replaced by jittery nerves and a definite edginess.

"Rules," she said.

"Rules?" he repeated, sounding incredulous. "What sort of rules?"

"No kissing."

His head jerked around. Disbelieving green eyes stared at her. "What?"

"You heard me," she said, feeling her cheeks begin to heat.

"Not right, I didn't," PJ muttered under his breath. "I'm your husband," he reminded her.

"Only for the moment," she said primly.

"You can kiss me like you did and still want a divorce?"

Now her face really was burning. "You caught me off guard. And I never said you weren't appealing. It's just…" she hesitated. There was no way she could discuss this with him. They weren't speaking the same language. "I won't say that I'm filing for divorce. I'll leave that up to you."

"Big of you," he muttered. His fingers tightened on the steering wheel. His knuckles were white.

"I just—" she plucked at the hem of her skirt "—don't think we should lead them to expect that we're a couple."

"Ally, in their eyes we *are* a couple. We're married."

"I shouldn't have come."

"Well, too bad. You're here now," PJ said as he flipped on the turn signal and, the next thing Ally knew, they were off the highway and heading south. She clenched her fists in her lap and tried to settle her nerves. She took a deep breath intended to calm her.

"You're not going underwater," PJ said. "Relax. They don't bite. I don't either," he added grimly.

"You kiss," Ally muttered.

"And damn well, or so I've been told," he retorted, then tipped his head to angle a look at her. "You didn't seem to have any complaints."

"You kiss very well," she said primly, staring straight ahead. "And you've proved that."

He made another right turn, then a left. They were getting closer and closer to the shore, running out of houses. And she was running out of time. She turned to entreat him. "I don't want us to make this any more difficult than it is, PJ."

He slowed the car and looked straight at her. "I didn't realize it was such a terrible imposition."

"It's not! It's—" she couldn't explain. She couldn't even make sense of her tangled feelings herself "—not difficult. But it is awkward. I feel like a fraud. That's why I don't want kissing."

He let the car roll to a stop now. They were sitting in the middle of the road. Fortunately there was no traffic. He let his hands lie loosely on the steering wheel for a long moment before he drew a long breath, then said quietly, "Is it when you kiss *me* that you feel like a fraud, Ally?"

He didn't wait for her to answer. He gunned the engine and they shot down the road another hundred yards and then he swung the car into a large paved parking area behind an immense stone and timber pseudo-English-style two-story house.

"Home sweet home," he said, and without glancing her way, he hopped out of the car.

Challenged by PJ's question, Ally sat right where she was, feeling as if she'd just taken a body blow to the gut. But before she could even face the question internally, let alone articulate a reply to PJ, he jerked open the door on her side of the car and said tersely, "Come and meet my parents."

Knees wobbling, and not just from being stuck in a car too long, Ally got out. She wasn't sure exactly what she'd expected—apart from being nervous—when he introduced her to his parents. Probably she hadn't even let herself think that far.

But whatever fleeting notions she had, they didn't come close to what she got.

"Good luck with your 'no kissing' rule," PJ said just before he turned to face the horde of relatives descending upon them.

And the next instant, they were surrounded.

"Ma, Dad, this is Ally. Al, these are my parents, Aeolus and Helena," PJ said and somehow he swept them together.

And instead of politely shaking hands and saying, "How do you do?" as Ally had expected, she was instantly enveloped in Aeolus's hearty embrace, her cheeks were kissed, her body was squeezed, her hands were pumped.

"And so you are real!" he said jovially, dark eyes flashing with humor. "My boy is just full of surprises!"

And somehow he managed to wrap PJ into the same fierce hug so that she might not have kissed him, but she certainly had plenty of body contact before Aeolus struck again, this time drawing his wife into their midst.

PJ's mother was not quite as effusive as her husband. But her expression, though clearly inquisitive, was warm and her smile was just as welcoming.

"A new daughter," she murmured, taking Ally's cheeks

between her palms and looking straight into her eyes. "How wonderful."

And just as she was smitten by guilt, Ally was kissed with gentle warmth. Then Helena stepped back, still smiling and slid an arm around Ally's waist, drawing her away from PJ and his father. "Come," she said, "and meet your family."

Her family.

More guilt. More dismay. And yet, how could she not smile and allow herself to be passed from one to another. There were so many, all dark-haired, eager and smiling, as they shook her hand, kissed her cheeks, told her their names.

Some names she recognized—PJ's siblings, Elias and Martha, their spouses and a swarm of little boys who must be more of PJ's nephews. There was another brother, some aunts, cousins, friends.

She heard Mr. and Mrs. Cristopolous's names, but they were just part of the blur. She did get a bead on Connie, though, the woman Aeolus hoped his son would marry.

Connie Cristopolous was the most perfectly beautiful woman Ally had ever seen. She was blessed with naturally curling black hair. Ally's own, stick straight, couldn't compare. Not only did it curl, but it actually seemed to behave itself instead of flying around the way most of the women's hair did. Her complexion was smooth and sun touched. Her features— a small neat nose, full smiling lips, deep brown eyes—were perfect. And she had just enough cheekbone to give her face memorable definition, but enough fullness in her cheeks to make her face warm and feminine.

She smiled at Ally and greeted her warmly. "So glad to meet Peter's wife," she said in a lightly accented voice that reminded Ally of the spread of warm honey. Even her thick luxuriant eyelashes were perfect.

Maybe she was a perfect shrew, too. But somehow Ally doubted it. PJ's father didn't look like the sort of man who would have chosen a shrew as a potential daughter-in-law. Ally suspected Aeolus Antonides had terrific taste in women.

She slanted a quick glance at PJ, who was being mobbed by his aunts and mauled by his brothers. He didn't seem to be noticing Connie. But no doubt he would.

Maybe he would even marry her. After all, she could be his, once the divorce was final.

The thought made Ally stiffen involuntarily, and she narrowed her gaze at the other woman, as if she could discern at a glance whether she was worthy of a man like PJ. Would she love him?

Would he love *her?*

The question made Ally stumble as she was being led up the steps to the house by a couple of PJ's aunts.

"Are you all right, dear?" one asked her, catching her by the elbow to make sure she didn't fall.

"F-fine," Ally stammered. But she wasn't all right. The truth was that while she might be able to cope with the idea that PJ didn't really love her, she didn't want him falling in love with anyone else, either.

Mortifying, but true.

"Come and meet *Yiayia*." The aunts drew her into the house.

The house PJ had grown up in was as lovely and warm within as it was without. There was a lot of dark wood paneling, floor-to-ceiling bookcases and a massive field-stone fireplace, which could have been oppressive but was softened by overstuffed sofas and chairs and balanced and lightened by high ceilings and French doors. These faced south and opened onto a deck that led to a lawn, then down a flight of wooden steps to the sand—and the ocean and horizon beyond.

Ally, seeing that, felt a moment's peace. She would have preferred to stop there, admire and take a breath, try to regain her equilibrium.

But the aunts were towing her on through the dining room and into the kitchen where a small still-dark-haired elderly lady was in the middle of a rather elaborate baking project. Her hands were stuck in something that looked like honey and ground nuts. A very sticky business.

Ally wondered how they would handle the requisite hug.

But though the older woman looked up when they came in, her eyes, bright and curious as they lit on Ally, she made no move to take her hands out of the bowl. She simply looked Ally over.

It was clear she needed no introduction to the new arrival. She was already assessing her carefully. She did not smile.

And Ally, who was still feeling overwhelmed, was almost grateful. And her gratitude had nothing to do with avoiding the sticky stuff.

"This is *Yiayia*," one of the aunts said. "Grandma," she translated in case Ally couldn't.

Ally could. PJ hadn't said much about his grandmother. He'd indicated that she would be there, but nothing more.

She smiled at the old woman who didn't smile back. She was still studying Ally closely and in complete silence. Ally wondered suddenly if PJ's grandmother spoke English.

Well, if she didn't, they'd certainly figure out another way to communicate. The family seemed big on kisses and hugs. At least, all of them but Grandma.

"Hello," she said at last, when it was clear that PJ's grandmother wasn't going to take the conversational lead. "I'm so glad to meet you. I'm Alice. Or Ally if you prefer. Or Al if you're PJ," she added with a small conspiratorial grin, inviting PJ's grandmother to share a grin with her.

She was surprised to discover how very much she wanted the old lady to smile.

"Alice," PJ's grandmother said quietly at last, her gaze still fastened on Ally's face. But even then her expression didn't change. She turned and looked up at the aunts. "Alice will help me. Go now."

They looked at her, then at Ally, then at each other and, with only that much hesitation, they nodded and left.

Outside Ally could hear a multitude of voices, laughter,

scuffling. But no one came into the kitchen. In the kitchen it was just she and PJ's grandmother. It felt like having an audience with the pope.

Like going to see her own father who was distant and formal and also rarely ever smiled. Ally almost breathed a little easier. This was more what she expected.

And then suddenly the door opened and PJ strode into the room. At the sight his grandmother burst into an absolutely radiant smile. And when he crossed the room in three long strides to pick her up bodily, sticky hands and all, and kiss her soundly, she crowed with laughter, then put her honey-coated hands on each of his cheeks and kissed him right back.

Ally felt her mouth drop open.

Both PJ and his grandmother turned toward her. "So, what do you think of my wife, *Yiayia?*" he said. "Isn't she gorgeous?"

"A beauty," his grandmother agreed. She was still smiling, still patting his cheek with her sticky hand but her eyes were shrewd when they met Ally's. "So, this is Alice." It sounded like a pronouncement.

PJ nodded. He was still smiling, but there was a seriousness in his expression that told Ally something else was underneath the smile.

"You went to get her?"

"She came to me."

"Ah." His grandmother's brows lifted. Her gaze softened a bit, a hint of a smile touched her face. "*Ne.* This is better."

Better? Than what? Ally could tell there was a subtext to the conversation, but neither PJ nor his grandmother enlightened her. And all the vibes she was getting said it wasn't better at all. She was very much afraid that PJ's grandmother, like his sister Cristina, was misunderstanding the situation.

"So, you have come," the old lady said, approvingly. "At last."

"Don't give her a hard time, *Yiayia.* She's had things to do."

"More important than her husband?"

"Important for her," PJ said firmly. "Like when I went to Hawaii for school. That was important for me. You understand?"

The old lady eyed him narrowly for a long moment, then slanted a gaze of silent judgment at Ally, who stood motionless and didn't say a word.

"*Ne.* I understand, yes," she said. She sighed. "You are happy now?"

PJ grinned. "Of course I'm happy now." He took her fingers and nibbled the honey off each one, making her laugh again. "Why wouldn't I be? I've got two of my favorite women right here in the room with me. You're making baklava." He nodded at the project underway on the counter. Then he sniffed the air. "Mom's made roast for dinner. And there's no way Dad can foist any more women off on me."

His grandmother laughed, reassured. "Wash your face and go help your brother with his twins. Tallie must put her feet up and rest. She's going to be a mother again."

"Really?" PJ was clearly delighted. "When?"

"In the spring. Go now. Leave your wife," she said after he'd washed his hands and face and had turned toward Ally. "Alice and I will talk."

"But—"

"Go," his grandmother ordered. "Trust me. I will not eat her."

Still he hesitated for a moment. "She's worse than Cristina," he said to Ally. There was a warning look on his face.

"We'll be fine. I've always wanted to learn how to make baklava."

*Yiayia* smiled and nodded. "I will teach you."

"Just be sure that's all you do," PJ warned his grandmother. He dropped another kiss on her forehead, then with a quick smile at Ally, went out the door, yelling for Elias.

They both watched him go. Then as she cleaned her hands and began to layer the filo and melted butter with the honey mixture, PJ's grandmother said something in Greek.

"I'm sorry. I didn't understand," Ally said, coming closer

and picking up the brush to help butter the layers as *Yiayia* spread them out.

"I said," *Yiayia* repeated clearly, in English this time, "he is my favorite."

She smiled fondly out the window where they could both see PJ rescuing his older brother who was being used as a human climbing frame by his toddler-aged twins. "All of my grandchildren I love, *ne?* But Peter I love the most." She turned to Ally and shook her head.

"I don't say that to anyone else," she went on. "But I know. He knows. He is the most like my dear Aeneas. Strong and gentle like his grandfather. He makes me laugh. He makes me happy. He is a good man."

"Yes." Ally knew that. She'd always known it.

"A man who deserves to be happy, too," *Yiayia* added.

"Yes."

"He says he is."

"I hope he is," Ally agreed quickly, then felt more was needed. "I want him to be happy," she said fervently. And that was the truth. "I know he was happy to come home for the weekend."

"Now that you are here and his father knows what he says is true. But that is not what I mean. He says he is happy, but I wonder…" Her voice trailed off and her gaze turned to the windows again as she watched PJ and Elias on the lawn playing with the little boys. They all were laughing.

"He looks happy," Ally said stoutly.

*"Ne."* *Yiayia* agreed, nodding. "But then I ask myself—" she looked archly at Ally over her spectacles "—why does a man who is happy and in love, kiss his old wrinkled *yiayia* and not his lovely wife?"

As tough as the old woman was, Ally liked her.

She felt guilty for not confessing her plans. But she'd promised PJ she wouldn't mention the divorce. And the truth was, even if she hadn't promised, she wasn't sure she could have got the words past her lips.

It felt like a sacrilege to even think it, much less bring it up. And she completely forgot about it after another ten minutes of conversation, during which PJ's grandmother changed the subject and asked about her art and her retail business.

Her questions weren't casual. They demonstrated she was not only knowledgeable but that PJ had obviously told her a great deal about what Ally did.

"He is very proud of you," she said.

"He made it possible."

*Yiayia* smiled. "And now you make him happy." Her eyes met Ally's over the pan of baklava. They were back to "happy" again. And this time *Yiayia*'s words very definitely held a challenge.

But before she could figure out how to respond, PJ's grandmother said, "Here comes Martha. You will love Martha."

And as she spoke, the door from the deck swung open and Martha stuck her head in. She carried her toddler son on her hip.

"Oh, good, you are here," she said to Ally. "I've been looking for you." Then, "Can you spare her, *Yiayia?* I want to get acquainted with my sister-in-law."

When they'd first met, Martha had simply beamed and kissed her. Was she now about to grill Ally the way PJ's grandmother and Cristina had?

But before she could demur, *Yiayia* said, "You go, both of you. Hurry now, Martha, or your mother will put you to work."

"God forbid." Martha laughed. "Come on," she said to Ally. "We'll go down on the beach. Eddie can eat sand."

She led the way and, bemused, Ally followed.

"I saw one of your murals at Sol Y Sombra," she told Martha. "It was amazing."

And any concern she might have had about Martha's reaction to her relationship with PJ evaporated right then. Martha's face lit up. "You were there?" And when Ally explained, her eyes widened. "Gaby's showing your work, too?"

She was clearly delighted and peppered Ally with a thousand questions—about her art, about her shops, about her focus. And she was absolutely thrilled to meet PJ's wife.

"Dad didn't think you really existed," she confided. "It's so cool to discover you do. And even cooler that I like you!"

If Cristina had been suspicious, Martha was just the opposite. She was eager to welcome Ally into the family. She practically danced along the beach as they followed Eddie from one pile of flotsam and jetsam to another.

"We'll have to get together. Maybe in Santorini—or we could come to Hawaii sometime, Theo and Eddie and I," she said, eyes alight with possibilities. "Theo would love that. He sails. He and PJ bonded over PJ's windsurfer. They have a lot in common. And apparently we do, too."

And what was Ally supposed to say? No, they didn't?

"That would be fun," she managed. And she was telling the truth when she said it. It would be absolutely wonderful, if only…

Something of her hesitation must have shown through, because Martha immediately said, "Don't let me bully you into it. Theo is always telling me I shouldn't just assume."

"No," Ally said quickly. "I really would love it. I just… We don't know what we're doing yet, PJ and I. We have to…discuss things."

"Of course," Martha said quickly. "It must be so weird, getting back together after all these years."

Ally nodded. "We don't really know each other…"

"Why did you stay away so long?"

And how, Ally wondered, could she even begin to answer that?

"There always seemed to be things to do," she said, "and PJ married me so I could do them." She knew that all the Antonides clan had heard the story of her grandmother's legacy by now. But she didn't know how much else any of them knew. She shrugged and turned to stare out to sea. It was easier that way than when she had to look into Martha's face. "And once I finally got going, I was a success. I ended up on a fast track.

Doing what he'd expected me to do. And—" she shrugged "—as that was what we'd married for, I just…kept doing it. I guess I thought he would have moved on. Got a divorce."

"Could he?"

Ally nodded. "If he had filed and I didn't respond, yes. He could have got a divorce without my ever having to sign anything."

"Bet you're glad he didn't. Bet he is, too." Martha shook her head. "Wow. What if you'd come back and found out you were already divorced? What if he'd married somebody else?" She looked appalled at the thought.

And Ally had to admit to a certain jolt when she thought about it, too. Of course it would have been easier. She could have married Jon without any of this ever happening.

"You wouldn't be here now," Martha said, making almost exactly the same mental leaps. Then she laughed. "And PJ would be facing a weekend with Connie Cristopolous."

"She's beautiful," Ally protested.

"But not PJ's type."

Ally wasn't sure what PJ's type was. But before she could ask Martha's opinion, the other woman went on, "So how did you find him?"

And Ally told her about going back to Honolulu, about her dad's heart attack, about looking for PJ. "I thought he'd be there still," she admitted. "But he wasn't."

"And so you had to track him down! How romantic is that?" Martha was clearly pleased.

Cristina thought PJ was the romantic. Martha thought she was.

"Eddie! Ack, no. Don't put that in your mouth!" Martha swooped down and scooped her son up, taking whatever he'd been about to eat and tossing it into the water. "Kids! What will I ever do when I have two of them?" she moaned.

"Are you…?" Ally looked at Martha's flat stomach doubtfully.

But Martha nodded happily. "Not till January, though. What about you guys? Have you talked about kids?"

"Not…much."

It wasn't exactly a lie. They had talked about children—the ones she hoped to have with Jon, the grandchild she wanted to give her father.

But now in her mind's eye she didn't see a child she might have with Jon. She saw PJ as he had been with Alex that evening at his house in Park Slope or, for that matter, PJ now. He had one of Elias's twins on his hip while he tossed a football with his brothers.

Martha's gaze followed her own. "Well, it's early days yet. You will."

Ally didn't reply. Her throat felt tight. The glare of the sun made her eyes water. She swallowed and looked away.

As a child, Ally had been a reader.

From the time she had first made sense of words on a page, she'd haunted the library or spent her allowance at the bookstore, buying new worlds in which to live. And invariably the worlds she sought were the boisterous chaotic worlds of laughing, loving, noisy families who were so different from her own.

Oh, she was loved. She had no doubt about that.

But the everyday life of her childhood had been perpetually calm, perennially quiet, perfectly ordered. When her mother had been alive, there had, of course, been smiles and quiet laughter. And even her normally dignified taciturn father had been known to join in. But after her mother's death, after the number of chairs at the table had gone from three to two, mealtimes had become sober silent affairs. After her mother was gone, there had been no more light conversations, no more gentle teasing. There had actually been very few smiles.

Never a demonstrative man, after his wife's death Hiroshi Maruyama became even more remote.

"He is sad," her grandmother had excused him.

"So am I," Ally had retorted fiercely. "Does he think I don't miss her, too?"

"He doesn't think," Ama had said. "He only hurts."

Well, Ally had hurt, too. And they had gone right on hurting in their own private little shells, never reaching out for each other, for years. Hiroshi's way of dealing with his daughter was to give her directions, orders, commands.

"They will make your life better," he told her stiffly, if she balked.

But they hadn't.

Marrying PJ and running away from her father's edicts was what had made her life better. Doing that had freed her, given her scope for her talents, new challenges that she could meet and, eventually, a life she loved and determinedly filled with her art and her work.

In the fullness of that life, she'd forgotten about the warm, boisterous families she'd read about and envied, the closeness she had yearned for all those years ago. She hadn't really realized anything was missing until she'd come home after her father's heart attack.

Then, forced to take a break, to slow down and look around during those long days in his hospital room, she had seen cracks in her well-developed life begin to appear. A chasm of emptiness opened up before her.

She was back with her father—in subdued silence. And longing for something more. That was why she'd been so glad to find Jon.

He was as addicted to work as she was. For his entire adult life he had been filling the empty spaces in his life with patients and professional demands on his time. Now he was thirty-five. It was time to marry, to have a family.

"One child," he said. "I have time for one child."

"Two," Ally had responded instantly. "I want at least two." There was no way she was going to subject a child of hers to the same loneliness she'd experienced.

Jon had looked doubtful and skeptical and as if he thought she was being irrational and irresponsible.

"Two," Ally had repeated. "Or three," she'd added in a moment of recklessness.

"No more than two," Jon had stated firmly. "We don't want chaos."

But a part of Ally did.

And tonight on the deck of PJ's parents' house, she was reminded of it.

The whole day, from the moment she'd got out of the car to be swept into the embrace of his parents, siblings, aunts, uncles, cousins and assorted relations, she had felt a sense of déjà vu that was odd because she knew she'd never experienced anything like it before.

It wasn't until after dinner, when she'd sat on a bench on the deck listening to Martha and Tallie compare toddler notes while in the kitchen the aunts discussed recipes, and in the dining room PJ's father, Mr. Cristopolous and several friends compared golf swings and on the lawn little boys toddled about and bigger boys tossed footballs, and on the sand where PJ's brother Lukas was deep in conversation with Connie Cristopolous and PJ and Elias were starting up a bonfire in the rock fire pit that Ally recognized what she was seeing—the families she'd read about in her books.

They were real—at least this one was. And for the moment—for this one single weekend—they were hers.

She smiled. Not just on her face, but all the way down to the depths of her soul.

"Come on, then, Ally." Martha broke into her realization. "I'll show you guys the mural I'm doing in Ma's sewing room."

And happily, willingly, Ally went with Martha and Tallie. She ran her hand along the oak banister as they climbed the stairs, certain that the wood beneath her fingers had been worn smooth by PJ and his brothers sliding down it. She paused to look at the family photos that lined the upstairs hall. They stretched back for generations, right to a couple of fiercely scowling men with bushy moustaches who looked as if they'd just got off the boat.

"My great-grandfather Nikos and his brother, right after

they emigrated," Martha said when she noticed the direction of Ally's glance. "I want to do a mural of the whole family—" she waved her hand to encompass the myriad photos on both the walls "—sometime. Show all the generations. I did something like it out in Butte as a local history project. You would have loved this photo of a traditional Chinese bride one of the students brought in."

Martha rattled on happily about that, while Ally and Tallie admired the ongoing mural in Helena's sewing room. Martha had done small vignettes of children—the Antonides children. Here was Alex throwing a ball, Eddie taking his first steps, the twins smearing birthday cake all over their faces. And their parents, too, when they were children. All of Helena's and Aeolus's children were there.

"Is that PJ?" Ally asked, arrested by a small painting on the wall by the bay window of a young boy on a surfboard.

Martha laughed. "Who else?"

Who else, indeed? Ally moved closer, drawn to the picture of PJ as a boy, recognizing the triumphant grin and, in his expression, the sheer joy of being alive.

"Of all of us kids," Martha said, "he was the one who loved it here the most. The one who loved the ocean the most. We always thought he was insane, going all the way to Hawaii when he had one out the back door. But—" she smiled at Ally "—I guess he wasn't so crazy after all. Look who he brought home."

And there was such warmth and such approval in her voice that Ally felt about two inches high.

She couldn't respond to it, could only smile and feel betraying tears prick.

"Hey," PJ's voice came from the doorway. "I wondered where you'd got to."

"Brought her up to show her family history," Martha said. "You haven't seen this, either." She waved a hand around the room.

PJ ambled in and startled Ally by snagging her hand and drawing her along with him while he moved from vignette to vignette. She tried to look at them, too, but mostly she was aware of his hand wrapping hers.

She should tug it away. It was sending the wrong message, and not just to the onlookers, but to Ally herself. It promised a relationship, a future. A married life of love.

Experimentally she tried pulling her hand out of his. He hung on tighter. "They're terrific," he told Martha, nodding at her paintings. "Ma loves 'em. Says she's going to make you fill the whole room."

"Yes, well, Theo and I are doing our part. Tallie and Elias are doing theirs. Up to you now," she added giving him a significant look.

Ally tensed at her obvious inference, but PJ's grip on her hand didn't change. "All in good time," he said easily. Then, as if he took it all in stride, as doubtless he did, he said to all of them, "Fire's going. Sun's set. Come on out."

The scene around the firepit was even more reminiscent of all the stories she used to read. Most of the family gathered around it, sitting on blankets, laughing and talking as the evening lengthened and the sky grew deep and dark.

The breeze off the ocean turned the air cool, and Ally would have gone for her sweater, but before she could, PJ slipped his sweatshirt jacket over her shoulders.

"Come here," he said, and drew her down onto the blanket, shifting around so that she sat in the vee of his legs and he tugged her back against his chest, looping his arms around her.

It felt far too intimate for Ally's peace of mind. But at the same time, perversely, it felt like exactly where she wanted to be.

"Warmer?" His lips were next to her ear, his breath lifting tendrils of her hair.

She shivered again at the feel of it and, misunderstanding the cause, he wrapped his arms more tightly around her. "I can go get you a warmer jacket."

It would have got her out of his arms. Saying "Yes, please" would have been the sane thing to do, but Ally didn't do it.

She couldn't bring herself to destroy the evening. It was her dream come to life. The warmth and joy of the camaraderie, the laughter and easy music that began as Lukas picked up a guitar and began to play, and two of PJ's aunts began to sing, enchanted her. And the hard strength of PJ's arms around her simply enhanced the experience.

"I'm fine," she said.

It was true. It was wonderful.

It lasted the rest of the night.

It was late when the party began to break up. Tallie and Elias had put the twins down to sleep. Martha had gone inside to rock Eddie. *Yiayia* had gone up to bed an hour earlier, but not before she'd stopped on her way in to smile down at Ally, snug in the embrace of PJ's arms.

*"Ne,"* she said approvingly. And her fingers had brushed over the top of Ally's head. A benediction of sorts?

"Night, *Yiayia,*" PJ said, tilting his head up to smile at her.

*Yiayia* said something to him in Greek that Ally didn't understand. She was surprised when PJ seemed to.

His smile broadened and he nodded. "Don't worry," he said. "I will."

His grandmother nodded and padded off into the house.

"What did she say?" Ally wanted to know.

"She said I shouldn't forget to kiss you."

Ally's breath caught in her throat, knowing that PJ's lips were a scant inch from her ear. But even as she held her breath, he made no move to kiss her.

Instead he eased back away from her and stood up, then held out a hand and hauled her to her feet. "Time to go up," he said.

"Yes. It is late. Nearly midnight." She felt stiff from having sat there so long, yet she was reluctant to leave. Lukas was still softly playing his guitar. And Connie, apparently oblivious to any machinations that would have directed her toward PJ, seemed enthralled with sitting at Lukas's feet and listening to his music. Elias and Tallie had come back out and were sitting on the other side of the fire, their arms around each other as they stared into the magic of the fire.

Ally understood. She didn't want to leave the magic, either.

But she could do exactly what she'd always done as a child after she'd read one of those books that made her dream impossible dreams. She could take her dreams to bed with her.

But first, she reminded herself as she followed PJ up the stairs so he could show her to her room, she should call Jon.

She hadn't called him all day. But it wasn't too late. With the time difference, he would probably just be getting home from the hospital. Maybe she could communicate a little of what she'd felt today to him—this feeling of family belonging, joy, connection. Maybe he would understand.

Maybe, she dared hope, he would share her dream.

PJ took hold of the handle on one of the doors in the hallway. "Here we are." He pushed the door open and held it for her. "My old room," he said with a grin.

"Yours?" She looked around, intrigued. It had obviously been redecorated since PJ had lived in it. The walls were a freshly painted pale sage green. But the bookcase still had some books that the young PJ Antonides would have read, and the hardwood floors showed evidence of being used for more than walking.

"Used to have bunkbeds, too," he told her. There was a double-size bed in the room now, with a taupe-colored duvet and heaps of inviting pillows. "I had the top one. Always wanted to be on top. Luke was stuck with the bottom."

She could imagine him in here, her mind's eye seeing the boy on the surfboard that Martha had painted. She wondered about the dreams he had dreamed as a child. He needn't have dreamed ones like hers. They'd been his reality.

Then she realized he was just standing there looking at her. "What?" she said.

He shook his head, smiling, too. "Nothing." But still he made no move to go.

"Where are you going to be?" she asked him.

He blinked. "What?"

She shrugged. "I just wondered where you were sleeping? Which room?"

"This one," he said. "I'm sleeping in here. With you."

# CHAPTER EIGHT

PJ WAITED for the inevitable, "No!" and the predictable protest that would follow.

Ally stood stock-still in the middle of the bedroom, staring at him, her eyes wide, looking stricken. She opened her mouth, and he prepared himself for the argument, the refusal, for more of her damn "rules."

Then just as abruptly her mouth closed again.

Her expression shifted subtly, becoming unreadable. Or at least unreadable to him.

Ten years ago Ally Maruyama had been an open book. Serious and sunny by turns, yes, but still fathomable. PJ had always understood where she was coming from, what she hoped for, what her dreams were.

This Ally was as fathomable as cement.

She kissed him like she wanted him. Hell, the way she'd responded to his kisses had nearly burned him to the ground. And she hadn't been immune, either. That much he did know.

And yet she persisted in wanting the divorce.

And now she was looking at him, not saying anything. Just looking.

"I suppose you think I should have got you a separate bedroom," he said gruffly, scowled as he deliberately began unbuttoning his shirt.

"No," she said with maddening calm. "I'm sure that would

have been awkward. Your mother would definitely have asked questions. I guess it just…didn't occur to me. I'm an idiot." Then she shrugged as if it didn't matter. And damned if she didn't just take hold of the hem of her shirt and pull it over her head!

PJ's mouth went dry. She wasn't going to kiss him, but she'd strip for him? God Almighty.

She wasn't baring anything yet that she couldn't bare in public. Beneath her top she had on a lacy ivory bra. It was at least as discreet as any bikini top. But he hadn't seen her breasts, even in that state of coverage in ten years. He remembered them as small ripe handfuls that had begged to be kissed. Now they were fuller, riper. A woman's breasts.

And he needed to kiss them again—now.

Like a slow fire, his desire had been simmering all day. From the minute he'd spotted her in the hotel lobby, he'd felt a quickening in his pulse, an awareness that he never felt with any other woman. He'd told himself it was just the heat of the moment, that it would fade.

But the trip out to the Hamptons hadn't really dampened it. Talking with her, listening to her, finding out more about who she'd become after all these years—even when they were doing nothing more than that—actually seemed to deepen his awareness of her.

Seeing her with his family had made it deeper still.

If she'd been stiff and silent, treating them with distant politeness, he would have backed off. But even though she'd looked a bit overwhelmed at times, she'd slipped into the pool of Antonides family warmth and hadn't come close to drowning.

She'd talked sailing with his father, canning tomatoes with his mother, and had been thrilled to discuss quilting with his aunts Narcissa and Maria. She and his brother Lukas had compared notes about riding camels in the outback of Australia. From the shy girl she'd been when he'd first met her, she had clearly blossomed. She seemed to enjoy them all.

And he knew they had enjoyed her. Even his grandmother,

whose reaction he'd been a little wary of, truth to tell, had warmed to her.

She'd taken him by the arm after dinner and said, "You surprise me, Petros."

And he'd stiffened because he didn't want to hear what she might have to say. "How so?" he'd demanded, a bit more belligerent than he usually was with his grandmother whom he adored.

"You swim in deep waters."

He'd frowned and narrowed his gaze. "What are you talking about, *Yiayia?*"

"Your wife."

Which was exactly what he'd been afraid they were talking about. "Don't be cryptic," he'd told her. "If you've got something to say, just spit it out. Not that it's going to make a damn bit of difference," he'd added gruffly.

Her brows had lifted. Dark eyes bored into his. A small smile touched her face. "You have it bad," she'd said.

"I have a wife," he'd retorted.

"A beautiful wife," she agreed. "A strong wife. But a wife, I think, who is still finding her way. *Ne,* Petros?"

His jaw had tightened. He'd lifted his shoulders slightly. He didn't speak.

He hadn't had to. *Yiayia* had always known what he was thinking, had always known what was important to him. She'd put her small but still-strong fingers over his and squeezed.

"I like her," she'd said. "Your Ally is honest. When she knows the truth, so will you."

What he knew right now, staring at Ally in her bra and capri pants, was confusion.

"What happened to the 'no kissing' business?" he said hoarsely.

She was rummaging in her suitcase, taking out some sort of nightshirt that didn't look very sexy at all but still managed to make his blood hot. At his question, she turned, looking over her shoulder at him. "Nothing happened to it."

"We're going to sleep in the same bed all night and nothing's going to happen?"

She turned and straightened. "Well, I suppose you could force yourself on me." The look she gave him was a defiant challenge.

His breath hissed through his teeth. "You know damned well I won't do that."

"I didn't think you would." She picked up the nightshirt and a toiletries bag and headed toward the bathroom, saying as off-handedly as she could manage, "I'm going to grab a quick shower. I'll be right back."

And she left him with his jaw dropped, his mouth dry and his body—well, his body could do with a shower, too.

A long ice-cold one.


Someone—probably PJ, come to think of it—had once said, "The best defense is a good offense."

Ally understood the concept. And she knew it applied to football and war. Neither her father nor Jon had any experience with either. So she was certain they hadn't said it. In fact she thought she could remember the instant PJ had branded the words on her brain.

"Stop running from your old man's edicts," he'd told her that fateful afternoon ten years ago. "Face him down. The best defense is a good offense," he'd added. Or words to that effect.

And then he'd proved it by asking her to marry him.

The same words had popped into her mind a few seconds after PJ's words, "I'm sleeping in here. With you," reached her ears.

Her first reaction, of course, was to argue with him. But they'd been there, done that. And doing it again wasn't going to settle anything, much less clarify their relationship.

*And sleeping with him is?* Ally asked herself sarcastically as she confronted her naked image in the bathroom mirror.

She didn't know the answer to that. But she wanted to know.

And somehow as risky as that was, it seemed a better way

to do it than go down the same path of argument again, she told herself as she finished drying off and pulled on her nightshirt.

He'd touched a nerve when he'd challenged her about when exactly it was that she felt like a fraud. Because, truth to tell, she felt something strong and vital when she was kissing PJ, and it was a feeling she had not yet captured with Jon. There was sweetness in kissing Jon, a sense of connection.

But nothing like the soul-searing full-on connection she seemed to feel with PJ.

And today everything that happened had only made those feelings—that connection—more intense, on levels that had nothing to do with kissing.

Maybe it had begun on the way out here today—a drive she'd dreaded for the wayward feelings PJ had been evoking ever since she'd walked into his office two days before. And yes, the feelings were there, but as they'd talked during the drive, she'd felt an understanding in him that she'd never experienced with Jon.

Jon was a wonderful, kind, committed man. He had given his life so far to his profession. But he'd sensed something lacking, just as she had. When they'd met at the hospital it had been like finding a kindred spirit.

But not quite as kindred as PJ.

She and Jon wanted the same things, but sometimes she wondered if he really knew who she was. He'd never listened to her the way PJ had today—the way she now remembered that PJ always had.

And while she had tried to know Jon—and his work—better, too, he never shared much of it. Whenever she'd asked, he'd given brief weary answers. "I don't want to talk about it," he often said. "I want to get away from it when I'm with you."

She understood that, but somehow she felt shut out. Sometimes she wondered if Jon thought she was too stupid to understand what he might tell her.

Admittedly maybe she would be. But she wished he would try. It might bring them closer together.

PJ had told her about his windsurfer today. She hadn't understood all of that, either. But he'd made the effort. And simply seeing his eyes light up as he'd talked about the breakthroughs he'd made and when he realized he'd actually made really significant developments was worth every bit she didn't totally comprehend.

She'd felt a growing sense of connection with him on a whole other level than simple sexual awareness.

And then there was the connections she made with his family. *Her* family now, according to his mother.

Of course Ally had told herself that wasn't true, that she had no right to be feeling the sense of welcome and belonging she had felt almost at once. She'd connected with his sister Martha. She'd been delighted with his sister-in-law Tallie and amazed that Tallie had actually baked her cookies to say how happy she was that Ally was part of the family.

It wasn't just that they were marvelous—Tallie, after all, was an accomplished baker who had given up being president of Antonides Marine to become apprentice to a baker in Vienna— it was that she'd made them expressly for Ally.

"I owe you," she'd told Ally frankly. And when Ally had looked at her blankly, Tallie had elaborated, "If you had stayed in Hawaii, I'm sure PJ would never have come back to New York when he did. Which allowed me to shanghai him into taking over for me so I could leave, which meant Elias could go crazy wondering where I was and come halfway round the world to track me down. So in reality, I owe you my husband and my marriage and—" she patted her bulging belly "—my family." She'd positively beamed adding, "That's easily worth a truckload of cookies."

Even PJ's mother had welcomed her. And Helena Antonides would certainly have been within her rights to demand a whole lot more allegiance to her son—not to mention presence—than Ally had ever given PJ. And, ultimately, even his grandmother had, in her way, been kind.

His grandmother had—at least he'd said she had—told him to kiss her.

Ally's face warmed at the thought.

And then there were the babies. Maybe it was seeing all those little Antonides babies that had intensified her feelings. Maybe it was balancing one of Elias and Tallie's twins on each hip and finding herself imagining what it would be like to hold a wriggling little facsimile of PJ. Or maybe it was being handed month-old Liana, the Costanides's only granddaughter, and rocking her to sleep. Or maybe it was seeing PJ do the same thing with his overwrought overtired nephew Edward when no one else could calm him down.

She'd studied a host of paintings of mothers and children in her university art classes, but as far as she was concerned, they were missing the boat by not having one of fathers and children as well.

PJ could model for them all. The look of quiet tenderness on such a masculine face touched her heart. Dear God, he would make beautiful babies. The thought was seriously tempting.

But the truth was, the biggest temptation was PJ himself.

And far from getting him out of her mind by coming to give him the divorce papers in person, she had actually opened a Pandora's box of feelings and needs and connections that she was having an increasingly hard time shoving back in.

And exactly how spending the night in the same bed with PJ was going to shut that box she wasn't sure.

But when she opened the door to the bedroom, she stared around in astonishment.

PJ was gone.

Lukas took one look at her when she came down stairs in the morning and said cheerfully, "Wow. Must've been quite a night."

It was just past eight, but she'd never really slept. Had barely closed her eyes. Half a dozen times during the night she'd told herself she should call Jon. Jon was the one who mattered.

But she hadn't called him. Hadn't even been able to think about him. Had only thought about PJ—about what she'd said to him, about his reaction.

She wished he'd come back, wished she could take the words back, soften them, apologize. And she'd vowed to do so as soon as he reappeared.

But though she lay there waiting, tensing at every sound in the hallway, none of the sounds had been PJ. She'd waited and waited. He'd never come.

By dawn it was too late to call Jon—and she couldn't have done it then, anyway. It felt all wrong. If it were right, Jon would make the first move and call her.

Not that it mattered. After she had sorted things out with PJ, she would call. She'd brought her phone down with her and set it on the small desk in the kitchen as she tried to muster a bright smile to meet the interested gazes of all of PJ's family.

"Night?" she echoed, not quite sure what he meant.

But his grin made it abundantly clear as he shoveled in another bite of his breakfast. "Both you and PJ look, um, well…not exactly well rested." The grin broadened.

"Lukas!" His mother pointed a spoon at him. "Don't be rude."

"Who me? I'm not rude. Just observant." He shrugged unrepentantly. "And envious."

He certainly had nothing to be envious of, Ally thought grimly.

"Where is PJ?" she said. "I was…in the shower," she explained, hoping it would sound as if that was how she'd missed hearing where he had gone.

"Gone surfing," Lukas said. "How come you didn't go along?"

"I'm sure Ally was still asleep when he left," Helena said. "He likes to be out there early. Sit down. Have some breakfast."

"I'd have stayed in bed," Lukas said with a wink.

His mother thwacked him on the head with her spoon.

"Guess you'll have to find a girl of your own," Martha said unsympathetically. "Got any sisters at home for him?" she asked Ally.

"I'm an only child. I think I'll just go look for PJ," she said to his mother, "instead of eating now." She couldn't have forced down a mouthful anyway. "If you don't mind."

Helena smiled at her. "Not at all. Go right ahead. You two can have breakfast when you come back."

Ally escaped gratefully out onto the deck overlooking the beach and the ocean beyond. The morning air was almost still. The slightest breeze was blowing in off the water as she made her way across the lawn and down the steps to the sand. It was already warm and humid.

Out on the water she could see a lone surfer sitting on his board, drifting, as a set of waves began building behind him. The waves here were nothing like the ones in Hawaii. These were small, tame waves. Not a challenge for PJ, which might have been why he let them slide underneath his board, not paddling to get into position to ride any of them in.

Or maybe it was just that he didn't want to talk to her.

She didn't blame him, she supposed. In her confusion last night, she had created an awkward situation. PJ had gone and he had never come back. And Ally had sat there, huddled and miserable, knowing she had driven him away.

And having done so, rather than feeling relieved that she wouldn't have to share the bed with him, she felt bereft.

Now she sat down on the cool sand beside his towel and, pulling her knees up against her chest, wrapped her arms around them as she watched him.

He had to see her, but he made no move to catch a wave or paddle in. He kept sitting out there, letting his hands dangle in the water, moving them just enough to keep his position, his gaze mostly on the horizon, not on the beach. Not on her.

Another set of waves rolled in, he made a slight move to catch one of them, but didn't, instead letting it roll past.

Ally felt her frustration increasing with every wave he ignored. Finally she stood up and stared out at him. She knew he was looking at her and, she imagined, was pleased that he'd waited her out and that she'd got tired of sitting there expecting him to finally come in.

She kicked off her flip-flops and walked down to the water. She wasn't wearing her bathing suit. But the shorts and T-shirt she did wear were just going to have to get wet.

The water was cool as she waded out. The sea lapped her calves, then her knees, then her thighs. She kept walking. He had stopped glancing back at the swells building behind him now, and was completely focused on her.

She was close enough to see his brows draw down. He sculled with his hands, turning his board toward the shoreline. She was up to her waist now. A wave broke just beyond her, and as it surged past, it soaked her up to the neck.

"What the hell are you doing?" His irritation was obvious.

Ally didn't answer, just dove under the next wave and came up on the other side, far closer to him now. Water streamed down her face. She shook her hair back, wishing she'd thought to put it in a ponytail. But who knew she'd be going swimming?

She pushed off the bottom as the water lapped against her chest and, keeping her gaze fixed on him, began paddling the last ten yards. He watched her come, his hands not drifting in the water any longer. His arms were folded across his chest.

He made no move toward her as she closed the distance between them and grasped the nose of his board.

"What're you doing?" he repeated, sounding annoyed and not at all welcoming. "You're crazy."

"You're chicken," she replied.

He frowned blackly. "I'm chicken?" he echoed her words. "How do you figure?"

"You knew I wanted to talk to you this morning. You wouldn't come in."

"I'm surfing, in case you didn't notice."

"As a matter of fact, I didn't," she said smiling up at him. "Didn't see you catch a wave. Saw a few good ones you ignored."

"They weren't good enough." He looked away, jaw set.

"Ah, what a pity," she said in a light mocking tone. "Waiting for the wave of the day?"

"What difference does it make to you?" There was a hard edge to his voice. He still didn't glance her way.

"PJ," she said, willing him to look at her, waiting until he spared her a bare glance before she said, "I'm sorry."

His gaze jerked back to meet hers. He didn't speak, but he was clearly interested now.

"I apologize," she said sincerely, all flippancy gone. "I shouldn't have said what I did last night. Shouldn't have acted the way I did. It was the way I acted when you came to my opening. I was…chicken then."

He stared at her in disbelief.

"I was," she admitted. "And I was last night, too. Chicken. And confused."

A muscle ticked in his jaw. Then, "You're not the only one," he muttered, and turned to stare out toward the horizon.

Maybe it was better that way. Maybe it would be easier to continue, to explain, if he didn't look at her.

Ally pressed on. "I wanted—" she began, but then she stopped because the truth was she didn't even know exactly what she wanted "—I didn't know what I wanted. I guess the bed situation was the last straw. I don't know what's happening between us," she admitted. "I guess I…wanted to find out."

His head came around and he looked at her again, his expression unreadable. And then he said skeptically, "And you expected to find that out with no kissing?"

"I told you I was confused."

He reached out a hand. "Come here."

For an instant she didn't move, caught by the feeling that she was standing on the edge of a chasm, as if taking that single step of putting her hand in his would be the equivalent of stepping off into space.

But teetering forever on the precipice wasn't an option. And now that she'd come out here, what else was she going to do?

Offer her lame apology, then turn around and swim away?

Or take the hand he offered and find out where they would go from there?

He was waiting, hand still outstretched, his green eyes challenging. He'd made one move. It was up to her to make the other.

Ally lifted her hand and put it in his, felt strong cool fingers wrap around hers. Then almost effortlessly he drew her up out of the water, and the next thing she knew she was able to scramble up onto the board to sit facing him.

"Right," he said hoarsely, letting go of her hand to grasp her by the arms. "Rules be damned." And then he hauled her into his arms and kissed her.

And there it was—that mindless all-consuming longing—all over again.

Every time PJ kissed her she lost her bearings. The sane and sensible Ally vanished and this one went up in flames. The young, earnest, buttoned-down, pent-up Ally—the teenage girl who had always hankered after "the boy with the surfboard" PJ had been—was instantly resurrected by the touch of PJ's lips on hers.

Those demanding persuasive lips made her forget her determination to marry Jon, to be the prodigal daughter come home to make her father happy. They made her forget everything except the man kissing her.

And the taste of him now, mingled with the sea water and warmth of the morning sun brought back to her all her youthful unspoken yearnings, and she thought, *Why not? Why can't I have him? Why can't I love him? He's my husband.*

And the counterbalancing thoughts, *He wants to stay married because it's convenient. He wants me. But he doesn't love me,* were nowhere to be found.

Not that she looked.

She couldn't look, had no brain cells left to look, to think rationally, to do more than kiss him back.

There was only hunger and need and desire—for PJ.

She kissed him openly, eagerly. She let her hands rove over his bare back, relishing the feel of smooth sun-warmed skin under her fingers. She nuzzled her nose against his cheek, and delighted in the scrape of a day's worth of rough whiskers. And if she was enjoying it, reveling in it, there was no question but that the enjoyment was mutual.

PJ bent his head and kissed his way down her neck. Ally instinctively tipped her head back to allow him access. His fingers snaked under her wet T-shirt to splay against her ribs just below her breasts, and his thumbs lifted to caress her, to rub lightly against her nipples, and Ally loved it, arching her back.

"You *would* have to wear a damn T-shirt," he muttered.

She smiled and brushed her fingers lightly against the obviously straining erection beneath the fabric of his shorts. "You would have to wear damn board shorts," she countered.

He gave a pained laugh. "Didn't want to shock my mother when she looked out of her kitchen window. Besides, how did I know you were going to come out here and do this?"

Ally shrugged awkwardly, suddenly self-conscious, yet at the same time oddly liberated. She smiled and looked him in the eyes for a split second. But what she felt for him was too strong, too overwhelming, and she had to look away.

"Hey." His voice was low and almost tender. "Al?" And she felt cool fingers on her cheek, turning her head so she had to look at him or close her eyes. "What's wrong?"

Wrong? "N-nothing." Only that she knew she still loved him. And recognizing it for the truth at last, she was powerless to fight it anymore.

PJ was the man she was in love with, not Jon. He was the man she hungered for, not Jon. He was the man she wanted to spend forever with, and not anyone else at all.

If he read it on her face or saw it in her eyes, she didn't know. She only knew he caught his breath at the same time she caught hers.

"Oh, God," he muttered, and took her mouth again.

His kiss was tender at first, then deeper, more passionate, a simple tasting at first, then eager and devouring as his arms wrapped her and he pulled her close.

Ally wobbled and clung to PJ, pulling herself closer, pressing against him and feeling the press of his body even more insistently against her—wanting, needing—

And then, abruptly, PJ flipped them both into the water!

Ally sputtered to the surface at the same time he did. "What the—"

PJ simply dipped his head toward the beach. And Ally knew the answer even as he said, "You know what."

Yes, indeed she did. In another few moments, without PJ's timely intervention, they would have scandalized his family and undoubtedly broken several laws of the state of New York. Her lack of control appalled her, and her face burned even as her body still continued to simmer.

"Sorry."

PJ gave her a rueful smile. "Me, too. And not because we would have shocked them, either." He reached across the surfboard and grasped her hand, giving it a tight squeeze. "Just—hold that thought."

As if she could do anything else.

They rode the board in together, and it was the first time Ally had surfed in ten years. It was magical—the swoop and the speed of the board on the wave, the excitement and the thrill of the ride and—most of all, the touch of PJ's fingers against her back.

And the audience of Antonides family members who had come down to the beach weren't scandalized at all. They cheered and applauded at the end of the ride as they came out of the water, PJ hoisting the board under one arm while he slung the other over Ally's shoulders.

*Yiayia* smiled approvingly after they had dried off on the deck and came into the kitchen. She looked up from her rocking chair and nodded and winked at PJ. "A little kissing, *ne?* I told you so."

PJ grinned broadly. "My grandmother is a know-it-all." He bent and gave her a kiss too.

She beamed and sighed with satisfaction. "*Ne*. A grandmother knows."

Wouldn't you know?

He'd suffered through, if not the night from hell—which would have been spending it in bed with Ally without so much as a kiss—at least a very miserable night of purgatory during which he'd walked the beach until dawn.

He should have known better, he'd told himself. He'd pushed it, glibly telling her he was sharing the room—and the bed—with her. He could have handled it differently, not been quite so blithely confrontational, backing her into a corner that way.

But hell's bells, why shouldn't he? he'd thought. She was his wife!

But when she'd simply accepted sleeping with him—in a nonbiblical sense—all the while insisting on "no kissing," he'd stalked out. He had enough control. That wasn't what he was worried about. But he was damned if he was going to lie there chastely beside his wife who didn't want him and was preserving her intimacies for another man.

He'd been furious—and hours of pounding the sand had left him exhausted but no less angry. He'd gone surfing at first light because if anything would calm him and allow him to regain control of his badly frayed composure, it was time alone, just he and his board and the waves.

The ocean was strong, far more powerful than he was, and could be erratic and unpredictable. He didn't control it, but he understood it. He didn't understand Ally.

The time he'd spent in the water had settled him somewhat. He'd had to focus, to get in sync with the waves, to stop thinking about her and what her coming back into his life was making him want. And as time passed, he found his balance again, settled, steadied.

And then he'd spotted her walking toward him on the beach.

The fury had come back, swamping him. And it was all he could do to sit there and ignore her. He'd have preferred paddling to Tierra del Fuego.

She hadn't gone away. She'd stood there waiting. And he'd thought to himself, she could wait till kingdom come. He was damned well not going to catch a wave and ride in to her.

He'd been shocked when she'd swum out to him.

But that had been only half the shock he'd felt when she'd apologized!

What did it mean? He didn't know. And from what she said, she didn't know, either. But there was a light in her eyes now that made him even hungrier for her than he'd been last night. There was an eagerness in her that matched his own.

And of course he could do nothing about it. Not now.

He couldn't haul her off to bed in the middle of the morning. Not with all his family and what seemed like half of the world turning up for one of his mother's legendary brunches.

His father and Elias and Ari Cristopolous wanted him for a foursome on the golf course. PJ was a reluctant golfer at the best of times.

"I don't play," he told his brother, hoping to get out of it.

"It's not play. It's work," Elias replied, then added archly. "Besides, you can't do what you want to do anyway, so you might as well give in gracefully."

PJ shot him a startled look, aware that his ears were reddening. "How do you know what I want to do?" he grumbled.

Elias just shook his head and grinned. "Been there, done that."

PJ doubted it. But he remembered that Elias's courtship had not been exactly smooth, even though it had at least taken place on the right side of the wedding, unlike PJ's own. "All right. Fine."

And it might have been if Ally hadn't decided to come, too. "Only to watch," she said. "Not to play."

But having her right there, sitting next to him in the car, her thigh alongside his, her hair blowing in his face, the scent of her shampoo tantalizing him on the way to the golf course did nothing for his mental preparation. He couldn't even remember which club to use.

"It's called a driver for a reason," Elias pointed out mildly once or twice.

But PJ was oblivious to everyone and everything except Ally. He lost badly. He didn't care. He looked at Ally and smiled, and had won enough when she smiled back at him.

He was eager to get off the course, to get back to the house. To the bedroom. To the bed.

But of course, that didn't happen. When they got back to the house, Mark and Cristina and Alex had arrived. Then Elias and Tallie's friends, the Costanideses, all showed up. So did the Alexakises.

"Why didn't you just invite everybody in Greece?" he grumbled.

His father smiled with beatific unconcern. "We did."

Probably they hadn't. It just seemed like it. And there was nothing he could do but smile at them, talk to them, introduce them to Ally.

He made sure he introduced them to Ally. And they were all as charmed as he was.

Cristina wanted to haul her off to the sewing room to talk art. Martha was eager to continue yesterday's conversation. It turned out that Connie Cristopolous was a mosaic artist as well. They were all eager to chat.

"Another time," PJ said gruffly. He had his fingers manacled around Ally's wrist and he wasn't letting go. He was afraid of what might happen, of a possible change in heart, if he let her out of his sight.

"You could come, too," Ally suggested, eyes twinkling.

"Nah. I'd rather play with the kids on the beach." He looked at her. "Wouldn't you?"

He'd have let her go. Really, he would have. And he might

even have gone with her if that was what she really wanted. But his spirits soared even higher when she smiled and nodded. "Yes. We can talk about this later," she said to Cristina and Connie and Martha. "Let's play with the kids."

They played with the kids. Besides the nephews, there were several little Costanides boys and the Alexakises had a boy and three girls. There were others, too, belonging to cousins and friends of his parents.

PJ couldn't keep them all straight and didn't try. What he noticed was Ally. The Ally he remembered had always been quiet, almost inhibited, a girl who rarely let go and played. But this Ally came alive with the children in a way he'd never seen before.

She got totally involved in building a sand castle with the little kids. And when he and Lukas and some of the bigger boys splashed them playfully with water—which of course turned into a water fight—she took great joy in dousing him. She was also the one who suggested "burying Uncle PJ in the sand" would be a grand game.

"Whoa, hang on," he'd protested.

But to no avail. Not when Elias and Lukas and even his mother agreed and helped dig the hole. At least she'd dug him out after and spent an inordinate amount of time brushing sand off him.

He'd loved every minute of that. Too much, in fact, and he'd finally had to head straight into the ocean before he scandalized his entire family.

When he came back it was to discover she had yet another idea—they should make face paint.

He stared at her. "Face paint?"

She grinned impishly. "Chicken?"

"Of course not," he said, affronted. "But how…?" Face paint was totally out of his area of expertise.

"We'll be right back," she promised the kids and, grabbing him by the hand, she led him into the house.

It was not the mystery he imagined it would be—not the mystery that Ally herself was. Cornstarch, cold cream, a few drops of water and food coloring and they were in business. He regarded the colorful tubs a bit warily.

Ally giggled. "Here," and in an instant she dabbed his nose with blob of green. "How handsome you are."

"Am I?" PJ growled and, dipping his fingers in the blue, set off after her while she dodged away, laughing, nearly colliding with his mother and falling over *Yiayia* in her rocking chair.

"Out!" His mother flapped her hands at both of them, shaking her head as well. "You're terrible! Who'd have thought PJ would marry a woman as crazy as he is?"

Ally stopped dead, looking stricken, all laughter gone. "Am I?"

"As crazy as he is?" PJ's mother looked surprised at how serious Ally seemed. Then, as if realizing Ally needed reassurance, she smiled and gave her daughter-in-law a hug. "Yes, I think you are." Then she stroked a motherly hand over Ally's silken midnight hair. "But that's a good thing, you understand?"

Ally looked from his mother to PJ himself, and he saw that her eyes were wide with something that looked like wonder. Then she smiled with a joy PJ had rarely seen as she gave his mother a hard hug in return. "Thank you. Thank you so much."

PJ, watching them, felt for the first time that the tide might really actually have turned. "Ally?"

She looked his way, eyes still glowing.

Grinning, he reached out a hand and stroked blue face paint across her cheeks.

# CHAPTER NINE

TONIGHT she was going to make love with PJ Antonides.

She'd been waiting for it all day.

No, not really waiting, because that seemed somehow to imply that she'd done nothing else. And she'd done a lot, enjoyed a lot.

It had been a magical day.

Not a day. The whole weekend had been magical. In all of it—with the exception of the horrible sleepless night she'd spent last night which was, let's face it, her own fault—Ally had discovered the happiest two days of her life.

The weekend she'd faced with trepidation and anxiety had turned into one of joy and good feeling. With their easy smiles and eager embrace, PJ's family had given her the warmth and sense of belonging she'd always wanted. Completely unexpectedly, under distinctly dubious circumstances, they had opened their arms to her, taken her in, made her their own.

And PJ?

She was about to let him make her his own as well.

She wasn't standing on the precipice any longer, torn between the man she'd conveniently and desperately married and the future she'd envisioned with Jon.

On the contrary, with her apology, she'd taken a step, made a move. And she was free-falling now, inexorably pulled by the attraction she'd felt from the first time she'd met PJ Antonides, an attraction that, unbelievably, hadn't diminished over the past ten years.

But it was more than simple physical attraction. And it was more than the camaraderie of old friendship renewed.

She was very much afraid it was love. Real love. A love that had begun all those years ago and had endured despite their separation, and that had only needed proximity to rekindle, to spark to life again.

At least, it was doing so for her.

She still didn't know how PJ felt. She knew he wanted to continue their marriage—for the moment at least. He'd made that much clear.

But it was also clear that being married was convenient for him. And he'd offered no declarations of love. In fact, he'd agreed that day in his office that he couldn't possibly love her.

And yet…

She hoped. She remembered the way he looked at her sometimes…the way he touched her…the way he'd kissed…

And so she had to find out.

What she'd had with PJ that single night ten years ago—and what they'd shared so far this weekend—both felt so different, so much more authentic than what she'd determinedly tried to construct with Jon, that she couldn't just turn her back and walk away.

And so when, at long last, night fell and the party broke up and PJ came with her to their bedroom, she didn't demur, she didn't act coy, she didn't protest. On the contrary, this time she was the one who grasped his wrist and drew him in with her, then shut the door.

One of PJ's dark brows lifted quizzically. His eyes were dark and heavy-lidded now, slumberous almost. Bedroom eyes. It was an expression Ally had never understood before. Now she did—and didn't need an explanation, either. She had only to look at the man whose lips were scant inches from her own, whose breath she could feel against her heated skin, whose lips she wanted to taste.

She drew an anticipatory breath, then ran her tongue over her own lips.

PJ groaned.

"What's wrong?" she demanded. "Are you sick?" With the amount of food his mother and grandmother and aunts had been making and PJ and his brothers had been eating, she wouldn't have been surprised.

But he was smiling as he shook his head. "Not unless you say 'No kissing.' You're not gonna say that, are you?"

And then she smiled, too, and went up on her toes to brush her mouth against his. "What do you think?"

His lips curved against her own, the merest yet most tantalizing graze of flesh against flesh. His words seemed to vibrate through her as he murmured, "I think that's an even better idea than the face paint, Mrs. Antonides."

And then he took over. His mouth closed over hers, softly at first, gently almost, but with a hunger that built quickly because she had been waiting for it, hoping for it, all day. Maybe, in fact, she'd been waiting for it since their wedding night. The brief quick hungry kisses they'd shared in the past few days were mere appetizers in the face of the feast that PJ was making of this.

It was definitely a kiss worth waiting for.

Ally forgot all about her worries, her nerves, her confusion. She could only respond to the sweet persuasiveness of his lips, his tongue, could only open to him, welcome him, meet his hunger with her own.

But even though he was clearly as desperate for it as she was, his kiss was deliberately slow and leisurely, as if he was a man about to partake of a feast and for whom slow meticulous preparation was every bit as important as the meal he was about to enjoy.

And Ally enjoyed it, too.

She relished the taste of him, all salt and sea spray with, somehow, a hint of lime. In his hair she caught the scent of wood smoke from the evening fire. She drew it in, savored it, even as she savored the silky softness of it threading through her fingers. Then she turned her face to enjoy the scrape of rough whiskers against the softness of her cheek.

He slid his hands up under her shirt, then tugged it effortlessly over her head. The night air through the open window cooled her own heated flesh, but didn't cool her ardor. She snagged the hem of his T-shirt and pulled it up and over his head.

"Mmm." He murmured and backed her toward the bed.

It was the bed in which she'd lain sleepless virtually all night, last night. It was the bed that had seemed as vast and cold as an arctic wasteland when she had spent hours in it alone. But tonight, as PJ bore her back down on it, it seemed a warm and welcome cocoon for the two of them to share.

"Do you want to leave the light on?" he asked. "Or off?"

She hesitated. A part of her would prefer to leave it on, to see PJ strip off and bare the splendor of his naked body. A part of her imagined that he would enjoy the same view of her.

Maybe it was self-consciousness that had her whisper, "Off?" almost as if it were a question. Or self-preservation. Or maybe it was an almost unconscious desire to re-create the intimacy of their wedding night. Then they had embraced in the darkness with only the rising moon to light the room.

Now as PJ flicked off the lamp, she found that there was indeed the same soft silver of moonglow bathing the room. She just prayed that this time the love they shared would last beyond the dawn.

If PJ had similar memories, he didn't say. He didn't speak at all. His hands, his lips, his body spoke for him. He pressed her back onto the bed and made slow sweet love to her.

His touches made her quiver with longing. His fingers trailing down over her ribs and then up the length of her legs made her bite her lip with frustration. But at the same time, she gave herself over to enjoying their touch, reveling in the fact that she was in PJ's arms, in his bed, where she'd never imagined being again.

And then his fingers finally found her, touching her where she most needed his touch, stroking her, opening her. And she sucked in a sharp breath at the sweetness of it, even as she twisted on the sheets and reached out to touch him as well.

Very quickly the rest of their clothes slipped away—and for a second she regretted not having more light to see him. But sight wasn't the only sense she had. Even in the near darkness she could feel his firmly muscled body, his heated flesh, his hair-roughened skin. She could trail her fingers down his abdomen, could run a single one along the proud jut of his erection, making him tense and shudder.

"Ally!" He groaned her name.

She smiled and pressed kisses into his chest, his belly, his—

"Ally!" He hauled her up and pressed her into the sheets. "You're going to kill me, doing that."

"Oh, I wouldn't want to kill you," she whispered. "I have a much better idea." And she wrapped her hands across his back pulling him closer so that their bodies fit together completely.

His knee nudged between hers and she shifted to accommodate. It had been so long, and yet in another way it felt as if no time had passed, as if the memories of that night melded into this one, just as their separate movements meshed and melded into one, as if her body knew what she had not known—that she was his and always had been.

He moved against her, pressed in, and she wrapped her legs around him, her fingers digging into his back as they rocked together, eager, hungry, desperate as the sensation built.

It was like catching a wave, feeling the surging power of the ocean as it lifted them, then plunged them over the crest to ride together, spent yet exhilarated, to shore.

It was like last time, and yet, as the moon slipped slowly across the sky and they loved and touched and stroked and murmured—and kissed and kissed and kissed—Ally knew that this night promised more than the first night. There was eagerness, yes. But the urgency of the moment in their earlier lovemaking—the grasping of a single night out of time—was no longer there.

This was different, Ally thought after they had taken each other a second time and lay tangled together in joyful exhaustion. This wasn't a single moment or even a single night.

It was the beginning of a lifetime together.

Or if it wasn't, if she was wrong, this night would have to last her a lifetime.

Even though PJ didn't speak, didn't offer her endearments, she didn't care. Words didn't mean that much. It was what you showed each other, what your actions said to each other, what you gave that really spoke of how you felt.

And the truth was, PJ had given her years of his life. He'd given her time to grow up, to become a woman he could meet as an equal, be proud of and, she hoped, come to love.

And Ally was determined to, desperately wanted to, be worthy of that love—and to give the same to him. She knew what she wanted now—just as she finally understood what she had to give.

This time she didn't need to turn her back on PJ to go away to find herself. This time she needed to stay, to give herself—to take up her marriage again and make it work.

Tonight he'd made love with Ally Maruyama. No, with Ally Antonides.

He'd waited all day for it.

No, not all day. Ten years.

He lay there now in the room he'd grown up in, where he'd planned his wild adventures and dreamed his impossible dreams, and knew that the boy he'd been could never have dreamed or planned this.

He lay with his arms wrapped securely, possessively, protectively around his wife. Ally's head rested on his chest, her hair tickling his nose. She was sound asleep, breathing softly. Satisfied and sated, he hoped.

Heaven knew he was. For the moment, at least. But probably not for long. He had ten years of loving to make up for. Ten years of doing without.

He hadn't thought about it that way before. He hadn't known, of course. He'd been young and raw and blind when they'd married. He hadn't thought, hadn't considered the consequences, had only acted on his instincts.

And his instincts, come to think of it, hadn't been bad at all.

But he'd never really thought beyond the night. Even when spending it with her had caused him to catch a glimmer of what actually loving a woman like Ally might mean, he'd known it wouldn't work.

She hadn't asked for that. And neither had he.

So he'd given her what she wanted—his name on a legal document and one night in his bed, in his arms.

That was then.

At thirty-two he was a different man. Wiser, he hoped. Steadier. A whole hell of a lot more responsible. And he was no longer interested in living solely for the moment. He wanted a future as well. He was grown up now. A man, with a man's knowledge of time and sense of missed opportunities, of waves not caught, of loves lost.

Well, he wasn't losing this time, he thought, stroking her hair, and smiling when she stirred and her fingers moved against him.

"Again?" she asked with a sleepy smile. Her fingers found him, stroked him.

He arched. "Ally," he warned because amazingly enough he was ready again.

"PJ," she acknowledged. And she turned her head and kissed his chest, licked his nipple.

His breath hissed, and he pulled her on top of him, settling her over him, thrusting up to meet her, closing his eyes as she took him in. Then they opened again so he could watch her in the silver of the moonlight, could relish the shadowy mounds and curves, the silken curtain of her hair. He lifted his hands and cupped her breasts, shaped them, learned them all over again.

She pressed down on him, then rose and slid down again, making him clench his teeth at the feel of her body taking him in. She sighed and her head dropped back exposing the delicate curve of her neck. He longed to kiss it.

"Ally." He urged her down so he could. And did.

Their bodies rocked together. Found a rhythm.

*Wasn't going to lose her this time. Wasn't going to let her walk away. Not too late. It wasn't too late.*

The words echoed in his ears faster and more frantically as the rhythm quickened, as the need built. Then, as once more the climax came, PJ clenched his teeth and pulled her down to hold her tight against him.

This time he had to make her want to stay—not just for a night, but for a lifetime.

This time he was giving it all he had.

The tapping sound woke her.

Ally was tangled amongst sheets and blankets and PJ, her face in the curve of his neck, his arm flung over her, her knee captured between his.

It was awkward and ache-making and absolutely wonderful—just as the whole night had been. Better even than their wedding night because he was still here and—

The tapping came again. Louder now. More emphatic. Someone was knocking on the bedroom door.

One of the kids, no doubt. She'd heard them up and about yesterday, the patter—and thud—of small feet up and down the hallway while she'd lain here alone and miserable. Yesterday morning they wouldn't have considered awakening her. They hadn't known her. But she and PJ had become serious favorites of the younger set by dinnertime.

And that wasn't the only thing that had changed.

She turned her head and laid a gentle kiss on the whisker-roughened jaw of the man who had changed them. He didn't stir, but then, he had to be exhausted.

The tapping came again. Harder. More brisk. "PJ? Ally?"

Not one of the kids, then. In fact the voice sounded like Elias or Lukas. It also sounded urgent.

Ally eased her way out of PJ's embrace, not wanting to wake him if she didn't have to. She knew exactly how little sleep he'd got last night—and he probably hadn't had much more the night before.

She tugged her nightshirt over her head, grabbed her robe and pulled it on, threw a sheet over the most exposed bits of PJ, then padded over to open the door a few inches and peer into Elias's face.

"Oh, God," he said. "I'd hoped it would be PJ."

Ally frowned. "What's wrong?"

Something clearly was. His normally tanned face was uncharacteristically pale. A muscle in his jaw seemed to tick.

"I wanted to tell him, then he could have told you."

Ally's heart suddenly bumped. "Tell me what?"

"Someone named Jon called."

He paused just long enough for Ally to find herself thinking ironically, Jon *never* calls. *Why now?*

And then Elias told her. "Your father's had a heart attack."

# CHAPTER TEN

"I SHOULD have called!" Ally was whirling around the room throwing things in her suitcase, her cheeks flushed, her hair flying.

"Called? Called who?" PJ wasn't even awake yet. How the hell could he be? He'd been awake most of the night. The wonderful lovely night. The absolutely fabulous spectacular night. The best night of his life—

And now Ally had turned into a whirling dervish. He rolled over and shoved himself up, still foggy with sleep or lack thereof, and tried to figure out what the hell was going on. His gaze, following her from the closet to the suitcase, passed the doorway. His head jerked. He squinted. *"Elias?* What the hell—"

Elias came in and shut the door, leaning against it. "*Yiayia* answered her phone," he explained, plucking it from his pocket.

Ally stopped tossing things in her suitcase and snatched it from his hand, then began to punch in numbers.

"Ally's dad had a heart attack," Elias went on.

PJ sat up straight, appalled, his gaze on Ally. Her movements were almost frantic.

"He's alive," Elias said. "But only just, apparently. *Yiayia* didn't know more than that. She grabbed me and told me to tell Ally."

PJ had a thousand questions. The only one that seemed likely to be answered was, What the hell was *Yiayia* doing with Ally's phone?"

It didn't make sense. None of it.

He wanted to shut it off and go back to sleep, to dream the dreams he'd been dreaming, to relive the night he and Ally had shared—a night that, from the look of her hunched shoulders and nervously tapping toes, she probably didn't even remember.

"She left her phone in the kitchen. It rang." Elias shrugged helplessly. "*Yiayia* answered it."

"Ally's phone?"

Elias spread his hands. "*Yiayia* has no concept of cell phones. Or messaging. She thinks that if a phone rings, you answer it. Sorry," he said to Ally.

But Ally wasn't listening. She was pacing and breathing rapidly, alternately biting her lip, clenching her fist and hugging herself with one arm across her chest. "Answer the phone, damn it!" she exclaimed. "Jon, I'm here. Call back for God's sake and tell me what's happening? And tell Dad I'm on my way!"

Then she flicked it off and continued to fling her clothes into the suitcase.

"Beat it," PJ said to his brother. Then added a gruff, "Thanks," as Elias nodded and opened the door.

"Don't thank me," Elias said over his shoulder. "This is nothing to be thankful for."

And wasn't that the truth?

As soon as his brother left, PJ got out of bed. Ally was stabbing at the phone again, then flinging it down in disgust.

"I should have called," she wailed. "I shouldn't have left him."

"Your being there wouldn't have stopped him having a heart attack," PJ said reasonably.

But Ally was pretty much beyond reason. She shook her head. "I shouldn't have left! I should never have come here! I should at least have called! I didn't…I…I have to go home. Now." She looked at him, eyes flashing, a frantic look in them that he'd never seen before, along with a desperation that seemed to dare him to try to stop her.

But PJ had no intention of stopping her.

On the contrary, he was going with her.

He'd let her go to her father by herself the first time—the day they were wed—to inform him of their marriage. She'd said she didn't need him there, that it wasn't his problem, that she could handle it, and he'd believed her.

This time he wasn't even giving her a chance. He had too much at stake now—his life, his future, the woman he loved.

The word snuck up on him. *Love.*

Not lust. Not physical satisfaction. Not simply "making love with" though they'd certainly done that often enough last night. No, this was greater than that, far deeper, far more demanding.

It was the love he'd glimpsed all those years ago—the potential for a relationship that had not only a physical component, but emotional, intellectual and even spiritual dimensions.

It was what he felt for Ally. He knew it. He accepted it. He *wanted* it.

And he wasn't letting her walk away again.

"I'll take care of it," he said, and he wrapped his arms around her and gave her a fierce hard hug.

And then he set about doing exactly that.


Ally felt sick. Desperate. Guilty.

It was true, what she'd told PJ. She should have called. She shouldn't have come. Not to his parents'. Not to New York at all.

She should have left well enough alone, sent the divorce papers, stayed with her father.

Except…except that then she wouldn't have PJ back in her life. She wouldn't have had this past weekend. She wouldn't have had last night.

Could she regret that?

Could she *really?* No, she couldn't.

Guilt and desperation and worry and anguish began bubbling up all over again.

She tried Jon's mobile over and over. She got the same terse businesslike response she got whenever something else in his life took precedence and was too important to permit him to talk to her. Ordinarily she just tried again, didn't take it personally. Of course he was busy.

But her father had had a heart attack! What could possibly be more important than that?

"Call the hospital," PJ suggested. He was using his own phone, making calls, other calls. His own business obviously took precedence, too.

No, that wasn't fair. He'd hugged her. She'd felt his hard arms come around her to hold her close and, for just a second, she'd allowed herself to sag into his strength, to let him hold her, support her. She'd even nodded her head when he'd said he'd take care of it.

But of course he couldn't. How could he take care of her father? She needed to get home.

"I have to call the airline."

"I called. The flight leaves at one." He glanced at his watch. "We've got to get on the road soon. Call the hospital. At least you can find out how he is."

"Yes." But finding out might make it worse. Her fingers fumbled with the address book on her phone. She'd put the number in there when he'd had his first heart attack, used to know it by heart. But her heart was pounding now and her mind was numb and she couldn't even remember how to bring it up.

"Here." PJ took her phone from her. "What's the name of the hospital?"

At least she could remember that.

He got the number in a matter of seconds, and she could hear it ringing through. He handed her the phone just as it was answered.

She gave her father's name in a tremulous voice, afraid he wouldn't be there. Afraid she'd already lost him, afraid it was too late.

But the receptionist said, "Yes. Cardiac intensive care. I'll put you through."

Her legs almost buckled with relief. She gave PJ a tremulous smile. He watched her gravely, his hand on her arm.

She hoped one of the nurses she'd got to know during her father's last heart attack might be on duty now, might remember her, be willing to give her an update.

*Where were they? Why didn't they come to the phone?* Her shoulders hunched, her fingers tightened. And then she felt PJ's hands on her back, his thumbs pressing, kneading, easing the knotted muscles there. She almost whimpered it felt so good.

And then she heard the click of connection and a voice said, "Alice? Is that you?"

"Jon!"

The hands on her shoulders stilled. She barely noticed. "How is he? He's not—" She couldn't say the words.

Jon heard them, anyway. "Of course he isn't," he said soothingly. "He wouldn't be here if he were, would he? Where have you been? I rang for over an hour."

She certainly couldn't answer that. Not now. "I—it's barely dawn here."

"You should keep your phone on."

"It was. It—I didn't hear it. Just tell me how he is."

"He's had a heart attack, Alice. It's serious. He's resting now and he's conscious, but I don't have to tell you that after his last one, there is cause for concern." Then he went into doctor mode and rattled off a bunch of medical terms and analyses that left Ally realizing maybe she really was too stupid to understand when Jon talked about his work.

But then the medical analysis ended and Jon said, "He thought you'd call. He expected to hear from you."

"I never said—"

"I know. But I thought—well, even *I* expected you'd keep in touch."

"I know. I…meant to. I got sidetracked. I'm sorry." Guilt swamped her again, drowning the small thought that they had phones, too. Jon could have kept in touch, called her. So could her father.

"Never mind. We're still assessing the damage. The first twenty-four hours is critical of course. Medically there is nothing to say this is true, but I imagine he'd do better with you here."

"Of course. I'm on my way. My plane leaves at—" She looked helplessly around for the answer, for PJ.

His fingers squeezed her shoulders. "The flight leaves a little after one," he said, and she remembered that he'd already told her that. She repeated it for Jon.

"So you won't be here until at least eight. I don't know where I'll be, Ally. Maybe you could get a cab from the airport."

"Of course." She knew he wouldn't have time to come and get her. "I'd like— Can I—" But she knew better than to ask to speak to her father. "Just tell him I love him," she said urgently. "And tell him I'm on my way."

"I will."

"And…and I'm sorry, Jon. I'll see you as soon as I can," she said. "I—" she'd been going to say, *I love you.* It had become a virtually automatic end to all her conversations with Jon. But the words stuck in her throat.

There was a pause. Then Jon said, "I have to go. I need to check on your father. I'll see you tonight."

There was a click, and Ally stood there, motionless, gutted, feeling as if, were she to move, she would shatter into a million tiny pieces. She could barely even breathe.

And then she felt the rhythmic magic of PJ's hands on her shoulders again. She felt his breath on her neck. His lips touched her in silent acknowledgment. He was so close she could feel the warmth emanating off his body. And she desperately wanted to lean into it, to let him embrace her, to take away her pain.

But she had caused her own pain. And if she hadn't caused

her father's, she soon would when she told him what she had to tell him when she got home.

"Come on," PJ said after a moment, and he took the phone out of her nerveless fingers with one hand and caught her wrist in the other. "Let's get the stuff into the car."

PJ's parents, his siblings, his whole family were instantly and completely sympathetic. They hovered, they patted, they hugged. His mother and grandmother plied her with food she couldn't eat. His sisters suggested milk and juice and homeopathic tranquilizers.

His father snorted at that and offered her a shot of ouzo to calm her nerves instead.

"She'll throw up, Dad," PJ said firmly.

It was probably the truth.

Ally tried to be polite, to thank them for their concern at the same time she tried to keep a stiff upper lip and maintain some slight version of her father's vaunted Maruyama control.

But, as she feared, she wasn't a very good Maruyama. Her lips quivered when she said, no, thank you, and tears welled when she shook her head. She might have made it with her dignity intact if, just as she was going to get into the car, PJ's grandmother hadn't said, "Wait!" and trundled down the steps to wrap her in her arms and hug her tightly.

And Ally couldn't help but hug her back. It was like hugging her own grandmother, the same small bones, the same tender look, the same fierce love. It undid her completely, and then she couldn't stop the tears that streamed down her face.

"I'm sorry," she murmured. "I'm sorry. I don't mean to."

"*Ne, ne.* It is good that you cry," *Yiayia* said, patting her back, touching her cheek. "You love him."

"I do, yes. But—" But that was only part of why she was crying. There was no way she could explain the guilt she felt. She shook her head and wiped her eyes. "Thank you," she whispered. "For everything."

*Yiayia* nodded, smiling gently as she touched a finger to Ally's chin. "It will be all right, you see. And when you come back, you bring your papa, *ne?*"

The idea was as preposterous and it was tempting. Mostly it provided Ally with a glimmer of hope. She swallowed and managed a tiny tremulous smile of her own. "I hope so," she said. "Oh, I do hope so."

"It will be all right." PJ tried again to get through to her, break down the wall of reserve Ally had barricaded herself behind.

She didn't answer, just sat there in the car silent as a stone.

Every now and then he heard her gulp or sigh or sniffle. But she said barely a word.

"He might be sitting up eating dinner by the time you get there," he persisted, patting her knee in an awkward attempt at consolation. How did you console someone who wouldn't be consoled?

"No," she said tonelessly.

"Ally, listen to me. You always used to tell me what a tough old buzzard he was. How can you possibly think he's going to pop off without a fight?"

She swallowed convulsively and shook her head. "I don't know. He's been fighting—" Her voice broke.

"I thought he wanted to see a grandchild," PJ said firmly. "You don't think he'd stick around for that?"

Tears spilled down her cheeks then and she didn't reply at all.

He knew she was crying for her father. But he suspected there was a lot more to it than that. Guilt, for one thing. A bit desperately he said, "Look, get it through your head, this is not your fault!"

But Ally didn't reply. And if she believed him, he couldn't have said.

All the rest of the way to the airport, she sat with her lips pressed together, staring out the window. He didn't know what she was seeing, but he was pretty sure it wasn't Long Island potato fields or suburban housing tracts. He wanted to reach her, to comfort her, to support her, but she'd created a wall between them and he didn't know the way over.

She didn't speak until they got to the airport and he turned at the long-term parking sign.

Then she roused herself to ask, "What are you doing? It'll be so much faster if you just put me off at the terminal."

"But I'd have to catch up," he said, pulling into the stall and shutting off the engine. "And the plane won't leave any sooner. Come on." He opened the door and got out.

Ally got out, too, and stared as he opened the back and took out their suitcases. Her eyes widened as she pointed to the extra one. "What's that?"

"Mine. I'm coming, too."

She stared, then shook her head as if she didn't believe it. Then shook it again more rapidly as if she did and didn't want to. "No! You can't. I mean, you don't need to do that."

"I want to do it. I'm going to do it."

"But—it's Hawaii! It's hours away!"

"Eleven until we get there," he said, picking up the cases and leading the way to where they could make a transfer. "No big deal."

She kept pace with him, though she nearly had to run to do so. "Really, PJ, it's not necessary!"

But he didn't believe that. Not anymore. He wasn't going to argue about it though. He just shrugged. "Yes it is. And I've got a ticket. I'm coming."

She called the hospital before they boarded the plane. Her father was stable, the nurse said.

"As well as can be expected," Ally reported when PJ asked. "Whatever that means," she muttered.

"It means he's hanging in there," PJ said. He squeezed her icy hand.

She gripped his, too, so tightly it was almost painful. He

didn't care. If he could take her pain, he would. Anything he could do, he would.

He leaned across the armrest between them and planted a kiss on her temple. "You've got to hang in there, too, Ally."

She drew a slow breath, carefully, almost warily, and nodded her head. "Yes."

If there was an unexpected blessing to their having spent most of the past two nights sleepless, the first in misery and the last in each other's arms, it was that eleven hours of forced inactivity meant they had a chance to sleep.

Ally did, eventually. In fits and bits, a couple of hours into the flight. PJ couldn't close his eyes. To do so felt almost like falling asleep on duty. She was his to care for and protect. And so he tucked a blanket around her, sat next to her and kept watch.

She woke once and found him looking at her and said, "I can't believe you're doing this."

"Believe it."

"You have a life."

"I have a wife," he countered.

As far as he was concerned, that was the bottom line.

Ally smiled faintly, almost sadly. And then she closed her eyes again and slept.

If Ally had ever needed a demonstration of the expression "He's got your back" she had it today. PJ had been behind her or beside her—stalwart, strong and steadying—every step of the way.

He'd packed their bags, got their tickets, taken her to the airport, held her hand every inch of the way. He'd let her sleep on his shoulder and wipe her nose on his handkerchief. He'd got a rental car while she'd tried futilely to call Jon, and then he had driven her straight to the hospital. This was Honolulu. He knew his way around.

She was grateful for it. She loved him for it.

The truth was she loved him, period.

He slowed to turn into the hospital parking lot.

"No," she said, "Just drop me at the front entrance. It will be quicker."

He nodded. "Okay. I'll meet you inside. Wait and—"

"No," she said quickly, needing to get it over with. "I have to go by myself."

"No! Last time you went by yourself."

Last time? "You mean—"

"When we got married, you told him on your own. I'm not letting you deal with that this time."

"I have to. You can't come."

He jammed on the brakes and stared at her. "Why?"

She glanced away, unable to take the hurt in his eyes.

"It's not that I don't want you there," she tried to explain. "It's just…he doesn't know. About you, I mean. And me. He thinks Jon— He expects Jon…" She couldn't finish. She could see she didn't have to.

His jaw tightened. His lips pressed into a thin line. "You're saying it will kill him."

"I don't…know." Her voice wobbled. "But I can't take the chance. I can't tell him now. I just need a little time. He'll come around. I know he will. He'll want to meet you…"

But they both knew it wasn't true. The last person in the world her father would want to meet was PJ, the man he blamed for the loss of his daughter for all those years. And now PJ was the fly in the ointment again. He was the man who had given her the chance to leave once before, and now he was the one who stood between her and Jon…

"We'll talk about it later. Promise. I won't be long," she said. "They never let anyone stay long. I'll see him now, talk to Jon. Half an hour. Please?"

His fingers flexed on the steering wheel, knuckles whitening. A muscle in his jaw ticked.

She put her hand on his arm. "I don't want him to die, PJ. I don't want to be the *reason* he dies."

His jaw tightened. "I know that." He let out a harsh breath and stopped the car in front of the hospital entrance. "Go on then."

Ally climbed out, then turned back. "You don't have to stay in the car. You can wait in the lobby. Or come to the cardiac floor. There's a waiting room there. He won't know. All right?"

"I'll park the car."

She leaned across the seat and gave him a quick hard kiss. "Thank you, PJ. You're the best." Then she turned and hurried through the doors.

She'd said that to him on their wedding day, too.

They'd said their vows, had become man and wife and, coming out of the courthouse she taken his arm and looked up into his eyes, a smile bright on her face and she'd said, "Thank you, PJ. You're the best."

He wondered if she even remembered that now.

Certainly she didn't at the moment. At the moment, understandably, she was only thinking about her dad.

He couldn't blame her. If his own dad were in intensive care, he'd be doing whatever needed to be done to make sure the old windbag stayed alive. He loved his unpredictable flamboyant father even when the old man complicated his life. And he didn't doubt that however difficult Ally's father had made her life over the years, she loved him, too.

He could even understand why she didn't want him to come in and meet her father now, though it rankled. No, more than rankled, it hurt.

He'd never even met the man. His father-in-law!

PJ parked the car and pocketed the keys, jingling them in his fingers, weighing his options. But he didn't weigh them for long. He hadn't come all this distance to be turned away at the door.

Ally was his wife, damn it, and he loved her. He wasn't going to interfere, wasn't going to cause problems or upset her or her father. But if Ally needed him, he was going to be there, a heartbeat away.

He turned and headed for the hospital doors.

He'd been in a couple of emergency rooms during his time here before. He'd split his head on a rock one summer, had run a drill bit through his thumb one fall. He'd never had a heart attack, though, so this part was all new to him.

It was less nitty-gritty than the emergency rooms and far more high-tech. Nurses moved with quick efficiency, barely sparing him a glance. He asked for Mr. Maruyama's room.

"Number four," a nurse said, barely glancing up from her charting. "But you can't go in. Only family allowed."

He could have argued. He *was* family. But that would only make things worse.

Besides, he could see the family—Ally—from here.

It wasn't far down the hall and the wall of the room was half glass. The privacy curtains were open.

Ally was standing next to the bed, one of her hands clasped in her father's, the other gently stroking his thinning gray hair. The pinched worried look he'd seen on her face ever since he'd awakened to Elias's news this morning had softened.

But she'd got here in time. And now as she smiled at something her father murmured, a gentle joy seemed to light her face.

A man in a white coat brushed past him, bumping his elbow. "Sorry." But he didn't even glance around, just headed straight toward Ally's father's room.

And as PJ watched, the man swept into the room and wrapped Ally in a hard fierce hug. Her father's gray face seemed almost to light up at the sight of him.

Jon.

PJ didn't move. Just stared.

He could hear nothing they said. He didn't need to. He saw Jon take charge, his manner easy and efficient, his expression concerned as he talked to Mr. Maruyama, but softening with a smile whenever he looked at Ally. PJ's guts twisted.

He saw the old man beam as he looked at the two of them. He reached out a hand and took one of Ally's, then extended it feebly in Jon's direction.

Ally hesitated only for a moment, then, as Jon's hand came out to meet it, let his fingers curl around hers.

"How's that for a happy ending?" The charting nurse smiled up at PJ and put her pen away.

PJ had no words.

He wanted to stalk into the room and rip their hands apart. He wanted to wipe the smile off Jon's cheerful face and the satisfaction off Ally's father's. He wanted to say, "She's mine, damn it! She's my wife. She belongs to me. I love her!"

But it was love, God help him, that stopped him.

Love—not the physical bit, not the touches and caresses and ecstasies they'd shared last night—but the deeper stuff, the harder stuff, the selfless stuff held him right where he was, on the outside, looking in.

Love, real love—"grown-up love" as his sister Cristina had called it just the other day—wasn't about what you wanted. It wasn't about that at all.

And loving Ally wasn't about possessing her, or even about protecting her or giving her such a good time in bed that she couldn't say no to him.

It was wanting what was best for her. Deep down. Gut level. Heart-and-soul level.

It wasn't killing her father's hopes and dreams to make his own come true. PJ knew Ally well enough to know the guilt would destroy her. It would also destroy the very love they shared.

His throat was tight. It hurt to swallow. His jaw was clamped so tight his teeth hurt.

The nurse laid a hand on his arm. "Are you all right? Do you want to go sit down? I'm sure Dr. Tanaka or Mr. Maruyama's daughter will come out and talk to you soon. I can tell them you're here."

Numbly PJ shook his head. "No," he said, his voice rusty with pain. "I have to go."

But still he didn't move, just had to look, to memorize, to hold forever in his heart.

And then Ally looked up and saw him. Her eyes widened. Her whole body tensed.

Of course it did. Because if he walked in there, he would destroy everything she loved.

He drank her in—her soft mouth, her flawless skin, her midnight hair and her wondrous eyes. He closed his own for just a moment, held the vision tight, as if imprinting it on his soul. And then he opened them and gave her back the sad smile she'd given him on the airplane.

He understood it now—felt it all the way to the bottom of his heart, to the depths of his soul.

Then he turned and walked away.

# CHAPTER ELEVEN

OF COURSE it had been longer than half an hour.

Ally knew that. And she knew from the grave look on PJ's face when she'd spotted him in the corridor that he wasn't happy.

But surely he understood she couldn't just leave that very second.

Of course he did, she thought as she hurried outside to find him. And he'd followed her wishes and hadn't come in.

But when she'd come out forty minutes later, he wasn't there.

He hadn't been in the heart center waiting room, and he wasn't in the lobby downstairs. The gift shop—he might have gone to buy a magazine, she thought—was closed. And the cafeteria was empty except for the man mopping the floor.

He'd probably just got tired of waiting and gone out for a walk.

She didn't blame him. She wished she could have brought him in.

But of course it was impossible. Her father was too ill. The slightest upset could cause his condition to deteriorate further. She hadn't needed the nurse to tell her he was fragile.

Nor had she needed the benefit of Jon's medical opinion in the corridor for ten minutes after her dad had fallen asleep again. She knew he was trying to be helpful, to include her. But he was only making her feel guiltier.

She knew she needed to talk to him, to tell him what had

happened. But now was not the time. And she didn't want to hurt Jon, either.

Still, all the time he'd talked, she worried about how to do it, and how to tell her father, and wondered where PJ had got to.

And now that she was outside, she realized that she didn't have a clue where he'd parked the car or even what kind it was. Some late-model metallic silver four door—like hundreds of others—but the model was a mystery.

She looked around, feeling desperate.

"Calm down," she told herself. He'd probably just got tired of waiting and had gone to get something to eat. It had been hours since either of them had eaten. And since the cafeteria wasn't still serving, he'd probably gone to pick them up some sandwiches.

Maybe he'd even gone to Benny's, she thought with a tired smile, then turned and trudged into the hospital again. She'd just go back and sit with her father a while longer. PJ knew where she was, after all.

She wasn't exactly sure how long she sat there before she noticed the suitcase in the corner of her father's room behind the door. It caught her eye because it was tweed and battered and looked exactly like hers.

She eased her hand out of her father's frail grip and went to examine it. Her heart was doing skip-steps in her chest. Her mouth was dry. It couldn't be.

But it was. Her suitcase. Her luggage tag with her address in Honolulu.

She hurried out to the nurse's station. "The bag in my dad's room! Where did it come from?"

"Bag?" The nurse looked confused.

"Suitcase," Ally corrected. "It's mine."

"Oh, yes. The gentleman left it," said another nurse who appeared just then. "You were in with your father and—"

"When?"

"Oh, a couple of hours ago. He said you'd need it."

"Where is he? Where did he go?" Her heart wasn't skip-stepping now. It was flat-out galloping.

Both nurses shrugged. "No idea," one said. "He looked a little ill. Washed out. I asked him if he was all right, if he wanted to sit down. But he just said he had to go."

"Go where?"

Both nurses shrugged. "He went out, came back with the suitcase so you could have it, and then he left."

Just like that.

Left. For good?

Ally felt as if all the breath had been sucked right out of her. As if there wasn't enough air in the whole hospital—in the whole world—to draw in another one.

"Are *you* all right?" one of the nurses demanded.

Ally managed to wet her lips, to stop her knees from shaking. "I'm…fine," she said. "I just…need to go sit down."

And she went back into her father's room. He opened his eyes when the chair squeaked as she sat down.

"My girl," he said in a raspy whisper. His fingers fluttered toward her.

Automatically Ally reached out and put her hand over his. Her father needed her. Her father wanted her. But even as she felt his cool, dry barely responsive fingers in hers, she remembered how the strength of PJ's had supported her all day long.

Until now.

Now he was gone.

It was simple, really, she told herself in the days following PJ's departure as she sat in the hospital and watched her father sleep or stroked his hair or held his hand. PJ didn't love her.

He'd never said he did, after all. He'd taken her to bed, yes. He'd caused her to be limp with longing and hot with desire. He'd made her crazy for him. He'd refused to sign the divorce papers because it was convenient to have a wife.

But he didn't love her.

Did he?

Ten years ago she'd been sure he didn't. The night of their wedding, PJ had made love to her with an eagerness and a gentleness and an awe that still had the power to amaze her, and yet she'd turned her back on it, convinced that it meant nothing.

PJ didn't love her.

Five years ago she'd believed it again. Of course he'd come to her gallery open, eager and smiling and delighted to see her, complimentary and kind, and with a very useful—albeit very beautiful—art critic in tow, but Ally had doubted his intentions, had been suspicious and resentful, sure he was implying that she needed rescuing, that she couldn't do it on her own.

How could he love her when she didn't yet love herself?

And now...?

Now she tried to believe he didn't love her again.

But she couldn't.

Because for the first time nothing in her wanted to believe it. Nothing in her *needed* to believe it. She wasn't afraid of it or of what it would ask of her.

She had the strength and the power and the convictions that came with knowing who she was and that she could be who she wanted to be. It had been a struggle, but it had been worth it.

And she hadn't achieved it alone.

She'd never have got there at all without PJ's gift—and not simply his gift of marrying her ten years ago, but the enduring gift of his love.

PJ Antonides loved her.

He'd walked out of her life, yes, but it wasn't because he didn't love her. It was because he did.

Why would he have brought her all the way back to Hawaii if he didn't care, if he didn't love her?

He could have put her on a plane, washed his hands of her, said so long, farewell, and gone back to his life.

Why would he have taken her out to his parents' house? He hadn't needed her to fend off Connie Cristopolous.

He'd taken her to show her what she was missing. He'd wanted her there because he'd wanted to share his family with her.

Why would he do any of that if he really didn't love her?

It wasn't PJ who didn't love her or who didn't trust love, she realized now.

She was the one. Ally herself.

Or rather, the old Ally. The frightened Ally. The Ally whose mother had died too young and whose father had always seemed to equate love with duty and demands.

But the new Ally—*this* Ally—knew better.

This Ally was beginning to understand now what love was really about. She'd seen it. She'd felt it. She'd held it in her arms.

It was PJ's gift of faith in her ability to become the person she wanted to be. It was his interest and his generosity and his support for who that person was. It was being there—always—but not interfering.

Just believing—in her.

She wasn't exactly sure when she started crying. Didn't mean to. Apologized profusely for frightening the nurses who came running at the sound.

"You're overwhelmed, dear," one of them told her. "You need to get some rest. You should go home for a while. Your father will be all right."

He hadn't heard her sobs. He'd slept right through them. He looked a little better, she thought. More rested. Less fragile.

But what would happen when she told him?

She didn't know.

All her earlier plans were still nice and sensible and eminently doable. She could still get the divorce in due time, marry Jon, have a child, be a mother, make her father happy. She could do it all, just as she'd planned—without PJ.

Because he'd loved her enough to give her that gift.

But if she did, she would do it without the other half of her soul.

\* \* \*

Nobility and self-sacrifice were terrific virtues. They had a lot to recommend them.

But sometimes—like now, PJ thought as he slapped another coat of varnish on the deck of his house, not nearly enough. The sun beat down on his bare back, burning him, and he knew he should put on sunscreen or go inside or put on a shirt.

But the pain of a sunburn might take his mind off Ally.

There was no point in thinking about Ally. The other shoe might have hung around for ten years, but it had finally dropped. He'd signed the divorce papers as soon as he'd got back to New York, and dropped them in the mail.

Yes, he loved her. Yes, he wanted her. And yes, he probably could have convinced her to stay married to him.

But at what cost?

Killing her father?

No. He might be selfish. He might want what he wanted and go after it single-mindedly. But he didn't kill innocent bystanders in the process. Or even not-so-innocent ones.

His back ached. It was a big deck. He wasn't used to this sort of manual labor anymore. "Getting soft," he muttered. It was time to get out from behind that desk.

Elias and Lukas hadn't been thrilled when he'd left.

"How long are you going to be gone?" Lukas had asked.

"Dunno. Need some time."

"Heads of companies don't just up and take off," Elias had said disapprovingly.

"No?" PJ had met his stare with a level one of his own. "Seems I recall you did."

His brothers had muttered and grumbled. "You'll manage," he said flatly. "I'll be back. I need some time."

"Going on your honeymoon?" Lukas had said with a wiggle of his eyebrows.

Elias had kicked him in the shin.

"Hey!" Lukas yelped. "What'd I say?"

"Grow up," Elias growled, "and you'll figure it out."

Was it growing up that did it? PJ wondered. If so, growing up didn't have much to recommend it. It seemed to him he'd been a whole hell of a lot happier before Ally had come back into his life.

But the real hell of it was, he couldn't regret it. Didn't regret it. Still loved her.

And he wasn't sure what the cure was for that.

Jon had been philosophical when she begged off.

"I knew it," he said. "Knew when you went to New York."

"I didn't know it then," Ally argued.

But Jon just smiled a sad knowing smile. "I think you did. I just hope you won't regret it."

So did Ally.

"I wish you the best," he said as they sat across from each other in the hospital cafeteria.

"And I you," she said sincerely. "And I know you will continue to be a good friend to my father."

"Of course," he said. His mouth tipped at one corner. "I am a good doctor."

"And a good friend," Ally insisted. "I'm sure you'll meet someone else. The right person for you, Jon."

Jon smiled politely. "I hope I will."

Ally had no such hope for herself. There was no one else. Just PJ.

So she was gutted when she went home that night to find a priority envelope containing the signed divorce papers in her mailbox.

Ally tried to tell herself that the papers were a part of the gift of his love. And maybe that was true. But they were also a signal that he'd moved on.

How many times could you spurn a man before he said that was enough? Ally knew she didn't want to find out.

She'd have gone back to New York the minute she'd come to her senses if she'd thought her father's health would permit it. But it was one thing to know she wasn't going to marry Jon, and another to tell her father the truth.

But he was out of intensive care now. He was sitting in his private room doing the crossword puzzle these days when she went to see him. He was still frail, but he could walk to the end of the hall.

"Will he die if I tell him we're not getting married?" she'd asked Jon yesterday.

And this time he didn't give her a ten-minute opinion. He simply said, "I hope not."

But he didn't offer to tell her father for her. And she couldn't blame him. The choice not to marry had been hers. So was the obligation to inform her dad.

Just like last time.

This time, though, it was worse, because this time she was afraid that what she was going to say might kill him.

She wanted to wait. But there was no waiting. He'd sensed something was wrong as he'd got better. "You're quiet," he'd said yesterday. "Pale. You have been pale since you got home. You're not well? Ask Jon for something to help you."

She'd shaken her head. "There's nothing Jon can do."

Today he looked up when she came into the room and shook his head in dismay. "No better."

Ally frowned. "You're not?" She thought he looked better.

"Not me. You." He shook his head. "What is wrong, Alice? Are you fighting, you and Jon?"

"No. I—we're not." She wanted to stop there. Knew at the same time she couldn't. "We're not getting married, Dad."

For a long moment her father didn't move. His expression didn't change. He didn't even seem to breathe.

But at least he didn't drop over dead.

"We don't—I don't—" she corrected, knowing she couldn't blame this on Jon "—think it would be a good idea." Pause. She watched her father. *Come on, Dad. Breathe, damn it.* "I don't...I don't love him."

"Love—" Her father got one word out. It seemed to strangle him.

She started to reach for the nurse's bell. He shook his head, held up his hand. Ally waited, coiled with tension.

"Love," he said again. He breathed now, sounding less strangled this time. "Yes. You must have love." His words were raspy, but absolutely clear.

Ally stared at him, then shook her head in disbelief.

"It's true. I know this," he said, nodding slowly, "because of your mother."

"My mother?" Ally's own voice was no more than a croak.

Hiroshi Maruyama had never talked about his wife. He'd shut himself away after her mother's death. To Ally it seemed as if the sun had fallen out of the sky. To her father it had just been the excuse for more work.

"I loved your mother," he said slowly. "And sometimes love hurts. When your mother died, I died. Inside. I—didn't want to live without her. So much pain." His eyes seemed to focus on something far off in the distance. They shimmered with unshed tears. And then he looked back at her. "I didn't want you to know such pain, my Alice."

Ally reached out a hand and took his. Thin fingers wrapped hers. Fingers that had some strength to them now. They squeezed. They pressed.

"That is why I wanted you to marry Ken. It was sensible. Not a love match. And if—if something happened—you would not be hurt as I was." He shook his head. "I can be very stupid sometimes."

"No, Dad. You just…cared…"

*For me.* Ally began to understand that, too. Began to appreciate his motives, if not what he had actually done.

"But I was wrong. I know that now. There is no defense against love. I had your mother for thirteen years. The best thirteen years—" his eyes shone at the memory "—of my life. Not long enough, but worth all the pain. Worth everything. I loved her. For herself. And for you, Alice. For the gift of you."

And then holding his hand wasn't enough. Ally fell to her knees and buried her face in his chest and felt his thin arms come around her, his lips on her hair. Then his arms loosened and he stroked her hair.

She looked up at him, at the tears on his cheeks and closed her eyes when he wiped her own away.

"You love, too," he said. It wasn't a question.

How did he know? She bowed her head and felt his frail fingers stroking her hair and realized that of course he knew. A man who had loved as he had loved would see that love reflected in his daughter's eyes.

She raised her head again and blinked tears from her eyes. "Yes."

"Go to him. Bring him to meet me."

"I'm already married to him, Dad," she said, her voice thick and tremulous.

A faint smile touched his lips. "Good. Then I will have a grandchild soon."

"What do you mean, he's not here?" Ally stared at Rosie, PJ's assistant, feeling as if she'd been punched in the gut.

She'd arrived last night—as soon as she could after her conversation with her father. Coming with his blessing had made her almost sing all the way to New York. She'd gone straight to PJ's apartment, eager to see him. Nervous. Worried.

She'd tried to get hold of him, but she'd never got his cell phone number. And she couldn't call anyone who might have it. She had to see him, to talk to him before anyone else.

And he hadn't been there.

She'd waited until dark. She'd lurked in a nearby café. She'd gone back several times. No PJ.

And now he wasn't here, either?

"When will he be back?"

Rosie shrugged. "No clue."

Not exactly the most professional response. But the way Rosie was looking at her made Ally think she wasn't being given Rosie's best professional demeanor.

"I need to talk to him. Where is he?"

"Don't know that, either," Rosie said. "They might." She jerked her head toward PJ's office door.

"Who?" Ally said. But it didn't matter, really, as long as someone did. She went straight past Rosie and pushed open the slightly ajar door.

Lukas was behind the desk doing something on the computer. Elias was on the floor, and two little boys—his twin sons—were climbing on him while he talked Lukas through some procedure.

They all looked up, startled, when Ally walked in.

Elias recovered first. "About time," he said. "This is all your fault."

Now it was her turn to stare. "What are you talking about?"

"Why I'm here. Why he's—" a thumb in Lukas's direction "—here."

"What? Where's PJ?"

"He's gone. Cut out. Split. Leave of absence."

"Leave of his senses, more like," Lukas muttered.

"Where's he gone? I need to talk to him."

"Talk?" Both his brothers looked at her suspiciously. "About what?"

She hesitated. But she couldn't not say it. She was a believer now. "I love him. I need to tell him."

"Hallelujah," Lukas muttered. "There's hope."

"I hope so," Ally said a little desperately. "Do you know where he is?" It occurred to her that they actually might not.

"Not sure," Elias said, hauling himself up off the floor and making the twins start to cry. He scribbled something on a piece of paper and handed it to her. "Try this. Settle down, guys. I'm coming." And he dropped to the floor again. "Tallie's baking today," he explained. "Some cousin's fancy wedding. So I'm babysitting—and getting Lukas up to speed."

Ally's brows lifted. "To speed."

"Running things," Lukas said grimly. "Hurry up and get him back here. If you don't, I'm going to be stuck being president of Antonides Marine."

Kauai?

She had stared at the address as soon as she got out into the corridor. Why on earth would Elias give her an address in Kauai? She'd just come back from Hawaii. She didn't know anyone in Kauai.

PJ had never mentioned Kauai. It didn't make sense.

But she had to start somewhere, had to take something on faith. So she went.

If she ever found PJ and he told her to get lost, she thought grimly as she battled bloodshot eyes that were gritty from lack of sleep, a rental car with a slipping second gear, and the conviction that she was going on a wild-goose chase, the consolation would have to be all her frequent flyer miles.

She didn't imagine they would make up for the heartbreak, though.

She felt as if she'd been traveling forever. In fact she didn't know what day it was anymore. She'd flown from Honolulu to New York, then back, through San Francisco, to Honolulu and on to Kauai. She hadn't passed Go, she hadn't collected two hundred dollars. She hadn't even stopped to look in on her father.

She didn't want to see the look of disappointment on his face when she turned up without PJ.

And now, it seemed, she was running out of road.

The man at the rental car office had blinked when she'd showed him the address. Then he'd looked it up on his GPS and given her directions. "Out in the boonies," he'd said. "And then some."

He hadn't been lying. The macadam had turned to gravel

a few miles ago, and now the gravel was gone. It had ceased to be any sort of public road and was now not much more than a track.

She knew that there were places in Kauai that were celebrated as "off the beaten path." She just wished she weren't on her way to one of them—especially since she expected to be sent on from there.

She felt like she was going nowhere—just winding through a thick jungly forest, over mountain and down dale. The trees held the heat in. Perspiration trickled down her back. She flexed her shoulders and tried to get rid of the crick in her neck. She wondered if she'd missed a turn. But she hadn't seen anything remotely resembling one.

And then, just as she despaired of ever finding the house, or her way back, she came around a curve and the view opened out into a lush hollow and there was a house—a long stunning Indonesian-style house overhung with palm trees on a rise between her and the sea.

She pulled up as near to the house as she could get. And when the engine shut off, she could hear the sound of birds, the rustle of palm fronds, and waves breaking, and her heart pounding in her chest.

She'd given up even imagining she'd find him. She'd hoped all the way back to New York, all the way to his apartment, all night in her hotel, all the way to his office, all the way back to Kauai, all the way to God knew where.

The house was like something out of Shangri-La—open and airy, with woven shades and soaring lines, all very natural and fitting, built with native stone and wood. The hideout of some wealthy eccentric billionaire no doubt. Certainly not PJ.

Ally grabbed her tote bag out of the car, went up onto the porch and knocked on the door. No one answered. The windows were open, though. Probably the door was, too. Who, after all, would be breaking in out here?

"Anyone home?" she called.

Again no response.

She wasn't driving all the way back again. She simply wasn't. She'd do a Goldilocks and sleep in someone's bed if she had to. Wait for them to come home. Find the next clue…

That was what it felt like.

She tried the door handle. It opened. She hesitated, then just pushed the door open. The inside of the house was as beautiful as the outside, with woven mats on broad-planked teak floors, rattan furniture, a native stone fireplace and eye-catching art—a pair of masks on the wall by the door, a very old surfboard above the sofa. And high on the wall above the fireplace a wall hanging that—

—looked astonishingly familiar.

And yet she hadn't seen it in years.

She stared. Then, numbly she made her way down the shallow steps into the living area to get a closer look.

Believing—and disbelieving—at the same time.

Good heavens, it was here. The one she'd made that first year in California when she'd been so homesick. The one of the beach where she'd met PJ. The ocean in all its shades of blue and green, the houses, shops. The execution was amateurish. She knew that now, had known it then. But it had captured a memory. A time. A place. Things that had meant something special to her but no one else.

And yet someone had bought it. She'd always priced it high—too high for anyone to be tempted. It wasn't that good.

But one day it had been sold.

And now it was here. She reached a hand up and could just reach the bottom of it. She brushed her fingers along the ragged edge of it. And she smiled as she did so.

She didn't need to wonder whose house this was anymore.

She looked around with new eyes. Open eyes. Ran her fingers over the soft patina of the wood. Savored the setting, the way the house and its furnishings fit as if they'd always been there, as if they belonged.

It wasn't a new house. But it had been painstakingly restored. She smelled a bit of varnish, now that she was paying closer attention. She moved to the windows that looked out toward the ocean. Yes, the deck looked as if it had been recently refinished.

And the man who had done it was walking up from the beach.

He was bare-chested, bare-headed, sandy and sunburned. He carried a surfboard under his arm. He looked beautiful. He didn't look happy.

Ally wondered if seeing her would make him any happier.

Or if it was too late. If she'd left it too long.

She took a deep breath and pushed open the door to the deck. It squeaked.

PJ looked up. And stared.

He didn't move. A wave broke against the shore behind him. And then another. He didn't so much as blink. Just stared—and stared—at her.

And then she saw him swallow convulsively. He let out a breath. "Al?" His voice was rusty.

She smiled tentatively, took a step toward him. "You sound worse than the door."

He swallowed again. "Don't…have much occasion to talk." He still didn't move.

She was going to have to make all the running, then. Well, fair enough. She crossed the deck. "Will you talk to me?"

He looked wary. "About what?"

"Coming back to New York." She smiled. "Lukas wants you there."

"I won't go for Lukas."

"Will you come for me?"

There was one more split second of stillness. And then he moved.

He took the three steps that closed the gap between them and wrapped his arms around her, crushed her hard against him, clung to her as if he'd never let her go.

He was shaking, she realized. And so, she thought as her knees wobbled, was she.

"What happened?" he demanded. "Your father…?"

"Wants to meet you."

He stared disbelieving.

She nodded, smiling up at him. "I told him I loved you."

A grin cracked his face. "And he didn't croak?"

She shook her head. "He's sticking around for a grandchild," she told him. "Just like you said."

PJ made a sound somewhere between a laugh and a sob. He wrapped his arms around her again and held her so tightly she nearly couldn't breathe. She didn't care. It felt wonderful. It felt perfect. It felt as if she'd finally come home to the place—and the man—in her life.

Then he eased his grip on her just slightly and drew her into the house with him. "How'd you find me?"

"I went to New York. To your place. You weren't there. I went to the office. Saw Lukas and Elias. I thought Elias was sending me on a wild-goose chase. This is really the…back of the beyond. It's…yours?"

"Bought it five years ago."

"You weren't in New York five years ago," she protested.

"No. But I was tired of hanging around Honolulu. There wasn't much point in staying," he added pointedly.

And there was a look on his face that made her ask wonderingly, "Because of what happened that night—at the gallery?"

"It didn't help."

"No. I'm sorry. I was insecure," she told him. "And there was Annie—" she hated admitting that, but it was true.

"A friend. Period. I swear it."

"I believe you. The problem wasn't you," she told him. "It was me. And now…it's not."

He held her again then, ran his hands over her as if he could barely believe she was here. Then he drew her down onto the sofa and kissed her, and Ally kissed him back, wanting far more than kisses, but needing to get all the explanations out of the way first.

She pulled back to look into his eyes. "I didn't understand," she told him, "about love."

PJ shook his head. "Neither did I. Or maybe I did and it scared me to death. It did that, all right." He let out a breath. "That first night…"

Ally stared at him. "The…first night? Our wedding night?"

"Hell, yeah. You comin' to the door like that. Blew me away. I wasn't ready for it at all."

"It was wonderful," Ally rubbed her thumbs against the backs of his hands.

PJ nodded. "Yeah. But terrifying. Trying to make it good for you—"

"It was good for me," Ally said fervently.

"Well, good. But—not just making love. Making a life…together."

"You…thought about it?"

He let out a breath. "How could I not? But how could I suggest it? I hadn't thought about it before. Wasn't ready to think about it then. And you had things to do. It would have been springing you from one trap to put you in another."

Ally let out a shaky laugh and pushed her hair away from her face as she looked into his. "Oh, God, PJ. I…I wanted it, too. So much. But I couldn't ask for anything more."

They stared at each other a long moment, each of them re-thinking the past, wondering, questioning.

Then PJ said, "Just as well we didn't. We'd probably have blown it."

And Ally bit her lip and nodded, certain he was right. But she had to ask, "What about when I came back to Honolulu five years ago? Were you ready then?"

"I thought I might be." He shoved a hand through his hair, then added wryly, "Not that I had anything to offer you then."

"You'd already given me everything I could ever have

wanted." She framed his face in her hands and kissed him again.
It was a long kiss, a lingering kiss. A kiss that allowed her to
realize, dear God, how much she loved him—and how long.

"I love you," she murmured. "So much. I think I always did.
But I didn't know how to tell you. Or to trust it."

"And now you do?" It was a statement, but Ally heard the
question in it.

"I do," Ally said, and smiled at the echo of her vow so many
years ago. "See?" And she turned her side to him so that he
could see a small fabric patch she'd appliqued to her sleeve.

PJ studied the pair of entwined fabric hearts. His mouth
twitched. "You're wearing your heart on your sleeve."

"I am," she agreed. "Always. For you. I just didn't know how
to tell you."

"Just say the words," he told her hoarsely. "You can't ever
say them enough."

So Ally said them again. And again. She put her arms around
his neck as he swung her up and cradled her against him as he
carried her inside. "I love you, PJ Antonides. I will tell you so
every day of your life."

"Works for me," he said. "You can show me, too." He grinned,
carrying her all the way into the bedroom. "Anytime you want."

She showed him how much she loved him while they stayed
on Kauai. She showed him back in Honolulu when they stayed
a week to visit with her dad.

Far from having died at the news of who she was in love
with, Hiroshi Maruyama seemed to have a new lease on life.
Certainly he did his best to make PJ feel welcome. And so what
if he dropped more than a few hints about how nice it would
be to have a grandchild.

"I'm willing," PJ said. "Whenever Ally is."

"We're working on it," she assured her father, blushing when
he smiled knowingly.

She was gratified that PJ and her father got on well. But

she was equally happy when PJ said he needed to get back to New York.

"Wouldn't want Lukas to think I'd abandoned him forever."

"I'm looking forward to getting home," Ally replied.

PJ's brows lifted. "Home." He grinned. "I like it that you're coming home with me."

"I liked—I love—everything about you," Ally assured him. "And I want to get back to look at the mural."

And now they were home in PJ's Park Slope brownstone—her home, Ally thought with abiding joy. And she was standing in front of the mural, looking. And looking. And looking.

"I'm not here," she said.

She looked at everyone in the beach scenes. She didn't find anyone who looked like her. She identified many of the others—surfers they knew, friends they'd had, even her own friend May. But she couldn't find herself.

Or PJ for that matter. He wasn't on the beach. He wasn't in the water. He wasn't anywhere.

She studied Benny's Place. Maybe he was eating a hamburger there. Maybe she was behind the counter. But neither was there. She looked at the anonymous passersby just ambling by on the sidewalks or sunning on the shore.

"We're not here," she grumbled.

PJ came and stood behind her, wrapping his arms around her, nuzzling beneath her ear. "You're looking in the wrong place."

"I've looked every place we were. The beach. The sand. Benny's." Ally sighed.

"You'll find it. You've got the rest of our lives."

She smiled and settled back against him, loving the feel of his hard strong arms holding her. She turned her head and planted a kiss on his jaw, then went back to the mural. She found the university, the surf shop where PJ had worked, the tiny hole-in-the-wall storage unit where he had built his first windsurfers. She found the apartment where he'd lived above Mrs. Chang's garage.

"Ah." She tapped at the tiny painted window. "Are we in there?"

PJ nipped her ear and laughed. "It's not an X-rated mural."

But she was beginning to feel a bit X-rated right now. His hands were sliding up under her shirt, cupping her breasts. She could feel PJ's body, behind hers, developing its own X-rated agenda.

And then, just when she was about to give up and suggest they adjourn to the bedroom, she found them—PJ and Ally—kissing on the steps of the courthouse.

Ally stared in amazement. She felt shivers all up and down her spine because it was such a pivotal memory for her. And that he would have chosen it, too…

"That's your memory of us? Not the beach? Not Benny's? You remember kissing at the courthouse?"

"What's wrong with the courthouse?" PJ wanted to know.

"Nothing's wrong. It's just—I can't believe that's what you remember." It was like a gift. The greatest gift—his love.

"It's not all I remember. But it's what I remember most," he said as he turned her in his arms and kissed her again—and again and again and again. Then he drew her with him down the hall and into the bedroom.

"It was the start of what I want to remember always, Al." And as they fell together onto their bed, he wrapped his arms around her and kissed her with all the urgency they'd both felt that day. "It's when I first began to believe in love."

# THE RUTHLESS ITALIAN'S INEXPERIENCED WIFE

BY
CHRISTINA HOLLIS

**Christina Hollis** was born in Somerset, and now lives in the idyllic Wye Valley. She was born reading, and her childhood dream was to become a writer. This was realised when she became a successful journalist and lecturer in organic horticulture. Then she gave it all up to become a full-time mother of two, and to run half an acre of productive country garden. Writing Mills & Boon® romances is another ambition realised. It fills most of her time between complicated rural school runs. The rest of her life is divided between garden and kitchen, either growing fruit and vegetables or cooking with them. Her daughter's cat always closely supervises everything she does around the home, from typing to picking strawberries!

# CHAPTER ONE

Was that something burning? Cheryl jumped from her chair and started searching the bedroom. Within seconds she discovered where the smell was coming from. The light glowing on Vettor's bedside table was covered in a thin layer of dust. She wiped it clean with a dry paper towel, fooling herself that everything was all right again.

Here she was, alone in a foreign country—no, it was worse than that. She was marooned in a creepy old villa with only a sick toddler for company. Leaning over the bed, she sponged his hot face with cool water. The poor little boy had to be kept calm. She didn't want to frighten him with her own worries.

Her fingers dug into the flannel as she remembered how helpless she had felt when RTN had broadcast warnings of a ferocious storm heading for Florence. The day staff had already left for their homes. The only worker living permanently at the Villa Monteolio was the caretaker. Cheryl had felt safe with him and his wife so close at hand. But then the storm had attacked, and when his wife had been struck by a tile, blown from the roof, the caretaker had rushed her to hospital.

Cheryl was now totally alone. She made another

quick check of the sickroom. Expecting the power to go off at any second, she wanted to make sure she could find her way around in darkness if the worst happened. This summer storm had been screaming violently all evening. The electricity had been dipping in and out for hours. *Any ancient country house was bound to suffer from power cuts*, Cheryl told herself. *If only this old place wasn't quite so Gothic...*

She looked up at the nearest carving. A stone angel perched on a ledge, holding a shield. It gazed across to the opposite wall, where a once identical partner crouched. The other angel's head had been knocked straight off its shoulders—recently, she guessed. The exposed stone was pale, and still crumbling. Now and then a scatter of loosened grit rattled down against the flagstones.

Cheryl thought of the nervous warnings the villa's staff had given her that morning. *'Don't upset Signor Rossi whatever you do,'* they muttered. *'He's a demon in disguise.'* Cheryl, thinking they were teasing, had laughed at the time.

She wasn't laughing now.

Another icy blast slammed against the northeastern corner of the house. All the shutters and doors creaked in a diabolical chorus. Wind streamed through them, finding every crack and crevice in the Villa Monteolio. The power dipped again. Shadows engulfed the stone angels.

Cheryl gripped the nearest solid thing. It was the arm of the chair she intended sleeping in, though the idea of getting any rest on her first night in a place like the Villa Monteolio during this hellish storm was beyond a joke. As she held on tight, the chair seemed to tremble. She gasped. Did they have earthquakes in Italy? She didn't know. They were on the ground floor of the house, and, glancing around quickly, she reassured herself everything looked built to last. Perhaps she ought to check the room above, and make sure nothing was likely to come crashing through the ceiling onto Vettor's bed.

Life had taught Cheryl to prepare for the worst and deal with it, but her little charge might wake while she was gone. What would happen if there was a power cut at the same time? She couldn't bear to think of Vettor opening his eyes in darkness. That was why she'd hunted out the old emergency lamp and set it up beside his bed without thinking to clean it first. It was why she kept this vigil. She was sure the power would go down as soon as she left the room. She dithered. If Vettor woke, surely the battery light would be enough to keep him company until she got back? If she went at all…

Cheryl fretted over what to do. Breathless seconds passed as she waited to see if an earthquake really would join all her other problems. Luckily, after that first shiver, the chair didn't move again. That *might* mean she only had Vettor and the storm to worry about.

After an eternity, she risked sinking onto the chair's seat. It felt stable enough, but she couldn't help wondering what the next panic would be. Outside, tiles had been falling like autumn leaves all evening. When interviewing her for this new job, Signor Rossi's human resources manager had told Cheryl to expect chaos. The old place was a wreck. So she'd known the Villa Monteolio was a work in progress, but the holes in its roof had still come as a shock.

Rain must be gushing in everywhere by now. Cheryl

glanced around nervously. How long before the upstairs ceilings started to bulge? She *really* ought to go and check on everything. Finding out what was going on would be better than sitting here worrying. On the other hand, if she went to investigate, what could she do? Water and mess might be ruining the top floors, but no workman would struggle all the way out here in this weather. Cheryl decided to stay put and keep the little boy company. Any damage to the villa would have to wait. It wasn't her problem anyway—she already had enough of her own.

Work was Cheryl's refuge from pain. Taking this job in Italy was supposed to help her forget what a mess her life had become. Her parents couldn't resist forcing her most recent disaster down her throat at every opportunity, so she'd left England to make a fresh start. The past could really hurt her, but now reality was attacking her on every side as well. It was horrible.

A tremendous squealing crash echoed in from outside, catapulting Cheryl out of her seat. The electric lightbulb dimmed and went out. It hardly mattered. Flickering flashes of blue-white light flooded the room, bursting through the window shutters. Cheryl dashed over to them and peered between their slats, squinting against the glare. The gale had torn up one of the great trees lining the Villa Monteolio's rutted drive. Its branches were bouncing on a power line, and sparks arced into the darkness, lighting up the driving rain.

She grabbed her phone. When the caretaker and his wife had been forced to leave, Cheryl had asked them for a telephone directory and programmed in every emergency number she could find, just in case. *Good job I did*, she thought, though it still took what seemed like for ever to get through to the electricity company. Half the area was in trouble tonight. The call operator promised to send someone out to the Villa Monteolio as soon as they could, but didn't know how long it would take.

A small voice croaked from the other side of the room.

Dropping her phone, Cheryl ran straight over to the bed.

'Vettor, it's me—Cheryl. You remember? Your new nanny?'

The three-year-old's eyes glittered with fever.

Cheryl peeled the compress off his forehead, freshening it in a bowl of water before she spoke again.

'I'm here, Vettor. We're at your uncle Marco's house. I've been trying to get hold of him, so he can come and see you,' she said brightly, silently thinking of all the unanswered messages she had left with his uncle's secretary.

There was no reply from her patient. Taking a fresh glass of cold water and the wet flannel back to his bedside, she wiped his face and hands, then gave him a drink.

'He'll be busy.' the little boy said sadly. 'He's always busy.'

The words came straight from his heart. They saddened Cheryl so much she couldn't look at him.

'Signor Rossi is a very hard-working man.' Cheryl stopped herself using the most obvious word, *workaholic*.

She sighed, thinking of the procession of personal assistants she had dealt with since answering that advert in *The Lady*. Half a dozen different professionals had interviewed her, but never the man himself. They were equally polished, but every one of them was doing a job, not living a life. What sort of man took on a nanny for his orphaned nephew without checking her out for himself? A man who could ignore all Cheryl's most urgent calls today, that was who. Someone whose staff had told her they were afraid of him.

She tugged at Vettor's bedsheet again, smoothing it over his restless little body. 'At midnight, the radio said all the roads for miles around were closed. It's because of this bad weather. Your uncle must be held up somewhere.'

Luckily, her little charge drifted back into feverish sleep. She did not have to dodge any more difficult questions. *All I must do is survive until someone gets here*, she told herself, jumping like a kitten as a door banged somewhere, far off.

It would be light in a few hours' time. Things would feel better in daylight. Wouldn't they?

As Cheryl tried to reassure herself, another great gust exploded against the house. Every window in the building shook. Her hand flew to her mouth, stifling a scream. Whatever happened, she mustn't scare little Vettor.

Biting the side of her thumb in terror, she braced herself for another blast. But when her next shock came, the gale wasn't responsible. A very human sound burst through the storm's racket, flinging Cheryl from her chair again. Someone was hammering at the front door.

She exhaled, feeling as though she'd been holding her breath for hours. It must be the electricians. What a relief! She was desperate to get the power back on again, for Vettor's sake. She checked her little charge and then grabbed a torch. Groping her way through the gloomy old building, she was glad to reach the great entrance hall without getting lost.

The arcing power lines bounced huge shadows crazily around the vast space. At any other time Cheryl would have been alarmed, but she was beyond that tonight. She didn't give herself time to think. Sprinting across to the imposing studded oak door, she pulled it open, sobbing with relief.

'Oh, thank God you're here!' she screamed at the large silhouette.

Then thunder crashed, right overhead. Cheryl jumped like a frog, dropped the torch—and fell straight into the stranger's arms.

He caught her, and held her close. Wind screamed around them in a fury of torn twigs and leaves, but Cheryl didn't care. Instinctively, she knew she was safe. The new arrival was sheltering her with his body, shielding her from harm. As his cheek pressed hard against the side of her head, he murmured quiet reassurance.

'Shh…*lei è sicuro con me*,' he whispered into her hair.

His voice was so reassuring all Cheryl's old fears were soothed away, along with her current terror.

But gradually fingers of reality fastened onto her again. What was she thinking? She stiffened, and tried to draw back from him.

'I'm sorry. My Italian is very basic…'

'Then I shall speak English. Is that better?'

Cheryl relaxed instantly. A voice speaking her own language was exactly what she wanted to hear so far from home.

'It's more than better, it's wonderful!' she said with real feeling. She'd been in Italy for less than a day, but her head was already throbbing. Trying to memorise new words while leafing through a phrasebook was hard enough at the best of times, but Cheryl had also been busy meeting new workmates—familiarising herself with a different workplace and dealing with a case of scarlet fever at the same time.

'Oh…I'm so sorry for that outburst, *signor*…you must think I'm a complete idiot. The boss here wanted to employ an English person, and as everyone else is apparently scared to death of him…'

The dark outline of the stranger's head dipped, and she heard a soft sound that might have been laughter.

'Don't worry. There's no need to apologise. This is the worst storm I've ever seen.' His voice bubbled with amusement. 'Isn't there a caretaker on duty?'

'He's had to go to hospital—' Cheryl began, but the wind swirled around them again. She shivered instinctively, sensing a hint of autumn in the air.

Instead of letting her go, the stranger tightened his grip. His bulky shape was an irresistible force, hustling her backwards into the building. She was more than willing to let him direct her into the darkened hall. As long as she didn't have to go on facing this storm on her own in this echoing old barn of a house she could stifle her usual feelings of panic in the presence of such overpowering masculinity.

There was a crash as the front door slammed shut. Her rescuer was still holding her securely against his powerful body, so Cheryl barely flinched. With the sounds of wind and torrents of water muffled, rational thought became easier for her. She supposed he must have kicked the door shut. She couldn't be certain, because she couldn't see past him. His vice-like hands were holding her so tightly she could barely move of her own accord. He was drenched, and dripping with rain, but Cheryl hung on. It was madness, but she couldn't let go. She was in the grip of a man and she didn't care. This *must* be a once in a lifetime storm.

Her legs gave way with the relief of it all, but the stranger held her up. Changing his hold to encircle her with only one of his strong arms, he supported her weight. Hugging her to his body, he comforted her with a voice that was lyrical, with a low, slow accent.

'There, there…it's all right now…'

Turning her in towards his body, he started patting her back softly.

Cheryl trembled with fear, but it wasn't only the storm terrifying her. Memories from the past, of Nick, came flooding back. Her mind did its best. It tried to keep her safe, telling her to make a stand and push this stranger off. But she was frozen to the spot.

Suddenly, thunder broke overhead again. Cheryl screamed, and the man's hand went straight to the back of her head. He pulled her face in tight against his chest, murmuring soft words still deeper into her ear. Now he was running one hand up and down the length of her back, his fingertips warm and persuasive through the thin cotton of her shirt. He smelled of damp linen and woodland, spiced with a tang she couldn't identify. It was a wild fragrance, heavy with musk. She felt her body tense in response, ready for flight. Her heart and head were swimming, both in the same direction.

'Shh…it's all right. I'm here now.'

Words rolled from him like velvet, but instinct still

told Cheryl to pull away. She started fluttering like a butterfly in a spider's web.

'No—I can't! Let me go… Now you're here I must get back to my little boy—' She stopped. Instantly the silent strength of this man told her that from now on *he* would be giving the instructions.

'*I'm* here,' he repeated slowly. There was real effort behind his words, as though he was working to keep his voice emotionless. 'Don't tell me I'm too late? The weather has been so bad—there are electric cables down everywhere. My car was stuck in a traffic jam. So many roads are blocked I had to abandon it and come across country. A local farmer gave me a lift for part of the way, but the crossroads below this estate is flooded. I had to climb over the wall and walk from there.'

'In this weather?' Cheryl jerked back in order to look up into his face. 'But the nearest road must be a mile away!'

Lightning ricocheted through a window, throwing his strong features into sharp relief. For a second a flash of white teeth flickered in the darkness of his smile. Cheryl saw he relished a challenge.

'I took a short cut through the woods.'

*That must be why he smells of pine needles and honeysuckle*, Cheryl thought. At any other time, in any other place, she might have savoured the fragrance, where it lingered on the big strong workman, holding her like this. But she could not trust herself.

'When you *knew* we'd already lost one tree in this hurricane? You must be mad! It's a wonder you weren't killed!' she burst out, more in fear than anger.

Her rescuer pulled a torch from his pocket. In its

sudden glare she saw him shoot her a strange look. Now she could see him better, it wasn't only the quizzical look in his clear blue eyes that set Cheryl wondering. This man seemed strangely familiar.

'The pines were rattling, for sure.' He sounded thoughtful. 'But it didn't matter to me at the time. I had to get here. There was no alternative.'

Cheryl returned his look with interest. For the life of her she could not think where she had seen that expression before. Those distinctive features and the determined jawline…

Another clap of thunder shook the building. Cheryl had been gradually releasing her hold on his jacket, but at that sound she grabbed him again.

'That one was a little farther away, I think.' A hint of amusement returned to his voice.

Cheryl shook herself, wondering why she still couldn't bear to let go of this stranger. Not only had she flung herself at him, she was almost beginning to enjoy the experience.

She pressed herself against the stranger, hardly daring to breathe. Waiting for the next lightning flash, she tried to gauge if the storm really was passing over. Rain still hurled itself against the windows, and wind shook all the doors, but the thunderclaps must have broken the storm's fever.

As she trembled against the stranger's chest, his grip loosened a little. It was then that Cheryl remembered herself. She was the only staff member in the villa. That meant she was in charge, and clambering all over an electrician was definitely not part of her brand-new job.

Pushing herself out of his arms, she bent and picked

up her own torch. Then she straightened up and looked her rescuer right in the eyes. The entrance hall was gloomy, but their hand lights and the crackling of broken power lines outside gave her enough light to make a judgement. He was tall, he was powerful, and his face was full of self-confidence. In fact, this man was ideally fitted for his role as lifesaver and genie of the power supply—except for two things.

He was dressed in a suit. It must once have been light grey and made to measure. Now it was dark with rain, and clinging as only wet linen could. And the reason he was able to keep such a firm grip on her? He was completely empty-handed.

'Where are your tools?' Cheryl began inching backwards, away from him.

He cast his torch beam around the vestibule. The action plunged his expression into shadow. Whenever sparks flared outside, it darkened still further. His frown looked threatening. She shrank again.

'I am Marco Rossi. My things have all been left behind. I've already told you that. Now, tell me, where is Vettor?'

Cheryl stared at him. *This* was Marco Rossi, her new employer? His staff had painted him as a grim ogre, but this man was gorgeous. She gulped. There must be some mistake. He'd scooped her up and comforted her like a guardian angel, not a demon. But then she thought of the time she had spent with the chef of the house. That woman was a professional to her fingertips. *She* hadn't offered any opinion on her boss, only facts. She hadn't passed on idle gossip or made judgements. Apparently, Signor Rossi liked everything to run smoothly.

*He looks a pretty sleek operator*, Cheryl thought, and then brought herself up short. This one man couldn't be allowed to trample down all her defences—even if her heart shimmered at the sight of him.

It was the way he looked at her. Surely there could never be any deceit in those eyes? They were too blue, too steady and too honest. When Marco Rossi gazed at her like that, Cheryl felt like the only thing in the universe. *His* universe.

*This has to stop*, she told herself. Her training at a top-class academy for advanced childcare profession-als kicked in. She must treat him as her boss at all times. All her womanly responses would have to be denied.

'I—I'm very pleased to meet you, Signor Rossi.' She started to put out her hand to shake his, then withdrew it quickly to dry her damp palm on her jeans before offering it. 'I'm Cheryl Lane—Vettor's new nanny.'

'I'm delighted to meet you at last, Cheryl. My people have given me some amazing reports of your interviews. I'm only sorry I was away in Brasília when they were conducted. The president wanted some advice.'

Cheryl didn't know what to say. Her first job had been with an English businessman. She'd thought working for an Italian property developer might be a step down from that, but Marco Rossi was no ordinary man. The advertisement she'd answered had been ex-tremely discreet. Figures and facts, including his name, had only come out at the final stage, when his staff had been sure she was The One. Later, she'd surfed the net to discover he was one of the wealthiest men in Europe. Marco Rossi was in worldwide demand. Now she knew why. *By women as well as heads of state*, she thought feverishly. In a daze, she reached out to try to find a switch on the wall.

'Don't bother trying the lights. The electricity supply is off—this whole estate is in darkness. Take me straight to Vettor.'

After his praise Cheryl felt several inches taller, and confident in her training.

'Of course, Signor Rossi. Though I'm sure you won't object if I ask to see some identification…'

Her voice had begun briskly but soon died away. Marco Rossi raised his torch, flooding his face with light. Shadows fell back, exposing the real man. Cheryl looked up into his iron features and piercing blue eyes. At once, she knew the word *no* didn't have any meaning for him.

'Take me to him. I'm his uncle and legal guardian. That's all you need to know.' His voice crackled with latent danger.

In a flash of alarm, Cheryl remembered the hushed tones of his staff. There must be some truth in their warnings. Right now he looked ready to explode at any moment. She stared at him, transfixed, like a doe caught in headlights.

'I've been travelling non-stop for the past ten hours. My jet was diverted, and my documents are in my luggage. That's all trapped, along with my driver. He's still stuck in a huge traffic jam. I got out of my car empty-handed. So, are you going to tell me how my nephew is, or do I have to wring it from you?'

There was no trace of warm reassurance in his voice now. His Italian lilt skated over words in a way that made Cheryl's heart sink for Vettor. Marco Rossi hadn't returned any of her calls. He didn't even bother calling the poor little mite by name. And he thought she was being awkward, when she was only doing her job. *So maybe this is my chance to strike back*, she thought.

Cheryl was the perfect employee, but this was serious. She raised her eyebrows. Then she gave Marco Rossi a hard stare. This was a man, she'd discovered, who was famous for always putting his work before anything else. It was a big black mark against him in Cheryl's book—although, gazing at him now, it was difficult to remember that. As she looked him up and down, his broad, powerful body and intense stare did strange things to her. Such feelings were aroused deep within her body that Cheryl began to fidget.

This was an important moment. She knew she mustn't wreck it. It was exactly the wrong time to be reminded of the feel of his damp jacket, or the wild fragrance of him...

So she channelled all her frustration into one dark glare. Marco Rossi didn't deserve the surge of hormones that were powering through her body. She tried to convince herself of that as she took in his powerful bulk. She wasn't going to allow it to make her eyelashes flutter like some silly schoolgirl.

'If you had returned any of my telephone calls, *signor*, I could have given you an up-to-the-minute report on Vettor.'

His lids flickered.

*They're lovely eyes*, Cheryl thought, *as clear and blue as that enormous swimming pool on his terrace...*

With an exclamation of annoyance, she broke eye contact. She had to. This man was a magician! He was trying to bewitch her with his come-to-bed eyes. But

Cheryl knew exactly what men were like. She thought back to the time she'd spent with Nick Challenger. That curbed her thundering pulse. Memories of Nick could kill any feeling within her stone-dead.

There was a tense silence. Then Marco Rossi cleared his throat.

'I tried many times. I couldn't get a signal for my mobile phone. The storm must have knocked out some of the transmitters.'

She risked shooting another look at him. The watchful amusement was long gone from his expression. He was staring straight ahead, his aquiline features carved in stone. Giving him the benefit of the doubt, she softened slightly.

'OK,' she allowed, 'I'll tell you what happened from the beginning. Your nephew didn't look well when I first arrived. I took his temperature, and he was feverish. I recognised the early signs of scarlet fever straight away. A local doctor confirmed my diagnosis.'

Cheryl had been relieved when the doctor had been impressed with her. She waited for Marco Rossi to congratulate her, too. Her new employer merely looked uncomfortable. She pressed on.

'Vettor has been calling for his grandmother. He seems to be missing her badly. Might it be possible for her to visit?'

Rossi stiffened, and then turned away in the direction of Vettor's bedroom. 'Things are that bad?'

'No—no. Wait, Signor Rossi.'

Instinctively Cheryl put out her hand and caught his arm. He stopped, looking down at her fingers. She forced herself to relax, and released her hold on him.

'I'm sorry, *signor*,' Cheryl said, without knowing if she was apologising for touching her employer or surprising him. 'I didn't mean to give you the wrong impression. It's just that—your staff tell me you don't often visit the Villa Monteolio.'

'What difference does that make? They always know how to get in touch with me. I write to Vettor, and he doesn't want for anything.'

*Except physical contact*, Cheryl added silently.

'He's just a child. He's lost his parents and he needs someone to care for him. To love him.' When a child was involved, Cheryl never knew when to keep quiet. The look on his face told her she had overstepped the mark.

Marco's jaw tightened. Turning his back squarely on her, he headed off along the corridor toward Vettor's room. 'I've wasted enough time already. Let me see him.'

Cheryl bounded past her new employer. Reaching the sickroom first, she blocked its doorway. She had to draw the line somewhere, and this was it. Marco Rossi couldn't leave a child alone in this ruin for weeks on end and then burst in on him like an avenging angel. Vettor was delirious. Cheryl knew how *she* would react if she opened her eyes and saw Marco Rossi's powerful figure bending over her in the gloom, but her fantasies had to be quashed in the face of a very real danger. If Marco confronted Vettor in this mood, it would terrify him. Cheryl couldn't allow that to happen.

'Wait here. I'll see if he's—'

Marco Rossi never waited for anything. With an angry exclamation he brushed Cheryl aside and went straight in.

## CHAPTER TWO

MARCO leaned over the little figure in the bed. As she got closer, Cheryl thought she heard the murmured words, *'Eh, bimbo?'* or something like them. But when her employer realised she was at his elbow, he raised a barrier of grim silence.

Vettor stirred, muttering something in his sleep. Marco started adjusting the bedclothes. It was too much for Cheryl. She couldn't bear to think of Vettor being frightened awake. She tried to squeeze in between Marco and his nephew, hoping her friendly face would be the first thing the little boy saw when he opened his eyes. It was no good. Marco was big, and solid as a rock. Desperate to protect Vettor, Cheryl did the only thing she could. Reaching around, she grabbed her employer's hands.

The feel of them came as a shock. They were hard, and the smooth skin was stretched taut over sinew and bone. They contained such strength. Cheryl realised they could snap her like a twig. Although she quailed inside, she braced herself and held on.

'Please don't scare him, Signor Rossi!' she whispered desperately.

'I want to check his rash. The last message I got was

from my secretary. She told me you suspected a bacterial infection. His mother had meningitis at this age. She only survived because, like you, I can recognise signs.'

That stunned her.

'Oh… Then I'm sorry, Signor Rossi.'

Cheryl relaxed her grip, but did not move. They were locked together, still bending over their patient. When Marco Rossi bobbed his head slightly in acknowledgement, Cheryl felt the movement stir her own body. Her heartbeat reacted instantly, but one look at his face shook it back into line. His expression was tense and inflexible.

'If that's the case, then hearing Vettor was sick must have given you a terrible shock,' she said. 'But the moment the doctor made his official diagnosis I rang your office number to give you the news. Vettor has scarlet fever. He's being treated with antibiotics, which are already taking effect.'

'Scarlet fever sounds serious.' Marco turned his aristocratic face towards her. 'Why isn't he in hospital?'

His expression was like flint, and its effect on Cheryl was instant. He trapped her in his gaze and looked right into her soul. A warm glow began creeping up from her breasts and flushed her cheeks with colour.

'The doctor said home was the best place for him,' she said, desperately trying to keep her mind on track.

Marco Rossi might be scary, but he was gorgeous, too. It was amazing to be pressed up against him like this, with neither of them willing to give way. He sent shivers right through her.

'I can see an improvement in him already, so there's no need to move him now. Besides, where would you rather be if you weren't feeling well, Signor Rossi? In an unfamiliar hospital ward, or safe at home with someone who cares *about* you, not just *for* you? This is the best place for Vettor,' she added, half afraid her employer would wheel away with a snarl.

He didn't. Instead, he went on staring at her with those piercing blue eyes. Eventually his lips twitched into a slow, teasing smile. Then he pulled straight out of her grasp, as though all her strength was nothing. Standing up straight, he confronted her, head on.

'You English, with your manners and your stiff upper lips!' He spread his hands wide to emphasise his point. 'Let me tell you something, Cheryl—'

'My name is Miss Lane, Signor Rossi.'

He raised one eyebrow in a gesture she wasn't supposed to defy.

'And my name is Marco, Cheryl. I don't have time for airs and graces. That's why I couldn't care less if you don't like the fact I haven't been here for my nephew. Your opinion means nothing to me. But why don't you just come straight out with your complaints, instead of tossing that lovely brown mane of hair and flashing those beautiful eyes?'

Cheryl had been about to answer back, but his last words disarmed her completely. All her nervous tension about Vettor, the storm, meeting her new employer dissolved, and she giggled. Actually *giggled*! She couldn't help it. But what sort of dedicated professional did something like that? Horrified, she clapped a hand to her mouth, stifling the sound. As she stared round-eyed at Marco Rossi she could hear her whole career shattering around her, louder than the storm.

And then he smiled. It was a triumphant gesture, as though she had fulfilled all his expectations.

The effect on Cheryl was alarming. Feathers of feeling began rippling up and down her spine. She tingled in such an intimate way it scared her. To cover her confusion she started flouncing the bedclothes and bustling around her patient's bed to neaten the far side.

'I'm sorry to cut your visit short, Signor Rossi, but Vettor needs peace and quiet. I shall have to ask you to leave.' *While I've still got a sensible thought left in my head*, she thought. Marco Rossi filled her mind and distracted her body. The silent strength of his tall figure stopped her looking at him as she spoke. She couldn't trust herself not to fall into the magnetism of his eyes again.

'Of course.'

That was a surprise. She had expected an argument. Despite all her good intentions, Cheryl looked up. He nodded in agreement with her. As he did so, the light in his eyes faded. Looking down, he swore softly, as though noticing the state of his sodden clothes for the first time.

'You're right. And I shall be no good to Vettor if I catch my death of cold,' he announced. 'Did all my day staff get away safely?'

Cheryl nodded. 'They left at around 5:00 p.m. That was when the weather warnings started to get really serious.'

'I don't blame them. Storms are trapped here by that ridge of hills.' He nodded towards the far side of the building, moving restlessly inside his wet suit. 'I need to dry off and change into some clean clothes.

My staff take care of all my domestic details, but with no one else about I'll have to ask you a favour, Cheryl. I know it's not in your job description, but could you have a look around and try to find where they keep the towels?'

Cheryl blushed. This was awkward. She was only one of dozens of people who worked for Marco Rossi. She had already glimpsed a side of him the others had never even hinted at. She had been glad—far *too* glad— of his gentle reassurance when alone and scared. Flinging herself into his arms had been the most delicious, daring thing she had ever done in her life. But all that had happened before she knew who he was. Now it was a case of an employer giving his wage-slave instructions. The change was painful.

Cheryl hoped he would forget the way she had mistaken him for an electrician in the entrance hall. That had been a terrible mistake, but she'd never underestimate him again. She would make sure of that. From now on she would treat Marco Rossi with respect. There was a barrier between them for all sorts of reasons. One short tour around his estate and house had convinced Cheryl the rumours in the media were true. He really must be one of the wealthiest men in the west. Anyone who had the self-confidence to take on a wreck like the Villa Monteolio would need barrowloads of cash to back it up. *Which Marco Rossi obviously has*, she thought.

She didn't need to look at the quality of the brand-new handcrafted staircase, or the Olympic-sized pool being installed on the south terrace to know that Marco Rossi was obviously mega-rich…and right out of her league. *Thank goodness he's not really my sort*, she told herself. So why had his almost perfect features long ago burned their way into her brain? Somehow Cheryl knew that even if she never saw Marco Rossi again, his face would haunt her for the rest of her life.

Uninvited, the memory of jostling against him over Vettor's bed rose up to tease her. For a few glorious moments they had been locked together. The touch of Marco's hands was all power. She had felt them twice now. Once in gentleness, once with determination. They were so unforgettable they fired her blushes all over again. Trying to calm her emotional turmoil, Cheryl thought back to Nick Challenger. He'd been her one and only boyfriend, and the relationship had been disastrous.

As a distraction, her memory worked far too well. Her heart froze. The smile died on her lips. She shivered, hugging her arms around her body. Not that they could give her any protection against a man like Marco Rossi! Nick was only half his size, and she still carried the scars. Marco would make a much more formidable enemy. She didn't want to put him to any sort of test.

His shoulders were wide and powerful, and two metres was such an awkward height. She already had a crick in her neck from looking up to him. As for his clothes—Cheryl looked them over carefully. His suit and open necked white shirt were obviously expensive. The cut was perfect. This man didn't have any physical flaws to hide, and his tailor had concentrated on accentuating the tall masculinity of him. The materials used were the best quality linen and fine cotton, but it was all ruined now. Everything he wore was soaking wet, and dirty from his mercy dash.

Even Marco Rossi's smile isn't *quite* perfect, Cheryl

realised. It might be white, it might be tempting, but there's a tiny chip out of that front tooth, on the right…

'How long will it take for your luggage to catch up with you, Signor Rossi?' she said briskly, trying to divert her attention from his body to his situation.

'I've told you—call me Marco.'

Cheryl smiled, and then wished she hadn't. He smiled back, and the effect was electric. Luckily, another hurricane blast smashed against the house and the moment was broken. She glanced over her shoulder, terrified. Marco grimaced.

'It will take my things some time to get here, judging by this weather.'

'Then it's just as well the rest of the staff showed me around before Vettor fell ill,' Cheryl managed with a trace of her usual bright efficiency. At last there was something about this horrible day to smile about. 'As we say in England, "it's an ill wind that blows nobody any good". While you go and have a shower, *Marco*, I'll sort you out some dry things. Finding my way around by torchlight might take some time, though!'

'I'll get my clothes, if you could find where Housekeeping store my towels. And don't worry, you won't need a torch. Listen—the generators have kicked in.'

He reached across to the nearest wall switch and snapped it on. A low-wattage bulb glowed bravely in the darkness.

'Oh, that's wonderful!'

Marco gave a very Italian shrug. 'It's always a good idea to have back-up when you live in the country.'

The increased light tempted Cheryl to run an appreciative gaze over him again. She chose exactly the wrong moment to do it. Marco sensed where she was looking, and turned his head. The glint in his eyes made her glance away sharply.

'That's very efficient of you, Marco.' She tried to sound prim.

'But of course! What else would you expect from a man with my reputation? And you *can* smile when you speak to me. It's allowed!' His response was light and teasing.

Cheryl didn't know what to think. To hear his staff talk, Marco Rossi was deadly serious about everything. But from the moment he'd burst into this house she'd been swept up by a whirlwind. He'd been protective, determined, and now he was smiling at her again.

She decided not to risk returning his gaze. It brought back memories of his hands touching hers. Cheryl didn't dare let herself be carried away like that, so she made herself stick to purely practical things.

But trying to talk about one thing while her mind was on something else proved to be a *big* mistake. 'When I've found the towels, I'll take your wet clothes off you, Marco.'

Then she gasped, suddenly aware of what she had said.

'Oh, no! I didn't mean—that is, when you've taken them off, I'll— No, what I should have said was—'

A devilish look haunted Marco's face as he watched her floundering. It spurred Cheryl into ever more desperate torrents of apology. She got more and more flustered, but Marco said nothing. He didn't need to. When he'd had his fun, he stretched like a cat and smiled with equal assurance.

'*Non te la prendere*, Cheryl!' His beautiful accent caressed her into silence. 'I'd say chill out, but you look like a girl who doesn't know what that means. What a shame you didn't leave your English reserve at the airport,' he said with mocking severity. 'Life in Italy is going to be tough if you're always worrying about double meanings. As for this—' he glanced down ruefully at his ruined suit '—it's not a problem. I'll sort it out. I'd never expect you to run around after me like that. In any case, it's the middle of the night!'

To her surprise, his concern sounded genuine. There was no sarcasm in his voice at all. That confused Cheryl even more.

'You're a man who employs staff…surely you expect that sort of treatment as your right, Signor Rossi? I mean, Marco.' She corrected herself as he lowered his dark brows in warning.

'Not from you. I'm employing you as a nanny—nothing more.' He was firm, but she couldn't leave it at that.

'I have to do something—you're filthy, soaking wet, and you might have been killed coming across country as you did!'

As she gazed into the blue of Marco's eyes Cheryl's mind was filled with images of him powering through the storm. Those pictures superheated a secret place inside her. It was somewhere she had almost forgotten existed.

When he spoke, his teasing tone aroused her most primitive instincts to an even higher pitch.

'It was worth it for the reception I got when you opened the door to me.'

There was that smile again. Coupled with his low, melodious voice, it plucked at feelings Cheryl hadn't allowed herself for a very long time. It felt right, and urgent, and…

*If I don't do something fast I'm lost*, she thought desperately. Marco Rossi had a way of looking at her that made her forget time and place. Once trapped in the mystery of his eyes, surely it would only be seconds before she was yielding to the kiss to end all kisses…

'I have to keep my mind off this storm, Marco.' She gulped. 'Tell me which bathroom you'll be using. I'll bring some towels when I've discovered where they're kept.'

Dodging past him, she tried to distract her body. His voice wandered out of the sickroom and into the corridor. 'That sounds ideal. I'll use the shower in my suite.'

He followed her, but in his own sweet time. Cheryl felt as though she was in the presence of some large, predatory feline who watched her every move. She closed the door to Vettor's room, tense with expectation. Marco was standing so close behind her she could almost feel his soft, warm breath on her neck. She hesitated, alight with nerves. They were both waiting for something to happen.

Compelled to turn and look at him, Cheryl had to lower her head the instant their eyes met. His expression was too intense. The only way she could cope with those burning blue eyes was to look up at him from beneath her lashes.

'I'm only trying to be helpful, Marco.'

He smiled.

'Oh, I'm sure you're going to be invaluable…' he murmured. And her heart stood still.

# CHAPTER THREE

HORMONES surged through Marco's veins, goading him on. He looked down on Cheryl's upturned face. Her lips parted. It was an invitation he definitely didn't need, but he was a red-blooded male. One kiss from her lovely full lips would be a great reward for dropping everything and focusing totally on getting home.

Hours of travelling through foul weather had washed him up on the front steps of the Villa Monteolio in a desperate state. He needed a break—and it had come in the shape of this gorgeous girl. Sex had been the last thing on his mind at the time, but when she'd flung herself into his arms his body had recovered like lightning. Marco's mind might have been full of worry for his nephew, but physically he had warmed to Cheryl straight away.

Now he'd seen Vettor, Marco could afford to indulge himself. Desire had been rising in him since his explosive arrival. Now it was a simmering need, threatening to boil over at any moment. Whatever the circumstances, there was one part of his body that was forever ready. It throbbed with anticipation right now. He was going to enjoy this.

Although…

Alarm bells rang in his head. His newest female employee ought to be as out of bounds as all the rest of them. Marco *never* dabbled with his staff. *But then*, he reminded himself, *none of them offered such warm temptation, so obviously.* Cheryl Lane was soft as butter. The novelty of her English reserve delighted him. It was almost as much a turn-on as the questions in her eyes. All he saw there was *When? Where?* and *How are you going to take me?*

Marco recognised consent. Miss Cheryl Lane was sending out all the right signals, and there was no harm in a little flirtation. He wouldn't admit it to himself, or anyone else, but his feelings for women were often tinged with revenge. At times like this, thoughts of another English girl shouldered themselves into his mind.

Years before, Sophie had seduced him in her parents' grand villa. He was a realist. He'd already known then from experience that the sight of him stripped to the waist and working up a sweat would cast a spell over any woman with a pulse. So the fact a titled English 'princess' had made a play for him had meant nothing to Marco at first. But Sophie had turned out to be…different. She'd had brains. Her natural lust had quickly directed his feelings to her own advantage. A poor little rich girl, she'd led Marco on and then dropped him as soon as Mummy and Daddy threatened her allowance.

The whole business had been a tourniquet round Marco's heart, twisting it until he'd sworn never to leave his emotions open to attack again.

It had been a hard lesson in how manipulative people could be when it came to getting their own way. But Marco was a quick study. He had a lot more to lose than his naivety these days. He didn't do the R word—relationships. Now he was as careful with women as he was with business deals.

And he could afford to be selective. If he decided to seduce Cheryl, it would be his first taste of a woman for quite a while. As usual, he was wary. From the moment he laid hands on them, women could never quite keep the acquisitive look out of their eyes. Whether he met them in Manhattan or Melbourne, Florida or Florence, once a woman learned who he was she wanted his wallet. But there was something about Cheryl… She was definitely one of a kind. When this softly upholstered girl had greeted his arrival by throwing herself into his arms the unusual sensation of pliant, warm helplessness beneath his hands had stimulated his body straight away. Now all he had to deal with was his mind.

He wondered what it would be like to push his hands through her rich brown hair. The need to feel its smooth silkiness rippling through his fingers rose up as he cast appreciative eyes over her. That mane of hers swung like a heavy curtain each time she moved. He liked that. And leaving the sickroom to follow her out into the vestibule had been no hardship at all. Those jeans of hers were good and snug. There was just enough curve about her to make it worthwhile walking along behind.

She intrigued him, and he could hardly wait to get her in his arms again. Miss Cheryl Lane was so different from the nerveless, hard-faced celebrity women he'd left behind in the city. Perhaps it was something to do with relief, and finally getting back here to his secret retreat. If only she wasn't on his payroll…

He treated his staff so well that core members were

loyal to the point of obsession. But new arrivals like Cheryl were a different matter. They were untried and untested. If she walked, it might be straight into the offices of a tabloid newspaper. Marco usually laughed off 'kiss and tell' stories. But things were different now he had Vettor to think about.

He looked down, deep down, into Cheryl's eyes. They were dark pools of arousal. She wanted him. He wanted her. It took superhuman powers to resist brushing that soft cloud of hair back from her brow. Everything about this little beauty sang to him. It must be three months since he had bothered to take a woman to bed. That was an unheard of spell of celibacy for him. But other things had seemed more important—until now.

Here was the perfect opportunity to put that right—if he wanted. He could tell there was a conflict between her mind and her body. Despite the invitation in her eyes, her hands were clenched and her brow was troubled. To put his thoughts into action was obviously going to take some delicate persuasion. Marco felt his body kick with the idea of another challenge. He smiled.

'Don't worry, *cara*. Anything that may or may not happen from now on will be completely between our-selves…'

Bending forward, he whispered into the sweet-smelling cloud of her hair. He already knew what it was like to have his hands moving slowly over her voluptu-ous body, melting her. From there it was a small step to imagining her softening beneath his touch, moulding herself into his arms as she relaxed into the rising tide of desire flowing between them. His fingers would travel back to the soft luxuriance of her hair, and from there flow down across the smoothness of her cheek. His caress would glide over her skin like silk on silk...

And then a thin cry pierced the night. It was Vettor.

Marco answered immediately, breaking the spell. 'I'm coming!'

Cheryl flinched, waking from her trance.

'I'll go!' She jumped to answer the call, still worried that larger-than-life Marco might overwhelm the little boy. He was only half a stride behind her as she rushed back into the sickroom.

'It's a dream!' Cheryl whispered, putting her secret thoughts into words as she soothed Vettor.

She told herself she ought to be grateful. He was still as febrile as she was, and this interruption gave her a chance to cool down. She definitely needed it. Had she lost her mind? Marco was filling her body with sensations that threatened to sweep aside all her good sense. But he *had* to be resisted. He was her boss, and Vettor's uncle. She couldn't allow herself to be seduced, however desperate she might be for his body. And there was bound to be something in the European Working Time Directive forbidding this kind of thing!

*It's a bit late to start checking my contract now*, she thought with growing horror. This is a nightmare situation, and it's all my own fault. If only I hadn't thrown myself at Marco so recklessly in the first place!

That had been a genuine mistake, but what sort of impression had it given her new boss?

Cheryl didn't have to ask. It was obvious. She could blame the storm, or the stress of being on her own, but what she had done was wrong. This very male man had seen it as an open invitation to tempt her with his eyes, his voice and the brush of his hand in passing. She could hardly expect him to do anything else after the reception she'd given him, but he must be put right straight away.

She sponged Vettor again, and gave him a cold drink. After settling him down, she sat on the edge of the bed and stroked his face until he was deeply asleep. It took quite a while. When she got up to creep out of the room, she was amazed to see Marco was barely a handspan away from her, a lazy smile in his eyes. He had been there all the time, watching.

Everything within Cheryl wanted him to pull her into a world of shameless passion. The feeling of relief when she'd fallen into his arms on the doorstep had been indescribable. Being held in that firm grip and re-assured by his warm voice had been one moment of perfect calm in the midst of the storm. Now her body was throbbing with his presence. Strange sensations were making themselves felt, low down in her body. She had to fight the urge to brush her hand over a place that was fast filling up with liquid warmth.

The nearness of Marco reminded her of things she had wanted to experience a long time ago. But none of her dreams had come true, only nightmares. Her relationship with Nick had ended in disaster. That love rat had treated Cheryl's emotions as badly as he'd treated her body. The experience had made her retreat from life, hiding away in her work among children. It was the one place she could be sure no one would ever hurt her again. Now this pirate of a man, Marco Rossi, seemed to promise things she was scared to experience.

His eyes focused on her full lips, and Cheryl felt her cheeks begin to pinken. 'It looks as if you're going to be one of my most capable members of staff.' He spoke with easy charm, glancing back as he strolled towards the bedroom door.

Cheryl stared after him, finding his voice softly arousing. What did it all mean? Every word he spoke acted like an aphrodisiac on her. She had never received *any* praise from Nick. Marco's confidence in her sent Cheryl's spirits into overdrive.

Her mind and body tussled for control. She felt like kicking against every rule. Marco Rossi's warm stability and the promise of his kisses made her want to go and offer herself to him right now. But her past cast such a long shadow. She had been a total failure in her one and only relationship, and now it looked as though she had totally misread the signs. Marco didn't want to kiss her at all. If he had, he would have taken up where he'd left off, wouldn't he? Her mother must be right. Thinking about sex blinded Cheryl to common sense.

*I have had a very narrow escape*, she thought. Making a fool of herself in front of Marco would have been agony. She couldn't bear to be hurt again, so instinct quickly chained up her impulses. It nailed her feet firmly to the ground, and right now that was exactly what she needed. But still her nerves taunted her. How could she trust her reactions to him? He would be spending the rest of the night here. *Not far from Vettor's room*, she thought, putting one hand to the neck of her shirt as though it was suddenly too hot and restricting.

*Behave yourself! Girls like you never…* Her mother's voice suddenly rang through her head, leaving Cheryl to fill in the rest. It was the voice of cold, hard reality and it punctured all her dreams. As usual.

Once again Cheryl retreated into her work. There was no alternative. She knew she was brilliant at her job, and it was so much safer to stick with what she knew.

According to Nick, she was frigid. He had called her a total loser in love. It had been horrible enough to fail with a bully like him. She ought to be thanking her lucky stars Marco Rossi hadn't kissed her after all. How much worse it would be to let a gorgeous man like *him* discover how bad she was at…

Cheryl swallowed hard. She couldn't even bring herself to think the word. She would just have to put a lid on her lust. If she didn't, it was sure to lead to disaster.

Thinking back to the tour she had been given earlier in the day by his chef, Cheryl followed Marco out of the nursery suite. Only then did she remember the laundry room was in the same direction as his suite. It might have been better to give Marco a head start. But it was too late now—he must have heard her close the door. She could hardly hang around in the corridor. It would seem suspicious. Keeping her head down, and without looking in the direction he had gone, she put on her most efficient voice.

'I'll put some towels out for you in your suite… Marco.'

His name was the only informality she could manage.

'Fine.'

She expected to see him stride off. That would have given her a good excuse to hang back. She was so much shorter than him, and the distance between them would stifle her embarrassment—or so she thought. Instead, Marco waited for her to catch him up. Shortening his stride, he fell in step beside her. He was close enough for her to sense the musky, warm male smell about him. It tantalised her nostrils until she had to glance at his face. As usual he was smiling, but it was to himself now, not her.

'I never thought it would be a relief to find a woman whose eyes *don't* light up every time she says the word *Marco*!' he murmured.

'Don't worry, I'm not unique. Graduates from the academy for advanced childcare professionals I attended are trained to deal with celebrity parents at close quarters,' Cheryl replied, glad he had hit on a bland subject. 'Our illusions soon go. We stop noticing people like you as individuals. In my experience, they all treat their children the same way in any case,' she finished, managing a barb.

'Oh? And you're so much better than they are, I suppose?' he probed.

'That's why they employ top-class nannies like me, yes,' Cheryl retorted, but regretted it straight away. Marco Rossi's expression had hardened. She knew then it was a mistake to go on digging in the knife over Vettor.

Luckily, they reached the door to Marco's suite before either of them could react to her words. Cheryl stood aside. It was a good excuse for another change of tone.

'I'll go and fetch you some towels and pyjamas—'

He exploded with laughter. 'I don't need *pyjamas*! I haven't worn those since I left home as a teenager!'

'Then what—' Cheryl began, and stopped. What else would Marco Rossi wear to bed, apart from that crooked smile of his? Flustered, she looked down at the toes of her shoes and blushed.

He stopped laughing the moment she realised her mistake. 'Just towels will be fine.'

Only gentle amusement tinged his words now. It gave Cheryl the confidence to look up and carry on.

'I'll be as quick as I can, although I must look in on Vettor every few minutes. He'll be so pleased to know you're here when he wakes up properly!' she said, hoping it was true.

'When are the electricity people turning up?' Marco strolled past her into his room, already peeling off his sodden jacket.

'They wouldn't give me an exact time.'

'In that case, you concentrate on Vettor. I'll tackle the workmen when they get here.'

'But you haven't had any sleep!'

'Don't worry about that. A shower and something to eat will keep me going for a while longer.'

Cheryl gazed at him, half afraid to see how much more he might take off while she was standing on the threshold. 'I hope there's something in the kitchen for you to eat. Things went a bit haywire when the staff left, and with Vettor being ill…'

Marco nodded. 'I'm glad you were here to look after him, Cheryl. I'm grateful. Your glowing references weren't exaggerating, were they? You really are a re-markable woman.'

Cheryl took a second step back, away from him. It was another compliment. This could only mean trouble. She began to wonder if perhaps her instincts were right—that only a split second *had* separated Marco's silver tongue from feeling so sweet against her lips. The next time they were alone together her resistance might crumble altogether. She could not afford to fall under his spell again.

'That's why you pay staff like me such good rates,' she said, emphasising the social divide between them on purpose. 'People who only offer peanuts get the monkeys they deserve. And now I really must go and look for those towels.'

Her excuse was as feeble as her will-power. The only reason she had to get away was to escape the torment of his presence.

# CHAPTER FOUR

CHERYL cooled down for long enough to remember where the airing cupboards were. She half hoped time away from Marco would allow her mind to clear properly. When she was in his orbit he filled her senses and turned her to marshmallow. While he was out of sight she wouldn't have the distraction of those clean-cut features and his sinuous movements. She could concentrate and become efficient, dependable Cheryl again.

Arriving back in Marco's suite, she found it almost silent. The only sound was the faint hiss of running water, coming from his *en-suite* bathroom. What Cheryl *should* have done was march straight into his dressing room, deliver the towels and go. But Marco would be busy in the shower for as long as she could hear the water run. That reassured her, and the temptation to explore his kingdom was too great.

This master suite was one of the few completed parts of the Villa Monteolio. Marco's chef had showed her around earlier in the day. Greatly daring, Cheryl risked taking another quick look. The rooms were practically empty of furniture, but they were full of sweet fragrances. All the woodwork was freshly painted in white, and the walls had been given coats of pale, neutral colours. There were no drapes at the windows yet. Chef had told her in hushed tones that they were still being made—in Milan, of all places. A single large abstract painting hung over the reception-room fireplace. Its organic shapes in shades of copper and gold picked up the colours of the original light fittings and the hearth. It put a contemporary twist on gracious living, and Cheryl decided Marco Rossi's craftsmen and interior designers must really know what they were doing.

Still the shower powered on. She edged farther into the suite. There were built-in wardrobes along one whole wall of Marco's dressing room, and a door had been left open, giving her a glimpse into a walk-in space the size of a small bedroom. She could see designer suits in every weight from linen to wool, and dozens of shirts.

Looking nervously over her shoulder, she took a few more steps. A chest stood against the back wall of the massive cupboard. Its drawers had been pulled out from the bottom upwards in his search for clothes. They had been left open like steps, burglar fashion. Craning her neck, Cheryl could see casual tops neatly folded and laid out according to type, style and colour. It was hard not to wonder how much it had all cost. *The rich certainly are different*, she marvelled, then realised she should be making her escape.

Alert to the still crackling patter of water from the shower room, she walked over to deliver the warm towels she had brought. She would leave them just inside the door. As long as she was quick, she could be in and out without him knowing. But the moment she entered she saw his wet clothes, discarded in a heap. Her mind began to work, and those strange feelings started tormenting her again. *He* had padded through here, barefoot and naked.

Then she noticed the wetroom door. It was ajar, and she could see a mirrored wall inside. It was completely clear. There was none of the condensation that a hot shower would have caused. The idea of Marco taking a cold shower ran through her veins like mercury.

She hovered on the threshold, wondering. Did she dare to go a little bit farther into the shower room? She looked at the towels she had put down on a shelf near the door. Surely they ought to be laid over the heated towel rail beside the wetroom entrance? Then Marco would be able to dry himself with something warm the moment he came out of the shower. And if she should catch sight of him through the glass wall…well, she was only doing her job.

It was the perfect excuse. Why should her employer have to stay dripping wet all the way through to his room when she could deliver everything warm and ready, within reach? He probably wouldn't even notice her.

A final mad impulse pushed Cheryl forward. Slipping through the half-open door, she entered the bathroom's wet zone. Her heart rate increased by the second. Another metre or so and she would be able to get a glimpse around the corner, right into the shower. She knew she should stop right now, turn and run. But that would douse every hope of seeing any more of this man who so totally entranced her.

She took a deep breath—and then a silent step forward.

There she stopped, transfixed. Marco Rossi was standing in a torrent of water. He was facing away from her, and nothing could disguise the perfection of his body. He had the bronzed, muscular form of a Greek statue. She watched, spellbound. He was soaping his close-cropped head, digging all ten fingers into the lather of shampoo. Bubbles sped down over his tightly moulded muscles. His skin was the colour of milky coffee, and the contrast of white foam against it was amazing.

She couldn't take her eyes off him, especially as his hands swept down over his body, working lather all the way. The farther he went the more he bent forward, until she could see every vertebra in the curve of his back. He shone like a seal under the harsh electric light, his smooth skin perfect, and with just the right amount of body hair. Her study travelled on down his legs. Every muscle was clearly defined, the Achilles tendons strong and sharp in each narrow ankle. As she watched, he lifted one foot and used the instep to rub the calf of his other leg. It was such an everyday movement, but it stunned her with its intimacy.

He lifted his head to rinse any remaining shampoo out into the flow of water surging around him. She should have guessed what would happen next, but her mind had stopped working minutes before. Besides, she couldn't move now even if she wanted to. When he turned off the flow of water and moved to grab the hand towel hanging beside him she should have been ready to make a dash for it. Instead she froze with awe at the sight of him.

It startled her—almost as much as finding a strange woman staring at his naked body surprised Marco. He was the first to recover. Snatching up a towel, he wrapped it around his waist. It wasn't quite large enough to secure properly, so he had to keep one hand on it. Dripping with water, his hair darkened and his face alight, he began walking towards her across the wet area. Every movement showed off the perfection of his body and his total self-assurance.

He held out his hand. Lost for words, Cheryl pushed a warm bathsheet into it. Swapping it deftly for the one he was using to cover himself, Marco wrapped it tightly around his waist and tucked the corner over to hold it. He was still smiling. He flipped the smaller towel back at her. She caught it instinctively.

'I think you'll find it's still warm.' He chuckled.

Despite all her bad experiences in the past, and even though he was wearing nothing more than a towel, Cheryl still did not turn and run. A switch had been flicked somewhere deep inside her body. She was throbbing with the sort of desire she had always feared. Until now her only experience of men had been with Nick. That miserable time had not prepared her for feeling like this. It was so different from anything she had ever known before. But this was a total stranger, and he was more than half naked. She ought to be a million miles away by now, but something made her stay.

Her mind whirled with the insanity of it all, but her body knew exactly what it was doing. It took control. Pulsing with a desire it was impossible to hide, Cheryl took a step towards him. The tiled floor was wet—her shoes weren't designed for it. She slipped, but before the gasp left her lips his hands had swooped around her body, scooping her up before she could hit the ground. For a second she clung to him, torn between relief and fear. He had saved her a second time. What would be the price?

Her mouth went dry. She tried to moisten her lips with the tip of her tongue. He saw, and his mouth curved in a slow, satisfied smile.

'That's the power of positive thinking. I wanted you, and here you are. I'm a man who always gets what he wants.'

Trapped, she stared up at him, white and tense. For a second time tonight she was laying herself wide open to danger. Sounds of the storm still lashed around outside, but they were muffled here in the shower room. Cheryl and Marco stared at each other in silence. The steady drip from the spray head dropped freezing water on their confrontation.

Gradually Cheryl saw his eyes cooling as he attempted to gauge the situation. She tried her best to salvage a shred of dignity.

'I—I brought you the towels. I didn't know you'd be—' Her eyes flitted over his naked chest.

'You didn't think I'd wear my clothes in here, did you? My suit's been soaked once already today.'

He was about to laugh, but something stopped him. Every sensible thought in his head told him Cheryl must have made a genuine mistake, blundering in here. He should treat it as nothing more—turn his back on her and walk away. But common sense was one thing. Gut feeling was something else. It felt so right that she should come to him like this. Primal urges were what the Villa Monteolio was all about. Princes and aristocrats had schemed and fought to live and love in this house. He was a better man than all of them put together. Why shouldn't he taste her sweet lips?

In a single mad moment he could overwhelm her now with the feral desire that was threatening to strip off his veneer of civilisation. But the look on her face stopped him. He admired her strong, capable nature when she tended Vettor. If he laid one finger on her now she would be sure to hit right back with every ounce of it. Marco enjoyed a little play-fighting, but rape and pillage were not his style.

'I think you'd better let me go, Marco.'

Her voice was faint and unsteady. With regret, Marco set her back on her feet and loosened his grip. He did not let her go straight away, but allowed his hands to drift down over the thin cotton of her shirt. That cold shower had been no proof against the surge of excitement she kindled in him. The pressure of her body against his was arousing him all over again.

'I don't expect to be spied on in the shower,' he said, the conflict between testosterone and good manners turning his words into a growl. 'Why did you come all the way in here if it wasn't in the hope of getting a warm welcome from me?'

'I was only bringing your towels.'

She had an answer for everything, this one. Standing there pink with shame at being caught out, she reminded Marco of the robin that haunted the villa grounds. Her brown eyes were bright with intelligence, and the proud swell of her breasts dared him to try anything. Marco grinned. She didn't need to toss that glossy mane of hair so defiantly. The line had been drawn between them. At least for the moment…

'You didn't need to go to so much trouble, Cheryl. Anything's a luxury after a freezing shower!'

That took the wind out of her sails—but not for long.

'I thought it would be a little bit of comfort after your cross-country journey.'

*Just as I thought. Never at a loss.* He smiled to himself.

'Don't you think I've got enough comfort, with all this?' He indicated the luxurious *en-suite* bathroom.

She nodded, but could not move. The sight of his bronzed body, wrapped only in that white bathtowel, was trapping her. His nipples were hard dark beads, pointing proudly out of his pelt of chest hair.

In one movement he brushed past her. Flinging the wetroom door wide open, he stepped back quickly to let her through—and Cheryl was only too aware of the electric charge igniting the air between them.

She walked out and heard him padding, barefoot, into the room behind her. Her body became one quivering mass of nerves. Every centimetre of her skin came alive. She could almost feel his gaze travelling over the back of her shirt. Despite the thinness of its cotton, she suddenly felt red-hot and claustrophobic. His hands had already run over her ribcage, comforting and supporting her. How would it feel to have them peeling away her clothes, removing the restriction of the bra that was right now pressing painfully against her erect nipples? Then his hands might travel south, sliding between her jeans and—

'H-have you got everything you need?'

Desperate to block the image from her mind, she dashed over to the bench, where Marco had laid out a set of neatly folded clothes. Bending over them meant she didn't have to look at him…until the moment he strolled into her field of vision again to see what she was doing. On the way, he picked up one of the other towels she had brought. As he used it on his long powerful limbs and broad chest, he followed her nervous movements with interest.

'Thanks, but you don't need to fold that shirt so carefully. I'll take it now.'

He held out a hand to her. His pale palm was in delicious contrast to the cool gold colouring that shaded the rest of his body.

Her eyes were drawn up the length of his forearm and over a smoothly curved bicep before reaching the soft darkness of his chest hair. *You can't look at things like that!* A warning voice rang in her head, but Cheryl ignored it. *Oh, yes, I can, and I'm going to!* the rebel in her replied.

'You're making progress!' His voice was a low rumble. 'I can see your mind isn't gripped by work all the time.'

There was a wicked gleam in his eyes again. Cheryl was mortified. All her nervous fiddling with his shirt was crumpling it right out of shape. She pushed it at him without making eye contact.

'I—I must go back to check on Vettor. I'll leave you in peace to finish dressing, Marco.'

Peace was the last thing on *her* mind. Her thoughts would be completely full of him until they met again.

'Fine.' He looked her over carefully. 'But we need something to eat. You'd better meet me in the kitchens.'

He was unfolding a pair of shorts.

'Of course,' she said quickly, diving out of the room before he could take off his towel.

Cheryl checked Vettor was still asleep, and then took a quick shower in her own quarters. There was one sure way to reinforce the divide between her and the almost totally irresistible Signor Rossi, and that was her smart official uniform. Anyone with a high profile wanted their child cared for by a graduate of The Academy. It was a way of displaying their success. And if Marco was like other rich people she had worked with, he'd value his prestige more than her.

She grabbed her summer uniform, a long-sleeved, knee-length lavender dress, like a life preserver. Brushing her chestnut waves back from her face, she pinned them up as neatly as her nerves would let her. Adding her name badge completed the starchy effect. *No wolf will look at me twice while I'm dressed like this—especially with thick black tights and flat lace-up shoes*, she thought, straightening her belt.

As she went to find Marco down in the kitchens, she noticed the eastern sky was trying to lighten with the dawn. Good. That meant the official start of another working day. Combined with her crisply efficient uniform, it would keep her mind off the beguiling Signor Rossi. At least that was what she hoped.

But a terrible thought began forming in her mind. What if he expected her to make breakfast for him? This was her first trip out of England. She had absolutely no idea what Italians ate.

Cheryl was deep in thought as she walked through the villa's great dining room. Then she stopped, and sniffed. The unmistakable, irresistible aroma of frying bacon drew her in the direction of the kitchens. Outside their door was a small dark heap. As she got closer, she

realised it was Marco's sodden clothing. Gathering it all
up in her arms, she pushed her way through the swing
doors and into the room beyond.

The kitchens at the Villa Monteolio had come as a
shock to Cheryl when she was first shown around. Food
was obviously more important to Marco Rossi than the
exterior of his house. A warren of rooms had been renovated to Michelin-star standard. Every surface was
smooth and shiny, every item of food catalogued and
colour-coded all the way from delivery area to presen-
tation table.

This morning Marco stood alone in the ordered perfection of his kitchens. He was using a fish slice to poke
the contents of an industrial-sized frying pan balanced on
a gas hob. As she walked in, he did a quick double-take.

'That's quite some transformation, Cheryl—' he began.
Then his face darkened as he saw what she was carrying.

'I was going to do that. Chef won't want you bringing
those wet clothes through here.'

Cheryl felt deflated. 'True. I'll take them back to the
laundry room. I would have made sure I came down in
time to do your breakfast if I'd known what you wanted.'

'Don't worry about it. I'm employing you as Vettor's
nanny, not a mind-reader.'

When she got back from dumping his things, Cheryl
found Marco loading a plate with food. His rich mix of
bacon, sausages, eggs and mushrooms was a very English
breakfast. *I could have cooked that for him*, she thought
bleakly, *although I wouldn't have guessed anyone could
eat such a huge amount.* He had made far too much for
one plate to hold. Putting the pan under the nearest rank
of heat lamps to keep warm, he carried his meal over to

the kitchen table. Then he returned to deal out a much smaller version of his own breakfast to offer her.

Cheryl couldn't hide her astonishment.

'Oh…but I never eat much at this time!'

'I can see that.' He shook the plate slightly. 'Go on— it'll do you good.'

There was no arguing with him. She took the plate, while Marco wiped a couple of splashes from the work surface and adjusted the heat lamps. He looked perfectly at home—which was another surprise.

'It's a good job you got down first, Marco. I had no idea how I was going to feed a sophisticated Italian man,' she said slowly, still watching him as she put her plate on the table and took cutlery from a drawer.

'I'm getting back to my roots.'

He balanced his fish slice on the edge of the pan, then went over to the staff section of the room. There, he picked up a big brown teapot and poured out two mugs of tea. Digging two huge teaspoons of sugar straight out of a storage jar, he dropped them into one of the cups and stirred it into a whirlpool. Cheryl dashed over to rescue the second cup of tea before he could sweeten that one, too. Opening one of the fridges, she got out some milk and added a splash to her own drink. As she passed the container across to him, she realised it was going to take an awful lot more to make her own tea drinkable. It was so strong it looked like bitter chocolate.

She sat down at the table with her mug of milk-filled tea, and watched Marco making great inroads into his packed plate.

'It seems funny the villa's kitchens have been renovated when the roof is still in such a terrible state,' she said, looking for any excuse to linger beside him.

'Only an English person would put the look of a house before cooking.'

Despite his words, Marco didn't sound scornful. While Cheryl wondered how to take his remark, he looked up quickly.

'Don't worry. The roof has been made weather tight from the inside. Replacement tiles are being created specially. Once they're flown in, this old place will look beautiful again within days.'

'Ah—so *that's* why you could risk having that new staircase installed!'

He took a long drink of tea, watching her over the rim of his mug. His clear blue eyes were sharp as needles. 'What do you think of it?'

'It's beautiful. I'm amazed there are still craftsmen about with so much skill.'

Her answer obviously pleased him. 'I made it myself.'

Cheryl didn't know whether or not to believe him. Marco Rossi was supposed to be impatient and short-tempered. She didn't know anything about carpentry, but the broad, smooth staircase in the main hall was a work of art. It must have taken patience and a real eye for detail.

She went back to her breakfast, and for a while they ate in silence. From her place at the table, Cheryl kept a discreet watch on him from beneath her eyelashes as she ate.

'I couldn't help noticing your suite hadn't been aired, Marco. I've moved in with Vettor for the moment, so I can be on call around the clock—'

'That's very impressive!'

'He's my responsibility, but that isn't why I mentioned it,' she said, careful to concentrate on carving neat pieces from her fried egg. 'When there wasn't any reply to my messages, your house staff assumed you wouldn't be coming back here any time soon. They didn't bother turning the heating on in your suite. Why don't you use my rooms to catch up on your sleep for a few hours? My suite is small, but it'll be much more comfortable than yours for the moment. Until the power went off, the under-floor heating was on in there, to keep it aired.'

He stopped eating. After a pause to take a long, slow draught of tea, he turned the full power of his ice-blue gaze on her. Before she could look away, he caught his lower lip between his teeth and shook his head.

'That is so tempting,' he said thoughtfully. 'But this place isn't your responsibility. It's mine. And the sooner I can get something done about that Tilia bouncing on the power lines, the better.'

'The electricity company said they were going to send someone as fast as possible. That's why I thought you were—' Cheryl stopped and blushed, remembering what had happened when she'd opened the door to him. 'Although they didn't say when it would be.'

'I'll ring them again. It will come better from someone with an understanding of technical problems.' Finishing the last mouthful of his breakfast, Marco pushed a piece of bread around his plate to mop up the last of the goodness. Cheryl didn't know anyone apart from her father who did that. All the male students at the academy used to moan about cholesterol. They'd left far more food than they'd eaten. Marco Rossi was very different from them.

*And in more ways than one*, she thought with a tingle of excitement.

'The staff say Vettor eats like a mouse. I hope I can build up his appetite to match his uncle's.'

'Don't you dare! Vettor's going to be an academic.'

Viewing his empty plate with satisfaction, Marco didn't see Cheryl's eyebrows fly up at his words.

'Using your brain doesn't need as much fuel as manual labour,' he went on brusquely, and then dropped his cutlery. After another quizzical glance at his hands, he held one out to her in a silent demand. She passed him her phone.

'Now, give me the number of the power company. I want to get my hands on that tree. If they don't know what they're doing, and I'm not there to keep an eye on them, they'll chop that beautiful creature up into useless chunks. If that happens they might as well stack it for firewood and be done with it.' His nostrils flared.

'You got here in pitch darkness!' Cheryl said incredulously. 'How do you know that tree is beautiful? You might not want it when you see it in daylight.'

'It is a Tilia.' He spread his fingers and frowned. 'Of course it's beautiful.'

His eyes were alight now, but not with the gleam he'd turned on in the shower room. It was an expression that gave Cheryl the nerve to try to keep his mind on more practical things.

'Can you be sure?' she ventured.

He nodded. 'I know about wood. I work in construction. At least I *used* to.' He frowned down at the mobile in his hands. 'That's how a poor boy from the wrong side of Florence rose from nothing and went on to employ a nanny like you for his nephew.'

Cheryl thought about the staircase out in the main hall. Marco had said he'd built it himself. Maybe he'd been telling the truth. There was no mistaking the way his face came alive with pleasure when he spoke about his speciality. That made a change. Most of the time it looked as though all his successes didn't bring him much to smile about.

'You make it sound as though you've got regrets, Marco. Why is that? You've got everything any man could want, and you must have left the donkeywork of manual labour behind a long time ago.'

Marco turned his head slowly and stared at her. There was a frankly disbelieving look in his eyes.

'Cheryl, you are the first woman who has had the sense to realise that!'

'It seems an obvious conclusion. Anyone who can afford—' She cringed at the reference to money and corrected herself. 'Anyone who is as successful as you must spend all their time in an office. My previous employer did nothing but network and attend meetings.'

'That's the complaint all my women make,' Marco said grimly. 'But I don't have space in my life for complications like them any more. You'll be safe from me, Cheryl.'

He turned that knowing smile on her again.

'For the moment I've only got room for one thing in my life, and that's work.'

*So your staff were right*, Cheryl thought bitterly. *I should have guessed. That's why this is the one and only time you've visited little Vettor since he's been here at the villa. Work absorbs your life; family gets left behind.*

'I'll make that call to the electricity company.' He stood up, concentrating on the mobile phone's display panel. Cheryl settled down to wait, expecting him to be passed from person to person as she had been. She was in for a shock. Marco had been right. They didn't mess with him. A few well-chosen words later, he handed the phone back to her with a smile.

'The workmen are on their way. I'll get ready to meet them.'

'No—you must be shattered. Vettor won't want to see you looking as tired as he feels. Why don't you go and get some sleep before he wakes up? I'll deal with the electricians, if you tell me where they should put the tree.'

He put his head on one side and regarded her. 'Have you any experience of men on overtime in bad weather, Cheryl?'

The delicious music of his accent when he spoke her name teased her even when he was trying to put her off.

'No, but—'

His eyes shadowed. Exhaustion was catching up with him, but he still smiled.

'Then you can leave everything to me. I speak workmen's language—and I don't just mean Italian.'

Still glowing from his earlier compliments, Cheryl had been ready to argue. But when he said that, she realised he was right. The last thing she wanted to do was haggle with a bunch of strange men. That was why she was a nanny—it kept her in the wings of public life, not centre stage. It was where she liked to stay. But Marco expected her to be invaluable, called her strong and capable, and she wanted to go on proving to him how good she could be.

She thought back to when simple tasks like driving or operating a DVD had been taken out of her hands, because

Nick had said she ought to leave 'complicated stuff' like that to him. Whenever he'd allowed Cheryl to visit his flat, she'd been left to clean it and do all the chores. Then she had discovered she'd been scrubbing his collars and cuffs for the benefit of another woman. The worm had turned. That day Cheryl had stood up for herself for the first time in her life and said enough, no more.

She had made a decision about what she would and wouldn't do, and she still remembered how good it had felt. Now she could get that feeling all over again. She didn't need to expose herself to an audience if she didn't want to, and Marco was giving her the perfect get-out.

'OK—if you've had more practice, it makes sense,' she said, trying to hide her relief.

'It does—and I'll be right on their backs if there's any mistake. Wood like that is a valuable commodity.'

Cheryl was amazed. Unlike other wealthy people she had worked for, Marco still seemed to have a grip on how much things cost.

'Oh… I didn't know that! Good grief—I would have asked them to tow it away as rubbish!'

'Working in the real world soon teaches you there's good money to be made from innocence.' He gave her a conspiratorial smile. 'So I'll deal with the workmen. But if you like you can come and watch how I negotiate with them. You might learn something.'

'I will.' She nodded, and he laughed.

'You sound very sure of that!'

She piled their breakfast plates up neatly, ready to carry them out to one of the dishwashers.

'I might not have known you for long, Marco, but I've seen enough to realise you mean business.'

He laughed.

'That's good. And now I think we'd better get ready to meet those electricians. If I stay in this warm kitchen for much longer, I might be tempted by that bed of yours.'

In the silence that fell between them, a gust of wind swept around outside the house. Her head jerked up, and she found herself gazing straight into Marco's eyes. Their Mediterranean blue made her feel alive in a way she had never known before. He put her on edge—so much so that when the next breeze rattled tree branches against the kitchen window she jumped guiltily.

Suddenly his hand was there, dropping over hers. He encircled her fingers lightly, holding her safe and warm while the storm struggled through its dying moments outside.

'It's OK, Cheryl. I don't think there will be any more thunder now.'

His voice was gentle and reassuring. She froze, knowing she should pull away from him, break this contact. It spoke to her deepest desires, and that meant danger. Her inner woman whispered that this was the moment. All she had to do was relax and let Marco carry her away on a cloud of pleasure. She was sure any encouragement, even the slightest movement, would do it. All the temptation was there in his eyes.

She took a deep breath. It was supposed to steady her, but instead it was suffused with the warm scent of him. Her heightened senses caught the faintest trace of something wholly masculine beneath the fresh sharp tang of shower gel. It filled her mind and body with fantasies of lying naked in the villa's lemon grove under skies as blue as his eyes…

Marco moved around the table. At no time did his hand leave hers, and as he reached her side he drew her gently to her feet. Then, with a last squeeze, he let her hand fall and touched her on the shoulder.

'Look at the time—our visitors will be here soon.' His voice was soft as thistledown, his eyes unreadable. 'I think you'd better go and fetch your coat, Cheryl. I'll meet you in the hall.'

# CHAPTER FIVE

CHERYL was on fire. That single contact with Marco's hand had been enough to send her temperature soaring. It couldn't last.

When she got back to the vestibule, the chill from the open front door struck her like ice. Marco's expression had a new tinge of winter about it, too. He was talking to a knot of workmen on the doorstep, his eyes hooded as the sound of her footsteps made him look back into the house. He held up his hand, as though he expected her to make a headlong dash down his impressive new staircase. Nothing could have been further from the truth.

She needed all her nerve to stand in front of this mob. But at least Marco was in command of them.

Cheryl came down the last few stairs, each step taking her away from the certainty of her own room towards the confusion in the hall. Her suite was empty, quiet and safe. The villa's entrance was noisy and full of movement. Every one of the workmen looked her over carefully, which made her shrink back nervously. She could almost feel the skim of their gaze.

'Cheryl? Come over here.'

Marco's voice cut through her fear. He was pointing

to a space between him and the main doors. She scuttled over to join him, glad for some protection from all the interested stares. None of the workmen would dare look at her while she was under Marco's personal protection.

'See out there—it's dawn. The electricians have made the power supply safe, so we'll go out and take a look at my prize.'

He shepherded her out of the house. Cheryl relaxed the moment she felt the wild, wet wind on her face. Standing on the deserted forecourt, she could forget about the house full of men, who she was sure must be studying her for faults. Digging her hands into the pockets of her coat, she stood beside Marco as they surveyed the fallen tree from a safe distance.

It must have been at least twenty metres high when standing, like the rest of the avenue. Now this fallen giant looked sad and dejected. Its roots had torn a great hole in the ground. It gaped like an empty socket.

'That's bad,' Marco said above the clatter of branches still rattling in the stiff breeze. 'Still, nature's loss is my gain. The nearest specimen tree nursery will be glad of the business, too. One quick phone call and this old avenue of trees will hardly look any different.'

'You can't *buy* anything of that size!' Cheryl laughed, wondering how out-of-place a sapling from the local garden centre would look transplanted between such giants. As the new girl at the Villa Monteolio, she could sympathise.

'*I* can—all it takes is money. And an army of garden staff to keep the new tree watered and secure until it is well established.'

Not for the first time Cheryl thought back to what the

Monteolio staff had said about their employer. Could anyone who would lavish so much money on a tree be called mean? Then she thought of Vettor, the poor little boy who had lost his parents and was now living in the stark and draughty Villa Monteolio. Quite clearly Marco wasn't going to take on the role of full-time father, and he cared more about his work than spending time with the little boy. If Marco put possessions before people, he must have a heart of marble.

As they watched, contractors arrived to move the great tree. Cheryl stood in silence as Marco gave instructions. Once or twice he even lent a hand. She noticed he called each workman by name. Missing nothing, she also saw the respect this earned him. Thanks to Marco, the job was completed with the maximum efficiency and minimum fuss.

Later, as the workforce got ready to leave, a large black Mercedes swept in through the gates of the Monteolio estate. It was so big and so impressive everyone except Marco stopped and stared. He was too busy pacing out the length of quality hardwood the storm had given him. When the car purred to a halt, he walked over to it. After a few words with his driver, he took a briefcase, suit carrier and leather cabin bag from the boot. As the car drove away, he smiled at Cheryl.

'Could you do me a favour? I don't want to put any of this stuff down on the wet drive, but these guys deserve a good tip. There's some money in the pocket of my suit—get it out and give it to them, would you?'

She pulled the zip of the suit carrier down far enough to see an Armani jacket inside. The same heady aftershave drifting around Marco clung to its fabric, tormenting her as she felt around inside its silk-lined pockets. When her fingers made contact with a fold of money, she pulled it out. Hesitantly, she started to peel off the top ten-euro note.

'How much shall I give them?'

'Give the whole bundle to Berni. He's the one standing right behind you. He'll share it out.'

'What—all of it? But there must be a hundred euros here, easily!'

Marco shrugged nonchalantly. 'So? Hand it over. How far would a single note go in an English pub between this lot?'

He said something in Italian to the workmen ranged around them. It went straight over Cheryl's head, but they chuckled appreciatively. She shoved the money at the men, and then shrank back towards Marco. The fact that his words mystified her didn't seem half so threatening as the workmen did. Somehow his tone always made her feel more at ease with him, not less.

'What did you say to them, Marco?' she asked, as soon as the workmen were inside their vehicles.

He made an effort to remember. 'It was just builders' talk. How cute, or what a treat. Something like that,' he said airily. 'They laughed because they're more used to tips being paid grudgingly, if at all.'

Cheryl was still uneasy. 'I wish you'd said don't spend it all at once.'

The way he'd handed out such wealth sent shivers down her spine.

'You don't like it here, do you, Cheryl?'

His sudden enquiry had a hard edge. Instead of

looking at her as he spoke, he watched the workmen's vans rattle away down the villa's overgrown drive.

Cheryl was horrified. The wind whipping her hair across her face almost took her breath away. 'I do! Whatever makes you think I don't?'

'You're uncomfortable. I can tell.'

'That isn't anything to do with the Villa Monteolio.' *Or you*, she added silently.

Marco started back towards the house. 'So neither the terrible weather nor the state of this place has put you off yet?'

'Nobody can do anything about the weather.' *Not even you*, she thought, watching his easy assurance as he strolled towards his villa. This man had the sort of self-confidence she could only dream about. 'And your staff told me you haven't owned this place for long, so that explains a lot.'

He stopped, instantly on his guard. 'What else did my people tell you about me?'

There was a pause. 'Nothing,' Cheryl lied. She knew how painful it was to be talked about behind your back.

Some of the tension left his face and he laughed. 'Let's see if you can come up with a more spontaneous reply to the next thing I'm going to put to you.'

He walked on a few steps and then looked back. His handsome face was alight, and Cheryl hesitated. While she wondered what was in store, he waited for her to question him. But she had been trained to listen to instructions, not ask for them. By the time she realised that curiosity was allowed under Marco's rules, she'd missed her chance to ask.

'I've come to a decision,' he announced, pushing

open the front door of the villa for her to go in. 'It's one you'll love, if you've got any sense. And I have a feeling you've got plenty of that, Cheryl.'

Something about the way he spoke persuaded her to believe him.

'Go on.'

'How long will it be before my nephew is well enough to travel?'

'It's difficult to say. The infection will take a while to clear, and he'll probably be listless for some time after that. Why?'

''I've got a proposition for you. Don't look like that—it won't hurt! All I need to know is whether you think he would enjoy some time by the sea?'

'I'm sure he'd enjoy it—any child would.'

'That's good. It's not natural for a child to spend his life cooped up indoors. He's got hectares here, but the seaside—children love it, don't they?'

'Yes,' Cheryl said quickly, but then frowned. 'Although with autumn around the corner you'd have to be careful he didn't catch a chill.'

'There's no chance of that where I'm taking him. And you, of course,' he added, almost as an afterthought. 'I've just bought a tropical island—miles from anywhere. I need somewhere to relax and be myself. A three-year-old will be the perfect guest. He can make sure the sea is warm enough, and explore. It'll be good for him, won't it?'

Cheryl didn't answer. The staff had warned her Vettor was a frail little boy, even when well. He didn't sound the sort to swim or go exploring.

'Do *you* think sun and fresh air will do him good, Cheryl?' he persisted.

'Yes, but—'

Marco hardly heard the doubt in her voice. He was already inside the villa. 'Then that's settled. We'll go as soon as you think he is fit enough.' His voice echoed out to her.

All Cheryl could do was agree. Marco would think it was because she knew her place. The truth was that he had stolen all her words away. The only thing going round and round in her head was the thought of him enjoying cocktails on a dusky veranda in an exotic location. The image set her senses simmering. A tropical paradise must surely be his natural habitat. And that idea completely robbed her of speech.

It didn't matter. Marco was so used to taking the initiative, he was thinking fast enough for both of them.

'Don't worry. I'll arrange everything.' He dropped his luggage on an old oak chair beside the entrance hall's great open fireplace. 'The moment the little one is well enough, I'm taking him to Orchid Isle. The only other people there will be a few of my most trusted members of staff. Don't look so shocked!' He smiled, checking in his pocket for keys before setting off towards the staircase. 'I like my privacy. That's why I keep the numbers of visitors down. Buying my own little bit of heaven makes sure the only holiday photographs in circulation are ones I approve of. If ever I *must* take a break.'

There was a strange inflection in his voice, but Cheryl hardly noticed. Her eyes were like saucers.

'You bought a whole island? Just to escape photographers?'

His smile took on a world-weary quality. 'Everyone

should have an escape route. Orchid Isle is mine. It's easy to see you've never been stalked by snappers, Cheryl!'

'Is it far away?'

'Don't worry. You won't have to walk. Although I see you've got the right footwear for it.' He looked down at her sensible working shoes and pursed his lips. 'They'll be great for the rocks, but you'll need something for dancing if I decide to throw a party.'

'How big is this island of yours?'

'It's only a couple of hundred hectares. But when I'm in the mood I sometimes fly friends in to join me.'

He had been smiling to himself, but stopped when he saw the look on her face.

'Cheryl? What's the matter?'

'Nothing… It's just a lot to take in—a tropical island full of the world's most beautiful people…'

'But in your line of work you must be used to mingling with the rich and famous.' He looked at her curiously.

'Good grief, no! I only work for them!'

His eyebrows shot up. 'I assumed your previous duties would have included taking the children to dinner with their parents and guests each night. Are you saying that wealthy people's kids aren't routinely included in their good living?'

'In my experience, people who employ nannies don't expect to be bothered by their children.'

He gave a silent whistle. 'Then you're going to have to get used to some changes, Cheryl. Everything I have will one day be my nephew's. The sooner he learns how to appreciate it, the better. I want him to eat dinner with me every night—under your supervision.'

That really appealed to Cheryl, but she was still apprehensive. 'What about the nights when you're partying?'

'That doesn't often happen. I want Orchid Isle to be a place where I don't need to be sociable. Should I decide to fly in a few friends for drinks, I'll need you to introduce the little one and show him how to behave well in company. Don't look so nervous, Cheryl. You can see it as your chance to taste the high life.'

'Oh, that's not my sort of thing at all.' She laughed. 'Thank goodness all the attention will be on Vettor!'

Marco smiled. But the expression in his cool blue eyes was anything but humorous.

Marco Rossi soon overturned all Cheryl's ideas about him. Everything she had read or heard had convinced her his would only be a flying visit to the Villa Monteolio. She was sure he'd want to get straight back to the glitter and glamour of his career.

Instead, he made his work come to him. Builders toiled around the clock to set up an office in one of the villa's many empty rooms, and within twenty-four hours it became a nerve centre complete with personal assistants and grim-faced consultants. Cheryl was curious, but she kept as far away from that part of the building as she could. She couldn't think why Marco would set up business at the villa. She had heard he didn't want home life distracting him. This 'home office' brought the two sides of his life together with a vengeance.

Over the next few days, Vettor got brighter by the minute. To Cheryl's relief, Marco's chef was keen to hear her ideas for the invalid's diet, and together they thought up dishes to tempt him. It took a lot to persuade

Vettor into trying homemade chicken soup, but once over that first hurdle he couldn't get enough.

During the next weeks he even put on weight and got some colour in his cheeks.

As requested, each evening, Cheryl and Vettor joined Marco for dinner. This was the Italian way, he told her. Children must learn to be a part of the family circle. Cheryl wondered why he bothered. There wasn't much to talk about, and Marco never revealed anything about his work. With so many strangers roaming the building, Cheryl felt safer shut away in the nursery wing with Vettor when they weren't dining with Marco. Although that meant she had no one but the little boy to talk to, for hours on end.

Summer's end flared with heat. It was stifling in the nursery suite, especially when Cheryl had to close the windows against the builders' racket. Finally, one day when drilling sent shock waves through their nursery tea, it sent Cheryl over the edge. She had to go out and say something.

Marching up to Marco's office door, she knocked loudly. One of his gazelle-like personal assistants answered in a haze of overpowering perfume. Outclassed in her dowdy uniform, Cheryl took a step back. The PA smiled sweetly, and told her Marco was in his workshop.

Cheryl had no idea where that was. She had to ask directions from every member of staff she passed along the way. Finally, hot and bothered, she rounded a corner and was confronted by a very strange sight. The ancient colonnade at the back of the Villa Monteolio had been turned into an outdoor workshop. Large sheets of plywood were stacked against the shelter of the rear wall.

Cheryl had no time to wonder why such modern material would be needed in such an ancient house. She was too busy looking at Marco.

Dressed only in jeans, he was bending over a work-bench. Every bit as bronzed and beautiful as she remembered, he was totally engrossed in marking up a piece of timber. She gazed at him in silent wonder. His upper body glistened as those powerful muscles glided beneath his warm skin. Cheryl's pulse ran away with her imagination. Her mind caught fire. He was wonderful, and it was all too much. Her eyes closed and an involuntary moan escaped from her lips.

'Cheryl? Are you OK?'

Dazed and confused, she opened her eyes. 'Yes! Yes, I'm fine…'

Guilt washed over her like a tidal wave. She looked down. Marco was so gorgeous, and here she was, trapped inside her working clothes and her clumpy, sensible shoes. It wasn't fair.

'I'm fine—apart from the heat. That's why I came out. I've had to shut the nursery windows. Some idiot was drilling fit to shatter our eardrums.'

Marco stuck the pencil behind his ear and picked up a saw. He was smiling. 'Are you *sure* it was an idiot?' He nodded towards the end of the colonnade. A board had been put up, and was hung with an amazing array of workman's tools. It gave off the powerful scent of newly drilled wood.

'So it was you?' Cheryl said slowly.

He dipped his head again.

'Then I'm sorry, Marco.'

'I'm sorry, too, for disturbing you, but it had to be

done. I wanted to make a place for everything as soon as I could. I get tired of driving a computer all the time.'

'And so you come out here?'

Beads of perspiration trickled over his pectorals. Cheryl watched, transfixed. They defined his muscles in a way that made her swallow hard. She tried to think of something boring.

'What would your clients think to know that?' she managed to say at last.

'They have no complaints about my work. Customer satisfaction is the only thing that matters to me.'

His expression was difficult to meet. Nervously, Cheryl touched her hair. He must have this stunning effect on every woman. Now he was turning it on her.

Rubbing a hand across his forehead, he wiped away a streak of dust before continuing. 'Chef tells me the boy is beginning to eat a more varied diet. She's got all sorts of contacts, and she's come up with these.'

He jerked a thumb towards the deep shadows at the back of his workshop. Something soft and white was spilling out of the wooden slats of a crate. Cheryl went closer. Beady black eyes blinked at her through the gloom.

'Do you think he will like them?'

'Chickens?' she said nervously.

'Don't sound so scared. They're harmless. They lay eggs.' Marco told her patiently.

'Oh, thank goodness for that!' Cheryl gasped, relieved. 'So they're not for soup?'

He shrugged. 'When they come to the end of their natural life, maybe…'

'No—stop! Let's concentrate on their eggs for now.'

Cheryl looked more carefully at what Marco was

working on. The plywood sheets were being turned into a henhouse, complete with wire-covered run.

'Why on earth are you doing this?' she marvelled.

'Weeks ago a fox killed the first chickens I brought here. I thought they would roost in trees and be safe. I was wrong,' he explained. Using a piece of glass paper he attacked a rough edge with long, steady strokes. 'I don't want the little one to be upset.'

'No—I meant why don't you pay someone to do this kind of thing for you?'

Marco's mouth became a narrow line. He bent over his work and frowned. Somehow Cheryl knew it wasn't with concentration.

'You know all about children.' There was a long pause as he walked over to fetch another one of the plywood sheets. Measuring it up, and then checking, he scored a pencil line across it with a flourish. Then he looked at her. His eyes were two vivid pools of self-justification. 'This is what *I* know.'

It came to Cheryl in a flash that she understood exactly what he meant, but he would never put it into words.

'You're too clever to restrict yourself to carpentry, Marco. I'm sure you'd make a success of anything you put your hand to. Even childcare,' she added mischievously.

Self-assurance mellowed his expression a fraction.

'It's true I've never found a job I couldn't do,' he conceded.

'I'll bet Vettor would love to watch you working out here.'

His brow creased. 'I don't know… What did you say about protecting him from chills?' As he spoke, he brushed a tiny droplet of sweat from his cheek.

'He'll be fine. I'm the one who's likely to have trouble—finding my way back from here to the nursery.'

'It's just there.' Marco pointed to the wing adjoining his workshop.

'So that's why the drilling was so loud! Did you know we were in there?'

He nodded. 'I guessed. There was a very English thud when you closed the window a while ago. An Italian would have thrown out a torrent of abuse and then slammed it.'

'Sorry, Marco. I'll get back to Vettor.' With a nod, she started back the way she had come.

'Why don't you use those French doors?' he called after her, pointing along the colonnade.

'I can't. I locked them before I left Vettor on his own.'

'That was sensible.' He looked impressed. 'But it's not a problem.'

As Cheryl wondered what he meant, Marco picked up a workman's tool bag from the floor at his feet. Dropping it on his bench, he began sorting through it. The bag was ancient, and stuffed full of all sorts of mysterious gadgets. Selecting a spool of wire, he nipped off a short length. Working it between his hands he strolled over to the locked French doors and bent over them. Within seconds there was a click. Pressing down the handle, he opened them wide for her. Cheryl heard Vettor cheer with excitement. She was horrified.

'But that's—that's…' she gasped, groping for a polite term for housebreaking. She couldn't find one.

'That's *legal*, as long as it's my own house—which this is,' Marco told her. Hands on hips, he waited for her to go inside. 'I was left to fend for myself when I was a kid. You soon learn what to do when you're locked out of your own lodgings.'

'Are you coming in to tea, Uncle Marco?' Vettor's voice drifted out from inside the nursery.

Marco laughed.

At the exact moment Cheryl walked past him, he raised a forearm and pulled it across his brow. She caught the essence of raw male sexuality and had to stop. It thrummed through the air, intoxicating her and drawing her eyes to him. Their eyes locked. For seconds on end he held her with a look so powerful Cheryl forgot every bad memory haunting her. She was his. It was all that mattered.

# CHAPTER SIX

'I'M TOO dirty, *bimbo*!'

His voice was rough. It was in complete contrast to the teasing seduction he used when alone with Cheryl. She was glad. Vettor should be her only concern. When Marco was around, her concentration was always divided.

'Oh, *please*!'

Vettor's plaintive cry tugged at her attention. She was used to seeing improvement in him by the day, but this burst of excitement was something else. For the first time his expression was alive.

If this was the effect Marco could have on Vettor, it ought to be encouraged.

'Why don't you come in, Marco? You could sit on this newspaper.' She grabbed her latest copy and dropped it down on one of the wicker nursery chairs.

'And wreck the only new carpet in the place?' He looked down at his dusty boots.

Cheryl's mind flashed back to Marco in the shower. Suddenly she wanted to see his slender, perfectly formed feet again.

'You could always take them off.' She paused, and swallowed hard. 'And your socks.'

'Not here,' he said, laughing. 'Not now.'

Vettor wasn't going to give up easily. 'Then I'll come out there with you. I can, can't I, Cheryl?' The little boy looked up at her anxiously. His eyes were as blue and penetrating as his uncle's, and equally hard to resist. It was no wonder she had found something so familiar about Marco on their first meeting.

'I'm better now, and I've eaten all my *torta*,' Vettor added triumphantly.

Cheryl nodded. 'I think it's a great idea, Vettor. You could do with getting some fresh air.'

For once Marco looked uneasy. He took a step back, away from them. 'I don't know about that.'

Cheryl tousled the little boy's thick thatch of brown hair. 'Why not? Unless you're keeping your work a secret from him?' she added, whispering the words over Vettor's head.

Puzzled, Marco shook his head. 'Why? Should I?'

'In case it was meant as a surprise!' Cheryl explained with a laugh. 'Go with your uncle, Vettor,' Cheryl said firmly, pushing the little boy forward. 'He's got something to show you out in his workshop. I have to clear away the tea things. Unless you'd like a cup, Marco?'

'Yes,' he said grimly as Vettor grabbed his hand. 'I have a feeling I'll need one.'

Cheryl watched the two of them walk across the quadrangle. Marco's fingers were as lifeless as sticks in Vettor's hand. The little boy was skipping along, trying to keep up with his uncle's long strides. Cheryl would have smiled if Marco's detachment weren't so sad. She wondered why he found it so hard to get down to Vettor's level. Over the past few days she had decided he didn't actually dislike his nephew. He simply didn't know how to behave with a child.

Cheryl poured out the strongest cup of tea she could make. Then she strolled out to see what was happening. Vettor was crouched beside the crate of chickens. Marco was at his workbench. He did not look happy.

'The child isn't interested in what I'm doing. All he wants to do is feed weeds to the chickens.'

'That's OK,' Cheryl said mildly. 'Here's your tea.'

Marco grabbed it like a parched man clutching at an excuse. The first mouthful made him pull a face in disgust. 'There's no sugar!'

Cheryl took the cup out of his hands and started to walk away. 'I'll go and fetch some from the kitchens.'

'*I'll* fetch the sugar. You stay here.' Marco came after her, but Cheryl played her ace.

'No—I still need to learn my way around the villa. It's good experience for me.'

'I'll never get anything done while I have to keep my eyes on the little one!'

Cheryl gave him a meaningful look, and crouched down beside Vettor.

'The quicker your uncle can finish the run he's making, the sooner those chickens can be put into it. He might even let you help, Vettor. But workshops are dangerous places, so you have to do *exactly* as you're told. Do you understand?'

The little boy nodded gravely.

'There's your problem solved, Marco. What would you like him to do?'

Cheryl tried to give them plenty of time to get to know each other, and when she got back Marco was fitting the henhouse together. He looked pleased, and she smiled with relief.

'What have you two been up to?'

'I'm finishing off,' Marco said with satisfaction.

Cheryl looked over at Vettor. He was squeezed in between the crate of chickens and the wall of the villa. One thumb was in his mouth. The fingers of his other hand stroked the downy feathers poking out from the chickens' cage.

'And what about Vettor?'

'I told him to sit down there and not move, and that's what he did.'

'Of course he did—there's no need to sound surprised. I thought you were used to instant obedience!' Cheryl joked gently.

Marco wasn't listening. Concern furrowed his brow, and his voice dropped to a whisper.

'Is he all right? I was *never* like that.'

'Vettor is a good boy.'

Marco stared at her. Then slowly the tightness around his mouth disappeared. Its corners lifted wickedly.

'Then he's nothing like I was at his age.'

'I hope that doesn't mean you'll be leading him astray!' Cheryl laughed, but then stopped abruptly. That was about as likely as Marco falling in love with her. Quickly, she turned her attention to the framework taking shape on his workbench. 'How did you learn to do all this? Did your father teach you?'

Marco shook his head. 'No. I never had one.'

*That explains a lot*, Cheryl thought. If Marco had grown up on the streets without a role model, it was no wonder he had difficulty relating to Vettor. The two of them needed time together—preferably away from home. Cheryl knew the perfect solution, but it would mean laying herself open to all sorts of danger. If she mentioned Orchid Isle again, Marco might think she was desperate for a free holiday on his tropical island. Worse, he might assume she was making a play for him.

'That's why I want my nephew to have all the advantages I never had and none of the distractions,' Marco announced suddenly. Then his voice dropped to a murmur again, so Vettor could not hear. 'I am responsible for what happened to his mother—my sister. That is why I have brought him here.'

Cheryl felt she might be getting to the heart of the problem. She waited in suspense, but Marco was concentrating on his work. Eventually, she felt bound to ask.

'What happened?'

'My sister was much younger than me—and while I was abroad working, building up this empire, she steadily went off the rails.'

Deep in concentration, Marco ran one hand along the piece of wood he was working on. Stopping suddenly, he frowned down at his finger. A splintery spike had plunged into his skin. When he pulled it out, a bead of blood sprang up. He sucked it away, and then picked up a piece of sandpaper before speaking again.

'I didn't see it happening. And by the time I found out that the money I'd sent to support her hadn't been spent on food and bills it was too late…'

He started scrubbing his work smooth with such energy that Cheryl decided not to ask any more questions. Whatever had happened between Marco and his sister put her own worries in the shade. She had to do what was best for Vettor. Both Marco and Vettor needed time away from here. Cheryl decided she must broach the subject of Marco's island in the sun. Her modesty could go to hell if it meant doing him and Vettor some good.

'Marco—if you're still keen to take Vettor to Orchid Isle, I think you should go as soon as possible. You both need a holiday, and it will give you a chance to get to know each other.'

Both Vettor and Marco stared at her. Vettor was the first to break the sultry silence.

'I don't have to go on my own, do I?'

'Your uncle Marco will be looking after you,' Cheryl said brightly, smiling at him.

Her employer did not smile back. 'Don't worry, *bimbo*. Cheryl will be there, too.'

Everything light and optimistic fled from her mind as she saw Marco's face. She wouldn't have to spend the holiday of a lifetime worrying about sending out the wrong signals. The way Marco was looking at her right now, he'd be immune to them.

'OK. You're the boss,' Cheryl said, trying not to sound too enthusiastic about the trip. Taking this job at the Villa Monteolio had been Cheryl's first taste of life away from England. To be whisked to a tropical island so soon after arriving here would be another step closer to heaven. But right now Marco didn't look as though he'd appreciate a gush of thanks, so she restricted herself to a small, tight smile.

Marco bent over his work again. She could not see his expression, and he didn't look at her as he replied.

'So that's decided. We all leave for Orchid Isle first thing in the morning.'

* * *

From that moment the atmosphere between Cheryl and Marco changed. She sensed he wanted to put some distance between them. The practical part of her mind knew this was how it should be. Yet every other piece of her ached to experience something more. Her whole body was restless for him.

She tried to divert herself by encouraging Vettor to make a little patch of garden outside the nursery wing. While he sat in the sun she worked the soil, and they made plans together. The little boy's English was improving as fast as her Italian. Marco hardly noticed. He was too busy working.

Cheryl flicked glances at him whenever she thought Vettor wasn't looking. Marco didn't notice. Feeling the sun on her back was lovely, but it was no substitute for the touch of his skin. Working the warm, promising soil could not stifle the thought of running her hands over the tightly packed bulk of Marco's muscles.

She was in such turmoil that when he finally spoke to her, she gasped.

'No need to panic—I only wanted to tell you both this henhouse is ready.'

Vettor leapt from his chair and rushed across the courtyard. 'Can I put the chickens in, Uncle Marco? You *said*!'

He reached Marco before Cheryl managed to get up from her hands and knees. Marco looked down on her in amusement as she brushed dust from her skirt.

'Looking like that, you can hardly complain if the child wants to get dirty.'

Cheryl was crushed. Of all the times to catch Marco's attention, she had to do it with grubby hands!

And then she looked into his eyes. Was that another twinkle? She blinked, and it disappeared. If it had ever been there at all. She sighed, watching him as he watched Vettor.

'Why don't you explain to Vettor how the hen-house works?' she prompted, if only to keep Marco's attention away from the dust on the front of her uniform.

He cocked his head, as though the details were obvious, but started running through them anyway.

'If your chickens aren't scratching about on the grass, they can stay nice and dry in their house. When they want to lay, they'll make a nest in one of these little boxes. Every day you can open the lid—' he demonstrated as Vettor watched, fascinated '—and collect the eggs. I'll carry it around to that patch of short grass below the terrace, then you can put the birds into their new home.'

'Can't it stay here?' Cheryl frowned. 'It would be so much better if Vettor could see the birds from his room. He could take some responsibility for them.'

Marco looked at her with quizzical amusement. 'I thought a top-class English nanny like you might be worried about germs.'

She looked up and caught his gaze, drinking in every feature of his face. She knew it so well she could have sketched him from memory, but she still wanted more. Only conscience made her tear her gaze away.

'Right now I'd rather Vettor had something to keep him occupied while he's convalescing, Marco.'

'Fine. So it will be your responsibility to make sure the staff are prepared to look after your pets while you're away, *bimbo*.'

The little boy looked from Marco to Cheryl and back again, puzzled.

Cheryl ruffled his hair affectionately. 'Remember? Your uncle is taking you to the seaside.'

'And you, too,' Marco directed at her. 'We can't possibly go without our indispensable Cheryl.'

Marco's words haunted Cheryl for the rest of the day. He'd called her *indispensable*.

She was still enjoying the memory of it when she got up at 5:00 a.m. the next morning. She indulged herself with a long, deep bath, full of bubbles. Orchid Isle was hours away, so she wanted to start the day feeling fresh. Travelling alongside Marco was bound to send her temperature soaring.

Dusting plenty of powder over her body, and adding a spritz of perfume, she dressed in a clean uniform and started work. While Vettor was eating his breakfast she filled a trunk with everything he would need for a few weeks in the sun. He might have more clothes and toys than any child she had ever cared for, but Cheryl wasn't impressed. She was worried. After watching Marco with his nephew, she guessed he gave his staff an open chequebook. Anything this child wanted, he got. That was a recipe for disaster.

Luckily, Vettor was so young he was more confused than spoiled by all the luxury. Cheryl hoped she could make Marco see that company was the real key to Vettor's heart before it was too late.

As she made arrangements for their things to be taken downstairs, the cold voice of reason tried to attract her attention. All accounts of Marco Rossi, billionaire, made him sound like a classic predator. His worldwide romances left a trail of broken hearts. *And that's only the ones the newspapers learn about*, Cheryl thought. *Who knows how many ordinary girls like me he's had?*

She nibbled her lip. *It's madness to carry on working here when I'm so tempted*, she thought. Then she looked at Vettor and smiled. This little chap couldn't be left to fend for himself. It was her duty to look after him, even though it meant being a hostage to her feelings for his uncle. She hesitated and thought about what might happen the next time her eyes met Marco's, or their hands accidentally brushed in passing....

*I'm bound to get my fingers burned*, she thought nervously. *And not only by the tropical sun.*

Staff took Cheryl and Vettor's luggage down to the entrance hall. Despite the heat, Cheryl still carried her coat over her arm. Her uniform was the one thing that could cool her thoughts about Marco. *My job is to look after Vettor*, she repeated to herself over and over again. That was the only thing guaranteed to keep her on the straight and narrow path. *And if I can persuade Marco to try entertaining his nephew, too, that will be a bonus. If only they could get on together*, she thought, remembering how uncomfortable Marco always looked when he was with Vettor.

The front doors of the villa were standing open, and Marco's voice drifted in from outside. The effect on Cheryl was electric. Her heart jumped. She picked up her bag, then put it down again. Taking Vettor by the hand, she crossed to the doorway.

Marco's shadow swept across the step. She hesitated. The sun was still low. His silhouette stretched across the forecourt, emphasising his impressive build. As she chivvied Vettor through the open door, she quailed at the thought of meeting Marco's gaze once more. His piercing blue eyes missed nothing. He was sure to know what she was thinking, and Cheryl didn't feel able to resist his scrutiny. Sure enough, when she managed to look up, Marco's eyes were running right over her.

She gripped the edge of the front door for support, and then saw his glance home in on her bleached knuckles. She dropped her hand immediately. His expression was unthreatening, but that didn't stop Cheryl being afraid. She thought back to one of Nick Challenger's favourite sayings: *knowledge is power*. She didn't want Marco to find out how nervous she was, so she turned her features into a carefully blank canvas.

'I'll start loading these cases into the car,' Marco said, after they'd exchanged a few meaningless pleasantries about the weather.

'You'll do that yourself?' She was amazed. Her previous employers had found it a strain even to speak to her, much less do anything for themselves.

Marco was already halfway across the vestibule.

'Of course.' He looked as puzzled by her question as he was by her single case. 'Where's the rest?'

Cheryl shook her head. 'This is all I've got.'

Marco looked frankly disbelieving. Cheryl hustled Vettor across the forecourt. In the past, Nick had taunted her about her appearance. She couldn't bear to think Marco was about to do the same thing. It would smash all her beautiful illusions of him.

Marco stowed her case away in the boot of the car. He was about to get into the spacious back seat when he remembered something.

'I forgot to say hello to you, little one.'

Striding back to them, he gave the little boy a formal handshake. Cheryl's heart sank. It reminded her of some grainy black and white film footage she'd once seen of a lonely, bewildered little prince being greeted like a diplomat by his returning mother, herself a queen. *If I had a nephew who was leaving the house for the first time in days I'd hug him and hug him and never let him go*, she thought.

Her mood darkened further as Marco bent to speak to the little boy.

'I'll need peace to work while we travel. And sometimes Cheryl and I will have grown-up things to discuss. So would you mind sitting in the front of the car?'

Vettor was being sidelined *already*! Cheryl erupted with anger.

'No, Marco! You can't do that to him!'

She should have saved her breath. Nobody noticed. Vettor was already launching himself into the front passenger seat, while the chauffeur and Marco were too busy laughing at his screams of delight.

'It was always my dream to ride next to a driver when I was a child. It's good to know some things don't change,' Marco told Cheryl. He stopped smiling when he saw the look on her face. 'I've had a booster seat put in place for him already. That is the law in England, isn't it?'

'Yes, but…' Cheryl began. Then she went quiet. The truth was that there could *be* no but. *She* was supposed to be the one who knew what children needed. Marco was ahead of her on points today. 'Yes, but I thought *I'd* be sitting in the front. You ought to spend more time with him, Marco, as you're away from home so much.'

Her cheeks burned. Marco had a suitably abrupt answer.

'I'm happier keeping my distance. I think he might be scared of me.'

'I wonder why?' Cheryl murmured, as Marco stuck out an arm and opened the rear door of the car for her. Every movement he made was quick. His decisions were made in a split second. Even his laughter could be threatening—a low rumble echoing up from that wide chest.

'I'm sure you'll find it all so easy when you have children of your own.' He grimaced as the chauffeur eased their car down the uneven drive of the villa.

'As a matter of fact I used to have one hundred and twenty-six children—all boys.' Cheryl smiled. 'While I was studying at the academy I did some work experience at an exclusive boys' boarding school.'

'Then you'll know they need careful handling. There's a fine line between setting reasonable guidelines and making them rebellious.'

Cheryl stared at him. It sounded uncannily as if Marco Rossi knew exactly what he was talking about.

When they got to the airport, sinister men in smart suits and dark glasses swept them past all the formalities and onto Marco's private jet.

'This is a world away from the hours I spent queuing

to get here from England,' Cheryl said as she settled Vettor at the window with a cold drink.

'I wasted too much of my life in queues when I worked in England years ago. This is the only way to travel.' Marco settled back in his seat, waiting for his laptop to be delivered to him.

'Where in England were you working?' Cheryl sat down next to Vettor. His hand luggage was full of activities and storybooks, but for the moment the little boy was happy to watch the ground crew checking around outside.

'I stayed all over the place. I found jobs wherever there was building work to be done. One week here, a month there. It's like that with casual labour.'

'You were a *builder*?' Cheryl marvelled. Looking at him now, in his beautifully cut suit and crisp white shirt, she knew Marco would never have been guilty of sagging jeans or showing off too much backside.

'You don't get to be a success in any business without starting at the bottom.'

Cheryl hiccupped with laughter at the coincidence of his words.

'What's so funny?' He looked at her quizzically.

'Nothing—I was just thinking about something, that's all.' Cheryl tore her eyes away from his, but Marco wasn't satisfied.

'Come on—share the joke.'

He looked so totally at ease, slipping off his smart jacket. Cheryl was lured into saying more than she should.

'OK—it's just that you're the last man on earth I'd expect to see leaning on a shovel, reading the tabloids or eating bacon rolls!'

His expression altered in an instant. In the time it took Cheryl to catch her breath it changed from mild amusement to dark suspicion.

'Don't forget who made a home for those chickens. Remind me to show you what else I can do some time,' he drawled.

Cheryl felt bound to respond. 'I meant that you're far too sophisticated to do a job like that.'

Marco glanced down at his work-roughened hands. She followed his gaze. His thumbs were making tiny circling movements over the tips of his fingers. She watched, entranced.

'You must be right, Cheryl. My hands agree with you, at least.'

A steward arrived with his computer. Settling it on his lap, Marco flipped open its lid. Straight away he was engrossed in his work. Cheryl's dreams shattered like the *torroncino* she scattered over Vettor's freshly made dish of vanilla ice cream.

Marco had shut her out again, and she had no idea why.

# CHAPTER SEVEN

ORCHID ISLE was a little patch of heaven in the middle of the ocean. As Marco's plane began its descent, he looked up from his work and pointed out of the window. It was almost dark, but Cheryl could still see a green oasis ringed by silver sand and creamy waves. It was beyond the wildest dreams of a girl from a poor estate.

'Give the steward your order, Cheryl.' Marco gently encouraged her away from the window. 'Then cocktails can be ready in your apartment when you get there.'

She was agog. 'I've never tasted a cocktail in my life! What are they like?'

'They can be made from fruit juice, alcohol, or any combination of the two. Ask and it's yours,' Marco replied in a voice as smooth as the azure sea beneath them. His eyes were as calm as the water, and for once Cheryl didn't feel embarrassed to find him looking at her. The mixture of excitement and adrenaline powering through her veins made her reckless. But the one thing she really desired was the single thing she could never ask for—him.

'I'll have whatever you're drinking.' she announced boldly. Marco frowned.

'OK. But I've got some things to attend to, and I normally stick to soft drinks when I'm working. Are you happy to do the same?'

'Of course. I'd never drink alcohol when I'm in charge of Vettor.'

Marco raised a brow. 'He'll be in bed by the time you taste it.'

'I don't know about that!' Cheryl pointed across the cabin to where Vettor was gazing out of a window, his face pressed against the glass. 'He's so excited I'll be lucky to get him to sleep before dawn tomorrow!'

Marco's laugh was as smooth as silk as he closed down his computer and they got ready to land. 'Well, if he's awake make sure you don't miss the sunset. The ones on Orchid Isle are unbeatable.'

Breathlessly, Cheryl waited for him to go further, daring to hope he'd say he'd join them, but he never did. Once the plane had landed he walked away, leaving Cheryl and Vettor alone on the landing strip.

Cheryl tried to be glad. She told herself it was all for the best. Sharing a tropical dusk with Marco Rossi was a temptation she really wouldn't have been able to resist.

Orchid Isle was all Cheryl's fantasies come true. It was wild and untouched, a real Garden of Eden. The only development was a small complex of buildings designed to nestle sensitively into their surroundings. There were luxury apartments for Marco and his guests, a natural pool camouflaged with ferns, mosses and orchids, and a fully stocked outdoor dining area and bar. The privileged visitors to Orchid Isle had everything they could ever need at their fingertips. Everyone blossomed from the moment they touched down.

Next morning, Vettor bounced out of his bedroom a different child. He was desperate to run and explore the beach and its wonders. Cheryl felt the pressures of her new job lift as she chased after him. Suddenly Marco's low chuckle echoed across the sand. Standing at the top of the beach, he raised his hand in a casual greeting. Stripped for swimming, he looked even taller and more impressive than usual. *Paradise really is his natural habitat*, Cheryl realised. They raced up to meet him.

'Cheryl! What on earth have you got on?' Marco looked almost bewildered. Sunlight flickered through the palm trees and glimmered over his golden skin.

'My uniform, of course. I'm on duty.'

'You don't need to bother with all that formality here.' He rolled his eyes, as if silently saying *Women!*

'No—really—I'm happier dressed like this. I keep telling you, I came here expecting to work,' Cheryl persisted.

'Oh, come on. Don't tell me you haven't got a few fancy things packed away somewhere,' he scoffed, secure in the knowledge that most women he knew always travelled with a designer wardrobe.

'It's not as though I'll be partying. Fancy clothes are the last thing on my mind.'

He stopped smiling.

'OK—so what exactly *have* you brought with you?'

'Some changes of uniform, jeans, a couple of tops—'

'No dresses? Don't you have a bikini? Or pretty shoes?'

His disbelieving expression shrank Cheryl instantly.

Her experience of socialising was limited. She rarely went to parties. Lurking in a kitchen with a lot of other singles was not her idea of a good time. Instead, she filled her days with work. Out of hours, she lived in scruffy casuals and comfortable lace-up flatties.

'I've been meaning to buy some,' she fibbed. 'It's just a case of getting to the shops.'

'That's easy enough. What do you need? I'll make a few phone calls.'

'Wait!' Cheryl put one hand to her forehead. Her mind was in a whirl. 'There aren't any shops here! It's nothing but beach and jungle. How can I possibly go off shopping?'

'I'm not asking you to go anywhere.' Marco gave her a wolfish smile. 'I want you to get some suitable clothes. And when I want something the shops come to me.'

To Cheryl's amazement, that was exactly what happened. It wasn't long before a big helicopter floated in from the mainland. While she watched from a safe distance with Vettor, dozens of interesting boxes were unloaded. Staff ferried them to her apartment. Cheryl didn't have to do a thing. She stared after them, wondering what would be inside all the mysterious packages. Then the sound of Marco softly clearing his throat brought her back—but not to reality.

'It's all yours, Cheryl. Your rooms are currently being filled with a selection of anything and everything the young nanny around Orchid Isle could possibly desire. So now it's up to you. You must choose what you'd like.'

Alarmed, Cheryl shook her head. 'I'm sorry. I can't possibly… How can I let you go to all this trouble just for me? I should have been better organised and brought more clothes. It's nobody's problem but my own.'

'Oh, but it is. This is supposed to be a relaxing break for me. Even my stewards are all in casuals,' he murmured, gesturing towards the nearest barman. He was wearing shorts and a shirt as bright as the sunlight. 'That uniform of yours is nothing but a grim reminder of working days.'

Cheryl looked down at the sand. She was hoping he would think her blush sprang from embarrassment. In reality the soft intimacy of his voice was making her flush with guilt. A torrent of wild warmth rushed through her lower body. She was thinking of those moments during the storm when he'd held her in his arms, pressing her against him and whispering his divine Italian reassurances into her ear…

'Everything is being set up for you, Cheryl. It's all ready to wear, so just decide what you'd like. Put it on one side, with a note of any alterations you'll need, and I'll settle up with the couturiers.'

That snapped Cheryl out of her dream. 'I can't possibly let you pay for me!'

'Why not?' Marco's scepticism changed to open disbelief. 'Isn't it every woman's dream come true—to take everything on offer and to hell with the cost?'

'Not *this* woman.' Cheryl underlined her statement by putting her hands firmly on her hips. 'You're right, Marco—this is like a wonderful dream come true for me. But I'd feel happier paying my way. You're already giving me this chance of a wonderful tropical holiday. It was my fault I didn't bring the right clothes. Let me make a contribution towards the cost.'

He frowned, puzzled. 'You'll be on call all day and all night, looking after my nephew. I don't call that much of a holiday.'

'I love my work—' She stopped, and pulled a wry face. 'Actually, that always seems a funny word to use—'

'You think love is a funny word?' Marco's blue eyes flashed a warning.

'No, I meant work.' Cheryl frowned at his interruption. 'I like Vettor. He's a dear little boy. Looking after him is no trouble at all. In fact...' She suddenly saw a chance for some bridge-building. 'Why don't you take charge of him for a while, Marco? I can hardly keep him with me while I'm trying on clothes, can I?'

Marco shook his head almost imperceptibly. Something in his eyes told of deep reasons why he kept his distance from the little boy.

'We are talking about your new clothes.' He recovered smoothly. Putting one hand to his chin, he stroked it thoughtfully with the same care he had used when touching her, on that first night at the Villa Monteolio. Cheryl ran the tip of her tongue over her lips. They tingled with anticipation.

'Everything will be fine, Cheryl. You can go in there on your own, lock all your doors and try on whatever you like in total privacy.'

Taking her courage in both hands, Cheryl persisted. 'While I do that, why don't you take Vettor off and show him the forest?'

The little boy had already started back towards the complex, looking for someone to serve him with ice cream.

'The staff can do that for me.' Marco turned away

from her and started to follow in his nephew's footsteps. He did not look back as he spoke.

Cheryl sighed. There was no point trying to force Marco to love Vettor. It would be easier to try to reject his offer of new clothes.

She ran to catch up with him. Marco might not be the world's best guardian, but Orchid Isle was a beautiful place. It might take time, but there was so much magic here it was bound to work on him eventually. She wouldn't give up hope yet. Especially if Marco was already keen for her to leave the formality of her uniform behind.

'How did you know what size to ask for, Marco? Have you been through my things?' she said as they walked towards the low thatched-roof buildings.

He stopped dead. His eyes flashed with such power Cheryl flinched. When he saw her reaction he bit his lip and walked on.

'Some men might get their kicks by intimidating women. I enjoy women in a different way. That's given me plenty of practice in some things, so I guessed you'd be about an English size twelve.'

Cheryl opened her eyes still wider. He was spot on! Marco was obviously an expert at this game. How many girls had been through his hands? She brought herself up short at that, but managed a smile at the double meaning. She was careful not to let him see it. What sort of special treatment had his other women received to make Marco such a very good judge of the female body? It made her wonder, and her heart galloped.

'I told them to bring everything, in all of the colours. Now, come on—you're wasting time.'

They reached her apartment. 'So, what are your first impressions of all this, Cheryl?'

'I—I don't know.'

Marco clicked his tongue. 'Oh, come on. You must have some opinion. *Dio*, you have always got plenty to say on other subjects!'

It was a good-natured rebuke, but Cheryl's mind was on something else. Tempting warmth was creeping through her body. This paradise, his generosity, the way the sunlight filtered through the leaves overhead, softening the look in his blue eyes…

'To be honest, I—I feel way out of my depth. I didn't grow up surrounded by wealth and luxury like this…'

'Then learn to enjoy it now. As a child I had nothing. A latchkey kid from the wrong side of town. I used my head and escaped. Common sense and hard work got me all this. And a nanny like you, too. Now you're here, you'd better make the most of everything I have to offer.'

For a single second their eyes met. Marco's mouth curved into a devastating smile. He took a step towards her, halving the distance between them. There could be no resisting him now. He looked down at her so knowingly that Cheryl knew her fate was sealed. Surely it was only a matter of seconds…

'This isn't a good idea…' she whispered. As the last of her self-control shredded, the fear returned. She felt the full power of him as he stared down at her…

And then he turned away.

'Decide what you want. I'll be back later to see how you're getting on.'

He walked off in the direction of the beach bar. Cheryl gazed after him. Once again her mind was on fire with thoughts of what might have been. It didn't take a genius to explain Marco's darkened eyes and shallow breathing. He was simmering with lust as much as she was. The sultry surroundings of Orchid Isle had raised the temperature—and the stakes.

If only he wasn't her boss…Cheryl knew she would be in his arms right now. The thought of it was heaven and hell all at once. The only thing she wanted in life was Marco, but surrendering to him would never bring her happiness. She knew he would only toy with her heart. She ran a hand across her feverish brow. To be seduced by him was a dream, but one that could so easily turn into a nightmare. Only one thing could really stop it coming true. Marco always claimed to have Vettor's best interests at heart. Distracting the little boy's top-class nanny was not the way to do that. Cheryl might doubt that Marco had a heart, but he definitely had brains. With luck, he would go on using them to stop her making a fool of herself.

The light of lust had dimmed in his eyes before he turned away, but Cheryl didn't take any comfort from that. With one last longing look at him, she tried to harden her heart. There was a paradise of clothes in front of her. It was no substitute for being in Marco's arms, but it would have to do.

Cheryl opened the door of her apartment, stopped and breathed in deeply. Then she stood and stared. That lovely new fabric smell, magnified a hundred times, was combined with a wonderful sight. Her lounge was filled with racks of clothes. The colour and quality of things on offer was beyond her wildest dreams.

She wandered from one end of the hanging racks to the other, and then back. Now and again she raised her hand to touch a silken skirt or sleeve. Each time she stopped herself actually making contact. Any one of these items must cost more than she spent on clothes in a whole year. How could she dare choose a single thing knowing that?

It was a long time before her brain forced her to do as she'd been told. First and foremost, Marco was her boss. He said she needed clothes and he was willing to provide them for her. The least she could do was try to find some. And, after all, this wasn't some terrible form of torture. It was shopping, for goodness' sake!

She decided to go for the cheapest items. This was easy in theory, but bracing herself to hunt for price tags was almost impossible. The items were light as gossamer, and she was afraid of damaging anything. She soon discovered there were no prices to find, but the ripple of fine fabric beneath her fingertips worked wonders. Once she began touching things, one spell was broken and another one cast. Thinking back to what Marco had suggested she would need, she picked out the minimum number of things.

When it came to swimwear, 'minimum' was all there was on offer. Much of the selection consisted of nothing more than tiny thongs laced around coat hangers. There were no bra tops. Cheryl was self-conscious enough in her boring old uniform. Going topless in front of Marco Rossi would be a fantasy too far. Moving farther along the rail, she found bikinis. These were so tiny the first wave would wash them away. The least revealing item was a silver one-piece with a racing back and minimal front. In desperation, Cheryl tried it on.

One look in her bathroom mirror and she sighed. It wasn't only with relief. The swimming costume looked wonderful, skimming her curves with the exotic glitter of a salmon. Cheryl never expected to look good in clothes, so this was a real surprise. Ill-fitting chainstore items in cheap fabrics were a world away from this heaven in a five-star dressing room. Working for Marco was showing her how life could be, and it was good.

She could hardly bear to take the swimming costume off, but there was more choosing to be done. By this time Cheryl was fired with enthusiasm. She ran her hands over luxuries she had never seen before and would never experience again. Moirés, silks and satins in every colour from burgundy to white sparkled and begged her to choose. Eventually she settled on a long, sleeveless white dress, splashed with one vivid cerise peony. Its skirt was split daringly high, but a matching high-necked jacket made it the least revealing gown on offer.

For possibly the first time in her life Cheryl was enjoying the sight of herself in a mirror. She added some silver stilettos from a selection of shoes on offer and twirled around like a queen—until there was a knock at the door.

'Who is it?'

'Me.'

There was no mistaking Marco's deep authoritative voice. 'Have you made your choice yet?'

'Yes, I have.'

'Good. I'm here to offer you my unbiased opinion.'

'Unbiased?' she repeated, trying to convince herself as she moved towards the door.

'Well, as unbiased as any Italian man can be when it comes to women.'

There was a confident lilt in his voice, and through the louvre door of her apartment Cheryl saw his silhouette make a gesture that clearly meant *Well, what can you expect?*

She realised a smile was creeping up on her. She stopped it straight away. Marco sounded relaxed enough, but she knew men could change in an instant. Life with Nick had taught her never to trust appearances. Then she caught sight of herself in a nearby mirror. This dress showed off a generous amount of cleavage. Putting the jacket on, she fastened each tiny pearl button from waist to neck. Then she opened the door, bracing herself for the blaze of Marco's scrutiny.

Lounging against the exterior wall, he was looking down towards the beach. The sight of her in the white silk evening dress had an instant effect on him. He stood up straight. His eyes opened wide with amazement and his grin became a long, slow whistle.

'That is some dress,' he breathed.

Cheryl spread her arms and looked down. It certainly was beautiful. The exquisite fabric rustled around her slender body with a sigh that was echoed by Marco.

'Turn around. I want to see it all,' he commanded. Meekly, Cheryl did as she was told. She pirouetted slowly under his gaze. All the time she could feel the sear of his scrutiny running over her, loving every centimetre.

'*Very* nice,' he said at last.

The warmth he gave those two simple words transformed them. Although she was nervous, Cheryl risked a direct look at him when she heard that. His expression had a magical effect on her. Critically, his interest was centred on the dress, not her. That gave her the self-confidence to glow. He looked genuinely impressed.

'So you like it?' She flicked out the material of the dress. It swept down from her fingers like an avalanche.

'You'll outshine any woman who dares to come near you. Does it work?'

Cheryl frowned. 'What do you mean?'

'Can you dance in it?'

In one sinuous movement Marco slid an arm around her waist. He swept her into her apartment, off her feet—and onto his. Half a dozen steps in her new silver stilettos convinced them both Cheryl was no dancer. She stumbled and fell into him.

'This is our first meeting all over again.' He chuckled softly into her ear. Her cheeks pinkened with a rush of guilty pleasure. He supported her, and showed no signs of letting go. Despite the feeling she must be leaving prints all over Marco's bare feet, Cheryl let him carry on. This chance to feel his arms around her one more time made her reckless, and she laughed.

'Oh, dear. I'm sorry, Marco!'

'Don't be,' he murmured. 'I can't expect you to be absolutely perfect in everything. And after all, dancing isn't part of your job description.'

*Oh, how I wish it was*, Cheryl thought. It would be the perfect excuse to accept his arms around her at any time, without any consequences.

He stopped. Dreading the loss of his touch, Cheryl shivered. Far from letting her go, Marco's hands closed around her body.

'How can you be cold at a time like this, *cara*?' He drew

her closer to him, enfolding her with those strong arms she had fantasised about from their very first meeting.

'I'm not,' she whispered, her cheek almost brushing the smooth bronze skin of his shoulder.

'But you're trembling as much as you were the night that storm threw you into my arms.' He spoke gently. 'Why? You've worked for me for long enough to know I'm not the monster people say.'

Cheryl had no answer to that—but Marco did.

'If I was so terrible, would I do this to you?'

He lowered his head. She tensed. Then slowly, sweetly, came the moment she had been waiting for. His lips made contact with hers. The warmth that bubbled through her whenever he was near became a boiling wave of passion. Carried along by the pressure of his kiss, Cheryl swept her arms around his practically naked body. She clung to his stability as her mind spun in a whirlpool of desire.

She had imagined his kiss long into her lonely nights. Now it was actually happening. It was better than anything her most fevered dreams had brought. Her hands roamed over the smooth expanse of Marco's muscular body. She delighted in feeling the change in texture from smooth skin to the soft downy hair of his chest. As she moulded herself to him, he pressed himself against her with delicious insistence. Cheryl could not believe a kiss could be so wonderful. His strength brought nothing but reassurance. Although there was no mistaking the power of his arousal as it nuzzled against her, the sensation filled her with excitement, not fear.

Desperate to experience every inch of him, she clung on. But it wasn't to be. Just as her mind started to leave her body altogether, he peeled away from her.

'That should have warmed you up, *bella*!' he said, with a wolfish smile on his face.

Pink and breathless, Cheryl gazed at him. She was speechless. It was incredible. He could turn off the heat as easily as he could turn her on. Now he was getting ready to leave, as if nothing had happened…

'So, now I've given my approval to your evening wear, change into your new swimming things and meet us on the beach.' He went on, already opening the door to go, 'There's no point in coming to an island paradise if you aren't going to experience the sea.'

*And no point in your kisses, either. They're nothing more than a game to you, are they, Marco?* Cheryl thought, burning with frustration as he walked away.

She spent the whole of that day either in the sea or on the beach. All the time she was supervising Vettor, she was painfully conscious of Marco. His computer had been set up in the shade of some palm trees, with a good view of the ocean. Although she never caught him looking at her, she sensed he was keeping a watchful eye on them both. She took it as a small sign that he really did care for Vettor, deep down, even if he didn't care for her at all. That went some way to softening the disappointment of his meaningless kiss. She was willing to make almost any sacrifice if things turned out all right between Marco and his nephew.

Late in the afternoon, one of Marco's staff splashed up to them with a summons. When Vettor asked to be swung up onto the errand boy's shoulders for the jog back up the beach, Cheryl was delighted. The sad little boy from Monteolio was coming on well. She was happier still when Marco told them why he'd called them back to the complex.

'My barman has invented this cocktail in Vettor's honour. He's kept the recipe a secret, but it's non-alcoholic, of course. I suspect it contains a healthy dose of ugli fruit juice.'

'Ugli fruit? I don't know if I like the sound of that.' Cheryl sounded doubtful.

'It's been given that name to keep it unpopular. That means there's all the more for us.' Marco gave her a knowing smile.

He watched Vettor take a sip of the golden juice. The little boy considered, licked his lips, and then drained the whole glass in one go. With a great gasp of satisfaction, he wiped one sandy hand across his face. Then he set off back towards the sea.

Cheryl instantly started after him, but Marco laid a hand on her arm. Signalling for one of his staff to take care of Vettor, he turned the full power of his charm on her.

'It gets Vettor's seal of approval. Now it's your turn. Ugli fruit is a cross between a tangerine and a grapefruit—more refreshing than one parent, but not as sour as the other. Try a little straight.'

He motioned to his barman, who placed a glass loaded with ice in front of Cheryl. A cascade of fragrant fruit juice crackled over the cubes. Savouring a mouthful, she found it tasted as good as it looked. He smiled at her expression. It was an innocent enough gesture, so Cheryl risked bringing up a sensitive subject.

'I'd like to thank you for arranging everything, Marco. The clothes you provided for me are truly lovely.' She looked away. 'Unfortunately...I'm afraid I don't actually have any money until pay-day. Certainly not enough for such wonderful things, anyway. Could you arrange to deduct the cost bit by bit from my wages over the next few months?'

Marco could not have been more surprised if she had strolled up from the sea stark naked. Rocking back in his chair, he gazed at her, incredulous.

'You are *still* offering to pay me?'

The shock of his reaction alarmed Cheryl more than a demand for money would have done.

'But of course—I must! You can't be expected to buy things for me!'

Marco's lips compressed with disbelief.

'Of course I can.' He shook his head, uncomfortable for a second. Then his expression became enigmatic again. 'You'll only be wearing these clothes while you're in my employment, won't you? That means they count as working clothes. So I'm supplying them as your employer.'

When Cheryl thought of it like that, she felt slightly better. But it wouldn't be right to agree instantly, so she pursed her lips. When she spoke again she tried to sound dubious.

'Well…as long as you're *sure*.'

'I'm positive.'

Cheryl relaxed a little. She couldn't guess how much the things she had picked out from those racks might cost. To know she wasn't going to be charged for them was a real relief. She took another sip of her juice. It tasted even better without the shadow of debt hanging over her.

'It seems a shame to add other things to this and make it into a cocktail.'

Marco grimaced. 'Don't let Andreas hear you say that. He considers himself a real *artiste* when it comes to mixing drinks.'

'What *would* your friends on the building sites say to hear you talking like that?' Cheryl slipped in slyly between more sips of her drink.

'I dread to think,' Marco muttered, but with none of the humour she expected.

'Do you miss it?'

'Yes. Yes, I do.'

It was a gut reaction, and instantaneous. Marco looked as surprised by his reply as Cheryl had been by her own impulsive question.

'Then why don't you go back to it?'

His astonishment morphed into caution. He narrowed his eyes.

'Nobody has ever said anything like that to me before.'

Something about the gentle breeze and the relaxing sigh of the sea lulled Cheryl into saying far more than she would have risked at home. 'Anyone who has watched you working at that laptop can see it's not doing you any good, Marco. You crouch over it in a way that must make your head ache. And the things you call it! If looks could kill… I'm amazed your screen doesn't burst into flames.'

Her exasperation grew as she remembered something she had seen only a couple of days earlier. 'But when you got that huge shard of wood in your finger you pulled it out without a mention. Office work is hurting you far more—I can tell. It isn't worth a heart attack, Marco. But making a home for Vettor's chickens? Now, that's *well* worth a splinter or two.'

He gazed at her with clouded wonder. Then he looked down at his hands again, turning them over to search for damage. Eventually he spotted a small scab, and chuckled.

'You remembered that? I don't recall doing it at all. Scrapes like that come with the job. They aren't so bad when your hands are toughened to the work. But these days? *Inferno!* I have the hands of an office worker.'

He continued to stare at his hands, rubbing the pads of his thumbs and fingers over each other in a gesture Cheryl recognised. She could see the distaste in his eyes. He was feeling the delicacy in his fingertips that so delighted her.

'Even pen-pushers must have holidays.' Cheryl sighed, watching Vettor and his new friend splashing in the shallows. After a while, an idea came to her.

'Vettor can't swim,' she said idly. 'I wish I was good enough to teach him. He loves paddling so much. It would be safer, and give him a lot more confidence, if someone could be found to give him proper lessons.'

Marco turned away and tried to concentrate on his computer. Cheryl saw the effort it took. He kept on staring at the screen, but without doing anything. Working on automatic, the display constantly refreshed itself. *Sucking the life out of him*, she thought bitterly.

There was a long silence. Eventually he pushed his chair back from his workstation. Arms outstretched, he flexed his shoulders in a ripple of power before relaxing his neck in a graceful arc. As Cheryl watched, the shackles of business fell away, taking a decade of stress from his face.

'*Mio Dio!* Who could work on a day like this?'

He slapped his hands on the tabletop and stood up.

'Take the rest of the day off to enjoy yourself, Cheryl. I shall be taking care of Vettor for a while.'

## CHAPTER EIGHT

ALTHOUGH there was a fitness suite, the natural pool and jungle walks to enjoy, Cheryl didn't spend her spare time on any of them. She sat in the shade of a palm tree sipping ugli juice, watching Marco and Vettor in the clear blue water. *It's a role I was born to play*, she thought. *Watching other people enjoying themselves*. All her life she had been insulated from other people by a bubble of self-consciousness. She could never risk breaking out to engage with other people. Unlike Marco, who was soon splashing about in the sea without a care in the world.

It felt like hours later when Marco finally strode up the beach, trailing his nephew by the hand. Passing Vettor's small wet paw over to Cheryl, he accepted a beach towel from one of his staff.

'*Eccellente*.' He rubbed himself dry with enthusiasm.

It was infectious. Cheryl began to simmer with the nearness of him. She swept a bathsheet around Vettor's shoulders, trying to blot out the image of sea-splashed, sandy Marco. As she did so she heard Marco's deep accent calling for someone to take his nephew off to bed. Before sending him away, Marco ruffled the little boy's hair and Vettor looked up adoringly. Cheryl was so pleased that at last Marco was letting his nephew into his life—putting the past behind him and allowing himself to care. She could see the fondness he had developed for the boy and noticed how much more relaxed they were together. Almost like father and son now.

When Marco spoke again, a warm breeze of sensation fanned the ashes of Cheryl's desire right back into life. It didn't matter what he said. It was the sound of his voice that bewitched her.

'You didn't feel like getting your new swimsuit wet again after all, Cheryl?'

'I didn't want to spoil your fun. I can't swim well enough to enjoy horseplay.'

He looked at her pensively. 'There's still an hour or so of daylight left. Why don't you join me in the water for a swim now my staff have taken charge of Vettor?'

'I don't know…' Cheryl held back.

Marco misunderstood, and his smile warmed.

'There'll be no splashing, guaranteed. It'll set the scene perfectly for dinner. And if we get the timing right we can enjoy a show as we eat. As I said, Orchid Isle sunsets are an unmissable sight.'

Cheryl's heart was singing as she went to her apartment to change. First Marco had abandoned work for play, and now he was pulling her out of her bubble of isolation for a glimpse of his world. Miracles could happen, after all.

Cheryl's new swimming costume looked every bit as spectacular as she remembered. At the last moment she realised she wasn't brave enough to walk about on dry land dressed so scantily. Luckily, silk robes were supplied in each of Marco's guest suites. She slipped on a vivid fuchsia and purple sarong, and started for the sea.

It felt like a long walk through the Orchid Isle complex. Cheryl's heartbeat increased with every step. Soon it was almost as loud as the forest. All around her the churr of insects and the exotic warble of birds throbbed like a wild pulse. Reaching the hem of trees skirting the beach, she stopped. The water was deserted, the sun-shadowed waves breaking on an empty expanse of shore.

'One of your favourite fruit juices, fresh from the press.'

Marco's voice purred up from behind her. It almost sent her into orbit.

'You frightened me to death!'

'You're looking very well on it.' The corners of his mouth lifted. Sipping his own drink, he handed over her glass. 'How is Vettor?'

'He's sound asleep, with a smile on his face.'

Cheryl took the fruit juice from him, resisting the temptation to press its freezing glass against her burning cheeks. A satisfied smile spread over Marco's face. In that instant Cheryl realised he'd planned this all along.

'So *that's* why you took him swimming. It was a deliberate attempt to wear him out!'

'Yes, but it turned out to be more fun than I'd imagined.' His eyes sparkled with laughter, while his hands idly wiped away the droplets of water that their glasses had left on the bar.

'Thank you, Marco. It was a great idea,' she said, full of feeling.

Picking up on her tone of voice, he stopped what he was doing and shot her a knowing look.

'You see? We men have our uses.'

'I've never doubted it.'

Cheryl used a cocktail stick to fish a sliver of cantaloupe from her drink. She nibbled it, trying to give the impression that this was just another conversation in just another bar. But her eyes were everywhere, taking in details. There were solid silver name plates beneath every bottle on display, and porcelain dishes of snacks sitting beneath individual glass domes. This was a universe away from dusty bar snacks at her local pub.

'Really? You sometimes give the impression you don't like men very much.'

He sounded almost understanding. Cheryl hesitated. It would be such a relief to confide in someone. But how could she possibly tell Marco what a fool she'd been? Her parents continually reminded her of the hideous mess she'd made of her life. If blood relatives could do that, how would her employer react? She ran her finger around the sugar-encrusted rim of her glass. The hard, rough edge spoiled its sweetness for her. It reminded her of life.

'It's because something happened, way back in my past,' she told Marco with difficulty. 'I was a fool to expect a happy-ever-after, that's all. It won't happen again. Do you mind if we—'

'Change the subject?' Marco said smoothly.

They exchanged a look and Cheryl got another shock. She saw something new in his cool blue gaze. It wasn't lust or curiosity. It was almost as though he understood exactly how she felt.

'Not at all,' he added with a lazy smile that wasn't mirrored in his eyes. 'Let's swim instead.'

Taking her glass and the cocktail stick from her, he placed them on the bar next to his own. Reaching out his hand, he waited for Cheryl to accept it. She hesitated, but only for a second. Dropping her sarong and towel on the nearest barstool, she took his hand, holding her breath, nervous of his reaction to the revealing swimsuit.

'What do you think?' she said shyly.

There was a heavy pause as his eyes roamed her semi-naked body. 'You look wonderful.'

A blush spread across Cheryl's cheeks as he led her into the warm water. It was paradise. As Cheryl sank into the sea's fluid embrace, her awkwardness dissolved. There was still enough daylight left to pierce the shallows. She could look down on glorious shoals of reef fish. Snappers and parrot fish flitted around displays of every type of coral. There were delicate fans, brittle as brandy snaps, pillows that looked like meringue but were hard to the touch, and a miniature garden in candy colours. Cheryl felt like a child in a sweet shop.

'That was the most beautiful thing I've ever seen in my life!' she gasped, as they finished their swim and started wading back towards the beach.

'I wouldn't say that.' Marco gazed down at her, his expression dark and sensual.

When it came to women, he acted on instinct. He never planned, but events were definitely nudging him in a particular direction. Cheryl was attracted to him. That much had been obvious from their first meeting. He'd stopped short of seduction up until now, but things were changing. Their chat just before swimming had told Marco one very important thing. Cheryl had been hurt in the past. She knew how it felt to give her heart and have it shattered. It wasn't something she wanted to happen again any more than he did. She would be wary of commitment. That was how Marco liked his women. He smiled to himself. A little seduction would make a perfect start to his holiday.

When it came to sex, Marco was highly selective. He could go for months with only work to sustain him. But when an unmissable opportunity like this arose—well, he wasn't a monk. By bringing Cheryl here he had gambled that his rule against bedding his staff would stop him being tempted. Tonight it was a different matter. Sun, sea, sand and most especially her shining swimsuit made all bets void.

*Why not?* he thought. After a bad experience, Cheryl wouldn't want commitment. And he didn't want to sleep alone. They were the ingredients for the perfect holiday romance. Orchid Isle was a place where they could both forget their pain. For a few magic moments it could be replaced with pleasure.

He looked down at her with a slow, sweet smile.

'Cheryl,' he said quietly. 'What you said before we went into the sea…it's been troubling me. You and I may have had our misunderstandings, but I wouldn't like you to think I was totally unfeeling.'

She shrugged. 'It sounds as though you've had a hard life. It must have toughened you.'

'There's been nothing I can't handle,' he said, trying not to think back too carefully, or too far.

He took another step, as though heading back to the bar. Cheryl started to follow, but he had already stopped again. Now they were standing much closer together than before.

Something about the setting sun and the gentle breeze turned her heart to butter.

'Tell me, Marco,' she said softly.

Gazing along the sweep of the bay, he shook his head. 'Another time, maybe. It doesn't matter.'

'Yes, it does.'

In an impulsive gesture, Cheryl's hand went out and touched his arm. The circuit between them was complete.

Slowly, he turned to face her properly, and he murmured, 'That wonderful kiss we shared…it wasn't enough for me.'

She had been gazing up into his face, her eyes full of concern. When he said that she lowered her lids. Her lips parted, but the only sound came from the surging surf on the shore. Marco raised his hand. With a touch that was no touch at all, his fingertips traced a droplet of seawater as it ran from her hair down the plane of her cheek. When he reached her chin, he lifted it. At the same time his thumb smoothed away her worries. Cheryl closed her eyes.

Their first caresses were slow, soft and subtle. Marco was in no rush. Anticipation was almost as sweet as the act itself. He knew exactly where his first kiss was going to lead. It was inevitable. This affair had been destined from the moment they met. Like all women, Cheryl would be powerless to resist him. That flimsy swimming costume would slide off, and she would be his. Her lissom little body would mould itself beneath the warmth of his fingers. His hands would roam over her peach-smooth skin, relishing every curve, until finally, wet and willing, she would straddle her legs in an unmistakable invitation for him to seek out the most intimate parts of her—

'No!'

He stopped and drew back from her. Silence fell between them.

Cheryl had never experienced such absolute stillness before. Far out in the bay, the setting sun touched the horizon. It was so quiet she waited, as if for the hiss of flames touching water. Then, after an agonising pause, the hand that was encircling her began to weave a dancing pattern over her shoulder again. His slow movements were as light as shadows drifting over her skin.

'What is it, *tesoro*?'

The whisper of his voice was as insubstantial as his touch. Cheryl took a deep breath. She tried to hold it, but couldn't. It escaped in a shuddering sigh. She tried again. Wordlessly, Marco's touch became slower and still more gentle. Eventually, his patience gave her the courage to speak.

'I—I don't do sex,' she said at last. His caress became a pat of reassurance, and she let her breath go in a gasp of relief.

'But that was just a kiss.' He smiled, his eyes dark with heady passion.

Cheryl stiffened. 'In my experience, one thing leads to another.'

'And in mine.'

She was withdrawing from him. Marco was having none of it. He gathered her unyielding body back into his arms.

'Something bad has happened to you in the past,

Cheryl. I sensed it from the moment we met. And the way you backed off from those workmen confirmed what I already thought.' His voice grew molten. 'But this time will be different. I promise you.' His vow was so powerful it silenced her with a whisper. 'Believe me. I know how to treat a woman—especially a delicate little flower like you. Forget everything except here and now. You are safe with me. I told you so when you first threw yourself into my arms that night at the Villa Monteolio. Remember?'

How could she forget? The memory of his calm strength melted into the warm reality of his hands. All the panic ebbed from her body.

Marco felt the subtle change as her shoulders softened. She didn't feel threatened any more. The only thing between them now was an unspoken understanding. Nothing was going to happen—unless she wanted it.

In a confusion of emotion, Cheryl had never felt so secure, and yet so apprehensive. This second, this minute was wonderful. But when the time came, what then?

'I'll take care of you.' His voice held all the warmth of the sea as he murmured into her hair.

'It isn't that I don't want to,' Cheryl murmured, 'especially with you. It's just that…I can't believe you could want me.' She closed her eyes and rested her brow against his chest. Unable to see his face, she felt him lift his head, but did not see the frown troubling his features.

When he spoke again, there was no hint of what might have been going through his mind.

'No man alive could resist the silent temptation you've been to me since we first met, Cheryl.' His delicious accent caressed her name like liquid silver, 'I'm stalked by so many women, and they are only interested in what they can get out of me. But you—you are different. Your feelings are shown so clearly, and your body betrays you. I know you must be as innocent as I am experienced. Let me show you all the pleasure at my fingertips…'

His last words whispered away into the curve between her neck and shoulder. Cheryl was a willing prize. She closed her eyes, surrendering totally to the strong arms that surrounded her.

Their kiss drove everything from her mind except the touch and taste of him. Suspended in an orb of passion, time seemed to stand still. But when at last he gently pulled away from her, a sliver of moon had risen above the shadowy hills of Marco's own kingdom.

Cheryl shivered. Marco was in charge here. *This is his domain so there's no escape*, she thought. *I'd better get it over and done with, and let him decide what happens next. He is judge and jury in his own land.*

'I never know what to do…to say…' she whispered, hardly able to get the words out.

Marco caressed her face, then ran his hands through her thick hair. 'That isn't the brave girl who stood between me and Vettor at our first meeting!'

'I didn't know who you were then,' she replied, adding to herself, *Only what a man of your size and strength might be capable of.*

Cheryl was torn. She knew what Marco was like, and how many women he had bedded. Why would it be different for her? Could she trust him with her body? With her heart?

'Tell me, Cheryl. Tell me what happened in the past to make you so wary. You are like a frightened child.'

He held her close as he spoke. She could feel the vibrations of his voice through his chest and the sensation comforted her.

It took a long time. Eventually, she sighed again and said, 'I've always been different—right from the start. My parents were so proud when I got to grammar school. I worked hard, and got top grades in everything,' she told him. 'There was nothing else to do. I had no friends. No, really—it's true. My parents said we were too poor to mix with families from the grammar school side of town.'

Marco gritted his teeth, holding her tighter.

They were both silent for a while. Then Cheryl plucked up the courage to go on.

'College was just as lonely. I buried myself in my books. And the Internet,' she added heavily.

'I think I can see where this is going.' Marco grimaced. 'You met up with someone you'd been chatting to online, and had a bad experience?'

She nodded. 'His name was Nick Challenger. When I told him how miserable I was at home he sympathised. He really was the perfect friend—to begin with. We met, and at the time I thought there was electricity between us. Now I know better.'

She thought back to her first meeting with Marco. That was *real* attraction. If only she'd been able to recognise the fake in Nick. Two tears escaped from her eyes.

'Oh, *mio tesoro…*' he whispered, stroking the tears from her cheeks.

'P-please don't be kind to me. I can't stand it!' she sobbed.

'Yes, you can. While you are here with me I will let no one hurt you.'

Although she could hardly see out of her raw eyes, she looked into his. Expecting to see pity, all she saw was concern.

'I must look awful,' she snivelled, but he squeezed her hands. Then it didn't matter any more.

'Do you think I care about that? Believe me. You are good and kind. Nothing and no one can take that away from you. Instead they should treat you as the delicate treasure you are. You deserve the best that life can offer, Cheryl. Never forget that,' he whispered, before gently placing another kiss on her lips.

## CHAPTER NINE

CHERYL was in love. In a rush of emotion, she realised this was the real thing. Heat and hormones had fired her feelings for the past few weeks. But this was something new: a deep, calm assurance. The comfort Marco was giving her had set the seal on it. He cared for her, when she had no one. He was the only man in the world who made her feel like this and treated her so well. Her self-esteem had been at a low ebb. With a few well-chosen words Marco was restoring it, moment by moment. He didn't care about her track record.

If anyone had suggested that a few hours ago, she would have thought it was because he didn't care about *her*. Now she could dare to hope. Perhaps he did care but, being the man he was, the only way he could show it was by letting her know the past didn't matter to him.

For a few glorious moments Cheryl let herself dream. Marco Rossi was not the sort to lay his feelings open for all to see. She went back over every second they had shared together, from the time they'd got out of the water. It was glorious. Surely he couldn't kiss her like this unless it meant something? And all this concern for her…

To Cheryl, a little of Marco's business armour had

been rubbed away. She had glimpsed the real man, and he was worth a thousand others. From now on she would do anything he asked. He had so much, when all she had was her loyalty. So when Marco took her hand, he made her the happiest woman alive.

He led her over to some tall trees fringing the beach. When she saw a hammock suspended between two of the palms, her footsteps hesitated.

'Stay with me, Cheryl.' Marco's voice was deep with authority. 'You shouldn't be alone. And I want you near me tonight.'

She moved forward with slow, silent acceptance. Despite her past, this was a new beginning. Marco had told her so. She couldn't have resisted even if she had wanted to.

He secured the wide, softly padded sling and then drew her in beside him. 'Nothing will happen.' His voice was a low caress. 'Unless you want it to, *tesoro*.'

Cheryl allowed herself to settle down against him. Leaning against Marco like this was a perfect fantasy. It drove all other thoughts from her mind—except one. What if he turned out to be exactly the same as Nick? Lulling her into trust and abandonment in the same way he'd eased her into this hammock?

Her body tightened with apprehension.

'Rest here, against my neck.' He cupped his hand around her head and drew her gently in towards his body.

'What if I say I don't want to?'

His touch glided away, freeing her.

'Then that's fine. I don't need to prove anything.'

Cheryl hesitated. This time it was more because she was afraid of what she might do, rather than what

Marco might have in mind. The warm scent of the sea rose from him like an invitation. He stayed perfectly still, waiting. At last Cheryl could not resist any longer. She sank down beside him again and the hammock rolled them gently together, skin against naked skin.

Marco didn't move, allowing her to come to him. When she let out a long, satisfied sigh he laid one arm around her, letting it fall casually down the length of her curled body. She felt the faint rasp of wind-dried salt on his skin as he enfolded her. At the same time his voice teased her with slow, caressing whispers of reassurance. It was a tone guaranteed to keep her in his arms for as long as he wanted. Cheryl was content to stay there for ever.

When his hands drifted from her hair to her shoulders and then moved to the sleek sides of her swimming costume, they both knew there was no going back. No woman could resist the temptation of him. Cheryl stretched beneath him, eager to feel his touch over every inch of her body. Once again his fingers found their way beneath the soft stretchy fabric. Caressing the smooth skin of her derriere with one hand, he drew her gently in to another kiss with the other.

'See, *innamorata*? I'm not the monster you thought.' His voice was like moonlight on the water.

'But what if…if…?' Cheryl hesitated, afraid of saying what was in her heart in case it made him stop.

Marco put his head on one side. 'You wanted me to stop? I would. It's up to you. You're a free agent. Just like me. Either one of us could get up and go at any time.'

'Oh, no!' Cheryl saw her worst nightmare coming true. That he would leave her even now.

'But I'm not going anywhere.' His lips parted in another slow, seductive smile.

'And I don't want to go.' Cheryl glanced back at the complex. But what would people think if she stayed? How could she use her position as Vettor's nanny like this? She bit her lip. 'But…'

'Then stay.' He withdrew his fingers from her panty line. Skipping them lightly up the length of her body, he began toying with the thin straps of her swimming costume.

His every movement set her nerves dancing. Gradually, his caresses stroked away every thought of anything outside the universe within his arms.

'Making love is the greatest pleasure known to man. Why would I want to keep you in my arms by force?' he murmured.

'You'll never need to do that.' Her eyes were large, and dark with trust. 'I want this, Marco, but…I don't know how. Not properly…and what happens if I'm no good at it?'

He made a sound of pure disbelief.

'Do you think that matters to me? A man gets his pleasure no matter what. I can wait…though not for ever.'

His voice was a growl of happy anticipation. It set free a primitive urge within Cheryl. Her mouth was parched, but she didn't need to talk any more. They kissed until all that mattered was the sensation of being totally absorbed in one another. When Marco finally released her body to question her expression, she raised a hand straight to his cheek.

'Please don't stop…'

Everything from the sweet huskiness of her voice to her fawn-light touch combined to make Cheryl totally desirable in Marco's eyes.

'*Tesoro…*' he murmured, drawing her gently, easily back into his arms. The next moment her face was pressed against his shoulder, held there by the warm security of his hand. 'You don't mind?'

She shook her head.

Slipping a finger beneath her chin, he raised her head. Looking straight into her eyes, he murmured, 'Then this is how it will be.'

Once more his kisses were soft and sweet against her lips. His gentle longing inspired Cheryl. She responded again, tentatively at first, and then let desire send her hands around him. She encircled his waist, feeling the vital glow of his naked skin.

'I shall teach you how to love,' he whispered. 'But it is a skill that takes many, many lessons. Don't feel you have to take them all at once.'

Cheryl lost herself within his sheltering arms. She had never felt so loved. *No!* she brought herself up short. *Love isn't one of his words*.

'It's a skill,' he murmured, nibbling down the length of her neck. 'Honed by years of practice.'

His voice was indistinct, but Cheryl thought she heard amusement in it. He wasn't laughing at her, was he? She tensed, but in that same instant Marco transferred his attention to her earlobe. Suddenly nothing else mattered. Her body dissolved. All the support she needed was there, coming straight from him.

'Would you really stop now, if I asked you to?' she gulped.

He stopped anyway. The instant he did, Cheryl wished she hadn't said anything.

'Of course.' He was watchful, quizzing her with his eyes. 'But you don't really want me to, do you?'

In reply, Cheryl reached up and began their next kiss. Then Marco took back the initiative. Peeling off her swimming costume, he encouraged her to strip him, too. Unrestricted, their bodies twined in a dance of ecstasy.

Cheryl lost track of time as he worshipped every inch of her. Then, when she was faint with pleasure, he drew her to the greatest peak of all. Gasping, she accepted his body as he sank forward. Gripped in the velvet of her embrace, Marco took a few seconds to master his instincts. They were almost overwhelming. But he wanted this to be a time for her, not him. Gently, with infinite care, he transferred his attention to the creamy sweet skin of her neck, tasting and kissing until the temptation became too great even for him. He drew back, aching for the satisfaction of a second thrust.

'Marco, no…'

He paused, but only until he realised what she meant.

'Marco…no—don't stop…' she pleaded, in a voice he had never expected to hear her use. It was smoky with seduction and totally irresistible. Now it was only the sensation of him leaving her body that caused her to tense.

Her muscles held him as he tenderly cradled her body. Lifting his head from the silken surface of her skin, he looked at her. It was perfection. He sank back into the welcome of her, and she responded with little fluttering cries of pleasure. Her nails dug into his shoulders. She arched beneath him, eyes closed. Marco allowed himself to smile. He loved to see his own special talent at work in a woman. Cheryl would never forget this for as long as she lived. He could guarantee that.

Passion made her more beautiful than ever as he brought her closer and closer to ecstasy. *This is it*, he thought. *She was born to respond like this, and I'm the only man who can inspire it in her.* Then Cheryl cried out his name, setting the seal on their coupling. She called with such longing he couldn't deny her any more. As she gripped his manhood with waves of pleasure, he rose and fell in perfect harmony with her body.

When it was over he started to pull back gently. Cheryl stopped him.

'No! Don't leave me, Marco!'

With a smile, he slid down her body. Nuzzling the tiny bead at the heart of her femininity, he made her sing again with orgasm. When at last her thighs relaxed their iron grip, he raised his head.

'Now, what was it you said about not wanting to do this, *mio tesoro*?'

He reached up and caressed her cheek.

'I didn't want to disappoint you.'

He smiled. 'You didn't.'

Consumed with nerves, Cheryl tried to keep her voice light. In contrast, Marco's movements became heavy. *Is it regret?* she wondered, tentatively reaching out to him. Her fingers slid over his short dark hair. He leaned into her caress, lowering himself down to lie beside her.

'That was incredible,' he breathed.

'You don't mean that.' Cheryl frowned, subsiding against a meringue of cushions.

His attitude changed instantly. 'I don't lie. Particularly about something so important.'

Marco put out his hand to console her. He stopped short of pulling her close to nestle into his body. That would be too intimate. He was starting to realise exactly how much the past few days had meant to him. Over the years, sex had been a regular feature of his life, but no girl had ever touched his heart like this one.

He winced. That was a bad image. He had learned long ago that you couldn't afford the luxury of a heart when it came to women. He reached up with his other hand. Releasing the hammock's brake, he pulled on a silken rope. It set the hammock swinging gently.

The night sky above was sapphire plush, scattered with diamonds. He felt Cheryl's breathing become deeper, slower and more regular. She was asleep.

It was the ultimate sign of her trust in him. There was something about helplessness that always brought out the worst in him. With weak men, he bawled them out and made their working lives a misery. He knew people called him a monster behind his back. He didn't care. Either do a good job or stand aside in favour of someone who can. That was Marco's rule. No, it was his attitude to women that unsettled him. One diamond tear, one tremble, and he was lost.

Marco twisted his head slightly, to look down without disturbing her. She was sleeping like a baby. The long dark lashes sweeping her cheeks emphasised the cool fragility of her English colouring. One small fist rested on his chest. It uncurled as she slipped deeper into sleep. He noticed her fingernails were as pink and perfect as the inside of a seashell. It was a first for him. Usually his interest in a woman's appearance was limited to her face and figure, not the finer details.

He leaned back again to look at the sky. Serenaded by the soft sibilance of insects, he drifted between sleep and wakefulness, cradling Cheryl as she slept. A shooting star scored the blue-black velvet. Wasn't that supposed to mean a baby was being born? He wondered if his poor downtrodden mother had ever seen a meteor. He doubted it. She'd spent all her wretched life at work. Besides, it never got truly dark in the middle of the city.

Cheryl woke from a wonderful dream to find it was all true. She was lying in Marco's arms. A gentle tropical breeze was rocking them. Above her, palm fronds filtered the growing warmth as the sky changed from apricot to peach. The rising sun chased shadows from Marco's face, but not from his expression. That stayed tight-lipped and tense. Cheryl felt a small movement against the softness of her inner thigh. He was aroused again.

It all came rushing back to her—their swim, that kiss, his kindness…

A blush began to rise from somewhere that was as aroused as Marco. What in the world had she done? Sex with Marco had been sublime, but he was her employer, and Vettor's guardian… She swallowed hard, starting to panic. If he woke and regretted their night of passion, it would be unbearable. Out of the corner of her eye she saw her discarded swimsuit, hanging from a branch. That wouldn't be much protection in this paradise, but it was all she had. With the temptation of Marco pressing so insistently against her, it wasn't any help at all. She had to escape.

Her arm was resting against the comfort of his chest. Carefully, millimetre by millimetre, she lifted it clear of the downy curls of his body hair. He didn't move. Hardly daring to breathe, Cheryl grasped the thick over-hanging branch that held her abandoned swimsuit. Gradually transferring her weight from the hammock to the tree, she managed to get out without waking him. Grabbing the sliver of silvery material, she pulled it on.

Her first thought had been to escape before she could see the waking disappointment in his eyes. But now she was dressed, the desire to linger was too strong to resist. She stood on the cool sand for a moment, watching him sleep. It was a spell-binding sight. Marco was so gorgeous, and yet so troubled. She could see it in his face. When awake, he worked hard to keep his emotions secret. Now his inner turmoil was obvious. With one last, lingering look at his beautiful bronze body, she slipped away into the trees.

She went straight to the natural swimming pool. A stream cascaded from a rocky outcrop into a shallow basin, just right for bathing. Every surface was softened with ferns and orchids. Tiny birds flitted through the overhanging trees, lit like shards of stained glass in a green cathedral. Stepping into the water, she felt all her worries wash away. She swam a few leisurely strokes closer to the turbulence created by the cascade. Water foamed and bubbled like a time-lapse film of clouds. It felt heavenly. She dived beneath the surface, fascinated by the tumbling pebbles at the bottom of the pool.

Surfacing through streams of water, the first thing she saw was Marco. He was standing beside an ancient tree, its trunk encrusted with moss, dressed only in his swimming shorts. His body was patterned with the jagged moving shapes of leaf shadows.

'How did you know where I was?'

'It was a lucky guess. I wanted to repay your kindness at Monteolio by bringing you these.' He held up his hands. Her discarded silk sarong lay over one, a soft towel over the other. 'But now I'm here—and you're there, looking like that…'

Smiling, he helped her out of the water. Cheryl wondered why she had ever been afraid of him. If she was nervous now, it was for an entirely different reason. He swirled the towel around her, then stood back to admire the effect.

'If I'd felt you getting up I would have stopped you.'

'Would you? Why? Was something wrong?' She searched his expression.

'No—no, not at all.' His ravishing grin put her mind at ease straight away. 'After last night? And you showed every sign of enjoying it as much as I did.'

'Yes. It was wonderful,' she murmured shyly.

'I told you it would be.'

His confidence was infectious. Cheryl looked up and laughed, but only until she saw the look deep in his blue eyes. Her voice died away as he lifted one end of the towel and began tenderly drying her hair. It was so softly reminiscent of the way he had comforted her the night before that Cheryl gasped.

Marco's expression turned into a slow smile. Scooping the tawny riot of hair back from her face, he ran his fingers through the glossy mane. He was openly admiring everything about her, from the grace of her movements to the beauty of her body. For the first time in her life Cheryl found herself relishing an audience. Marco was the only man she would allow so close. He was everything she needed, now and for ever. Nothing else mattered.

Taking her hand, he led her to a sunlit glade. The forest floor was as soft and yielding as her body.

'This is my idea of paradise,' she breathed, as tropical birds spangled through the canopy of leaves hiding them from the world.

'And mine,' he whispered in response.

His first kiss was long, slow and irresistible. His lips sipped from her, and she was only too willing to respond. The touch of his fingers on her skin was like thistledown drifting on a warm breeze. He took such pleasure in the way she melted against his body that he went on caressing her as they stood in a shaft of filtered sunlight. It was Cheryl who finally drew back a little from him. She looked up at him shyly, but her eyes were limpid with sensuality. Marco's hand went to her hair, tenderly caressing a curl back from her cheek. His smile asked a silent question. Cheryl closed her eyes and lowered her head.

'No—wait.' Marco leaned close to murmur in her ear. 'You're still troubled about something, Cheryl. I can sense it. What's the matter?'

'Nothing.'

'Oh, no—that's not good enough! I've never wanted a woman more than I need you right now,' he whispered. 'But I would walk away rather than coerce you into something you weren't ready for.'

She raised her head and opened her eyes. His expression was penetrating in its honesty. She threw herself against the solid reassurance of his chest. Marco had said he wanted her! In that split second he burst the bubble of isolation separating her from life. He was drawing her towards a whole new future. She could hardly dare hope that happiness would last beyond these few precious moments together. But she could seize her chance and live her dream. If only for a little while…

'I want you, too, Marco—you can't imagine how much. But I'm scared.'

'Not of me?'

She shook her head. When she tried to put her fears of abandonment and pain into words, they came out all wrong.

'I don't know what to do…'

'Then maybe we should consider more lessons…'

With a wolfish grin he pulled her towards him and kissed her with a passion that swept every thought from her mind. In a head-spinning torment of desire, she felt her body warming to him again. Desire bubbled through her veins like champagne. Sliding her arms around his neck, she drew him down onto the soft bed of the forest floor. Hungry for his body, she claimed all his caresses and begged for more. As they lay on the warm yielding surface, he whispered about her beauty and his delight in her body. His fingers traced lascivious lines over her skin, teasing her nipples to peaks of awareness, awakening the coral bead of her femininity with his caresses.

Cheryl was in heaven. She had been unwanted as a child, and unloved as an adult. But in Marco's tropical paradise she became the woman she had always wanted to be. Pulsing with life, tingling with anticipation, she let him lead her towards the greatest prize of all. His lovemaking was slow and intense, teasing every nuance from the union of their bodies. When at last he exploded into her, her fingers dug into the smooth curve of his back in an equally epic orgasm.

Swimming back to earth through a haze of wonderful sensations, they laughed in shared delight. In his spellbinding moment of release, a perfect truth had come to Marco. Sex was something he could take whenever and wherever he fancied it. But what had happened with Cheryl was an entirely new experience for him. In showing her how she could find as much satisfaction as he did in sex, he had discovered something quite different. For the first time in his life, Marco was making love instead of simply luxuriating in sensations.

It was a staggering thought. He lay back, but instead of pulling away from Cheryl he drew her with him. The movement disturbed a tiny jewelled frog. It glittered and was gone in a flash of gold and green. An iridescent butterfly fluttered down and landed on her hair. It was a perfect ornament to her fragile beauty. She was right—this truly was paradise. Desperate not to disturb her, Marco's breath was so light it hardly ruffled the bright blue wings.

And then he felt Cheryl tremble in the silence, and took her in his arms again.

# CHAPTER TEN

'ARE you ready to tell me what was troubling you, Cheryl?' he murmured eventually. She was so completely relaxed now; he knew he had seduced all her immediate worries away.

'It's nothing—no, really!' She smiled and kissed him before he could question her further. 'My past was haunting me, nothing more. I've never had any luck with relationships before. You've been such a shock to my system. I abandoned England to make a fresh start, and I've certainly found one!'

'How do you know you haven't escaped the frying pan by jumping into the fire, *tesoro mio*?' He chuckled.

'Oh, Marco, only you could make me smile at a time like this. To hear you say such an English thing in that beautiful voice of yours—'

'No one's admired my voice before.' He laughed softly and, moving her away from him, held her gaze with his. 'What happened last night, and again just now, could stay a unique experience for both of us. That's up to you. You must decide what is going to happen next, Cheryl. I've wanted you night after night, day after day, but I know my own soul. I'm not interested in emotional ties. I've resisted taking things any further with you until now because I didn't want to hurt your feelings. But anyone who has suffered like you must think the worst of every man right from the start.'

'That's why I work with children,' she said simply. 'They don't know enough about me to inflict pain on purpose.'

'On the other hand, I know too much now.'

'I should never have told you.'

'Yes, you should.' A dark look clouded his features. He frowned, his hands moving restlessly over her body.

'Cheryl, I have a business proposition to put to you. I need a proper, stay-at-home mother for the little one, not a nanny—'

'Oh, you're not going to sack me?' Her face crumpled.

He shook his head, and carried on. 'A woman with your background needs to be sure of a settled, secure future. And I'm in the ideal position to provide both. Marry me, Cheryl.'

It was more than she had ever dreamed of, but she had never expected it to happen in a million years. Her mouth dropped open. For a long time she couldn't say anything. Simply breathing was hard enough. Finally she managed to collect her thoughts and put them into some sort of order.

'I didn't really hear you say that, did I?'

Marco's smile drained. Suddenly, he was the world-beating businessman again. 'It's the obvious solution. I'm a media face who has outgrown all the posing and the press coverage. I don't care what the papers or anyone else say about me any more, but the child is a different matter. I don't want him exposed to gossip. The façade of a happy marriage will keep the gossip columnists off my back and give him the illusion of a normal family life. It will also reward you. For the hell you've suffered in the past, and all the good work you're doing for us now.'

So it wasn't love. For a split second Cheryl might have been able to fool herself, but not any more. Not when Marco could let slip that phrase about *the façade of a happy marriage.*

'This is too sudden—' she began. Marco shrugged her concern aside.

'No, it isn't. I'll get my people to draw up documents to make sure neither of us suffers financially in any way from the arrangement. They'll sort everything out. Everyone will be happy. Think about it—you could go further and fare much worse. And this arrangement would, after all, be strictly business.'

She didn't know what to say. It would be marriage to the only man on earth who made her feel like making love.

'How "strictly" is that, exactly?' she asked doubt-fully.

'You mean will I still want sex?' Marco gave a hollow laugh. 'That depends on what my lawyers say. Don't worry, *tesoro.* You haven't minded me ravishing you so far. We are so good together it would be a shame to forgo the bedroom, don't you think?'

'Yes, but…'

He laughed, 'Oh, I so love your innocence, Cheryl! That's why this marriage is such a good idea. It puts the

Botox brigade off my tracks, and replaces them with a pretty little original like you.'

Cheryl thought, *but not for long*. Marco was right. Nick had seemed nice, but turned nasty. Marco's terrible public reputation was at odds with the way he could be in private. Appearances could be deceptive—but he was stunning in that department, too. It really was a no-brainer. The man who filled Cheryl's every waking moment and all her dreams was asking her to marry him. It might be a loveless match as far as he was concerned, but Cheryl had enough devotion for all of them. Right then and there, she decided to make sure Marco would never regret it.

'All right, I'll do it,' she announced boldly. 'If arranged marriages are good enough for some royal families, then they're good enough for me.'

From that moment on, Cheryl lived like a queen. They had champagne cocktails and croissants for breakfast. That was followed by a leisurely bath to the sound of birdsong from the surrounding jungle.

As she was deciding what to wear, a masseuse knocked on the door of her apartment. Marco had flown the woman in especially for the occasion. Cheryl had a wonderful time selecting essential oils for the preparation of her own exclusive blend. Then she lay in pampered perfection while every care was soothed away. Much later, softened and supple, she was treated to a succession of wonderful treatments. First a hairdresser, then a reflexologist, a manicurist and finally a beautician came to spoil her.

At first she was desperate to know what Vettor was doing, where he was and who was looking after him.

Gradually her worries receded. Each time someone said *Signor Rossi has taken him down to the beach*, she believed it a little more easily. By the time she was glittering like a superstar, the message was, *Beba has taken him fishing*. When Cheryl stepped out of her apartment, she was totally relaxed and happy. The only thing missing from her life was Marco—and he was the first thing she saw.

He was lounging in the shade of a tree, but stood up as she walked towards him. Cheryl had expected to feel overawed or nervous, but she didn't. The admiration burning in his eyes gave her the confidence to stride out. The billowing folds of her skirt swirled in the warm air, perfuming it with Chanel.

'You look stunning.' He stretched out his hands to her. Drawing her close, he placed a kiss lightly on her forehead.

'Hmm…someone is working well today. I forgot to specify perfume when I arranged everything. They must have remembered my favourite.'

Buoyed up by her luxurious morning, Cheryl put her head on one side. 'Actually, it's my own. I was petrified when I left England to come and work for you. I treated myself to a tiny bottle at the airport as a reward for my own bravery.'

'Then you have exquisite taste.'

He smiled, and Cheryl did the same. If only he knew! Her scent had been chosen because it was the only name she'd recognised. She'd never expected to use it, but this was one of those special occasions she had dreamt about. Now it was here, she was going to enjoy every second.

'I've never felt more pampered,' she sighed, languid with satisfaction. 'Have you two been having fun?' She looked over to where Vettor was investigating a rock pool with one of the errand boys.

'We certainly have. But you and I must get down to business now.'

Cheryl looked back at Marco, her dreams evaporating. *What else could I expect?* she thought grimly. She had never been offered love here, only a job. Even from her first interview for the post of nanny she'd got a hint of what Marco Rossi could be like. Work always came first with him. His absences had told her he had little time for his nephew. This was a man who delegated, rather than loved. No wonder he could offer marriage to her so easily. It was nothing more than a business decision as far as he was concerned. *Well, I can hardly complain about that now*, she told herself. To be fair, he'd never dressed up his proposal as anything but a marriage of convenience. She'd known his reasons before she accepted, and none of them involved love.

'I thought we were supposed to be on holiday.' Pulling away from him, Cheryl strode off down the beach.

'Wait.'

She slowed her footsteps, but only slightly.

'Cheryl.'

His voice gave her name all sorts of meaning. She stopped, digging her toes into the warm silver sand.

'We have things to discuss.'

When she turned around, he was already there. His bare feet had been silent on the sand, but his eyes spoke volumes.

'I'm having my people move your things into my apartment here, and into my suite back at the villa.'

She blinked.

'Is that OK with you?' he added.

It sounded as though he was arranging a business deal.

Cheryl wanted to be romanced, whisked off to bed, made to feel special every time. But who was she to expect things like that?

'I—I suppose so.'

'You don't sound too sure.'

Cheryl looked down at the sand. Tentatively, she put one foot out and rubbed her toes back and forth, drawing a line. Her newly manicured nails glittered like pearls in the sunlight.

'It sounds so clinical when you put it like that,' she managed eventually.

In response to her words Marco strode away up the beach towards the table where his work was laid out in the shade. Her heart plummeted. He really was a businessman to his fingertips. She had agreed to his proposition, and this was how her life was going to be from now on. No romance, just harsh economics.

She watched as he spoke into his mobile phone. Then to her amazement, he dropped the thing. Within seconds he was back at her side.

'You must stop selling yourself short, *tesoro*.' His lilt was questioning.

The fine hair on the back of Cheryl's neck prickled. There was determination in his eyes.

'It's the first rule of business,' he went on. 'Treat yourself as you want others to treat you. Although you needn't think I'm doing any more work today. That phone call was to clear everyone from the far side of the island. They'll all be concentrated around here, ready to fawn on little Prince Vettor while he fishes. That means you and I will have one corner of this paradise all to ourselves.'

His hand slid around her waist. Suddenly Cheryl was in the air, effortlessly swept off her feet. She tried to scream, but only a thin gasp escaped from her throat.

'What are you going to do with me?' Staring at him, wide-eyed with horror, she struggled to speak. The muscles in his arms were like steel hawsers, clenching her against his body.

'Something any intelligent man should have done a long, long time ago.'

He was heading toward the trees. Cheryl could see the waterfall flickering at the far side of the secret glade where he had helped her from the water. Even the forest birds fell silent.

She began to struggle. 'Put me down!'

He laughed. 'What? And get that pretty little pedicure ruined?'

Shouldering his way through fern fronds and palms, Marco carried on regardless. Her prim struggling had no effect on him.

'Stop wriggling—this will be worth it.'

They reached the water's edge. As Marco strode out onto the jetty with Cheryl clamped to his chest, she heard the sound of an engine.

'Right on cue.' A sapphire-blue speedboat swished into dock beside them. Marco thanked the pilot, who leapt out and disappeared towards the complex. 'I won't bother with formalities like tying her up and helping you aboard,' Marco said, and he tossed Cheryl lightly into the boat.

She landed, cat-like, on her feet. As Marco stepped in to join her, she crouched. There was nothing solid to cling to except for the side of the craft—unless she risked grabbing Marco.

Taking the controls, he swung the speedboat around in a wide arc. Pointing its nose down the creek, he headed for the sea.

'You're going to like this, Cheryl.'

'Is that an order?'

He gave her a wry smile, 'No, it's a prediction.'

Taking a pair of sunglasses from a compartment beside him, he put them on. His sure touch on the steering wheel didn't falter.

'Nick was your first boyfriend? Is that right?'

'He was my *only* boyfriend.'

'You've got a lot of catching up to do when it comes to the art of romance. It isn't the sort of thing that can be carried on in the presence of a child. I've arranged for us to take a special lunch at Crystal Bay. There won't be anyone there to disturb us. Not even a waiter. You can carry on learning love from a master.'

Cheryl had to smile—this was beginning to feel like a dream.

A few minutes later, Marco's speedboat rounded the coast on the other side of his island. Crystal Bay was protected from onshore breezes, and the still air was heavy with the fragrance of tropical flowers. Its silvery curve of beach was absolutely deserted. Marco nosed the launch towards a newly built jetty. A cloud of pretty parakeets scattered through the trees with a noise like thrown jewels. After tying up the boat, he stepped ashore and reached for Cheryl's hand.

'You need me, Cheryl. Let me show you how things should be between a man and a woman.'

Before she could think what to say, he pointed towards a belt of trees beyond the beach. Following the line of his arm, she noticed a wooden chalet with a thatched roof, well camouflaged among the dappled shade of the trees.

'What do you think?' he carried on, without waiting for her reply. 'I want to make up for our first date last night being so...unconventional. Lunch today will be our chance to get to know each other. You know what they say...there should be one date for every decade of your age before the man suggests—' he gave that lopsided grin of his which always made Cheryl forget her worries '—in my case *marriage*.'

To her amazement, Cheryl found herself smiling right back at him. Her mind raced, already filling with ideas. Marco might be treating their arranged marriage as a sham, but he was the man of her dreams. Who else would do something like this for her? He really was perfect. What more could she want?

*A proper wedding*, she told herself. Gradually, she realised part of the solution might be in her own hands. Marriage to Marco ought to be a cause for celebration. What better reason could there be for treating herself? The lives of her parents had taught her one important thing. Mr and Mrs Lane had always spent every penny of their money. They liked to treat themselves whenever they could. Cheryl had had very different ideas. She'd grown up a saver. Now she would splurge what little she had on clouds of white satin for the dress she'd dreamed of since she was a little girl.

'My people have been busy organising our civil ceremony, right down to the final details. A few forms, half an hour or so of our time—'

Cheryl's face fell. 'Oh, I was so looking forward to a church wedding. I've always wanted to walk down the aisle.'

Marco was amazed. 'A quiet wedding will mean so much more than a flashy, crowd-pleasing event.'

'I suppose so.' She sighed, knowing in her heart that it wouldn't be the sort of marriage that her dreams were made of.

Marco laughed and squeezed her hand, but there was concern in his eyes.

'It will be so much easier to have a discreet ceremony with the minimum of witnesses. Each extra person involved makes a media event more likely. I don't want my vows recorded by the world's press,' he finished darkly.

A trickle of ice ran down Cheryl's spine. Perhaps Marco wasn't so perfect after all. Not only was he trying to rush this marriage through like any other business deal, he was making sure hardly anyone knew about it.

*That will make it easier to deny in the future*, a warning voice told her.

'Wouldn't a builder from the wrong side of town like you be grateful for the advertising?' she said, but her heart wasn't in the teasing.

'Don't worry. I'll take full advantage of our arrangement. There's only one thing…' His thumb made small circles on the back of her hand. He looked troubled. 'It means inviting the press here for the first time ever—for me to show off my bride. How will you cope with all the publicity?'

'I'll manage,' Cheryl said firmly, as much to reassure herself as to convince him.

Marco lay awake for a long time that night. He had already begun to regret his hasty proposal. He'd been carried away by mistaken ideas about Cheryl. Women usually wanted him for his money, nothing more. He'd imagined Cheryl was genuinely interested in him as a man. But briefly today he had glimpsed a different side to her. Her face lit up whenever he mentioned marriage. She wanted to ditch his idea of a discreet, businesslike ceremony in favour of a full bells-and-whistles approach.

It wasn't the financial details that worried him. Cheryl's horrible past meant she was overdue some pampering. That was why he had arranged those beauty sessions for her, and their surprise lunch. She had certainly enjoyed all that. Over their meal she'd opened up, revealing herself to be an intelligent, thoughtful companion. They shared the same views on lots of topics. Taken all round, Cheryl was ideal. She was the perfect mother for Vettor, good company, good in bed, and very easy on the eyes.

But the fact she wanted him to lash out on a lavish fantasy wedding concerned him. Was this the beginning of the end? He thought back over the short time they'd spent together. Unlike his other women, Cheryl never rolled her eyes because he preferred a full English breakfast to an executive's croissant and coffee. She had remembered him picking up that splinter when he'd hardly noticed it. Though he always denied he missed hard labour, Cheryl saw through him and sensed the truth. And, best of all, her face really came alive when she was with Vettor.

Taking all those things together, Cheryl really was the employee from heaven.

Why the hell did he want to ruin things by marrying her?

# CHAPTER ELEVEN

MINUTES after Marco had finally drifted off to sleep, he was bounced awake in a flurry of noise.

'Can I come? Can I come?'

Vettor's voice rang through his head more vividly than any alarm.

'Where?' Marco hauled himself up on one elbow. He dragged one hand down over his face. It didn't make the dawn any brighter.

'When you and Cheryl get married, Uncle Marco! I want a big, big party.'

'No.'

Marco sat up abruptly, wide awake. He silenced Vettor before the little boy could get into his stride.

'When Cheryl and I get married, it's going to be a quiet wedding, with the smallest number of people we can get away with.' Marco dropped his hand heavily onto the bed, glowering at Cheryl. 'I've had barely any sleep. And I didn't ever expect to see *you* back in uniform again.'

'At the moment I'm still working under contract.'

Horrified at his reaction, Cheryl hid her feelings and bit her tongue. Like a true professional, she waited for his next instruction. Marco's attitude had changed. It sent a chill right through her. Yesterday he had made her feel special. Now his scowl drained their situation of every last drop of romance. She'd been awake half the night, getting more and more excited about becoming Marco's wife. Her excitement had reached such a pitch that she'd let Vettor into their secret almost straight away. Now the little boy knew almost as much as she did. But this morning there was a new truth written all over Marco's expression. Cheryl could see her future husband was having second thoughts. She was scared.

'Vettor, I think we'd better leave Uncle Marco to wake up in his own time,' she said diplomatically, grasping the little boy's hand. Guiding him off the bed and towards the door, she carefully avoided catching Marco's eye. But he hadn't finished with them.

'Come back here, *bimbo*.'

Leaning forward, he reached out to Vettor. The little boy sprang back at him, and was caught up in a laughing bear hug.

'OK, so I don't think our marriage is a time for wild celebration. But I can't bear to see you looking so disappointed, little one. I'll make sure you don't miss out. I'll make the party come to you—like the shops came here for Cheryl. We'll invite everybody, to satisfy their curiosity. Then maybe they'll give us some peace for the more important business of our wedding. I'll bring a whole carnival to Orchid Isle, Vettor. Just for you.'

Marco rough-housed him into another hug. He shot Cheryl a sharp look over the little boy's head as he did so.

'Settle Vettor with someone, and then come back here. We have things to arrange.'

Cheryl nodded, but said nothing. He had misunderstood her before. She had been quite happy with Marco's idea of a small, quiet wedding. She just didn't want to be robbed of the chance to dress up and enjoy herself. Yet now he was talking about entertaining on a massive scale. She'd always known marriage to him wouldn't mean being loved, nor being a cherished part of his life. Despite that, it looked as though she was going to be on his arm, in front of the world's media, playing the perfect hostess. Of all the pain he could inflict on her, that would be the worst.

The thought of socialising with all his grand friends settled on her like a lead weight. All she wanted was to be with Marco and look after Vettor. But the man who meant more to her than her own life came with a frightening social life. Knowing that was part of the deal made her feel sick with nerves.

Ten minutes later, Vettor was happily eating his breakfast beneath the vines. Cheryl couldn't delay her meeting with Marco any longer. Taut with dread, she took the walk of terror to his apartment and knocked at the door.

His voice thundered out from somewhere inside. *'Chi è là?'*

Her heart granulated. Who else *could* it be, when he had told her to come straight back? Then she remembered the stream of PAs, drivers, aides and minions who constantly invaded his life. She was only one in a long line of people clamouring for his attention.

'It's me—Cheryl,' she added, so there could be no mistake.

He threw open the door, making her jump. He was dressed in nothing but a pair of jeans, his naked brown torso rippling with strength. It was thrown into stark relief by the soft white foam of shaving soap on his face.

'You're busy, Marco. I'll come back—'

'No, come in. I'll do this later. Electric razors never do a good enough job for me.' He walked off into a side room, leaving her to enter. As she closed the main door, she heard him splashing water. Seconds later he was back, dabbing his face with a towel.

'You told me to come back.'

'Always the perfect employee,' he said, half to himself. 'Would you like some juice?'

Cheryl shook her head. A metre-wide plasma screen and a bank of sophisticated speakers formed an island in the middle of his reception area. From a fridge concealed in this entertainment centre he poured himself a glass of mineral water. After taking a token sip, he came straight to the point.

'I decided last night that I'd made a mistake—marriage to you is not such a good idea, Cheryl. But then Vettor bounced in. He obviously likes the idea of having you as stepmother.'

*It's typical of Marco to state facts without trying to cushion them*, she thought sadly. *So this won't be painless, but at least it will be quick.*

'I'm sorry, Marco. I wouldn't have told him, but…it slipped out by accident. I couldn't keep it to myself,' she said sadly. Marrying Marco would have been a sham, but at least she could have pretended he was hers. To Cheryl, he was irreplaceable. Losing him now would mean denying herself any shred of pleasure for ever.

'Things have gone further than either of us would have liked…'

*Not me*, Cheryl thought, but he hadn't finished.

'…but marriage still holds a lot of advantages, so long as neither of us is under any illusions. My legal team will have everything sewn up. When—*if*—the worst happens, you'll get a more than generous settlement. But you should know that no lawyer in the world will make any more money out of me than I'm prepared to give.'

Cheryl gaped at him in horrified surprise. She had expected him to make a speech about not wanting to marry beneath him. Instead, all he was interested in was the money side of things! It upset her so much she couldn't contain her anger.

'Well, of all the nerve! And to think I was willing to give you the benefit of the doubt when people said that money was all that mattered to you! Is that all marriage means to you, Marco? A cash settlement?'

'Of course not.' He recoiled. 'But the minute I mentioned the idea you started spending millions on white lace, carriages and a cast of thousands.'

'I don't have millions to spend,' she flared.

'Yes, but *I* do.' He bounced her own anger straight back at her.

'This isn't about *your* money. It's about *my* dreams!' Cheryl flung her arms wide with frustration. 'It's old-fashioned, but I always imagined I'd exchange vows while wearing a beautiful dress, standing hand in hand with my ideal man, in front of a priest. That idea kept me hiding my money away when my parents would have spent it all. I wanted one special day, after spending a lifetime watching other people having fun. That's all! I'd rather spend my few thousand pounds of savings on a wedding that would really mean something to both of us, for ever, than all your billions on a sham!'

Panting like a hawk, Cheryl glared at him. Marco stared straight back. It occurred to her that his expression was changing, but she didn't care. *I'm red and I'm hot and I'm furious*, Cheryl thought, *and if he doesn't like it, then that's tough!*

'How *dare* you suggest I'm doing this for dollars?' she started again. 'I'm not going to let you accuse me of being in a hurry to grab your money! Why should I be in a rush for something so meaningless when I've waited for love all my life?'

There was a moment of perfect silence. Then Marco moved forward, closing the gap between them like a trap.

Cheryl stood her ground. A few days ago she would have flinched or backed away. Now she looked up at him defiantly.

That was when she saw his face really had changed.

'Have the wedding you want,' he allowed. 'Pay for it yourself. I don't mind. All I need is a mother for Vettor. Our marriage will secure your future, and his, in the easiest way. That's all I care about.'

Cheryl blinked at him. All her rage and disappointment drained away. Was that all it took to make the great Marco Rossi understand? A bit of plain speaking?

The shock was so great, only the wistful look in his eyes stopped her being completely speechless.

'But—but what about *you*, Marco?'

'Oh…I'll get by.' He shrugged.

Something about his careless gesture spoke louder than words to Cheryl. For the first time that day a strange calmness began to steal over her. 'When it comes to life, getting by isn't enough,' she said quietly.

Their eyes met. Cheryl's body had longed for him from that first drama in the Villa Monteolio's entrance hall. Now she had tasted the delights of him, and she could not get enough. Being united beneath the stars had been wonderful beyond her wildest dreams. Coming together again in the sunlit glade had built upon that triumph. There was only one thing missing. She wanted so badly to be loved by Marco, but that didn't feature in his business plan. What could be more heavenly than to be adored by this irresistible man, to lie in his arms for ever? And yet there would always be something missing. His heart. Cheryl needed to reach out and comfort him, but his expression told her sympathy was the last thing he wanted.

She hesitated, and it was a second too long.

'I'm fine.' He broke the moment nonchalantly. 'And don't forget it's the ceremony that matters—the legal binding together of my family unit.'

His possessive words hammered her castle of dreams apart.

He couldn't love her. *He can't love anything*, Cheryl reminded herself. He scares his staff and dictates that Vettor will have a happy childhood, though he has no idea what that might mean.

'And remember—we've already had our wedding night. So you don't need to worry about me,' he added quietly.

'I'm not so sure about that.' Cheryl spoke from the shrapnel of her fantasies.

A mirthless smile lifted the corners of his lips. 'I've told you, *tesoro*, there's no need to be nervous. Not when I'm here.'

His voice was like smoke, weaving around her. The way he presented himself to her, the easy seduction of his smile, persuaded her she must be wrong. Marco had sympathised with her, comforted her and made love to her as though she was the only woman in the world. What did it matter if she was only one of dozens? The ultimate temptation of being alone with Marco in the suite that would now be theirs silenced all her misgivings. He was the one and only man for her. She had known it all along. He knew it, too.

Cheryl closed her eyes. If she didn't want to make love with him again—no, *have sex*, she corrected herself, because that was all it would be as far as Marco was concerned—she should make some excuse and walk out right now.

But Marco was already investigating the tiny buttons at the neckline of her dress. His long, sensitive fingers brushed her skin with all the delicacy of butterflies' wings. And in a rush of realisation Cheryl knew she didn't want him to stop.

He loosened her dress. She moved to let it fall free from her body. The prim cotton uniform slithered down to her ankles, revealing the delicate lace of her new underwear. Marco's hands went to her hair, releasing the pins that kept it neat. As the chestnut waves flowed free over her naked shoulders, he smiled.

'Like Venus,' he whispered with satisfaction.

His gaze evaporated every last fear lurking in Cheryl's mind. Now she knew what it was like to have someone look longingly at her, she couldn't get enough of the sensation. She gazed back at him, and then blinked. For a split second she fancied she saw something hiding deep in Marco's expression. Was that a flicker of affection deep in his clear blue eyes? She looked again. The expression was gone, but it hardly mattered. The slow tease of arousal was already misting her judgement.

'It seems a lifetime since we last made love, Cheryl.'

She was about to jump on his use of the word, but he stopped her. Pressing one long finger to her lips, he shook his head with a smile.

'Shh. I've already told you—forget everything but me.'

His voice was low with meaning. Cheryl shimmered in a haze of sensations. Her body cried out for him. Her mind reached for the satisfaction only Marco could give her. But still a web of memories trapped her imagination.

'If ours is to be such a sham of a marriage, I—I don't really want to do this again…' she whispered.

They both knew it was a lie. Her dark eyes begged him to take the lead. Although motionless, she reached out to Marco.

He stared into her eyes for a long, long time.

'Fine,' he murmured at last. 'If you want to call a halt, I'll finish my shave. You can go and practice changing from Nanny into Mamma. I won't distract you any more.'

He made to move away, to take his hands from her. She stopped him.

'I'm yours, Marco.' Her voice was soft, but urgent. 'We both know it. Take me…'

Marco silenced her with a kiss that swept every one of her doubts away.

For now.

# CHAPTER TWELVE

FROM then on, Cheryl's days and nights were filled with Marco. His passion was as relentless as the sea, and she couldn't get enough of him. Her life passed in a delicious warm haze of desire. Only one shadow darkened her horizon. The Party. She tried hard to stifle her fears, blocking them by concentrating on Marco instead. That wasn't difficult. His body was totally hers. He caressed her and seduced her to heights of pleasure she had never known before. Marco and Cheryl's nights were spent in passion, not sleep.

Vettor had picked up on the magic shimmering between them. From being a good child, he'd turned into an ideal one. Tempted by fresh fish from the ocean and all kinds of tropical fruits, he ate and ate. When Cheryl could bear to tear her attention away from Marco, she saw Vettor filling out and ripening in the endless sun.

'I wish we could stay here for ever,' she said dreamily some weeks later, as Marco rocked them both in the hammock.

He clicked his tongue. 'It can't be done, I'm afraid. There's only so much work I can do on a laptop. After the party this evening I must get back to the office. It keeps my workforce up to speed.'

Any mention of the party made Cheryl's blood run cold. She lifted her head from his chest to look round at him, trying to reassure herself.

'But you'll be spending plenty of time with me? Just the two of us? On our own?'

His arm tightened around her and he kissed the crown of her head.

'Of course. I'll make sure of it.'

No sooner had Marco made that promise, than he broke it. A noisy fleet of helicopters roared in overhead, and he sat up.

'I must go. Our party arrives in boxes, and they're all aboard those choppers. Let's start getting ready. Our guests will soon be arriving.'

Your *guests*, Cheryl thought with dread.

Vettor had no worries at all. With a whoop of joy, he forgot the glittering beetle he had been watching and charged off towards the apartments.

'I'll be right in to help you,' Marco called after him.

Cheryl was half out of the hammock, but when she heard him say that she stopped. 'That's my job. What about me?'

His eyes still on Vettor, Marco reached for her hand. She made it easy for him by catching hold, but his intention was not helping her to her feet. Instead, he gave her a cheerful squeeze and let go straight away.

'Surely you don't need to do anything? You're beautiful enough already, *cara*.'

Throwing her a quick smile, he abandoned her for the complex and Vettor. Cheryl's plan to bring them together had worked brilliantly for the little boy. But not for her. *If only Marco realised how I felt*, she thought sadly as she followed them. *I'm a spare part today. I'm no longer needed as a nanny, and Marco's staff do absolutely everything else for us.*

The only thing left for her was to act as hostess at his party. And she was dreading it more than a trip to the dentist. The guest list ran to several pages of closely typed paper. When she looked down the names she didn't recognise any apart from ones she had seen in newspapers.

Marco had brushed aside her worries with his usual ease.

'If we invite everyone, that'll satisfy their curiosity. It will save inviting them back to the Villa Monteolio after the event. The press will get their pictures, and won't need to gatecrash our big day. We'll give everyone the best of everything. They'll be dazzled by our generosity and your beauty.'

Cheryl had not been convinced. 'I wish I didn't have to attend. I might as well not be there anyway—I'll just fade into the background. You handle people so much better than I do.'

'You'll manage—you'll learn.' Marco's belief in her was total. 'It's a case of having to do it. And there will be an English couple here, so you'll have something in common with them at least.'

'The Duke and Duchess of Compton?' Cheryl squeaked. 'What makes you think I'll be able to talk to them?'

'Oh, you'll be fine. I knew Sophie when she was nothing but a girl on the party circuit. If she tries anything, just tell her *you're* the one I'm marrying,' Marco said airily. 'If that doesn't work, remind her who bought her husband out of a very deep hole last year.'

That hadn't reassured Cheryl one bit. The Duchess of Compton was a famous beauty, and rumoured to have a lot of lovers. What if she set her sights on Marco?

Worse was to come. Cheryl had thought her spirits couldn't sink any lower, but as the guests began jetting in to Orchid Isle she found out how wrong she could be.

None of the women reached double figures in their dress sizes. They were all as thin as sticks of celery, and as they descended from their private planes, their angular faces turned this way and that. At first Cheryl thought they were admiring Orchid Isle. The multiple explosions of paparazzi flash guns soon put that idea out of her head. They were posing. Image was the only thing anyone was interested in.

But Orchid Isle lived up to all their guests' expectations. Cheryl was relieved to hear nothing but coos and compliments. And despite all the famous people thronging his island, Marco was the star. Everyone wanted to be photographed with him.

'Just one more, *tesoro*.' He took Cheryl's hands and persuaded her into position beside him again. 'I know how much you hate it, but if I show you off on this occasion you'll never need to pose for them again.'

Reluctantly, Cheryl agreed. She fitted so neatly beneath Marco's arm it felt like the most natural place in the world for her. And at least she had the comfort of him as she smiled for the cameras yet again. She wished she could fall into a pose as naturally as Sophie, the Duke of Compton's wife, did. Cheryl could see that camera lenses and lovers alike adored the woman.

It made her look at Marco more carefully than ever. She noticed his behaviour changed whenever the dashing duchess came near. His smile was always devastating, but then it developed a new intensity. He seemed to consciously turn his back on Sophie so he could speak to Cheryl. It was lovely to have his full attention as he brushed a windblown curl from her face or a petal from her dress, but it was making Cheryl feel uneasy. Was Marco trying to hide something?

Her insecurity grew when he suggested they split up and circulate among their guests. Before she could protest, he disappeared into the throng with Vettor.

Cheryl surveyed the mass of people, wondering what to do. Waiters in dazzling white jackets and black ties brought around a constant supply of canapés and drinks. She took a nibble from one, and a glass from another. Instantly she felt better. Having something in her hands helped take her mind off her fears. The champagne was flowing freely, and there were all sorts of delicacies to choose from. The arrangements of smoked salmon, caviar and truffles set on silver salvers were works of art.

Everything looked so pretty it was almost a shame to spoil the displays. That didn't worry the male guests, who ate everything they were offered and were quick to ask for more, but their wives and other arm candy were more particular. Cheryl never saw any of them eat anything. Looks were exchanged whenever a waiter offered them a canapé, though champagne was apparently allowed on the latest celebrity diet. She, too, tried to resist, and when Marco's retained photographer started exhibiting portraits of the guests on a giant screen she needed something to cheer her up.

She hardly recognised her own image. Projected twenty feet above the crowd, in the new black and white silk dress Marco had chosen for her, she looked both stunning and serene. In reality, she felt like a zebra in a herd of gazelles. She was totally out of place, and had never felt more at risk. None of the men could take their eyes off her cleavage. None of the females could take their eyes off Marco. But at least the women were being nice to her—or so she thought.

When all the noise and crowding became too much, Cheryl dived into the vast marquee that had been set up as a ladies' restroom. There she cowered in one of its silk-draped cubicles. She knew she couldn't stay there for ever, but just as she was screwing up the courage to face everyone again, a racket of heels and squeals erupted outside. Jumping back into her haven, she pulled the pink curtains closed. She tried to tell herself it was because the cubicle's arrangement of lilies and roses needed attention. It didn't. The real reason was Sophie Compton. Cheryl had recognised her voice, and couldn't face her figure.

'Of course this Cheryl Lane is a total *nobody*!' The duchess's cultured tones rang through the whole structure as a group of women clattered into the marquee behind her. 'God knows where Marco found her. As I told him, you can always stoop and pick up nothing.'

Cheryl burned with indignation. She had guessed it would be bad. Now she knew.

'So she hasn't got a title?' another voice enquired.

'Good God, no!'

'Well, she's definitely *not* one of us!'

That was the transatlantic drawl of a famous TV anchorwoman. Now Cheryl knew her shame would be broadcast coast to coast.

'Have you *seen* the amount she eats?'

That remark was greeted by a tinkling riot of laughter. Inside the cubicle, Cheryl's shame turned to awful, crawling despair.

A fourth voice chimed in. 'She's stuffing in the canapés—I saw her.'

This sparked more laughter all round, and then, fuelled by their gossip, the hunting party snapped shut their compacts and quickly moved out of the marquee.

Cheryl buried her face in the curtains, gripping the pink silk until it creased beyond rescue. She dared not cry. Unlike her tormentors, she had no idea how to repair the make-up mask her personal beautician had so carefully applied. All she could do was hide, racked by painful dry sobs.

Was this what her life would be like from now on? People saying one thing to her face, another behind her back? While Marco sailed on a tide of admiration, sharks surrounded her. All her life she had felt as though she was on the outside, looking in. Now she was wallowing in the thick of things. Once she had dreamed of being the centre of attention. Living it was going to be a nightmare. She loved Marco so much it hurt. Yet why should he ever love *her*? He only needed her because it suited him to have the best possible mother for Vettor. How would she cope, knowing that he might find satisfaction in her arms, but never love? That wasn't life. It was a life sentence.

She cowered in her cubicle until she heard the click of more heels on the smooth veneered floor of the restroom. The fear of hearing herself talked about again catapulted her out of her refuge. She was sure she must have made lots of mistakes, but at least people would smile to her face. They wouldn't dare say anything nasty to her in public.

Would they?

Despite the cavalcade of entertainers and musicians, sumptuous catering and a final display of fireworks, Cheryl couldn't enjoy anything. By the time their final guests were preparing to leave, dawn was shimmering across the ocean. Marco slipped his arm around her waist as they walked along the shore together. Flower petals blown out to sea from the party danced around their feet, brought back by mischievous wavelets.

'Thank you, Cheryl. I know how difficult it must have been for you, among all those people. If it's any consolation, I prefer it when it's just the two of us.' He gave her a squeeze, and held her close as they strolled on.

His silence was contented. Cheryl's was full of doubt. *Which two does he mean? Me, the greedy nobody? Or Sophie Compton, elegant duchess?*

'Did you enjoy the party, Cheryl?'

'Oh, yes,' she replied quietly.

'Are you happy?' he murmured.

'Very.'

'Good.'

His voice oozed satisfaction. Cheryl was glad—although neither of her answers could have been further from the truth.

They wandered towards the helipad, watching the remains of the party being packed away in ice. Everything was being transported back to the Villa Monteolio so that the staff there could enjoy Marco's generosity.

'Why don't I go and arrange a very special breakfast for us? We could have it served in bed…' He nuzzled into her ear.

Cheryl turned to him. Before she could speak, he kissed her. The passion between them sparked, but Cheryl knew it was nothing without love.

*But this isn't how it should be*, she thought. *We're about to get married!*

And that was the terrible thing. It would never be a real marriage of the sort she so desperately wanted. She needed to be enclosed, enfolded and included for the first time in her life. Marco could certainly provide all that—when he wanted sex. But his lifestyle wasn't something she wanted to be a part of. All she wanted was this gorgeous man walking along beside her—but apparently he came as part of a horrible celebrity package. The party had been a taste of things to come—all show, but no substance. Nothing was real any more. The heart-stopping moments she had shared with Marco were a dim and distant memory, receding as though she was looking at them down the wrong end of a telescope.

Marco left her, heading for the apartment complex. Behind her, the last boxes were loaded, and the helicopter blades began to turn.

Almost as if acting on instinct and self-preservation, Cheryl turned her back on Orchid Isle and jumped onto the departing aircraft.

Marco smiled as he strolled towards the complex. His heart felt lighter than it had done in years. He no longer felt the need to submerge himself in work. His obsession with it had been an attempt to prove memories had no power over him. Cheryl had changed all that. She was transforming his life. He saw things so much more clearly now. By encouraging him to spend time with Vettor, she was improving all their lives. *Especially mine*, he thought.

Then the giant screen above the dance floor caught his eye. It showed three men, all immaculate in designer tuxedos, each with a champagne glass in their soft, pale hands. One was an international playboy, and the second was a gambler, famous for beating the house in Monte Carlo. It took Marco slightly longer to recognise the third. When he did, he swore softly.

'*Mio Dio*, that's *me*!' he said aloud.

There was no one to hear him except a chorus of parakeets in the surrounding trees. He thought back to the conversation going on when the photographer had taken that snap. The other two men had been trying to outdo each other, listing their latest extravagances. Marco was openly proud of his self-made millions, but their preening left him cold. He had smiled with them, but only because he was a polite host.

An old saying crossed his mind. *You can tell the quality of a man by the company he keeps.*

*Why am I wasting my time on people like that?* he

thought. Suddenly, all he wanted was Cheryl—now and for ever.

Realising that made him laugh out loud. Above him, the parakeets spun out from the treetops like streamers, and he smiled up at the sky as they flew by.

Cheryl had no idea where she would go or what she would do. All she knew was that she had to get away from Orchid Isle.

*I can't stay here a minute longer*, she told herself. *I'm not me any more! All those beauticians and personal dressers, and what's it all for? Marco didn't fall in love with my appearance. He didn't fall in love with me at all. He's marrying me for what I can do for him. All this pointless extravagance is making me a laughing stock in front of his friends. He's better off without all that. I can't spend my time trying to live up to the expectations of other people. It's like being a child all over again, and I can't cope with it.*

She couldn't bear to think how Vettor would react when he was told there would be no wedding. She stared out of the helicopter window, blind to the beauty beyond. All she could see was a future filled with disasters, mistakes, blunders and social gaffes. *Mum was right. I should never have tried to get on in life*, Cheryl thought.

She wasn't suited for high society. The only thing she would get from marrying her boss was a lot of people talking behind her back.

Marco could do without her. He'd never needed her physically, in the heart-stopping, emotional way she needed him. He had Vettor to absorb all his love now.

They were devoted to each other. It wasn't as though Cheryl could do anything for them in a professional role either. She'd been employed as a nanny when Vettor had no one. Now the little boy had Marco's full attention. How could he ever be expected to think of a humble ex-member of staff as his mother?

While talking to the chef about breakfast, Marco spotted some of his staff draping fresh figs with prosciutto. The kitchens were so well organised they were already getting ready for lunch. Knowing how much Cheryl loved the fruit, he took a few. Dropping them in a basket, he headed off to find her. After a few seconds, a sudden thought struck him. It gave him such a surprise he stopped dead. He'd partied all night, he'd just thrown his chef into confusion, and now he was taking time off for an impromptu meal when he should have been working.

He couldn't imagine doing this for anyone but Cheryl. Looking down at the violet-dark figs he was carrying, he rubbed his chin, considering. Now he came to think of it, life had changed for him in a lot of little ways lately. And the improvement had accelerated under the azure skies of Orchid Isle the moment he took Cheryl into his bed. *She's got a lot to answer for*, he told himself with a lazy smile.

When he got to the airstrip, he found it deserted. Wandering back to the complex, he was disturbed to find no sign of her anywhere. Vettor was still sound asleep, but where was Cheryl? If he didn't find her soon he'd have no excuse for skipping a meeting with his attorney. He smiled. This new and improved Cheryl could make him forget everything else on the planet. She made him resent every second he spent away from her. His lawyers were complaining he hadn't signed the pre-nup agreement yet. He would never have forgotten that lifestyle-saving detail with any other woman.

*You've got a lot to answer for, Miss Lane-soon-to-be-Signora-Rossi!* He said to himself as he set off on a circuit of the island in search of her. Then he stopped again. *Signora Rossi…* It sounded almost as good as she did. He grinned. The more he thought about Cheryl, the wider his smile became…

Right until the moment one of the airfield staff told him she'd left Orchid Isle on the last helicopter.

Marco could hardly believe his bird of paradise had flown. He dashed back to their apartment. There was no note, but there couldn't be any doubt about it. He tried to think back over their last conversation, their last lovemaking…it was hopeless. His brain had stopped functioning. He couldn't make sense of anything.

Reaching the heart of their suite, he stopped at the foot of the bed. Housekeeping had not visited their apartment since their last passionate lovemaking, but the duvet was folded back neatly, as Cheryl always left it. The bolsters still bore the slight impressions they had left. *Last passionate lovemaking?* He brought himself up short. The words had an unlucky finality about them, but Marco Rossi had never lost a woman yet—and he didn't intend to start now.

He grabbed the bedside phone to mobilise every member of his staff, all over the globe. He'd send them all out to track Cheryl down, to bring her back.

He'd spend all the money it took to retrieve her, to find out why—

Then he paused, and thought back to his sister Rosalia. When he had discovered his money had been paying for her drug habit, he'd thrown more and more of it at her problem. He'd funded Rosalia and her boyfriend through rehab, and arranged for them to stay at the world's most exclusive spa to try to encourage them further.

Marco had been due to take them there, but he'd hung on at the office that day, to clinch one last deal. Instead of running them to the airport himself, he'd delegated the task to one of his drivers. The man had been a new recruit, untried and untested. Desperate to impress, he'd taken one too many risks on the twisting road and killed himself and his passengers.

To Marco's way of thinking, if you had a coin, you had a friend. Yet his desperate need to create security for himself had killed Vettor's parents. *His* work ethic had helped bring about their problems. Later, it had made him entrust them to a crazy driver. His wealth had created their tragedy, and it hadn't been able to solve it.

Whatever had made Cheryl run away, Marco realised he couldn't fix things by simply casting his net of gold. The only thing he wanted was Cheryl. And he wanted her badly enough to show her by his own actions. Not by sending someone else to find her.

Without realising it, Marco had moved around to Cheryl's side of the bed. Leaning over, he brushed her pillow and inhaled. A last, lingering memory of her perfume crept into the deepest corners of his soul. *She's brought me so many pleasures*, Marco thought with a rush of adrenaline.

Losing sight of the really important things in life meant he had been too absorbed to keep his sister Rosalia safe. No way was he going to make the same mistake with Cheryl!

He had to find out where she was, and why. And he was going to do it right now.

The helicopter landed on Marco's luxury liner. Cheryl got out, knowing she should go below without looking back at the distant pleasures of Orchid Isle. That was what common sense told her—but Marco Rossi was the enemy of common sense. He had totally bewitched her.

She went to the rail, twisting her handkerchief into a hangman's noose. How could she sacrifice all those perfect days and nights with him? The feel of his warm smooth skin gliding against hers? Velvet nights of ecstasy and dawns filled with passion? The only reason she could do it was because he had given her everything except the only thing she wanted from him—his love.

*I must be mad*, she thought.

Cheryl might not have much experience of the world, but she knew one thing for certain. No other man would ever mean anything to her again. All she wanted was Marco. She tried to block out the past few weeks so her mind couldn't dwell on the big, empty space where her heart had been. It didn't work. She was desolate.

Squeezing her eyes tightly shut, she tried to make her mind a blank. Her senses rebelled. She even started hearing things. Above the small sounds of shipboard life going on around her, she heard the rasp of a speed-boat. She tried to tell herself not to be silly, but it got closer. Suddenly everyone around her was galvanised into action. Excited shouts and the racket of running feet opened her eyes to a surprise arrival.

Marco was swinging the Orchid Isle speedboat alongside his liner in a flurry of spray. Abandoning it to leap onto the steps leading up to the deck, he took them three at a time. He was at the top before anyone could open the rail for him. He burst through it, eyes blazing.

'Cheryl?'

His expression was grim, but he spoke her name with such soft sibilance her heart nearly stopped. In that instant time stood still. Cheryl shut her eyes again, knowing her own desperate need for Marco could never make up for the gulf that separated them.

'I'm sorry, Marco. I just can't do this.'

There was another rattle of hurrying feet, and then silence.

'What? *What* can't you do?'

'All this.'

She opened her eyes again to gaze at him, unable to keep the misery from her voice. He had dismissed all his staff. Finding herself alone with him, Cheryl waved her hands in a hopeless gesture of misery.

'I don't fit in here. If I marry you, I won't be a member of your staff any more. But that doesn't mean I can hope to be part of your world. Your party proved that to me once and for all.'

Marco stepped forward. Taking hold of her wrists, he squeezed them gently.

'Then forget it. Let me take you home.'

Stunned, she stared at him. In her confusion she could put only one meaning on his words.

'To England?'

Marco's beautiful blue gaze was hooded as he shook his head slowly. 'No. I mean *our* home, *tesoro*. The Villa Monteolio.'

Cheryl's head drooped. It was her turn to shake her head as she stared down at the deck. As he watched, a single tear fell onto their entwined hands.

'There's no point, Marco! I don't fit into your world. You said you wanted a mother for Vettor. But that time has passed. You don't need one now. Anyone can see you're the best and only parent he needs.' Her mind flew back to them playing in the surf on Orchid Isle. 'When you're together, it's the two of you against the world. You're going to conquer it together. I used to think I'd have to be the one who was always there for Vettor. But he doesn't need me any more.'

'Yes, he does. And so do I, Cheryl. For a long time I lost sight of the only truly important thing in life. Relationships are the only things that matter. And to me, right here and now, that means only one person. *You*.'

His voice throbbed with intent, and his eyes were burning.

'I want you, Cheryl. None of this means anything to me—not this vessel, nor the party, our guests, or even Orchid Isle. I'd give it all up in an instant for you, *mio tesoro*. You found my heart. When you left the island just now, I discovered you'd taken my soul with you.'

Their eyes met, and suddenly nothing mattered any more. They were within reach of each other again. That was enough. Cheryl lifted her hand to touch his shoulder at the exact moment he did the same thing to her. She sighed with longing, but Marco was already taking the initiative. In seconds he was kissing every thought from her mind.

Much later, when she could catch her breath, she looked up into his face with an expression of pure adoration.

'Oh, Marco, I missed you from the second I got onto that helicopter! I am so very sorry—'

He kissed her again.

'No—wait, Marco. I have to apologise—'

He wasn't listening. He was too busy celebrating her body. All he wanted was to hold her in his arms. After a paradise of kisses, he finally leaned back a little way and gazed down at her.

'I don't want your apologies, my love. Getting you back was all I ever needed. Every second we were apart was torture for me. I thought I'd lost you for ever,' he murmured tenderly.

He was looking at her in such a way…Cheryl knew she had to tell him everything.

'It started yesterday, at the party. You arranged it, all your friends were there, and you couldn't keep your eyes off the Duchess of Compton. The *last* thing you needed was an awkward girl like me who didn't know her place.'

'That's rubbish! I wanted to make sure Sophie kept her claws out of you, that's all. Cheryl Lane, you mean more to me than all of those people put together—men, women, megastars, the whole lot.'

His hands tightened on her shoulders. There was such fire in his brilliant blue eyes Cheryl didn't doubt him for a second. Even so, there was one horrible truth that had to be exorcised.

'I overheard somebody saying terrible things. They made me sound as though I was a dead weight around your neck.'

'Who was it?'

His voice was a dangerous growl. Cheryl felt her anger surge through him, and sensed she held Sophie Compton's future in her hands. Revenge would have been sweet, but Cheryl knew she could never forgive herself for telling tales. Marco's courage was infectious, so she came to a decision.

'I wouldn't tell you even if I knew. It's in the past, Marco. If I don't want people to say things like that about me in the future, then I've got to make more of an effort. I'll have to learn to face them with more spirit next time.'

'There isn't going to be a next time. You'll never have to face that sort again,' he stated firmly, stroking her hair. 'I had the party for Vettor's benefit, but it's the last time I will do anything like that, believe me. I knew you wouldn't enjoy the day but— *Dio!* I should have noticed the warning signs and been more understanding. And you've got plenty of spirit already. Along with all the other qualities I've been looking for all my life. You're the first person who's never wanted anything from me, Cheryl. Instead, you've shown an interest in me, and turned my lonely nephew into a cheerful little boy into the bargain.'

'You did that yourself. You're his father now.' Cheryl smiled. She couldn't decide which she loved best—the gentle way Marco was looking at her, or the unusual warmth in his voice.

'From now on I've decided to take a more relaxed view of life. Like you,' he added.

She laughed. 'You're making fun of me!'

'Not really.' He pulled her in close again, and she felt him kiss the top of her head. 'I've been too engrossed, far too passionate about my work in the past, *tesoro*.' He spoke with his chin on her hair. She felt the movement, and knew he was more comfortable speaking from his heart when he could not see her face. Cheryl relaxed. Marco didn't need her to say anything. She could tell from his silence. It was more reflective than usual.

'Come home to Italy with me now. I need you, Cheryl. So does Vettor. You've been gone for less than an hour, but from the moment he woke up he's been driving everyone mad with *"Where's Cheryl?"* How am I supposed to cope with that?'

Cheryl tried to laugh. 'He'll be missing *you* now, too,' she reassured him. 'You give him everything he needs, backed up with all the experience and common sense he needs to keep him grounded.'

'And now I've got the perfect female carer for him, too.'

Cheryl gazed up at him in wonder for a long time.

'Can I hope that means me?' she breathed softly.

'There could never be anyone else but you for me, my love.'

'Oh, Marco…' Her voice trembled into silence. All the pain of isolation poured out from somewhere Cheryl had never known existed. 'Marco, I want you to be my husband for real. And Vettor to be my little boy.'

It was the last tiny piece of her jigsaw. She hadn't known it was missing until this moment, but now it felt as vital as the final clue in a drama. She had never been loved as a child. Now she was desperate to make up for it with motherless Vettor and her gorgeous fiancé.

'Shh, my love.' He stroked her tenderly. 'We will love Vettor as if he were our own son, and he will be a brother to *our* children. Yours and mine,' he added with another kiss.

There was such feeling in his voice and touch; Cheryl was swept right back to the first time they made love. She felt him lace his fingers behind her back. With a sigh of contentment she relaxed against him.

Nestling his cheek against her hair, he spoke quietly into its warmth. 'Until I met you, Cheryl, I wondered why I bothered with life. I'd been working so hard for so long, I'd lost sight of the important things. But when I look at you it all comes flooding back. Let me make you happy. Let me keep you safe beside me at the Villa Monteolio for as long as grass grows and birds sing.'

Cheryl had dreamed of this moment from the instant they'd met. Now Marco was turning her life into something better than any fantasy. She took a moment to revel in it before saying anything.

'Is that another proposal, Marco?'

'Of course it is,' he whispered. 'Fill my life, my love, and I'll make every day perfection for you. That's guaranteed.'

'I know, Marco. You've already made all my dreams come true. So the answer to your question is…yes…' she murmured, closing her eyes in anticipation of another delicious kiss.

# THE MILLIONAIRE'S
# CHOSEN BRIDE

BY
SUSANNE JAMES

**Susanne James** has enjoyed creative writing since childhood, completing her first—sadly unpublished—novel by the age of twelve. She has three grown-up children who were, and are, her pride and joy, and who all live happily in Oxfordshire with their families. She was always happy to put the needs of her family before her ambition to write seriously, although along the way some published articles for magazines and newspapers helped to keep the dream alive!

Susanne's big regret is that her beloved husband is no longer here to share the pleasure of her recent success. She now shares her life with Toffee, her young Cavalier King Charles spaniel, who decides when it's time to get up (early) and when a walk in the park is overdue!

For Toffee,
and my other friends

# CHAPTER ONE

'LADIES and gentlemen—bidding will commence at half past ten exactly. That's in fifteen minutes from now.' The auctioneer's strong, commanding voice cut through the murmuring in the small sitting room and people began to take what seats were available, automatically consulting their own watches and glancing around at the competition.

Melody found a place towards the back, aware that her heart was pounding as she fingered the numbered card in her hand nervously. It stated the number thirty in large black figures and, looking down at it, she still couldn't really believe that she was here, doing this. To call it one of life's amazing coincidences seemed too trite a description. But she *was* here, she was not dreaming, and she was about to take part in the bidding for the rather quaint but very lovely Gatehouse Cottage. And it had certainly not been part of her present holiday plans.

Casting a surreptitious glance around her, she saw that the other interested parties were presumably the kind of eclectic bunch you'd see anywhere, she thought. Ordinary enough people, but today with a single purpose. To buy this property.

Presently there was a hush as the auctioneer took his place at the table, and straight away the atmosphere became charged with expectancy.

'We'll start the bidding at the guide price,' the man said, looking at everyone over his spectacles, 'and I'm going up in tens. Who'll start the bidding for me, please?'

There was an immediate response as someone raised a card, and Melody's breath was almost taken away at the speed with which everything proceeded. Well over the asking price was reached almost at once, before bidding began to slow as bidders shook their heads. Soon it was left to only four hopeful buyers to provide the entertainment. It got slower still as people dropped out one by one, and Melody's mouth was as dry as dust as she continued to raise her card.

Now that she'd started, she just could not stop. For once she was putting her business acumen and expertise into something for *her*—and the experience was a heady one!

Soon there were only two bidders remaining—herself, and a man with a deliciously deep voice at the back of the room, who was just out of her sight. She would actually have had to swivel in her seat to see who was keeping pace with her, so she continued to stare straight ahead.

Swallowing hard, Melody determined to keep on, up to the limit she'd set herself—but equally determined seemed her opponent! But suddenly she was the last bidder, and the all-important gavel was struck sharply once, twice…three times. Gatehouse Cottage was hers!

Melody got up from her place and went towards the desk, where the auctioneer beamed at her. 'Congratulations,' he said kindly.

'Thank you,' she said lightly, by this time feeling in an almost dream-like state. She could barely catch her breath. What had she just done, for heaven's sake?

There was paperwork and official business to see to, and the vital signature to append, but finally Melody left the building and went out into the strong summer sunlight, feeling as important as a middle-eastern tycoon! But she was still shaking inside… She was not usually of an impetuous nature—snap decisions weren't her style—yet she had just entered into an agreement that would now make her the owner of two properties—her apartment in London as well as this idyllic cottage in one of the most beautiful rural spots in England.

Presently, going down the path to reach her car, she almost bumped into someone standing there. A man was leaning nonchalantly against the gatepost, and Melody immediately looked up to apologise—almost swallowing her tongue as she met the searching gaze of the most blue-black eyes she'd ever seen! For a second neither of them spoke, but she was the first to find her voice.

'Oh, I beg your pardon,' she murmured, rather formally, stepping out of his way—but he didn't attempt to move, just stood looking down at her, a faint smile on his lips.

'There's nothing to apologise for,' he said casually, in a darkly rich voice that had the effect of making Melody's spine tingle unexpectedly. 'Except, perhaps,' he added, 'for pipping me at the post just now.' He paused. 'Congratulations, by the way,' he drawled.

So! This was the other determined bidder who'd helped to force the price of the cottage ever higher! He was tall—very tall—and dressed in dark trousers and a shirt which was open at the neck to reveal a tantalising glimpse of black curling hair. Melody looked away quickly.

'Oh—well…' she said, shrugging slightly. 'There must always be winners and losers, mustn't there? But I do hope I haven't ruined your long-term plans too much…'

He raised one dark eyebrow, still staring at her. 'I'll live to fight another day,' he said. He paused. 'But I think the least you can do is to let me buy you some lunch.' He glanced at his watch. 'It's almost midday, and I know a really great pub. I'm hungry after all that tension.'

Melody couldn't help feeling surprised at his suggestion. This man was obviously a fast worker who didn't believe in hanging around—the sort of opportunist that made her feel slightly wary. Then she bit her lip. She'd been too excited—or too nervous—to eat any breakfast at her hotel that morning, and now that she'd secured the deal her appetite was coming back to life!

'All right,' she said, after a moment. 'Why not? 'I'm Mel, by the way.'

'And I'm Adam.' He extended a tanned hand in formal greeting, and grinned in a warm, all-embracing way that had the effect of breaking down any remaining reserve Melody might have felt at accepting an invitation from a complete stranger.

Their cars were parked a little way away along the deserted road. Everyone else had obviously departed. Melody wasn't surprised to see that his was a low-slung, exotic red Porsche. Her own compact Mercedes seemed rather staid by comparison.

'We might as well go in mine,' Adam said briefly, as he flicked the automatic key to unlock his door. 'I can drop you back later.'

'Oh, no, thanks,' Melody said at once. 'I'll follow you to wherever you're taking me. I'll probably want to go on somewhere afterwards, anyway.'

She'd been taught from a very young age not to take anyone at face value, and knew better than to put herself in any kind of vulnerable position. Yet this smooth, suave, unknown male—obviously used to trading on his undoubted good-looks—had coolly invited her out to lunch and she'd agreed straight away! This was not like her, she thought, as she got into her car. But today was a pretty exceptional one, she excused herself. In fact, now that she really thought about it, she knew it was a *fantastic* day! A day to remember, to savour! Enjoy the moment, she told herself. Reality would become apparent all too soon.

Starting the engine and slipping her car into gear, she

followed the Porsche along the blissfully uncluttered roads at a much more respectable pace than she'd imagined they might. He'd seemed the type who'd take pleasure in roaring away in front of her and expect her to keep up with his dizzying assault on the numerous twists and bends they encountered. His whole persona came across as confident, self-assured—a natural leader, accustomed to success and its trappings, Melody thought, and he'd had no problem in getting her to join him for lunch today! But following him on an enjoyable run on this perfect July day had the effect of sending her spirits soaring. If only her mother, Frances, was here now, to share this special morning with her, she thought, her eyes clouding briefly.

In about fifteen minutes they arrived at an insignificant-looking wayside pub, and pulled up simultaneously in the car park at the front. Adam immediately came over and opened her door for her to get out, and Melody was conscious—not for the first time—of how he looked at her, how he was obviously scrutinising her appearance. She hoped he approved of her white designer trousers and navy and white striped shirt—an outfit she felt was simple but elegantly casual. Her long fair hair she'd tied up in a heavy knot on the top of her head—the style she always used in business. And, after all, today *had* been business—though not the sort that she was usually engaged in. Drawing her hair back formally had the effect of complementing the perfect bone structure of her heart-shaped face, her thoughtful grey-green eyes and full-lipped mouth.

Without making any comment, Adam handed her out of the car, and together they walked along the gravelled path to the entrance of the pub. The place was obviously popular, because already it was comfortably full of people. He ushered Melody to a vacant corner table by the window, and looked down at her as she took her seat.

'What are you drinking, Mel?' he asked.

'Just a sparkling water, please,' she said, and he raised his eyebrows slightly.

'No champagne…to celebrate your success today?'

She smiled up at him. 'I'll keep that for some other time,' she said.

She watched him as he went over to stand amongst the jostling crowd at the bar, easily the most noticeable person there. He was taller than anyone else, for a start, she thought, his lithe, athletic body obviously demonstrating a robust and healthy physique. Heavens above, she thought to herself crossly. The day had been enough of an explosive affair as it was…surely she wasn't being blown away by someone she'd probably never see again? Was she that fickle, that pathetic, after losing Crispin not all that long ago? Blame it on today, she excused herself. Today had a definitely weird feel about it!

Presently he came back with their drinks—her water, and a pint of lager for himself—and put a lunch menu in front of her.

'I can recommend the crab cakes,' he said, glancing down at his own copy. 'With the coast so near, the fish is fresh here daily. Or,' he added, looking across at her briefly, 'the barbecued sea bass is also very good.'

By this time Melody's mouth was watering, and she was prompt with her selection. 'I love fish cakes,' she said, 'and I don't often have the chance to eat fresh crab. So crab cakes, please, with a green salad.'

'You're obviously a woman of quick decisions,' he said. 'When I bring people here it usually takes them longer to choose what they want than it does to eat the stuff.'

He got up and went across to order at the bar, glancing back at her as she stared out of the window. This was an unusual woman, he thought. Apart from being very, very, beautiful, she was overtly well dressed, sophisticated, and clearly with a very firm head on her shoulders. The sort of female who knew exactly what she wanted in life and was determined to get it. He'd known many women in his thirty-eight years, but he had the distinct feeling that no one would ever get the better of this one in an argument! She was the kind of woman you wouldn't want to cross, but something about her—especially when he'd observed her at the auction—had excited his curiosity and made him want to find out about her. Who she was…and more importantly why she was taking possession of Gatehouse Cottage.

He returned to sit opposite her. 'So,' he said without preamble, 'you're not from around here, are you?' Well, of course she wasn't…he'd have noticed!

Melody sipped at her water. 'No. I live and work in London,' she said briefly. 'I'm here on holiday for a few weeks.'

Adam frowned. 'But…the auction,' he said slowly. 'How did you know about the cottage being for sale?'

'I was in the village looking around a few days ago and saw the sign. I went into the agent's office and made some enquiries. And…decided to go for it.' She looked up at him calmly, and he stared back at her for a second.

'Do you do that sort of thing often?' he asked. 'I mean, people usually like to buy little mementoes to bring back from a holiday, but a cottage seems rather excessive!'

Melody smiled. 'I agree,' she said. 'And I've never done such a thing in my life before… But…I was attracted to the place… It felt special as soon as I stepped inside. It felt…right, somehow,' she added guardedly.

Adam seemed lost for words suddenly, but her answer only confirmed his opinion of the woman. She knew what she wanted and was going to get it. Whatever the cost. And, talking of cost, she must have the wherewithal to do it, he thought. Not many people had that amount of money instantly at their fingertips!

'Do *you* live locally?' Melody asked, deciding that it was his turn to answer some questions.

'No. I work in Malaysia, where I obviously have to live for most of the time,' Adam said. 'But I always take a long break here, with friends, at about this time every year. Abroad is fine, but rural England is where I feel normal.'

Melody looked away for a second.

'I'm really sorry…to have beaten you at the auction this morning,' she said simply. 'I hope you'll be able to find somewhere else before too long. Not that there seemed much else on offer here… I suppose people just never want to leave the place.'

'You're not sorry at all,' he said cheerfully. 'Besides, someone has to win a battle—as you pointed out—and this time it was you. Maybe there'll be another occasion when I'll have the advantage.'

'Oh, I can't see that happening,' Melody said at once. 'I will not be purchasing another property for a very long time—if ever. A flat in London and a cottage in the country are quite enough for one person to worry about!'

Their meals arrived, and Melody couldn't wait to try the crisp, piping hot crab cakes nestling amongst just the right amount of delicious-looking dressed salad. She picked up her knife and fork and looked across at Adam.

'This all looks yummy!' she exclaimed.

He watched her for a few seconds without starting his own meal. Then, 'What do you intend doing about your living arrangements?' he asked bluntly.

'D'you mean when will I be moving in to the cottage?' Melody asked innocently, between mouthfuls. 'Oh, that's anyone's guess. The previous elderly owner had been there for some years and hadn't done much to the place—so there's obviously some work to do. Everything's still sound enough, but it'll need decorating throughout, and I shall have great fun choosing the right sort of furniture. It's going to be so wonderful to relax here whenever I can get away.' She looked across at him, popping a cherry tomato into her mouth, her eyes shining at the prospect.

'So,' Adam said slowly, 'you've bought the cottage purely as a holiday home? You never intended it to be a permanent dwelling…or maybe a home for your family to share?'

'I don't have any family,' Melody said, rather curtly. 'This is going to be just for me.'

'How often are you likely to be able to get here?' he persisted.

Melody looked away quickly. What right did this man have to interrogate her? she thought. It was none of his business.

'As often as I can,' she said firmly. 'A lot will depend on how things are at work.' She paused, before adding, 'I'm fund manager for one of the big banks,' thinking that she might as well tell him what she did, how she earned her living, before he asked.

He picked up his fork then, and began to eat slowly. Well, what else had he thought? he asked himself. This was clearly a dynamic businesswoman whose daily bread was not likely to be earned in this or any other backwater. 'You won't exactly be number one in the popularity stakes,' he said casually. 'The locals don't take too kindly to absentee property owners… people responsible for killing off villages like these. They want folk to live here and be part of the genuine life of the place—help to keep the school and the post office and the pubs going.'

Melody kept her eyes on her plate, trying not to seethe at the clearly admonishing tone in his remark. Of course she knew exactly what he was talking about. The press regularly ran features about the problem. And she reluctantly had to admit that she hadn't given herself time to really think this through—hadn't got to the point of wondering how often she'd be driving from town, or how long her visits might last. But that didn't stop her thoroughly resenting this stranger giving her a lecture!

'C'est la vie,' she said coolly.

In those few seconds the cordiality of the occasion seemed

to have vanished, and neither spoke for a while as they ate. Then she looked up. 'Let's talk about *you* and your plans,' she said, in a way she recognised as her formal business voice. 'If *you* had succeeded this morning you would obviously have had every intention of living at the cottage permanently, then? Which would have meant abandoning your job in the Far East?'

He returned her gaze, and the eyes which earlier had appeared a friendly blue-black colour now seemed to have acquired a hardened edge. 'Good heavens, no,' he replied casually. 'I can hardly abandon my job—seeing that I'm a partner in the family firm over there.' He finished his meal and put down his knife and fork. 'My father and I transferred the business from England some years ago.'

Well, well, Melody thought cynically. This man, who'd just told her off for helping to 'kill off' the village, thought nothing of taking his family firm out of the country, obviously throwing employees out of work! Talk about double standards! She couldn't let *that* pass!

'So *you* were obviously not "number one in the popularity stakes"?' she said, echoing his own words to her. 'With your ex-staff, I mean. What a miserable bombshell that must have been for them.'

Adam frowned. 'We didn't take the decision lightly,' he said slowly, throwing her a glance which held a hint of disdain at her comments. 'We were able to give them all handsome redundancy payments, and my father—who is very well known in the industry—used his influence to find places for many of the men with our competitors.' He paused. 'He is a very thoughtful man…it caused him a great deal of worry at the time.'

'Mmm,' Melody murmured enigmatically, not wanting to let him off the hook too lightly, yet knowing full well the difficult position companies like his often found themselves in. Her doctorate in Business Studies and Law, together with her masterly understanding of today's commercial world, made it difficult for her not to sympathise.

'So,' she said, as she finished her glass of water, 'if you had managed to secure Gatehouse Cottage this morning, what would *your* plans have been for taking possession?'

'Oh, I didn't have any,' he replied. 'I wasn't bidding for myself. I was there on behalf of friends of mine who have a very special reason for wanting to own it. Friends who've lived in the village all their lives and who have no intention of ever moving away,' he added significantly.

Why was she being made to feel so guilty? Melody asked herself. This morning's business transaction was legal and above board, with the best man winning! It was her good luck—and her considerable financial resources—that had made her the one to buy the cottage, yet the impression she was getting was that she had no right to own the place, and that everyone would hate her for it! This was not the way it was meant to turn out, and being with Adam Whoever-He-Was was making her feel uneasy.

She made a move to go, picking up her bag from the side of the chair.

'Thank you very much for my lunch,' she said, glancing across at him. 'I enjoyed the crab cakes enormously, and I shall come back for some more before I go home.'

He stood up then, tilting his chiselled lips in a half-smile. 'Glad you liked them,' he said. 'Um…wouldn't you like coffee before you go?'

'No, thanks. Not for me,' Melody said. 'I must get back to my hotel—I'm moving out from the Red House today—do you know it? It's very comfortable.'

'Of course I know the Red House. Everyone knows the Red House,' he said off-handedly. 'It's got a formidable reputation in the area. So why are you moving out?'

'I thought I'd come closer to the village. To my new

property,' Melody said neatly, throwing him a glance. 'I rang a
B&B that I'd noticed—there are quite a few of them to choose
from! Luckily they had a vacancy, so I'll be staying there for a
week or two.'

Adam settled the bill at the bar, and they went out into the
warm afternoon sunshine. He stood by the side of her car as
she opened the door to get in.

'Can you find your way back to the Red House from here?'
he asked. 'Or would you like me to lead the way?'

'Oh, there's no need for that—thanks anyway,' Melody said
quickly. 'I don't have any problems with route-finding, and I
was making mental notes of the direction we were going in as
we drove here.' She smiled up at him through the open window.
'And I'm used to reading road signs.'

He shrugged briefly—as if to say, *Well, I was only offering*—
then watched her reverse expertly in the confined space of the
car park and drive away with a brief wave of her hand as she went.

Adam got into his own car and waited for a moment before
switching on the engine. He felt instinctively that this was a
rather unusual woman who didn't fit in to his personal catego-
ries for the female race. He was certainly attracted to her and,
although her petite stature gave her an air of vulnerability, she
gave every impression of being someone who was well able to
look after herself. Not to mention the fact that she was clearly
a very experienced driver who had no difficulty in finding her
way around! Now, why should that disturb him in a woman?
he asked himself. Most females were rubbish at map-reading,
or at even knowing their norths from their souths! But not, apparently, this one!

He stared pensively out of the window for a second. Whether
she was brilliant behind the wheel or not wasn't particularly
relevant anyway…all he knew was that she was certainly a

very intriguing woman—at any rate, she'd intrigued *him* more than anyone had done for a very long time!

He swept out of the car park, smiling briefly to himself, painfully aware that his present, overpowering sensation was one of wanting to cover those dainty, seductive lips with his own! He snorted derisively. Fat chance of *that* ever happening! he thought.

As she made her way back to her hotel, Melody felt such a strange mix of emotions she could have screamed. She should have been thrilled and excited at her purchase that morning, and of course she *was*, yet she realised Adam did have a point about the time she'd be spending at the cottage—actually living there, and buying her bread from the little bakery, fetching her news-paper from the shop. She knew only too well that people like her were a serious irritation who did little to help the local economy.

After she'd driven for a mile or two she pulled in to the side of the road and took the local map which the hotel had given her from her handbag. Although she'd told Adam that she'd have no difficulty finding her way back to the Red House, the fact was she didn't have a clue where she was. But she hadn't wanted to extend her association with the man by accepting his offer that he should shepherd her back. Although he was, without doubt, the dishiest male she'd met in her whole life, she felt that this was not the time to prolong an unlooked-for acquaintance. At this staggeringly unexpected point in her life it would be better to be alone, to think clearly for herself.

The route they'd taken from the village to the pub was unknown to her. All these country roads looked exactly the same as one another, and her hotel was an isolated building that didn't seem to belong anywhere special. Melody sighed as she traced the minute, incomprehensible wiggles on the map with her finger. If the worst came to the worst she could always go right back to the village and set off again from there, she thought. But surely there *must* be a more direct route from where she now was to the Red House?

Feeling that she'd better go back to the pub, she turned the car around and began to drive cautiously along the empty road. Suddenly, rounding a corner, she spotted a woman cyclist ahead of her. Good, she thought. A local who would obviously know where the hotel was.

Pulling up slowly alongside, she opened the passenger window and called out.

'Hello—sorry to bother you, but I'm trying to find my way back to the Red House Hotel. Can you direct me? I'm hopelessly lost!'

The woman—dark-haired and attractive, probably in her mid-thirties, Melody assessed—had an open, friendly expression, and immediately got off her bike—an ancient vehicle with a basket on the front in which were several boxes of eggs. She looked in at Melody.

'I'm afraid you're a bit off-course,' she said, frowning slightly and shielding her eyes from the sun for a second. 'Look, your best bet is to go to the crossroads a mile up the road in front of us, take the left turn, then go on until you come to the smallholding on the right. You can't miss it. There are always two white horses in the field in front. Turn down that road, go on for another mile or so, then the road sort of doubles back on itself before you must take the next right turn. The Red House is there, more or less in front of you. Or should be if *I've* got it right!' the woman said, laughing.

Melody repeated the instructions slowly, hoping she'd find the place before nightfall. The woman's last remark didn't sound particularly convincing! Especially with the added, 'Good Luck!' that she heard as she drove away.

Anyway, she thought, her present confusion would do

nothing to spoil the excitement of the day. Soon, *soon*—when the necessary formalities had been completed—she would be given the keys to her cottage and would be able to revel in really looking around. She would go upstairs and open the door to the little bedroom at the back. The room in which she'd been born.

## CHAPTER TWO

MUCH later in the afternoon, Melody drove up the winding drive that led to the B&B called Poplars, a large Victorian building, and followed the sign to the visitors' car park.

She got out of the car and went towards the large front entrance door. As she entered, a stocky, bearded man came through to greet her, two chocolate Labrador dogs padding behind him. He grinned cheerfully.

'Ah—Mrs Forester? You booked by phone?'

Melody smiled back. 'Yes, that's right.'

He held out a work-roughened hand. 'I'm Callum Brown. I own this place with my wife Fee—or rather, it owns us! I saw you come up the drive, and as you're our last guest due to check in today, I gathered it must be you. Now—shall we fetch your things?'

Together they went across to the car park, the dogs trotting obediently behind Callum. Melody bent to pat them. 'I love dogs,' she said. 'What are they called?'

'Tam and Millie,' Callum said, glancing down at them fondly.

They went back inside, and Melody stood for a few moments at the desk in the hall to sign in.

'Your room is number three, on the second floor,' Callum said. 'I'm afraid we don't run to a lift, so I'll take your cases for you.'

'No need for that, Callum. I'll do the honours. It'll be a pleasure.'

Melody swung around in amazement. She'd recognised the voice straight away, and now found herself staring once more at the man who'd paid for her lunch.

'What…what are *you* doing here? I mean…' she began rather stupidly.

'Staying with friends—as I told you I was,' he replied easily. 'But I didn't realise that Poplars was where you'd transferred to. Anyway,' he added, 'let me make myself useful.' He took her room key from Callum and picked up her cases.

'D'you two know each other, then?' Callum asked curiously.

'Yes, we do. We met at the auction this morning,' Adam said. He paused, then, 'Let me introduce you properly. Mel is the new owner of Gatehouse Cottage, Callum.'

'Well…congratulations,' Callum said slowly. 'You've bought a very desirable property.'

Just then the cyclist whom Melody had spoken to earlier breezed into the hall.

'Oh, *hello* again!' the woman said to Melody, and Melody's heart sank. She hoped that nothing would be said about their afternoon encounter—but no such luck. 'You must be Mrs Forester,' the woman went on. 'The guest who managed to book our last room? I'm *so* glad that you obviously found your way back to the Red House! It was lucky that I was just on my way home after collecting the eggs from the farm.' She turned to the men. 'Mrs Forester got herself *hopelessly* lost this afternoon, trying to get back to her hotel, and she took a surprising risk asking *me* for directions! I'm saying that before either of *you* two do,' she added.

She smiled at Melody, whose face had slowly turned crimson as the woman was speaking. Why did it have to be this particular person she'd asked, a friend of Adam's? What an opportunity for him to gloat, she thought.

'Yes…I did find it, thanks,' she murmured, looking away quickly.

Without saying anything further, Adam led the way along the hall and up two narrow flights of stairs. He glanced back at her over his shoulder. 'I didn't realise you were married,' he said bluntly.

'I'm not,' she retorted.

After that there was silence, then he said casually, 'You'll like it here. Callum and Fee are wonderful people. This place is almost always full—though they always keep a room for me at this time of year.'

'You must be a very special friend,' Melody said flatly.

'Oh, we've all known each other for yonks,' he replied, stopping outside her room and inserting the key.

Melody knew at once that she was going to be happy here. As she'd expected, it was furnished in a cosy way, with a large double bed, comfortable furniture and a very small *en suite* shower room in the corner—obviously a desirable extra which had been recently added on.

'A lot of work's been going on here,' she observed, dropping her handbag onto the bed.

Adam had put down her cases and was standing at the window, looking out. 'They've made a huge difference to the place,' he said. 'Callum does all the renovations himself, and Fee keeps the domestic side going.'

'But she must have help, surely?' Melody said.

'Oh, a girl comes in each morning to help with the break-fasts, and another one arrives later to help with the laundry and cleaning.' He paused. 'And Callum's very hands-on…they're a fantastic team. And still very much in love even after ten years of marriage,' he added, a trifle obliquely.

Melody looked at him quickly, wondering whether he was or ever had been married. There'd been a distinctly cynical ring to his remark, she thought. 'How long have they owned the place, then?' she asked.

'Thirteen years,' Adam said. He turned to look out of the window again. 'They were born in the village, and never want to leave the area.'

The significance of his words wasn't lost on Melody. She was being got at again, she thought irritably. She raised her chin defiantly. It simply was not possible for everyone in the world to live and work in the place of their birth, to stay in one place and do the right thing—much as she acknowledged that the thought of really belonging here, living here all the time, provoked a definite feeling of envy! Her job at the bank was fluid, high-powered and fast moving. At twenty-eight, she was one of the youngest members of staff to hold the position she did, and she was *proud* of her progress—if only for her mother's sake.

She was very well aware how vital it was—especially for a woman—to study and work hard, to dedicate yourself to what you were good at. Success brought not only prosperity, but security and peace of mind. You'd never need to rely on anyone else, ever. No, whatever this man thought of her motives, she thought, there was no way she could ever live here permanently. The only option was for this to be her bolthole as often as she could get away. Gatehouse Cottage was hers, the ideal solution for her particular way of life, and if Adam disapproved—tough! Anyway, wasn't it time for him to make himself scarce and give her some peace to shower and change? she thought.

As if on cue, he went towards the door. 'The couple of pubs in the village do pretty good food,' he said casually. 'Especially the Rose & Crown.' He paused. 'If you'd like me to come with you—as this is your first evening here—I'd be very happy to oblige.'

'Oh—that's okay, thanks,' Melody said quickly. How *embarrassing*! Just because they'd met already, there was no need for him to feel responsible for her, she thought. 'After that lovely lunch I shan't need to eat until later on. In any case,' she added, 'I might go for a walk first, to get an appetite.'

Tilting his head in acknowledgement of her remark, he left the room, and Melody closed the door behind him thankfully. The man's presence unnerved her, she thought—but why? Was it just because she had bought the cottage? Or because he'd made it clear what he thought of holiday ownership? Or was it because he had managed to awaken feelings in her that she was absolutely determined would never affect her life ever again? Her work was her soul mate now, and always would be. Work absorbed the mind totally, and carried no risk of hurting her, of wounding her heart. It was a totally abstract thing that demanded only cold dedication. Work didn't have feelings.

Shaking off all these somewhat intense thoughts, she unpacked her cases, grateful for the huge wardrobe complete with wooden hangers, and then had a long, hot shower, shampooing her hair vigorously. She hoped that by the time she was ready to go back downstairs no one would be about and she could slip out unobserved. She needed to be by herself and take stock of her situation. Perhaps she'd go down to Gatehouse Cottage later and have a really good look at the garden. It had obviously been neglected lately, she realised, but she'd seen the potential at a glance. The gooseberry bushes were heavy with fruit, and the ripening apples and pears on the trees indicated a busy harvesting time later on. Melody hugged herself in renewed excitement.

It was a warm, sultry evening, and she decided to wear a cream, low-necked blouse and a long multi-coloured ethnic cotton skirt. She dried and brushed out her hair, tying it back in a long ponytail, and slipped her feet into open-toed silver sandals.

She went cautiously downstairs. It was quiet and deserted, with a delicious smell of cooking reaching her nostrils—

making her realise that, after all, she was hungry enough to find the pub which Adam had talked about sooner rather than later.

She was just letting herself out of the building when a door in the hallway opened and Fee appeared, her cheeks flushed.

'Oh, there you are, Mrs Forester… We were wondering whether you'd like to have supper with us this evening.' she said 'You'd be more than welcome.'

Melody was taken aback at the suggestion, but managed to say quickly, 'Oh—please call me Mel…all my friends do. And I appreciate the offer, but really I'd hate to intrude. I'm sure you're looking forward to the end of the day and some time to yourself.'

'You wouldn't be intruding,' Fee said. 'Adam's been telling us a little bit about you, and we realise you're a complete stranger here.' She paused. 'Actually, it'd be good to have another woman on the scene to chat to for once, instead of having to listen to Callum and Adam going on and on about boring men things.' She smiled. 'To have a nice gossip! And, since you'll be taking possession of the cottage, we could fill you in on how everything ticks in the village. I've roasted a wonderful piece of lamb,' she added. 'Because if I dish up one more salad meal I'll have a mutiny on my hands! What's the matter with men and salad?' she said.

She nodded her head in the direction from which male voices could be heard, and Melody found herself unable to resist the genuine invitation she'd been offered.

'Well—if you're absolutely sure,' she began hesitantly.

'Wonderful!' Fee said. 'Come on through. It'll be ready in about twenty minutes. Just time for an appetiser!'

Although she'd really have preferred to do her own thing tonight—mainly because she didn't particularly want to spend more time in Adam's company—Melody knew it would have been churlish to refuse Fee's suggestion. Besides, the smell of roasting meat was extremely tantalising!

She followed the other woman along a narrow passageway that led to the kitchen, where Adam was already sitting comfortably with his long legs stretched out in front of him, while Callum was busy uncorking a bottle of wine. Both men looked up as they came in, and Adam got slowly to his feet.

'Ah, good,' Callum said easily. 'I want your opinion on this wine, Mrs Forester. I bottled it two years ago, and we haven't tried it yet.'

'Look—*please* call me Mel,' Melody begged. 'Do you make your own wine, as well as everything else you do?' she added, impressed. She bent to smooth the glossy heads of the dogs, who were fast asleep sprawled in front of the Aga.

Callum grinned. 'Oh, my wife beats me about the head if she finds me shirking,' he said. 'And we can't let all the plums and damsons go to waste.' He eased the cork out gently. 'Besides, what we don't keep for ourselves we sell off at the village fête. It disappears even quicker than Fee's fruitcakes!' He threw her a quizzical glance. 'I don't expect you're used to the sort of daft things we get up to,' he said. 'Like pig roasts and skittle championships, and tugs of war at the annual Harvest Fair. Not your usual scene, from what Adam has been telling us. Still, I'm sure you'll get used to it, in your own time.'

Melody looked away. What exactly had Adam been saying about her? she wondered. That she was never likely to fit in here, never be 'one of them'? She began to feel uneasy.

Adam pulled out a chair for her to sit, glancing down at her, admiring her casual, summery appearance, and the feminine hairstyle which seemed to add something to the package, he thought. Or maybe it took something away—whatever it was, it held more allure for him than the rather sharp-edged look he'd observed that morning.

Callum took a sip of his wine. 'Mmm,' he said, rolling his tongue around his mouth in extravagant appreciation. 'I think you're all going to approve of this. How shall we describe it? Fruity, nutty, saucy, suggestive…?'

'Shut up, Callum,' Fee said. 'Give us all a glass, for goodness' sake. Why do we have to go through this ridiculous rigmarole every time you open a fresh bottle? Just let's drink it, then can you come and carve the meat, please?'

Melody took a few tentative sips of the wine and realised that it was the most delicious she'd tasted in a long time. 'This is fantastic, Callum! It beats champagne by a mile,' she added, taking another generous mouthful.

'Oh, I'm afraid we don't have much experience of drinking champagne,' Callum said easily. 'Though I think we had sparkling wine at our wedding, didn't we, Fee?'

Melody bit her lip, feeling her colour rise. She hadn't meant to give the impression that she was a connoisseur—though it was certainly true that she was offered plenty of expensive wines in her career. What sort of impression was she giving these people? Especially after her extravagant purchase that morning, she thought desperately.

The episode passed as Callum got to work with the carving knife, while Fee put bowls of vegetables and a large plate of crisp brown roast potatoes in front of them. Adam sat down next to Melody, and conversation paused significantly while they all helped themselves to the mouthwatering food. And although Melody felt uneasy, and somewhat out of place sitting here with these complete strangers, she couldn't help enjoying the feeling of being made welcome. And it wasn't long before the wine kicked in, making her feel warm, tingly and relaxed.

It was nearly ten o'clock before she decided to call it a day, and she realised how good it had felt to be with people who were not involved with work. Even though the staff often called in at a wine bar on the way home, or had the occasional meal together, it was always a case of talking shop. This had been different.

After thanking her hosts profusely, she stood for a moment outside, breathing in the soft evening air, and as it was still not quite dark she decided to go for a short stroll. This was the sort of thing you could do in a quiet retreat like this, she thought, as she walked noiselessly down the drive—there was no sense of danger lurking around every corner, no dark-hooded yobs hanging about, and the only sounds were the occasional baaing of a sheep or the hoot of a night owl.

She wandered along the few hundred yards towards Gatehouse Cottage. Not that she would be actually given the keys until the day after tomorrow, when all the financial arrangements had been completed—but it would be good to just stand in her very own front garden and plan the future. And not only that, she realised. The future was one consideration, but she also wanted to visit the past—a past which she had not seen fit to talk about to the others. It was not important to anyone but her, after all.

It took only three or four minutes to get to the cottage, and she paused before silently opening the small wooden gate and going up the path.

She peeped in through one of the windows—which was in need of a good scrub, she noticed—and stared in at the sitting room. She couldn't see much in this light, but, cupping her hands around her eyes, she could just make out its shape, and the open grate in the corner. She'd have a log fire there one day, she promised herself. On a grey morning that room would spring to flaming life.

Suddenly something wet touched her ankle, followed by a snuffling sound, and Melody jumped, letting out a faint cry of alarm. She sprang back and turned quickly to see one of the Labradors gazing back at her solemnly. Then Adam's voice sounded through the darkness.

'I knew I'd find you here,' he said quietly. He paused. 'I volunteered to give the dogs their nightly stroll,' he went on. 'Tam didn't frighten you, did he?'

'No, of course not!' Melody lied. She swallowed nervously. 'My instinctive thought was that it might have been a fox…or a badger…'

'Well, would that have worried you?' he asked casually.

'No…it was just…I didn't expect to have company—of any sort,' she said.

Melody's instinctive sense of irritation at being followed had been replaced almost at once by one of mild relief at not being down here alone, and she bent quickly to pat the animals. Although she'd convinced herself that this quiet rural paradise was her dream, in fact she felt slightly wary at just how solitary it was. The silence was deafening, and with no street lights at this point the darkness was very dark indeed. She'd already made a mental note to have a security light put over the front door.

After a moment, she said casually, 'I didn't think I'd be able to get to sleep very easily—especially after that rhubarb crumble and clotted cream,' she added, as she came to stand next to him. 'So I thought a walk seemed sensible.'

'Well, you haven't had much of one,' he said. 'From Poplars to here, I mean.' He paused. 'I could take you for a slightly longer one, if you like…' He glanced down at her feet. 'Will you be able to walk in those sandals?'

'Of course I can. As long as we aren't going to cross a river.'

'No rivers,' he replied shortly. 'Just half a meadow and a couple of small copses. It's a favourite track behind Poplars and back again. The dogs will lead the way.'

They fell into step, and Melody was struck again at how this was such a long way from her flat in a busy street where the sound of traffic never stopped. She looked up at Adam. 'I really can't believe my luck,' she said simply. 'Although if you'd bid one more time I'd have stopped.'

He waited before answering. 'Do you mean that? Was I that close?'

'Oh, yes,' Melody said at once. 'It was touch and go—but you stopped at just the right moment!' There was a short silence, then, 'Anyway,' she went on happily, 'you said you didn't want the cottage for yourself, didn't you? After you'd told me that I didn't feel so bad about it! But I hope the friend who was interested will find something else soon.'

'Oh, it's too late now,' Adam said briefly.

He glanced down at her, and by now Melody had grown accustomed to the light, so she could make out his features and rather dark expression. 'Too late? What do you mean?'

He waited before going on. 'I was bidding for Callum and Fee,' he said. 'They really wanted to have the cottage—it's been their ambition for years. Poplars and the Gatehouse were originally linked—as you'll have noted from the agent's blurb—and it was their aim to own both so that one day, when they retire, the cottage would be their family home. The hard-earned profit they've made on the guesthouse allowed them to go for it.'

Melody swallowed. Now she felt worse than ever! She'd unwittingly thwarted the plans of that lovely local couple…and not a word had been said about it during the meal. Well, what was there to say? she thought. What could they have said? They'd lost the chance, and business was a chancy thing—everyone knew that.

'But…but…they wouldn't have lived in the cottage, would they? Not while they were running Poplars?' Melody said, trying to quell her feelings of disquiet.

'No. Not yet. But in the meantime they intended renting it on a long-term lease to any local couple who needed a place to live. We're so desperately short of affordable housing for the younger generation and they're all moving away. In another ten or fifteen years the village will just be full of older people and tourists. And part-time owners like yourself.'

For once, Melody felt lost for words. She could see the point he was making—in no uncertain terms! But she could see her own, too. It had seemed so right that the place was for sale at the very time she was in the area on holiday. Was fate trying to tell her something, giving her the chance to find out what she'd always wanted to know? A chance to unwrap something of herself that had lain hidden for so long?

Neither spoke for the next few moments as they trod easily over the soft, dry grass of the meadow. Then Melody said, 'I'm amazed that I was invited to share that fantastic meal…to be their guest. They must hate me—or at least bitterly resent me,' she added.

'Oh, Callum and Fee aren't like that,' Adam said at once. 'They don't bear grudges.' He shrugged. 'They knew all along that it was more than probable that someone else would beat them. They've accepted it gracefully.'

He didn't look at her as he spoke, nor mention the fact that it had been his suggestion that she should be included in their supper arrangements. For one thing, he'd thought it would be useful to have some idea what this woman's plans were for when she came to the village, and for another—and a more pressing one—he wanted to know what she was *really* like. He readily admitted that she fascinated him, and not only because of her outward appearance. There was something about her, some inner thing that intrigued him. And if he wanted to get to know her, there was no time like the present!

'Callum and Fee…they don't have children?' she asked— and the question made Melody think briefly of her own life plan. She and Crispin had met at work, and both had been equally ambitious. She'd had vague notions of motherhood, maybe in ten years' time, but their careers had always taken first place. A family had definitely been a back burner issue.

'No,' Adam replied shortly, in answer to her question. 'They don't.'

They walked on slowly, neither wanting the evening to end, because it was one of those rare warm summer nights with hardly any breeze, and a pale moon to give them just enough light to see their way.

'This is so heavenly,' Melody murmured. 'Like a dream.'

'What happened to your marriage?' Adam said suddenly, without the slightest embarrassment at asking the question.

'My husband—Crispin—was killed in a climbing accident last year in the Himalayas,' Melody said quietly.

Adam looked at her sharply. 'Oh—I'm sorry—really. I shouldn't have asked,' he said.

'We'd been married for just a few months.'

'That was bad. I'm sorry,' he repeated.

She looked so small and defenceless as he glanced down at her that for a mad moment he wanted to pull her towards him and hold her tightly. But he resisted the temptation.

'And you?' she enquired. 'You're not married?'

'No, thanks,' he said cheerfully.

Well, Melody thought, that was a fairly unequivocal reply! Anyway, something about this man told her he wasn't the marrying kind. He'd be the sort who enjoyed women's company for the obvious reason, but would never be happy to settle down, commit to one person. She frowned to herself, not knowing what had given her that impression. But something about his attitude made her think that he was of a restless nature.

Suddenly she said, 'I did get lost this afternoon—trying to find my way to the Red House—as Fee informed everyone.'

He smiled faintly in the darkness. 'We all get lost sometimes,' he said.

'You knew I'd have difficulty, didn't you?'

'Yes. Especially as you roared off in the wrong direction,'

he replied. 'But I knew you'd succeed eventually. And everyone speaks English here!'

Their walk came to an end, and they let themselves in quietly.

'For your future reference,' Adam said softly, 'they lock up at midnight.'

'I'll remember,' Melody said. She turned to go towards the stairs. 'Thanks for the stroll, Adam. I'm sure I'll be repeating that many times.'

'I'm sure you will,' he murmured. Then, 'D'you think you can find your way to your room?' he enquired innocently.

Melody smiled ruefully. 'I deserved that,' she said. 'Goodnight.'

'Goodnight, Mel.'

Melody undressed quickly, washing and cleaning her teeth rapidly, before pulling back the duvet and collapsing into the feather-soft bed. It was heaven to lie down, and she was exhausted. What a day! Her head was so packed with thoughts and emotions that it felt as if thousands of insects were racing around, trying to find space. Almost at once her eyelids began to droop, and in her semi-doze Adam's handsome features, with the stern, uncompromising mouth, loomed large. She didn't know what to make of him, she thought. He didn't like *her* much; she was certain of that. Although he was perfectly polite—even charming at certain moments—there was a coolness between them which she'd felt from the first moment.

Of course he was cross that she'd upset his friends' plans…but what about *her* plans? This village was where she'd started life, and Poplars had been her mother Frances's sole means of employment until she'd had Melody at the age of forty, when she'd promptly moved with her newborn child to the east end of London to live with a cousin. Melody had been twenty-two, in the middle of her Finals at university, when

Frances had died suddenly. And in all those years Frances had never revealed who the father of her child was—had been so secretive about that part of her life that discussion on the matter had become almost a taboo subject. All she would ever tell her daughter was that she had loved deeply, only the once, and that certain things could not be spoken of, that some words were better left unsaid.

Melody had had to be content with that. But somewhere in this village there was a living part of her, part of her mother and the father she would never know, and somehow she knew that just by being here, breathing this air, she was completing her family circle so that she almost felt as if she was being embraced. So didn't *she*, Melody, have her own very personal reasons for wanting to live here again, even on a part-time basis? Wasn't she entitled to return to the family nest, to the village where her mother, too, had been born? How much more right did anyone need to belong here?

She turned over, flinging her arm across the pillow.

She opened her eyes and stared around the room for a moment. Her mother must have cleaned this place hundreds of times when she was housekeeper here, she thought. Servicing all these rooms and cooking for the Carlisle family, who'd owned Poplars for three generations, must have been desperately hard work. Melody's eyes misted for a moment, thinking of Frances's determination that her daughter should be qualified and independent. That education was the way up and the way out. So whatever life threw at her, her girl would always be able to stand on her own feet and follow her dreams. And that was what she was doing now!

In his own room on the ground floor, Adam slumped in an armchair by the window, feeling wide awake and knowing that he wasn't likely to get to sleep easily. He knew he was still upset at letting the cottage slip through his fingers—and especially upset to lose it to a woman—a stranger to the village—who'd bought the place on a whim.

He clicked his tongue in annoyance at the thought that if he'd bid just once more he'd have won. But he'd already exceeded the stake he'd put in of his own money, to help his friends out, and hadn't wanted to undermine Callum's confidence by upping and upping the price unreasonably. Callum was such a straightforward, honest man, and he and Fee had already repaid every penny that Adam had lent them way back, when they'd first purchased Poplars. They'd worked so incredibly hard to be able to do that. Now this woman had sauntered in and stolen the cottage from under their noses.

After a few moments, his mind took another turn. He had to admit that Mel seemed much nicer than she'd appeared at first…not so damned sure of herself. His lip curled faintly. She'd jumped nearly a foot into the air when Tam had licked her leg, and he'd sensed her edginess a mile off! He paused in his thoughts. It must have been a terrible blow to be widowed so soon after her marriage—though she obviously had no financial worries, he mused. His eyes narrowed briefly. Maybe all was not lost, after all…

Was it just possible that he might be able to change the course of things, make her change her mind and sell it to his friends after all? It was a long shot—he knew that—but it was worth a try. Another place would come up sooner or later, if buying a country retreat was really what she wanted. He stood up restlessly. She was going to be here for a few weeks yet, so she'd said. That should be long enough for him, Adam Carlisle, to demonstrate his masculine powers of persuasion. But he'd have to be clever about it. This woman was worldly-wise, unlikely to be a push-over, in any circumstances—and she was intelligent and perceptive. She'd spot his motives a mile off if he went blundering in. No—softly, softly, with a dose of gentle cunning, *might* work. He unbuttoned his shirt, shrugging it off. Something told him he was going to enjoy this!

# CHAPTER THREE

Two days later Melody stood once more outside her cottage, this time with a set of keys in her hand. Everything had been signed, sealed and delivered, and now the only person who had a legal right to enter the place was her! Melody Forester!

She waited a moment before opening the door, realising for the first time just what lay ahead of her. Before she was due to return to London in a couple of weeks there was a lot of work to be done! But she'd get things moving straight away, she thought decisively. First of all she'd hire someone to help her clean the place right through, and then she'd go shopping for curtains and floor coverings. The cottage was absolutely devoid of anything, except some ancient lino in the kitchen, so at least she had a clean sheet and could start from scratch. Of course she couldn't do everything at once, but she'd make a jolly good start, and then focus her mind on the kind of furniture she wanted. It would be simple, but comfortable.

She smiled to herself. She was supposed to be here on holiday, to rest and recharge her batteries after the heavy but very successful year which her team had had—and here she was, giving herself another set of problems with decisions to be made. Holiday? What holiday!

She unlocked the front door and stepped into a small hallway which led almost at once into the sitting room—which had windows at either end, making it light and airy. She stood quite still for a moment. In a strange way she almost expected her mother to appear, for this had been Frances's home for more than twenty years—all the time she'd been employed at Poplars—and in spite of the total nakedness of the place, the atmosphere felt warm and welcoming to Melody. She felt oddly connected here. It felt like home, and that was what she would make it. Even if Adam Wotsisname didn't approve, she'd come here time and time again—make it a home from home!

She bit her lip thoughtfully. She hadn't seen Adam since that first evening—for which she was thankful. She didn't want any hindrances, any bothersome ties here, and something about him suggested that he could be somewhat over-helpful if she gave him the slightest encouragement. Then she felt guilty—what had he done except buy her lunch and take her for a moonlit walk? In his way, he was sort of charming—and annoyingly handsome, it had to be admitted—but his attitude had rankled from the start. He patently considered her an outsider, and had no problem declaring the fact.

There was only one other room downstairs. It was small, but would be useful as a study if she needed one—or it could even be used as an occasional third bedroom. She didn't doubt that she'd have plenty of takers among her colleagues for the chance of a short holiday here now and then!

With her feet echoing on the wooden floors, she went up the narrow stairway and into the back bedroom where, apparently, she'd first seen the light of day. From its window she not only had a full view of her garden, but in the near distance over the tops of the trees she could just see the roof of Poplars. She stood quite still for a moment, a frown crossing her features. Why *was* it that her mother had never wanted to come back to the area—even for a short visit?

Melody had been told so much about the way of life in the village—the wonderful walks and peaceful atmosphere which Frances had loved—yet her mother had always made some excuse or other not to return. No—it had been beyond excuses. It had been a firm decision that that part of her life was over. For ever.

Melody shrugged, kneeling forward on the shabby cushioned window seat as she continued to gaze at the scene below. Suddenly there was a light tap on her front door, and Adam's voice calling from below halted her in her reverie. She tutted to herself—he hadn't wasted any time, she thought. She'd only taken possession of the cottage half an hour ago!

She heard him run swiftly up the stairs, his strong footsteps echoing through the place, and he came straight in to stand next to her. She turned to look up at him, trying to look pleased at his unexpected entrance. He was wearing jeans and a fine grey T-shirt, and his dark hair shone with healthy vigour…though he did tend to wear it rather long. Not that it didn't suit his persona, she admitted—it was just that the men she usually mixed with all seemed to favour neat and formal hairstyles.

He was holding a huge bouquet of roses and lilies, and he thrust them forward. 'Morning, Mel,' he said easily, smiling down at her. 'Just a small welcome gift for your first day.'

Melody was genuinely touched. 'Oh…how lovely! And how unexpected!' She took the bouquet from him, examining it appreciatively. 'You must have known that these are my all-time favourites! But—*thank* you…you shouldn't have!'

'Oh, I think I should,' he said, going over to the window, his hands in his pockets. 'Buying houses isn't an everyday occurrence, is it? At least, not for most people,' he added. 'I've brought a vase down from Poplars, by the way.'

'Yes…I've just been thinking about all the stuff I'm going to have to buy,' Melody said. 'I hadn't got around to the question of vases yet! But I shall certainly need some, because flowers always light up a house, don't they?'

He glanced down at her, thinking how exquisite she looked in a fresh, simple green cotton sundress which showed off the lightly tanned, smooth skin of her neck and shoulders to perfection. Her long pale hair was pulled back casually and held with a tortoiseshell clip. He'd noticed at their first meeting that she wore very little make-up, but what she did use certainly suited her, because from her appearance she might have stepped from the pages of a glossy magazine. This place didn't need flowers to light it up, he thought. She did that all by herself!

He pulled his thoughts up sharply. He didn't want to admire this woman to the point where he started to feel anything for her, he told himself. If it hadn't been for her, the cottage's ownership would have been in very different hands, and it still peeved him beyond words that he hadn't gone the extra mile. But how *could* he have known that he was so close? He'd only seen her, the other bidder, from the back during the auction, but there'd been something about the way she'd sat there that morning—the angle of her head, the slim, determined hand that had kept raising her card—depicting a businesswoman who was used to getting what she wanted.

He turned away briefly. What was done was done—for the moment. He knew it was a long shot, but he did have a little time to perhaps change things, to make her see just what she had taken on and maybe convince her that this wasn't what she really wanted. That it could become more of a burden than a bonus if it turned out that she simply did not have enough time away from her London life and job to justify the financial outlay and upkeep. He also felt instinctively that a town was where she fitted in—where everything you needed was on tap at all hours of the day. In this village tomorrow was always deemed soon enough for most people!

Allowing her to go first, they went downstairs, and Melody turned on the kitchen tap and filled the large glass jug which Adam had brought with him. Pausing for a moment, she said lightly, 'I really don't know where to start. I mean…this kitchen could do with some work, though it seems to have been refitted at some point in the past.' She looked around her doubtfully, then opened the fridge door and peered inside. 'This is clean enough—and I suppose I won't need anything any bigger.' She stood back. 'But there's no washing machine, and I'll certainly need one of those…'

'The last owner died,' Adam said matter-of-factly. 'That's why the place came on the market. And I think the washing machine was in a bad way, so it was chucked.'

'I wonder if there's room for a dishwasher—' Melody began, and he interrupted.

'Oh, I don't think this kitchen has ever sported one of those. I'm afraid you'll have to do everything by hand, Mel!'

Melody said nothing as they wandered into the sitting room, where the sun was streaming in through the windows, lighting up all the dusty corners.

'What are those two boxes on the floor doing there?' Melody said, frowning.

'Oh, I brought them with me—for us to sit down on,' Adam said, promptly kicking one to one side and taking up position. 'It's quite comfy, actually—who needs expensive chairs? Now, then—' he rubbed his hands together briskly '—I've come to help!'

Melody looked at him, a faint feeling of hopelessness sweeping over her. This man was here to stay! Her worst fears were being realised! She was not going to be allowed to be anonymous, to be by herself and work things out quietly and in her own time.

She placed the flowers carefully on the windowsill, and turned to look down at him.

'I really don't want to take up your time, Adam, or for you to use up your holiday on my behalf,' she said evenly. 'I'm sure you've other far more interesting things to think about than me and my cottage.'

'Oh, not true,' he said at once. 'As a matter of fact, I've already been here a number of weeks, and I was beginning to get quite bored. Your current project might prove to be an interesting diversion for me—and, well, you know, a pair of brawny arms can be useful at times.'

He looked pointedly at her own slender frame in a way which made Melody's colour rise, and she shrugged resignedly. The fact was that being here now, in the revealing light of day, had made her feel less sure of herself. When they'd bought and furnished their flat in London, Crispin had been there, and they'd worked as a team and had lots of interested friends all helping out. But now she was here, alone, in virtually unknown territory—even though her mother had spoken many thousands of words about the place, which had made it *seem* familiar.

Melody's earlier euphoria was threatening to give way to a feeling of doubt. Had purchasing the cottage been something that she was going to regret? she wondered. Then she scolded herself! What was the matter with her? This wasn't like her. Of *course* she'd cope alone—hadn't her mother had to do that, all her life?

'I vote that we first of all go to the Rose & Crown for coffee,' Adam said brightly, 'and then decide on a plan of action.'

'It can't be that time already, surely?' Melody said, glancing at her watch. 'Anyway, Fee's breakfasts are so generous, coffee will seem an unnecessary indulgence.'

She couldn't remember the last time she'd enjoyed lazily eating bacon, eggs, sausages and mushrooms, followed by lovely warm, crunchy toast and fresh farmhouse butter. Not to mention home-made marmalade!

'Well, holidays are a time for indulging ourselves,' Adam said firmly.

Melody looked at him shrewdly. There was a distinct change in his attitude from when they'd first met, she thought—the animosity he'd demonstrated seemed to have disappeared. Her eyes narrowed briefly. If he thought that he'd met someone who'd be good for a holiday fling, he was going to be disappointed. She was not on the market for such things, thanks very much.

Patting the other box for her to sit down, Adam leaned back nonchalantly. 'See—this feels cosy already,' he said, his eyes twinkling mischievously.

'Um, well…not as cosy as it *will* do—in time,' Melody retorted as she sat down as well.

'Talking of which,' he went on, 'how much time *do* you have?'

'Just under two weeks—' she began, and he cut in.

'Your employers are very generous,' he said. 'From what you've told me, you'll have had about six weeks off, won't you? Do *all* the staff enjoy such annual freedom?'

'Some do—sometimes,' she replied shortly. 'We've had an exceptionally tough time this last year. We—me and the rest of the team—often don't leave the office until ten o'clock or after, and we always start early. They are very long days,' she added, trying to hide the irritation she felt at having to defend herself. What did *he* know?

'Mmm… You're a fund manager, you said?' he went on. 'It must be fun, playing around with other people's money.' He'd only made the remark to annoy her. He realised only too well what a highly skilled and specialised job it was.

'Oh, it's great fun. A real laugh,' Melody said dryly. 'We all sit there, playing Monopoly with millions and millions of pounds which don't belong to us.' She paused. 'For your information, we spend hundreds of hours researching the companies we invest in on behalf of others, going over and over it until we're satisfied. Being in charge of pension schemes, where we're fully aware how we affect people's future well-being, is a nail-biting process which is taken very seriously.' Her eyes flashed as she spoke, as she relived just how much effort everyone had put in during the year to keep pace with the country's fluctuating economy and prospects.

After a few moments she calmed down. He'd made a flippant remark which she'd taken too seriously, she reasoned. She had the distinct impression that he'd only said it to get her going—and she'd taken the bait!

Adam had been watching her closely as she'd been speaking. 'Do you like what you do? Do you enjoy it?' he asked casually.

'Yes, of course! I wouldn't do it otherwise. I can't see myself doing anything else, ever.'

Well, he'd known she was a career woman. She was not going to tear herself away and come all the way down here just for a few days now and then. It was a total waste for her to own this cottage, he thought. It was like a spoilt child, seeing something in a shop window that he thought he wanted but which would never leave the toy cupboard.

'Anyway,' she said, 'I don't want to think about work—there are other things on my mind! I need to hire someone to clean the cottage from top to bottom. I expect there are locals who might be glad of some work?'

'Oh, don't count on that,' he said bluntly. 'Casual labour isn't that easy to come by—just ask Fee! All the guesthouses use up most of what's on offer.' He paused. 'And I'm afraid we don't run to agencies here, to cope with such demands.' He grinned. 'I'd hazard a guess that it's going to be just you and me, Mel!' Looking at her soft hands and beautifully manicured nails, he smiled inwardly. She might be a whiz-kid at what she did for a living, but he somehow couldn't imagine the woman down on her knees with a scrubbing brush!

Melody shrugged. 'Well, in that case the first thing will be to buy cleaning materials,' she said, fielding his remark briskly. She knew very well what he was thinking: that she wasn't used to domestic labour. Well, he'd got another thing wrong, she thought. Even though her mother had always put education at the top of the list for her daughter, Frances had also encouraged Melody to help with everything in the house—and she had. And when Frances had been unwell, which had been the case often in the years before the woman's untimely death six years ago, Melody had taken over. Shopping, cooking a nourishing meal and baking a cake were no problem!

'And what about you and *your* extended holiday?' Melody asked suddenly. 'I suppose being the privileged son in a family business means you have all the perks—which obviously means lots of time off. I wonder what the other staff think of that!'

'Oh, the staff don't have any problems with that,' he said, unperturbed at her remarks. 'In fact, they are extremely happy with their lot. They've never had it so good, and they're grateful.'

Suddenly a light footstep outside heralded Fee's appearance, and she popped her head in through the open door, beaming at Melody.

'I just had to call by and say welcome to our new neighbour,' she said, and Melody was struck by Fee's kind enthusiasm—which was more than generous in view of the circumstances.

She came in and looked around her, and Adam immediately stood up.

'Come and sit down on this lovely upholstered seat, Fee,' he said jovially. 'Not quite up to modern standards, but needs must.' He pulled the woman gently towards him on to the box he'd been sitting on, and just then his mobile rang. He wandered outside to answer it. Fee looked across at Melody.

'You must be thrilled, Mel,' she said simply. 'This is going to be such a lovely change from your home in London.'

'Yes, of course…' Melody replied quickly, feeling slightly awkward. 'You run a marvellous guesthouse, Fee,' she said hurriedly. 'Everything seems to run like clockwork. Which means, of course, that someone—you—works extremely hard all the time. Success at anything never happens by chance, does it? It's always hard graft in the end.'

Fee sighed, wiping her forehead with a tissue, and closing her eyes briefly. 'I'm used to hard work.'

Melody looked at her quickly. 'Are you all right, Fee?' she said. 'You do look rather warm…'

'Oh, yes—I'm fine,' Fee said, smiling briefly. 'As a matter of fact… Oh…it doesn't matter…'

'Go on,' Melody said gently, sensing that the woman wanted to talk.

Fee waited a moment before going on. 'It's just that I'm pregnant, Mel—after all this time, after all the false alarms and disappointments.'

'But that's terrific—fantastic, Fee!' Melody said enthusiastically. She had no doubt that Callum and Fee would make the most wonderful parents.

'We've not told anyone yet—not even Adam,' Fee said, lowering her voice, and Melody thought Adam must be a very special friend if he was usually privy to all their important news. 'He's known all about my past problems,' Fee went on, 'but it's a bit soon, and I don't want anyone to get excited on our behalf. Not until I've passed the three-month stage—which isn't quite yet.'

'Well—thank you for letting *me* into the secret,' Melody said warmly. 'And I won't breathe a word!' She paused. 'But shouldn't you be taking it easy—you know, with your feet up?'

Fee smiled. 'That'll be the day, Mel,' she said. 'If this time it's meant to be, putting my feet up or not won't make any difference—though of course if it proves to be the real thing I'll be taking full advantage of the situation! I'll have everyone running around after me, obeying orders…'

Both women laughed at the unlikely thought of Fee remaining idle for long, and Melody said, 'Adam seems very…I mean, you've known each other for a very long time, obviously…'

'Oh, yes. He and Callum started school together. They're both thirty-eight now. And then of course Adam and his twin brother Rupert went to boarding school at the age of nine, then on to university—they never really came back here to live much at all.'

'Oh…I didn't know Adam had a twin brother,' Mel said, surprised at herself for *being* surprised.

'No—that's seldom mentioned,' Fee said quietly. 'There's a bit of bad blood there, I'm afraid…'

Melody couldn't help feeling curious at this last bit of information, but didn't pursue the matter.

'Then, of course, their parents decided to sell Poplars, and—'

Melody was mystified. 'D'you mean that *they*—Adam's family—owned the place? Owned Poplars?'

'Oh, yes. Didn't you realise? The Carlisle family owned Poplars and the Gatehouse for three generations, but about fifteen years ago Isabel and Robert—Adam's parents—decided to sell up because they were away such a lot. They're great travellers—quite apart from the time they have to spend in Malaysia—and they thought it was a shame for the place to be empty for such long stretches. So they sold the two properties to a local couple—both vets—but their marriage fell apart almost at once, and everything came up for sale again. That was when we just managed to afford Poplars. The cottage was bought by a man from the next village. He died at the end of last year—and, well, the rest you know.'

For a few minutes Melody was stunned into silence. No wonder Adam had such tight-lipped ideas about the two properties—and such pride in the area. Poplars would have been his home, and his sense of possessiveness was tangible. And his family would have been looked after all that time by *her* mother! With a rush of emotion Melody realised that he would have known Frances, even though he'd apparently not lived at Poplars much since childhood.

The information that she'd just been given had left Melody feeling dry-mouthed and slightly taken aback. Yet why? she asked herself. Wasn't she here to find out things—about herself, about her mother's past? Perhaps these were two little pieces of the jigsaw of her life which had to be fitted in first. And maybe that would be it. Maybe there was nothing more of significance to learn.

She shivered slightly, and Fee looked at her sharply. 'You're not *cold*, are you, Mel?' she said. 'In this heat?'

'No—no, of course not.'

'Um, well…I hope you aren't sickening for something—there's a summer flu going around at the moment.'

Mel smiled quickly. 'I'm fine, Fee, honestly,' she said.

But somehow she wasn't really fine. She felt disturbed—and she knew the reason. Adam Carlisle had emerged from out of nowhere, and his family had had a direct influence on her mother's life. Despite all her best intentions, his presence was affecting her feelings in the sort of way she'd thought she was immune from for ever.

# CHAPTER FOUR

DECIDING that there was no time like the present, Melody wanted to make an immediate start. So presently, having gone back to Poplars to change into her jeans, she allowed Adam to drive her into the village to make some purchases. He had already established that the electrics were all in working order, and that the cottage's hot water system—after a few false starts—was functioning perfectly well. So now all they needed were some basic cleaning materials.

Adam pulled up outside the post office, which seemed to double up as a general store, and together they went inside, selecting a long-handled broom, dustpan and brush, two buckets, scrubbing brushes and floor cloths, and various cleaning fluids. Fee had tried to insist that they borrow everything from Poplars, but Melody had been adamant that she was going to need it all for the long term, so there was no point.

As they piled their purchases into the car Melody felt an almost childish thrill at the thought of the mundane task ahead. Cleaning might not be everyone's idea of fun, she thought, but when it was your very own place—empty, to do with what you liked—it became a more attractive prospect. And she was honest enough to admit that sitting there beside Adam as he drove them back was adding its own very particular dimension!

Although his unexpected interest in her and her acquisition of the cottage might have struck her as rather annoying at first, Melody now found herself grateful that she wasn't entirely alone. And he did seem genuinely anxious to help her. She shrugged inwardly—maybe he *was* getting bored with his long holiday, and with pleasing himself with nothing much to do. It was true, she reflected, that a prolonged period of inactivity with no particular focus could pall after a while.

She glanced across at him covertly. He had the most amazingly masculine profile she'd ever seen on a man… It had an almost carved look about it, perfect and symmetrical, with a very firm chin which might indicate a ruthless streak, perhaps? And every time she'd had the full benefit of his glittering eyes looking down at her she had been conscious of being almost wrapped up in his gaze—enfolded, momentarily held prisoner. She turned to look out of the window, thinking that the last few days seemed to be part of an unimaginable dream—a dream from which she didn't want to wake up!

Back at the cottage, they took everything inside and began taking stock.

'Of course I shall have the whole place redecorated,' Melody announced. 'I know a very good team in London—they did our flat—and they won't object to spending a week or two down here on this.' She glanced up at Adam, who she knew had been watching her. 'Unless Callum knows of local workmen who'd appreciate the opportunity?' she added, bending to pick up the packet which held the rubber gloves they'd bought.

'Well, we could ask him,' Adam said. He paused. 'If that is your intention why are we bothering to clean up here now? Can't we leave it all to the decorators?'

'Of course not,' Melody said at once. 'If we get the place reasonably clean and fresh it'll give them a start, and more incentive to make a really good job of it. I don't intend to pay the sort of rates these people charge for the simple task of cleaning up—something I can do quite well myself.' She looked away for a second. 'But you don't have to be involved, Adam. Honestly…I can cope by myself.'

'Don't be silly,' he replied shortly. 'I told you—I want to help.' He picked up the broom which had been leaning against the wall. 'Now, I propose we start upstairs and work our way down—or would you like it the other way around?'

Melody smiled up at him, relieved that he was going to stay. Although the cottage was not large, it was going to take some time to clean it thoroughly—and two pairs of hands were better than one. 'No—I agree,' she said lightly. 'Let's begin upstairs.'

As the back bedroom was the largest, it was decided that they should begin on that. Adam went into the bathroom to fill one of the buckets with hot water, adding some frothy detergent, while Melody began sweeping, dragging the broom from ceiling to floor, getting into the cornices and corners, painfully aware of the countless cobwebs she was disturbing. The dust was already beginning to make her nose tingle, and as Adam returned with the heavy bucket she sneezed violently, three or four times in quick succession. He grinned across at her.

'Bless you and bless you,' he said. He paused. 'I don't hold out much hope for your white T-shirt,' he added.

'Doesn't matter. I've packed plenty of spares,' Melody said nonchalantly, continuing with her brushing.

They'd thrown the window wide open, and the blessed summer air, filtering into the room, went some way towards giving it a more wholesome feel. When Adam, on his hands and knees, began scrubbing the floor furiously, Melody began to feel that truly this was her home. Home! What a wonderful thought! Because this place, even in its present state, felt more like home than the flat in London ever had, she realised. And she was aware that in wanting to clean it, to literally touch and handle every part of it, she was linking herself with her own life-blood, her own destiny. And her hard-working mother's spirit seemed to inhabit the place, fill it with her presence, which made Melody's heart glow.

She pulled herself away from this rather intense train of thought and watched Adam for a moment or two, noted his strong muscles tensing and flexing beneath the tanned skin on his arms as he squeezed water from the cloth he was using. As he continued with what he was doing his casual top pulled away from the waist of his jeans, exposing a band of lean, supple body which hardened and rippled with the effort, and beads of perspiration glistened on the back of his neck...

Impulsively, Melody crouched down beside him for a second, a surge of gratefulness overcoming any shyness she might have felt. 'Adam—it's—I mean—it's so good of you to be doing this,' she said earnestly. 'Why should you be spending time on my behalf? I mean—we hardly know each other, and scrubbing out a grubby property is hardly the stuff of a dream holiday, is it?'

He stopped for a moment and leaned back on his heels, looking at her squarely. 'In some people's view it might be the stuff of nightmares,' he agreed amiably. 'But don't worry about it, Mel.' He paused. 'I never do anything I don't want to do—and, as I told you, I like a challenge. And anyway...' he hesitated briefly '...if this was now Callum and Fee's place I'd probably be doing it for them.'

Melody shrank back. It was easy to forget that her successful bid for the cottage had spoiled his friends' plans. His *best* friends' plans. She couldn't rid herself of the feeling that she'd committed an act of felony.

She stood up quickly. 'There isn't any more I can do here,' she said. 'So I'll go and suss out the bathroom.'

He didn't look up, or make any comment, and Melody went

across the narrow landing. Staring around her, she noted that all the porcelain must have been replaced in the not-too-distant past—although an ugly brown stain in the bath, running from the taps to the plug, would need some serious attention. She put her head on one side pensively. She'd probably have this—her very favourite room in any house—refitted at some point. But it certainly wasn't bad enough to consider that now. Rome wasn't built in a day, she reminded herself.

Going over to the handbasin, she opened the window wide and leaned out, resting her arms on the sill, glorying in the vision of her somewhat overgrown garden. Those gooseberry bushes, with the fruit luscious and turning pink with ripeness, were begging to be stripped, she thought.

Suddenly something large and black fell directly down past her line of vision, brushing her nose and chin as it went straight down the front of her T-shirt, which had gaped open at the neck. Melody's heart jumped right into her mouth and she let out a scream of pure terror as she pulled at her top in anguish. 'Aaaaargh!' she yelled. 'Oh, no—no—*help*!'

There was an almighty crash from the bedroom as Adam's feet obviously made contact with the side of his bucket, and almost at once he was beside her, grabbing her by the arm. 'What the hell's wrong?' he demanded savagely.

By this time Melody had ripped off her top, flinging it on the floor, and just stood there, literally shaking from head to foot. 'Something…something *horrible*…has just fallen down my neck!' she cried, desperately trying to control herself, and failing miserably. 'Oh God, Adam… It was *disgusting*!'

He stared at her for a minute, trying to suppress a grin. 'Well…I thought you were being murdered,' he said, trying to unlock his gaze from Melody's low-cut lacy bra, which enhanced the perfect shape and roundness of her dainty figure and delectable cleavage. He turned away decisively and picked up her shirt, shaking it out vigorously. At once a massive spider ran across the room in a frenzied effort to escape. When she saw it, Melody fought to control another shudder of horror.

'Ugh…that's…horrible—*horrible*! I cannot stand spiders!' she cried. 'Or anything with more than two legs! Oh, Adam… that was *awful*!'

She was still trembling, and for a moment he thought she was going to burst into tears. Part of him wanted to take her by the shoulders and shake her, tell her not to be so ridiculous, but he was aware that for some people the fear of insects—especially spiders—was not something minor which could easily be controlled. Like any phobia, it must be treated with consideration. He knew that.

He put his arm around her waist and gently drew her towards him. The feel of her scantily clad body next to his sent his male instincts soaring wildly. He swallowed, wishing that his hands didn't smell of disinfectant—though that did have the effect of helping him to calm his momentary lust. 'It's okay, Mel…don't worry. The thing's gone now—disappeared,' he said reasonably. 'You know they're much more frightened of you than you can ever be of them,' he murmured into her ear.

'I don't care!' she repeated. 'They move so fast…and they *bite*!'

'Oh, not all of them bite—' Adam began, but she interrupted.

'I know someone who was bitten—or stung—I don't care which. Her arm became infected and she was on antibiotics for *weeks*!' Melody leaned right into him now, as he held her, but soon she began to calm down, her breathing becoming steadier. She turned and looked up into his face. 'Oh, dear…I'm sorry— really,' she said at last. 'I'm not proud of my behaviour… You must think I'm a fool, Adam…'

'Of course I don't,' he said coolly. 'Fear of spiders is a well-known phenomenon.' He paused. 'There are groups that can help, you know,' he went on. 'Help with any hang-up.' He didn't let her go, only too aware of the thudding of his heart against her breasts.

After a few seconds she pulled away. 'I'm sorry,' she repeated, 'I think I overreacted…but I really couldn't help it…'

'Don't apologise,' he said. 'You're not the only person in the world who's afraid of creepy crawlies.'

He knew that the spider was not the thing uppermost in his mind at that moment! How had he stopped himself from kissing her? he wondered. Because he *almost* had done. He had wanted to, in a moment of madness—and she'd not yanked herself away either, as she might easily have done.

Adam still had her T-shirt tucked under his arm, and he held it out to her. 'Are you going to put this back on?' he enquired, and she shuddered.

'Certainly not,' she said. 'But I'd like to go back to Poplars and put on something fresh.'

He looked down at her quizzically. Perhaps this was the moment to point out that if she did intend to be a country-dweller—even if it was on a part-time basis—she'd better get used to unwelcome company now and then

'There are no guarantees regarding spiders, woodlice *et al*,' he said, as they went down the stairs. 'Not in any cottage. Certainly not in one of this age. They come with the territory, I'm afraid, Mel.'

'Oh, you can buy stuff to deter them,' Melody replied quickly, having by now reasserted her self-control. 'Perhaps they'll all eventually get the message,' she added hopefully.

'Don't count on it,' Adam said enigmatically. 'It would be wiser to try and develop a more rational frame of mind, so that when you do come across anything you can handle it. You can get used to anything—if you persist,' he added.

Melody wasn't convinced by this argument, and she bit her

lip, angry with herself, and a bit piqued at the advice he was dishing out—especially as she knew that he was right. That spider would not be the only thing she'd come across in the future…in fact there was probably much worse to come—rats, even! she thought. But sitting beside Adam now, as he drove slowly back up the drive of Poplars, she felt her optimism begin bubbling back to the surface of her thoughts. She loved it— *loved* it—that the cottage was hers!

She didn't look across at Adam as he drew into the car park. She didn't need to look at him, because the drift of his maleness touched her nostrils, made her realise with a jolt what had been wrenched from her life when Crispin had been killed. Her husband had been the last man to touch her, to hold her in that certain way that needed no explanation, and when she'd felt Adam's arms around her just now it had evoked a physical need in her that she'd thought she'd filed away for ever. Hadn't she vowed that her one serious relationship was to be her last? That she would never expose herself to the trauma of loss ever again? Yet a man whom she barely knew had just driven a horse and cart through that determination!

She chided herself angrily at her weakness. It must be this unusually warm summer weather, plus the heady experience of spending all that money on her idyllic home in the country which was ruffling her normally level-headed and practical thinking. Well, that was her story, and she'd stick to it!

She got out of the car, and ran quickly up the stairs to her room. Fortunately there was no one about, and she shut the door behind her gratefully.

For a few moments she sat on the edge of the bed, where she had a good view of herself in the wall mirror. The face that stared back at her didn't seem like hers—more like that of someone she'd once known.

Snap out of this daydreaming, she told herself sharply, going over to the chest of drawers for a fresh T-shirt. Keep your eye on the ball! Just because she'd been held closely by a man— for the first time in more than a year—it hadn't changed a thing. That incident in the life of someone like Adam would have been a well-practised passing fancy. What he'd said on that first evening, about not being married, nor apparently wishing to be, left her in no doubt that his interest in the opposite sex was purely physical—and transitory. Holding her like that hadn't been anything more than a consoling gesture to a stupid female who was scared of spiders. He would have forgotten about it already.

She shrugged on the clean top, releasing her long hair from the back in a faintly irritable gesture…well, then, *she'd* better forget all about it, too!

Waiting for her outside, Adam couldn't believe that, yet again, he was allowing himself to be beguiled by a beautiful woman. Hadn't the lesson he'd thought he'd learned been harsh enough? It was true that he'd found her attractive from the moment he'd set eyes on her, but it had never been his intention to let his feelings be stirred in any way at all. Yet this morning had shattered his confidence in that determination, because for those few seconds he'd not only wanted her, he'd recognised that deeper, familiar longing, which spelt danger. Of course he'd dated many women since the break-up with Lucy, but they'd meant nothing—nothing at all. And that was the way he wanted it.

His lip curled slightly as he recalled Melody's horror at that creature running down her cleavage. Well, as he'd told her, she'd better get used to such things. Together with everything else that went with living in a place like this—however infrequent her visits were to be. No smart shops, no theatres or museums to alleviate boredom on wet weekends, to keep a city girl amused.

He leaned forward on the steering wheel, resting his chin on his hands for a moment. Why was the woman getting to him anyway? Why was he bothering to think about her like this? Something about her told him that as soon as she returned to London, Gatehouse Cottage would take a very back seat in her mind. He felt, overwhelmingly, that her purchase had been a rush of blood to the head of someone who had far too much money at her disposal. After all, why would anyone—any normal person—buy a property in the country without a second thought? Without apparently having had any idea that such a thing might occur in the first place? It didn't make any sense.

He glanced out of the window to see her coming towards him. She smiled at him as their eyes met, and he leaned across to open the passenger door for her. Why did this woman look so delectable? he asked himself. And why had their paths had to cross?

# CHAPTER FIVE

THE following morning Melody woke early, conscious of the sun filtering through the slightly parted curtains at her window. She smiled to herself. It was going to be yet another fine, warm day.

She lay on her back for a moment, staring up at the ceiling. She and Adam had spent almost all of yesterday spring-cleaning the cottage, and when they'd packed up finally she had felt as if an almost spiritual event had occurred. It was hard for her to explain it, even to herself, but by cleaning away the dust and grime of the lives of other occupants she felt that she was now ready for new beginnings.

She'd been dog-tired by the time they'd called it a day, and although Adam had suggested that they go somewhere for supper Melody had declined the offer. 'All I need now is a long, warm bath and an early night,' she'd said.

Anyway, the picnic lunch Fee had brought down for them—soft rolls with ham and cheese, fruit and coffee, plus a cool bag containing ice-cold drinks—had kept them going all day. Melody had certainly not had sufficient appetite to bother dressing up and going out somewhere to eat. As they'd put all the cleaning things neatly in the kitchen cupboard, Adam's response to her refusal had been non-committal.

'Okay. Fine by me,' was all he'd said.

Now, Melody jumped out of bed decisively. It was not even seven a.m. yet. There was plenty of time to go for a walk across the fields before breakfast—which she was in the habit of having at about eight or nine o'clock.

Washing quickly, she selected cream trousers and a turquoise cotton top, then stooped down for her running shoes, fixing the straps firmly. She and Adam had parted company yesterday without any reference to today, and Melody hoped that he wouldn't feel under any obligation to go on taking her under his wing. She'd been more than grateful for all his efforts yesterday—and had told him so, over and over again—but for the time being there was little more to be done at the cottage, so he had no need to interrupt his holiday further on her behalf.

She bit her lip. This could be awkward for both of them, she thought. She did not want to feel obligated to him, but neither did she want to give him the brush-off—not after all he'd done yesterday. And equally, she thought, he might feel that he couldn't very well stop what he'd started and abandon her to her own devices. Melody brushed out her hair vigorously and pulled it back in a ponytail. Stop worrying, she told herself. Things will pan out. Anyway, first things first. This early walk was the next important thing on her agenda.

The front door was already wide open—Callum and Fee's day had obviously begun—and she could hear muffled voices from the kitchen as she went outside. She stood quite still for a moment, taking in lungfuls of fresh air. She could already feel the life-enhancing effect of not inhaling toxic fumes from countless streams of traffic. Lap it up while you can, she told herself. All too soon she'd be back in the smoke.

Thinking along these lines made her realise that she probably ought to ring the office at some point—she'd neither made nor received any calls on her holiday from her colleagues, and the thought of her long break coming to an end, of having to leave her cottage, filled her with a silly sense of homesickness. How daft could you be? she asked herself. The next time she returned here the place would still be standing. Nothing was going to happen to it. And anyway, before that she had some fruit-picking to do. She'd take as much of the stuff back with her as she could manage, to distribute among her workmates…

She wondered what their reaction would be to her news. She imagined that they'd all be mildly surprised—her purchase was hardly the equivalent of a few sticks of rock, or a locally crafted souvenir, she thought, smiling briefly. But her closest colleagues—Eve and Jon, who'd lived together for ages—*they'd* be more than interested! Their main preoccupation outside work seemed to be looking at properties. She'd ring them tomorrow and tell them, Melody thought. Keeping her news to herself seemed unnecessarily secretive.

She set off rapidly, taking the long track behind Poplars towards a bank of trees she could see in the near distance. The turf was soft and mossy beneath her feet, and Melody felt that she could walk for miles with no trouble at all. Presently she came to a stile at the foot of a hilly area, and, climbing over it easily, she began making her way upwards, wondering what she'd see when she reached the top. When she did, she wasn't disappointed. Below her the overgrown fields fell away on either side, and the whole undulating scene represented a picture-book vision of flowering bushes and wild plants. She could see scores of poppies, cow-parsley everywhere, and beneath her feet bright buttercups and dandelions, adding their own vivid glory as they vied for attention. The air—like champagne—was filled with the hum of bees, already on their hunt for nectar.

Melody's heart missed a beat. How many times had Frances told her about her countless expeditions to collect blossom and foliage to decorate Poplars—and her own, humbler dwelling?

And, as if to complete this idyllic picture, Melody espied a small stream, meandering along the bottom of the field. Starting to make her way down, she was forced to run as her feet gathered pace, her cheeks beginning to redden with the effort. When she reached the stream, she saw that thanks to the long spell of hot weather the water was no more than a trickle, but the effect of sunlight on moving water was pure magic. Melody breathed in deeply, feeling at that moment that she must be the luckiest person in the world.

Nimbly, she stepped over the stream and went towards the bushes in front of her. She could see at a glance that there were suitable things to pick—even though she'd probably have to endure pinched fingers in the process!

She'd barely begun to make her selection when Adam's voice, almost immediately behind her, made her jump. Turning quickly, she saw him standing a few feet away, his hands in his pockets, a faint smile on his lips.

'So…you're a countryside pilferer, are you?' he said, and without waiting for a reply added, 'Why are you up so early? After all you did yesterday I thought you'd be asleep until lunchtime.'

She stood back. 'Oh—well, I had a very early night,' she said. 'And I certainly wasn't going to waste this lovely morning.' She stared up at him. He was wearing chinos, and a light open-neck shirt, and his black hair shone like polished coal in the sunlight. She turned away. 'Anyway—what are *you* doing up and about?' she asked.

'Oh, I take the dogs out first thing,' he said, not taking his eyes from her, and thinking how sweet and natural she looked. So different from his first impression at the auction. And she'd surprised him yesterday, with how she'd worked at the cottage.

She'd insisted on scrubbing every inch of the bathroom by herself—which had been no mean feat, because it had been the grimiest room in the place. And there'd been no complaints, no expecting to go back to Poplars for a rest, and she hadn't checked her appearance in the mirror either—rather unusual in a woman, he thought, or at any rate in the women he'd known all his life.

'What have you done with Tam and Millie, then?' she asked, glancing around her.

'Oh, they're enjoying themselves sniffing about in that copse over there,' he replied. He gave one short, sharp whistle through his teeth, and at once both animals emerged and ambled up towards them, going over to Melody to be made a fuss of.

She glanced up at Adam. 'Is it…will it be okay for me to pick a few bits and pieces from these bushes?' she asked. 'They're not all protected species, are they?'

'Shouldn't think so,' he said casually. 'Help yourself. The owners are very gracious people. They like the locals to enjoy their property, as long as it's respected.'

'Who *does* own all this, then?' Melody asked curiously.

'It belongs to the big house about a mile thataway,' Adam said, indicating behind him. 'The de Wintons own it now. The family is filthy rich, but lovely with it, and since this area is not suitable for farming it's mostly a local amenity.'

Melody turned back to the bushes. There'd be no point in picking too much, but a modest arrangement in a tumbler on her bedroom cabinet would satisfy a particular need—though they wouldn't last long. She knew that. Not like the exotic blooms Adam had given her.

He threw himself down on the grass and leaned back on one elbow, gazing up at her as she foraged around, her smooth brown arms raised, her head held high, the ponytail trailing luxuriously down her back.

'Finding anything spectacular?' he enquired, wishing again that this woman wasn't quite so attractive to look at. He kept remembering the feel of her feminine curves pressed into his chest. He shook himself briefly. This long sunny spell had gone right to his head!

'Everything's spectacular,' she replied without looking around. 'I mean, just *look* at this dog-rose...such a dainty pink. I must have just a small sprig—if I can manage to snap a bit off. Ow!' she said, sucking a finger noisily.

Adam immediately got up. 'Here—let me,' he said, coming over to stand next to her.

Melody stood back as he leaned upwards and snapped off a stem. He turned to look down at her and, swallowing, she moved away from him quickly. There was no need for them to be *that* close! 'That's fine, Adam...thanks,' she said, taking the cluster of roses from him. She shaded her eyes from the sun for a moment. 'There are lots of other things over there,' she said. 'And those daisies are so long-stemmed—I must have some of those!' She scrambled past him for a moment. 'But I must not allow myself to get carried away!' she added.

With both dogs flopping down beside him, Adam resumed his prone position on the grass and watched her idly. Presently she stood back and examined the quite considerable amount of foliage she was holding in her arms.

'There—that will do,' she said, glancing down at him.

He waited for a second before speaking, then, 'Come and sit down,' he said, patting the ground beside him.

Melody did as she was told, feeling light-hearted—and light-headed!

He leaned towards her so that they were almost touching, and, looking down briefly at the flowers, said, 'Well, what have you got there, Mel? Have you any idea what you've been picking?' he asked.

She returned his glance, interpreting what he'd just said as criticism of a townie who was more used to expensive florists' shops than dusty hedgerows! She held the bunch away from her and pointed with her forefinger. 'Let me enlighten you,' she said coolly. 'Here we have foxgloves—which will look well with the meadowsweet and the daisies—together with gorgeous stems of honeysuckle. Just smell those—don't they make your mouth water? This dainty blue flower I'm pretty sure is meadow cranesbill, and here we have ladies' smock—a bit gangly, but still charming—and of course the ubiquitous Queen Charlotte's lace—known to you, no doubt, as cow parsley. And—'

'Stop, stop!' Adam said. 'I'm impressed! Where did all that knowledge come from? You've obviously studied the subject…'

She shot him a quick glance. 'Not exactly,' she said. 'But my mother used to talk to me about flowers a lot, show me pictures. And her favourite pastime was to paint—she did beautiful still-life watercolours, which will be hung on my cottage walls eventually.' She paused. 'She even gave me a jigsaw puzzle once, with all the names of flowers, wild and cultivated. We did that together for hours. So it was just something I learned at my mother's knee, you might say.' She looked away for a second. Should she tell Adam how closely she was connected to the place—how, in a way, she was so closely connected to *him*, or at any rate to Poplars and Gatehouse Cottage?

The moment passed and she said nothing, for she still felt this need to guard Frances's secret. But the longer it went on, the more difficult it would become. She knew that. She shrugged inwardly. Maybe there would be no need to tell him, or anyone, why she had felt a pressing need to own the cottage, or why she already felt an integral part of the village. So much time had gone by, she thought wistfully. Her mother's world was a different one from the one in which *she* was now living.

Adam leaned forward, hugging his knees and staring ahead of him at the barely moving water of the stream a foot or two away from them. This woman was beginning to confuse him.

He'd always prided himself that he was good at first impressions, that he could sum someone up straight away. But there was a lot about Mel that defied his former assessment. She didn't seem quite the indulged rich-kid who'd plucked Gatehouse Cottage from under their noses—more that she genuinely wanted to be part of the place. To live it.

'You've put me to shame,' he said, not looking at her. 'I was born here—my parents once owned Poplars, as a matter of fact—and as a young child I used to tramp these fields, but I was never particularly interested in flora and fauna. Certainly not enough to learn about them. Then I was packed off to boarding school at nine, after which university…so my childhood memories are slight.' He paused. 'But there must be something about one's early childhood, because I feel a need—a compulsion—to keep returning each year. And of course the biggest excuse is to spend time with Callum and Fee, who've always remained my best friends.'

There was a silence before Melody said lightly, 'Well, then, it must be like coming home each time.'

She didn't say that Fee had already told her some of this, because that would have looked as if they'd been gossiping about him. So it was just another secret! She was good at secrets, she thought.

Neither of them said anything then, and after a few moments Melody, feeling her feet throbbing, slipped her shoes off and inched herself forward, dipping her toes into the stream. 'Oh…that's *so* good,' she breathed, glancing back over her shoulder at Adam.

He grinned back at her. 'I've never seen the water this low,' he said. 'It's barely covering your feet.'

'No, I know—but it's doing the job,' Melody replied. She wiggled her toes for a few moments, then sat back for the sun to dry her off. 'I shall relive all this when I get back to London,' she said. 'It'll be a whole world away.'

Adam looked at her thoughtfully. 'So—when d'you expect to be returning?' he asked, in a casual tone which he might have used to anyone as a polite enquiry.

'Can't be sure just yet,' Melody replied, leaning back on her elbows to bring her down to lounge alongside him. 'It'll all depend on work, of course. But I shall make immediate plans to engage the decorators.' Her eyes shone as she anticipated the time ahead, and she turned to see him gazing at her. 'I must take lots of photographs of the cottage later, of every room, so that I'll have something to show them. It'll give them an idea.' She paused. 'And then it'll be measuring up for carpets and curtains.' She closed her eyes briefly. 'D'you know, I feel exactly as I did when I was given my first dolls' house! Arranging everything to suit just *me*!'

A pulse twitched and hardened in Adam's neck as he continued looking at her. He knew that if he didn't break the spell this woman was weaving around him he wouldn't be able to stop himself from gathering her up in his arms and claiming her mouth. At that moment, sitting here with birdsong all around them, he knew that he wanted to possess her—really possess her—and he only just managed to restrain himself. He recalled the feel of her as she'd clutched him in that grimy bathroom yesterday, as she'd rested her head against his shoulder for that brief second—though you could hardly call that a come-on, he thought. He was used to the women he knew seizing an opportunity like that with both hands! But he'd been surprised, and cross with himself, at how she'd stirred him… Women were not to be trusted—he knew that better than anyone. Yet here he was, at it again! Allowing himself to be aroused by a beautiful, intelligent female—and, worst of all, by a woman whose arrival in the village had upset his plans!

All at once Melody seemed to sense the sudden emotional tenseness between them, and she stood up quickly, her heartbeat beginning to notch up noticeably. Spending time with the devilishly handsome Adam Carlisle had not been part of her holiday plan! If she couldn't shake him off soon it was going to confuse everything. Buying a property in the country was enough of an event on its own. Don't let things get complicated, she warned herself. Yet every time his dark eyes looked into hers in that very special way they seemed to penetrate her soul, holding her captive. But she knew that she'd always felt things deeply—too deeply—and she did not want to risk being hurt again. To risk losing again.

When her mother had died it had seemed the end of her world for a while. Then fate had dealt her another blow, when Crispin had been killed, and she'd shed enough tears to float a boat. Well, she'd made up her mind never to be asked to pay such a price for happiness again.

Quickly she thrust on her trainers and got to her feet, glancing down at Adam briefly, knowing that he'd wanted to kiss her, and knowing that she'd got *that* close to letting him do it. 'I think I must go back for some breakfast,' she said, matter-of-factly. 'The time has just flown by…'

He got up, too, then, and without another word fell into step beside her as she walked on rapidly, the dogs trotting happily in front of them. Once or twice she stumbled over the rough ground, and Adam automatically put a hand under her elbow to steady her. But, not wanting to feel the touch of his hand, not wanting to feel any part of him close to her, she deliberately moved away quickly, almost shrugging him off.

He knew her motive, and shook his head briefly as he looked down at her. 'I just don't want you to sprain an ankle,' he said shortly. 'We've some way to go yet, and even your weight might be too much.'

'Oh, don't worry,' Melody replied. 'I shan't expect any special favours. I'll get back under my own steam whatever happens. I promise you that.'

'Oh, I don't doubt that you're fully self-contained, Mel,' he said. 'But if you've ever tried walking with a sprained ankle you'll know what I'm talking about. You'd be lucky to get back to Poplars by bedtime, never mind breakfast.'

'Has it ever happened to you, then?' Melody asked.

'Yes. Playing rugby,' he replied. 'I thought I could get off the pitch unaided, but I was wrong. And I've never forgotten the pain.'

'D'you play a lot?' Melody asked, glad of the neutral conversation.

'Not now,' he said shortly. 'It's a young man's game.'

She looked up at him, thinking that his face bore no testimonies to the game—no misshapen nose or lumpy ears to spoil his model features.

They made good time getting back to Poplars—Melody still clutching her precious blooms, which even now were beginning to wilt slightly.

'I must put these in water and have a wash,' she said lightly, before running quickly up the stairs to her room. Adam merely nodded as they parted company.

Looking around her, Melody could see that there was nothing remotely suitable to arrange her flowers in, so presently she filled the washbasin with cold water and laid all the foliage in it up to the neck, realising that she'd need to ask Fee for a vase or jar.

She paused for a moment in front of the mirror, idly ruffling her fingers through her fringe. She was starving by now, but wanted to give Adam time to have his own breakfast before going down. She didn't want it to become the norm for them to spend all their time together, but that was how it seemed to be turning out. It was still not much after nine, but she didn't want to hold Fee up any longer. She'd noticed before that the other guests all tended to eat early, so she'd probably be the last one in the dining room again, she thought.

At about a quarter past nine she ventured downstairs. The large, inviting room was empty, with only one table—hers, obviously—still laid up for breakfast. Adam must have swallowed his pretty quickly, she thought, going over to the large side table which still had all the cereals and fruit displayed.

She poured herself a glass of orange juice, and put a small helping of muesli into a bowl, then filled a generous cup with coffee from the percolator which was bubbling alongside.

As she went to sit down Callum emerged, a sunny smile on his broad features. 'Morning, Mel,' he said. 'Enjoyed your early walk? Adam told me he'd bumped into you. Perfect morning again, isn't it?'

Melody returned his smile. 'It is,' she agreed. 'I can't believe my luck!'

'Yes, we've got very satisfied guests at the moment. But it does rain here—I can promise you that—and it often goes on for days!'

'Well, so long as it behaves itself for a little while longer,' Melody said, sitting down and unfolding her napkin.

'Now—full English, Mel?' Callum asked.

Melody smiled. 'I don't think so, thanks. But a soft-boiled egg and some toast would be great, Callum.' She paused. 'No Fee today?' she asked lightly.

A brief frown crossed the man's face for a second. 'She's…she's having a bit of a lie-down for an hour,' he said. 'Not feeling too good… It's this heat, I think.' He turned abruptly. 'One soft-boiled egg, coming up.'

He left the room and Melody stared after him, remembering her conversation with Fee yesterday and hoping that it *was* only the heat affecting the girl, and not anything more sinister. She'd known the couple for such a short time, yet it was impossible not to warm to them…they were so kind and generous. Adam certainly thought so, and clearly valued their friendship.

Just thinking of the man seemed to conjure him up.

Suddenly he appeared at the door, going over to fill a large mug with coffee before coming across to sit down opposite her.

'Mind if I join you?' he said—though it wasn't a question, more a declaration of intent! 'Have you found anything suitable to put your morning's harvest in?' he asked.

'No,' Melody replied. 'But that jug in the window over there would be perfect. D'you think they'd mind if I borrowed it?'

'Oh, we'll take it and ask later,' Adam said cheerfully, knowing full well that Fee never objected to anything.

Melody tried not to mind that he'd turned up. Even though she'd decided that for the rest of the day she was going to give him a wide berth. 'Have you had breakfast?' she asked, looking up at him over the rim of her glass of juice.

'I grabbed a slice of toast a few minutes ago,' he replied easily. 'As a matter of fact the three of us went over to the Rose & Crown for supper last night, and ate rather well. So it's no hardship to go without this morning.' He paused. 'You should have come with us.'

He studied her closely as she dipped her spoon into the muesli and began to eat, thinking what a graceful woman she was. Everything she did—eating, or gathering flowers from the hedges, or scrubbing discoloured pipes in the cottage—she seemed to do with a kind of unassuming elegance. He pursed his lips and stared out of the window. In a couple of weeks she'd have gone home to London and he'd be on his way back to the Far East. He grimaced inwardly at the thought. He didn't want to go back—well, he *never* wanted to go back. He wanted to stay here!

'I was much too tired to eat,' Melody said. 'I get to a certain point when sleep is the only answer for me.'

She finished the muesli just as Callum came back with her boiled egg, and Adam leaned back in his chair nonchalantly, looking up.

'Can we use your computer later, Callum?' he asked. 'Mel wants some pictures of the cottage. I've got my digital camera, and I thought we'd go down there later and take some. Then we could print off some copies for her to take back with her.'

'Course you can,' Callum said at once. 'Be my guest!'

Melody looked across at Adam. It was no good. The man was making himself useful again—*too* useful—and it was becoming impossible for her to refuse him! But she had to admit that the arrangement he was suggesting would be very convenient—and her own camera was not digital.

Presently, back in her room, she arranged her bouquet of wild flowers in the wide-necked jug she'd borrowed, and placed them on the windowsill. To her, they were as perfect as the bouquet which Adam had presented her with. She paused for a moment or two, her thoughts—as usual—on their normal helter-skelter of emotion. When she'd booked this holiday she could never have guessed what lay ahead—that she would buy the very home in which her beloved mother had lived, and in which she'd given birth to her only child. Nor that she would tread probably the very path that her mother had wandered along and pluck the same sort of flowers... Melody had the feeling that her existence was taking on a life of its own, and the most dramatic part of it was that in the midst of it all she knew she'd met the most breathtakingly gorgeous man she was ever likely to set eyes on! And his apparent determination to be constantly by her side was upsetting her equilibrium!

She sat for a moment on the edge of her bed, her hands clasped in her lap. Warning bells were beginning to ring. Don't get involved any further with him, she instructed herself anxiously. Think of something—anything—some excuse—to put distance between you. If you don't, it will all end in tears—and they'll be *your* tears!

That thought brought Melody to a sudden decision, and,

leaning across to her bedside table, she picked up her mobile and made a phone call. After a few minutes' conversation with the person on the other end she snapped it shut, a small glint of satisfaction in her eyes. Well, that might go some way to cooling things down a bit, she thought. If Adam Carlisle thought that he was going to be unelected Master of Ceremonies in her life he was going to be disappointed!

# CHAPTER SIX

'I THINK those shots of the cottage that we took this morning will come out well,' Adam said lazily. 'I'll print them off later, and we can chuck any you don't think you'll need.'

He'd discarded his shirt and was lying full-stretch on the warm sand, his hands clasped behind his head. He turned to look at Melody as he spoke.

Half-sitting next to him, she tried not to be too aware of his brown muscular chest, with the dark line of strong body hair reaching down to the waist of his jeans, and she looked away, concentrating on the line of the horizon instead. The sheer expanse of blue water beyond them was dotted with what looked like millions of tiny diamonds, shifting and dazzling as the sunlight danced on the waves.

In spite of all her good intentions, his suggested visit to this secluded cove was, she had to admit, an unexpected treat. She'd only been to the seaside once or twice so far on her holiday and she hadn't known that this place existed. Although they were certainly not the only ones there, it was blissfully unpopulated. Their nearest neighbours were an elderly man and his dog, and, a bit further away, a young couple with a baby.

'D'you think that not many people know about this beach?' Melody asked curiously.

'Oh, I'm sure it's known,' Adam replied casually. 'But of course there's absolutely nothing here but sea and sand... No ice-cream vans, or shops selling the gaudy stuff that most people seem to need. Actually,' he added, 'it used to be a private beach, owned by a titled family who lived in a big house nearby which no longer exists.'

He turned to look at her as he spoke. She had changed earlier, into a honey-coloured sundress, with fine spaghetti straps that exposed the perfect contours of her neck and shoulders and was cut just low enough to reveal a glimpse of her curvaceous figure. It could hardly be described as a provocative number, he thought briefly, but it did plenty to excite *his* interest. Especially as she seemed unusually uninhibited about letting the sun reach her thighs, and had drawn her skirt up so that the sun could reach the length of her slender, fine-skinned legs.

'Well, it's just another little piece of paradise, as far as I'm concerned,' Melody said, deciding that she wasn't going to waste a single moment of the afternoon feeling that yet again she'd been manipulated. She and Adam had spent most of the morning taking dozens of shots of the cottage and garden—and he'd also recommended that they should start picking some of the fruit.

'It'll take us some time to do it,' he'd said, and Melody had sighed inwardly at the 'us'. She'd have been more than content to go it alone. Anyway, she'd thought, wasn't it high time for him to be returning to the Far East? Surely they must be missing his fantastic organisation skills by now? Although she couldn't deny that she was starting to enjoy the time they spent together immensely.

'It was a shame that Fee couldn't come with us after all,' she said now, for his suggestion that they should go to the coast had included the other woman as well. That had been the main— the *only*—reason Melody had accepted the invitation. There was safety in numbers, and she'd have loved to have Fee's cheerful company. Yet once again she and Adam were to be a cosy couple.

'Yes, I'm really sorry about that,' he replied—without much conviction. 'She would have enjoyed a couple of hours away from the unremitting toil, and the sea air would have done her good. But there you go. At the last minute she didn't feel up to it, so Callum said.' There was silence for a few moments, then, 'Are you going to join me for a swim?' he asked. 'The tide's just right now, and the water is calm… There's never much opportunity for surfing, if that's your preference,' he added.

In answer, Melody turned to rummage in her brightly coloured holdall. 'Calm water will be perfect for me,' she said. 'I've only tried surfing once, and I wasn't all that good at it to tell you the truth.' She pulled out her swimming things and stood up. Adam grinned up at her.

'Feel free,' he murmured smoothly. 'I'll be gallant and look the other way.'

Melody shot him a dismissive glance. 'Look wherever you like,' she said. 'I'm always well prepared.'

Taking out a large, full-length white towelling robe, she dropped it snugly over her shoulders, giving herself immediate privacy, and in a few seconds had slipped out of her dress and underwear. Then she stepped out of the robe and stood in front of him, her simple black designer costume exhibiting her slender curves and the flat plane of her stomach.

Adam had not taken his eyes off her during this rapid operation, and now, with his mouth drying slightly at the delicious sight of her, he jumped to his feet, released the belt of his trousers and dropped them to the ground, revealing his tight-fitting black swimming trunks—which he'd obviously changed into before they'd left. Then he moved over to her side and took her hand in his.

'Come on,' he said lightly, 'let's make a run for it.'

Caught up in the blissfully relaxing atmosphere of the day, Melody felt her heart soar as they sprinted together across the soft sand. But when they reached the shingle, and then the hard ridge of pebbles at the edge of the water, she was forced to let go of him and raise both arms to steady her balance as they splashed into the waves.

For the next hour they swam and splashed about in the water like schoolchildren. Adam was obviously a much stronger swimmer than Melody, and once or twice he left her to strike out alone. She watched him moving easily through the deep—his over-arm strokes rhythmically purposeful—until she was afraid she was going to lose sight of him altogether. But then he turned and came back to tread water by her side.

'I never like going too far out of my depth,' she confessed, and he grinned at her, his hair plastered to the side of his streaming head and neck.

'A very wise maxim—in all matters,' he said enigmatically.

Presently—reluctantly—they decided to return to dry land. Melody couldn't help hobbling as they reached the pebbles, grimacing as the fine shingle crept between her toes. 'Ouch!' she said, glancing up at Adam. 'This hurts!'

He didn't seem to feel it at all, and swiftly caught her around the waist, half-lifting her towards the sand. And as their soaking bodies made contact Melody felt the hard vigour of his muscular frame close in on her. She gasped, pulling free. Then, to cover her fleeting confusion, she tossed back her dripping ponytail and, laughing, ran ahead of him towards the spot where they'd left their things. But he caught up with her easily and, grasping her arm almost roughly, pulled her along behind him until they flung themselves down on the sand.

'That was fantastic!' Melody panted, collapsing with her arms above her head. 'The last time I bathed in the sea must be about three years ago.' She turned to look at him as he lay prone beside her. 'You're a very strong swimmer, Adam.'

'Oh, I learned even before I could read properly,' he replied. 'And I've had plenty of opportunity to practise since.'

He returned her gaze, wishing with all his heart that he was free—properly free from the emotional shackles he'd cursed himself with. But once he'd made up his mind about something he seldom wavered. He just wished that his mind would leave his body alone.

Sitting up quickly, and grabbing a towel from his rucksack, he started rubbing himself down briskly. 'D'you have any family, Mel? Any brothers or sisters?' he asked casually.

Melody sat up and began drying herself, drawing the towel carefully over her arms and chest so as not to let the sand on her body irritate her skin too much. 'No,' she said slowly. 'There was only ever me and my mother. She died just as I was graduating.' She paused. 'And I never knew my father—well, I can't remember him, anyway,' she amended quickly. 'And, regrettably, I never had siblings.' She stopped what she was doing for a second. 'I've always thought it must be wonderful to have a sister, or a brother—or both!' she added, smiling.

Adam grunted. 'Well, don't they say that what you've never had you'll never miss?' he said shortly, and Melody darted a quick glance at him, noting the sudden darkening of his features and the cynical ring in his tone. She remembered Fee's brief allusion to Adam's brother.

She cleared her throat. 'What about you?' she asked lightly. 'I know that you're lucky enough to still have both your parents living…but do you have any other family?'

'Yes. One brother,' he replied flatly. 'My twin—Rupert.'

Melody feigned surprise. 'Oh—how wonderful! And are you identical?' she asked, wondering if it was possible for there to be someone else who had all Adam's physical attributes.

'No. We are not identical—in any respect.'

In the unusual prolonged silence that followed, Melody was dying to push the conversation on and find out what the 'bad blood' Fee had mentioned was all about. But something made her hesitate. It must obviously be something pretty drastic, she thought. And something he was not going to volunteer to enlighten her about. But she just could not leave it there! She had to find out what had made Adam's mouth become set in a hard, forbidding line.

'And does—Rupert—work for the family firm as well?' she enquired, busying herself with flipping the sand out from between her toes. 'Do you see each other often?'

'No. On both counts,' Adam said curtly. 'A couple of years ago he decided to break away from the rest of us and do his own thing. He and I haven't spoken since. And before you ask, no, I don't miss him, and I'm never likely to.'

There was a long pause after that, then Melody said softly, 'I think that's terribly sad.'

He turned on her then, and said savagely, 'There are many sad things in life. Some of which can't be helped, and some of which should never have been allowed to happen.'

Of course Melody had realised that there must have been some disagreement between the brothers, but still, she thought, civilised people could surely come to terms with it eventually?

'I personally think that if you're lucky enough to have family you should value it,' she said simply. 'I would have loved, *loved*, to have had close relatives.'

'Oh, don't be too upset about being an only child,' he went on brusquely. 'For relationships to work in a family—or anywhere, for that matter—there must be trust, understanding and unselfish love.' He flung his towel down on the sand. 'Believe me, families can be a mixed blessing. They're overrated—well, that's my opinion, anyway. That may sound harsh, but…'

She turned to face him squarely. 'It not only sounds harsh, Adam, it *is* harsh,' she said, trying to keep a trace of bitterness out of her voice. 'I'm sorry that it clearly didn't work for you, but to have someone as close as a brother or sister…to share everything with in bad times as well as good…must be so comforting. Surely there can be no one else that you would feel as close to…no other human bond?' She swallowed a lump in her throat. 'Because blood is the precious thing that unites you…blood is the *lifeline*.'

Adam snorted derisively as he stared back at her. 'Oh, don't you think I know all that?' he said. 'And wouldn't it be amazing if everyone in the world was able to feel close to their "nearest and dearest"?' He spat out the words angrily.

'I've always thought it would be great to have someone to share things with,' Melody went on slowly, but he cut in before she could go on.

'Ah, yes—sharing,' he said, looking away. 'A wonderful concept. If it works.' He stood up suddenly. 'But, hey—why are we spoiling a brilliant afternoon? All this introspection is depressing me!' He reached down and pulled Melody to her feet. 'Let's get dressed and find somewhere for a meal—those sandwiches we ate earlier have become a distant memory, and I'm always hungry after a swim.'

Melody did as she was told, and with the aid of her bathrobe dressed easily, then rubbed at her hair furiously. She knew it would take some time to dry, but the sun, still hot and golden on their backs, would help. Fishing in her bag for her hairbrush, she started to drag it through the unwilling tangles, and glanced up to see Adam watching her.

'That looks like agony,' he commented.

'It is,' she agreed. 'And it also makes my arms ache.'

'Here. Let me.'

He moved over to her side and took the brush from her, and

even though she'd rather have done it herself she didn't object, but stood perfectly still as he deftly worked his way through her long tresses, dragging the brush in long, sweeping strokes from the crown of her head to where the hair ended at her waist. Occasionally he stopped to run his fingers through it gently—which had an almost dizzying effect on Melody, making her nerve-ends tingle from the back of her neck to the top of her thighs. He didn't say anything at all while he was engaged in this operation, seeming to be lost in his own thoughts.

Melody was certainly lost in hers! But then, she thought, she'd always loved someone combing and brushing her hair...it relaxed her, made her feel good. And doing this for her seemed to bring Adam back to normal. When they'd talked about families just now she'd seen a different side to him. Clearly there must have been huge sibling rivalry between the two brothers. She shrugged inwardly. Well, if he was the jealous type it was no concern of hers. Perhaps Rupert had always been the favourite with their parents? It could happen; she knew that. But to bear grudges or to show resentment was un-attractive in a man, as were all the things he'd said about family life. He clearly had no time for relationships in general, she thought, remembering the flippant way he'd answered her when she'd asked if he was married. *No, thanks,* had been his terse reply! But none of this should come as a surprise, she thought. He wanted to be foot-loose and fancy-free, while clearly enjoying the company of women. Winner takes all, in his case!

By the time they left the beach it was nearly seven o'clock. 'There used to be a good place to eat a mile or so further on from here,' Adam said, as he stowed their things into the car boot. 'I haven't been there for ages, and it's probably changed a bit by now—but it may be worth a try.'

They got into the car and drove away. Suddenly beginning to feel deliciously tired and tingly, Melody leaned her head back against the seat. 'That was a most unexpected treat,' she said. She turned to glance at him. 'Many thanks for that, Adam.'

'My pleasure,' he said casually.

'I suppose when one has children beach holidays are a must,' Melody went on. 'We all usually go skiing, or on other activity breaks…'

'Who's "we"?' Adam asked, without looking at her.

'Oh—my friends…workmates,' she replied. 'We don't do very much socialising during the year, but an annual expedition based on healthy exercise seems to have become the norm over recent years.'

He turned to look at her then. 'Well, you're going to miss all that, then—coming down here instead,' he said pointedly.

'Oh, I shan't be let off that lightly,' Melody said. 'I'll have to fit it all in somehow.'

'Mmm…trying to please yourself and everyone else as well can be a pressure,' he said casually. 'I can see that eventually you'll end up letting the cottage to strangers, just to justify your financial outlay and keep the place ticking over,' he went on. 'Empty places soon deteriorate.'

'Oh, I shan't *ever* use it for letting purposes!' Melody declared. 'That was never my thought when I bought it. No…I intended it, and still do, as an escape—a chance for a complete change. Somewhere for me to—what's that current phrase?— "recharge my batteries" from time to time. As often as I can possibly arrange it,' she added.

'Yes, it's a popular concept,' he agreed. 'But for it to work, it must be properly planned.' He paused. 'I don't think you've *really* thought this one out, Mel,' he said, in what to her sounded like a headmaster's admonition! 'It's extremely hard for a life to work on two levels, and to be honest I shouldn't be surprised to see Gatehouse Cottage back on the market in a couple of years from now.'

Melody was stung by that thought. 'It certainly will not be!' she said. What did *he* know of her plans, of her intentions. But, annoyingly, there was a grain of truth in his remarks—not about the possibility of selling, but about her finding it difficult to pack up and come down here for flying visits, glorious as that prospect had seemed when she'd bid for the cottage. Well, she'd prove him wrong! Somehow she'd squeeze enough time out of her frantically busy career to make the trip at least every couple of months. She was not going to be defeated now—and certainly not by the remarks and opinions of this man who was little more than a stranger. Even though he didn't *feel* like a stranger!

Angrily, she turned to look out of the window. She was going to make damned sure that Gatehouse Cottage was hers for a very long time to come. She'd never give him the satisfaction of being proved right!

They reached the restaurant, and Adam clicked his tongue. 'So—it *is* here,' he said, 'but somewhat changed, I fear.'

The place had obviously been taken over by one of the large chains, and, pulling into the huge car park, he glanced across at her. 'Do we risk this—or find somewhere quieter?' he asked.

'This'll be fine by me,' Melody replied coolly, realising that by now she was feeling very hungry.

Inside, the restaurant was heaving with families, and small children's voices were raised piercingly above the general loud conversation and clattering of dishes. Adam looked down at Melody as they entered.

'Do we advance or retreat?' he asked.

'Don't be pathetic,' Melody replied. 'This'll be fine. Look—there's a table for two, right over there in the corner.'

They sat down, and Adam looked around him, his lip curling slightly. 'Ye gods,' he said. 'It's like a zoo. Look over there—there are seven kids in that family!'

Melody couldn't help smiling. 'Seven does seem extrava-gant,' she said. Then, 'So—you don't like children?'

'Don't know them—so can't express an opinion,' he replied. 'But, as I'm most unlikely to ever have any of my own, the matter is irrelevant.' He paused. 'What about you? Your well-expressed opinion about families leads me to think that you'll probably have a litter of your own one day.'

Melody shrugged. 'It isn't something I've given a lot of thought to,' she said slowly. 'I suppose we would have started a family at some point…but since Crispin died… Well, anyway, I don't somehow think that it's likely now.'

He tilted his head and raised one eyebrow, encouraging her to go on, but Melody decided that enough was enough, and the subject was dropped.

Against their expectations, the service was quick and the food good. Adam chose a rare steak for his meal, while Melody preferred tender lamb cutlets, and, despite the bedlam going on all around them, they both ate heartily.

'See?' she said. 'Despite the prevailing atmosphere, it didn't put us off our supper, did it?'

'I told you that swimming always makes me hungry,' Adam said, draining his glass of red wine.

'Yes—and it must have had the same effect on me,' Melody said, putting down her knife and fork.

She glanced up at him for a moment and he held her gaze. She knew that he had been watching her as she ate. She'd have loved to be able to read his mind…or maybe she wouldn't! Because when he looked at her like that she knew very well what would be uppermost in his thoughts. She admitted to herself that it warmed her, made her feel special. But she didn't need this, she reminded herself. She couldn't cope with it! Her plans, whatever his opinion of her, did not include him—or any other member of the male sex!

She picked up her glass of water. 'I am going to pay for this meal, Adam,' she began firmly, determined to assert the fact that she was her own woman, and didn't expect any favours.

'Over my dead body,' he said pleasantly.

'Then we'll fight over it, and I'll make a scene,' she countered.

'Go ahead. No one'll hear you over this din,' he said. Then, 'It'll be a privilege to pay for a beautiful woman to…recharge her batteries. I've certainly recharged my own,' he added. 'That was a good steak.' He reached for his wallet and glanced across at her. 'How about making a start on those trees tomorrow?' he asked casually.

Melody looked back at him steadily. 'Your holiday is being completely swallowed up on my behalf,' she said. 'You really don't need to spend any more time on me, or Gatehouse Cottage. I already feel guilty about all that cleaning you helped me with.'

He shrugged. 'I told you, it's been a pleasant diversion for me,' he said, thinking that if she did prefer to be by herself he'd better back off. Better for both of them—especially him! He was enjoying this woman's company far too much, when all he'd really wanted to do was find out about her and her future intentions for the cottage. Maybe, by some unimagined quirk of circumstance, he might still be able to undermine her decision and get her to sell it on again. Though he didn't feel too optimistic that that would ever happen.

'I think I'll leave the trees until next weekend,' Melody said lightly. 'As a matter of fact I've invited some friends down for a few days—I've said I'll book some rooms for them, and I'm sure they'll enjoy helping out in the garden.'

'What friends are those?'

'Oh—my special mates, Eve and Jon. We work together most of the time.' She paused. 'And they're bringing Jason with them—who I haven't known for quite as long, but…'

'Boyfriend?' Adam asked bluntly.

She gave him a measured glance. 'Sort of. He's working pretty hard at it,' she said. 'He's a nice bloke, actually...I like him.' She reached into her bag for a tissue, thinking of Jason's shock of fair hair and his ready wit. She'd asked Eve to bring him down as well, so that Adam would get the message and maybe make himself scarce for a change. But in doing so she hoped that Jason would not get the wrong idea and see it as encouragement. Because she had no emotional interest in him, and never would have.

The waitress came across then, with their bill. Just as Adam was about to scrutinise it, his mobile rang, and he reached into his pocket to answer it. When Melody saw his expression change, she immediately leaned forward.

'What is it?' she asked quietly.

He shook his head briefly, still listening intently. Then, 'Of course...we'll come straight back—take us about an hour, Callum. And don't worry. We'll sort everything.'

Melody held her breath. 'What *is* it?' she asked again.

Adam stood up quickly. 'It's Fee. She's been taken ill. They're waiting for the ambulance now.'

# CHAPTER SEVEN

THEY couldn't get out of the restaurant fast enough, and in a few moments were sweeping out of the car park, with Adam's foot hard on the accelerator.

Sitting forward in her seat, but staring straight ahead, Melody said, 'What exactly did Callum say, Adam? When did this happen?'

'A couple of hours ago,' he said. 'Apparently Callum had been out walking the dogs, then stopped to spend a few minutes in his workshop at the back—sorting out some wood he's bought. When he went inside he found Fee had collapsed on the stairs.'

Melody was horrified, and turned to look at Adam as he spoke, noting the grim set of his jaw and realising again how close he must be to the pair. He might not have much time for his own kith and kin, she thought fleetingly, but there was no doubt about his loyalty to his friends.

'So, what did the doctor have to say?' Melody asked.

'Not much—except that she should go to hospital immediately.' He paused and glanced across. 'Fee is pregnant, by the way,' he said shortly. 'They're both longing for a family—have been for a long time. But they've already had so many disappointments.' He shook his head briefly. 'This doesn't look good—and Callum sounded desperate with worry.'

Melody looked away, not volunteering the fact that she'd been let in on the hopeful news. 'Poor Fee,' she murmured. Then, 'Why is it that those who really, really, want children sometimes seem to have so much difficulty?'

Adam shrugged. 'They both had the feeling that this time was going to be the lucky one,' he said. 'But it seems to be following a pattern, I'm afraid.' He waited before going on. 'They only told me about it last night in the pub, and they were so upbeat and excited.' He banged his fist on the steering wheel. 'It's so damned unfair!'

'But Callum didn't say that Fee had actually miscarried, did he?' Melody asked. 'She has been feeling the heat all day—we know that. Maybe it's just a faint, a bad turn…?'

'No, it's more than that,' Adam said. 'Apparently she'd been lying there for ages, quite unable to get herself up… And I believe there were other symptoms…' He didn't go on, and Melody bit her lip. She knew that Fee was at a very delicate point in her pregnancy and that anything untoward would be viewed very seriously.

'On a practical level,' Adam said, glancing across at her, 'Poplars is going to be unmanned until Callum returns from the hospital later. That's why he's asked me to get back as soon as possible.'

'Well, what normally happens in an emergency?' Melody asked. 'Don't they have back-up? People in the village…?'

'There are one or two they can usually call on,' he replied. 'But there's this wretched summer flu going around like wildfire, and even the permanent girl who helps with the cleaning has been off for the last two days. It'll be hard to find anyone available. Anyway,' he said, pausing briefly as they approached a crossroads, 'I've told Callum we're on our way. He's going to follow the ambulance and stay with Fee until her condition becomes clearer, though the doctor hinted that she's likely to be kept in for a few days. I told Callum I'd see to the dogs—and everything else—until he gets back.'

Melody sat back in her seat, picturing Fee's attractive features—which must now be twisted with anxiety and desperation. Poor girl, she thought. She wanted to have children so badly. Then Melody's expression cleared slightly. Surely they shouldn't be too pessimistic just yet? she thought. As far as anyone knew, Fee's baby was still where it should be—this could easily be a horrible false alarm, something that could be sorted. Antenatal care had improved dramatically over the years, and women seemed to be giving birth against all the odds. Just thinking along those lines made Melody's heart lift. She somehow couldn't help believing that one day Poplars would ring with the chatter of small voices—and Callum and Fee would be the best parents in the whole world.

It took a bit longer to get back to Poplars than Adam had thought, and it was almost dark when they eventually arrived. Callum's car was nowhere to be seen.

'They've obviously gone,' Adam noted briefly. 'Callum said he'd leave me a message about anything I need to be aware of.'

Melody felt relieved that Fee was already in professional hands and on her way to hospital. The sooner Fee was assessed, and possible treatment begun, the greater the chance of saving her baby, she reasoned.

She followed Adam into the immaculately tidy kitchen, where the dogs—obviously having had their meal for the day—lay comfortably sprawled out on the floor. A hastily scribbled note lay on the table, and Adam picked it up, reading it out loud.

'"Adam—I'm just off. It's nine-twenty. Fee has already gone in the ambulance. I hope to be back before morning, but could you hold the fort until then? You know how everything ticks. Fee is comfy at the moment. Thanks, mate. C."'

As Adam looked down at her, Melody saw a look of deep

concern on the handsome features, and she touched his hand gently. 'Don't worry too much,' she said, trying to sound more optimistic than she felt. 'This doesn't have to have a bad ending, and Fee is in the best hands,' she added.

'Yes, I know that,' he said, bending to smooth the glossy heads of the animals, who'd ambled over to his side. 'But Callum sounded so desperate on the phone. I really wonder whether they can tolerate yet another disappointment. I mean, how much more of this can they take?' He stood back and ran his hand through his hair. 'They're good, kind, hard-working people…they don't deserve this trauma every time!'

Melody looked around her. 'What happens if Callum has to stay with Fee and doesn't get back tomorrow?' she asked.

'Well, I'll have to explain to the guests—all the rooms are occupied, so we have a full house—and tell them that cooked breakfasts are off the menu. They'll just have to be satisfied with cold stuff.' He paused. 'Do you know, if I *do* have to tell them that it'll be a first for Poplars? In all the years that Callum and Fee have run the place they've kept it going without a hitch—even when Fee was going through a bad patch.' He bit his lip. 'I know they just hate any disruption, or any reason for their guests to be dissatisfied.'

'Well, then,' Melody said, a rising note of determination in her voice. 'We'll make sure that doesn't happen.' She looked up at him. 'As long as every guest doesn't turn up at exactly the same moment for their breakfast in the morning, I can cope with grilling bacon and frying eggs, and—'

He looked down into her upturned face and instinctively cupped his hand under her chin. 'Are you saying…? Do you mean that you'd be prepared to help out?' he asked uncertainly.

She closed her hand over his wrist briefly. 'Adam,' she said patiently. 'I was trained from a very early age how to rise to any occasion.' She turned away. 'You know this place as well as anyone. Show me where they keep everything, and tomorrow—if it turns out to be necessary—I cook, you serve!' A faint smile played on her lips as she imagined Adam waiting at table, with a fresh white teatowel draped over his arm, maybe having to be polite to an unreasonable guest! Well, she'd make sure she gave no one any reason to complain, she thought firmly. She'd get up really early—give herself time to get to grips with any peculiarities in Fee's cooking equipment.

'You're finding something funny?' he asked, noting her amused expression but looking relieved that, between them, they might save the situation.

She hastily corrected him. 'No,' she said flatly. 'Of course not. I was just thinking what a strange turn my holiday seems to be taking. Ten days ago I had no idea that anything out of the ordinary was going to happen. I'd even thought I might go back to London sooner rather than later…but of course that was before I saw the sign outside Gatehouse Cottage.' *And before I met you,* she could have added, but didn't.

Adam went over to study the large boldly printed chart on the back of the door, running his finger along the columns. 'Good,' he said, 'no one appears to want early breakfast tomorrow, and with a bit of luck there shouldn't be any undue bottlenecks. Oh…the lady in room seven is allergic to wheat, so she has to have special bread, which is apparently in a sealed bag in the cabinet. "Not to be in contact with other bread", it says here,' he added. He continued perusing the chart, then, 'And the guests in room two are checking out tomorrow. Their bill is already worked out, apparently, with all details in the safe.' He turned around and looked over to Melody. 'D'you think we're up to this, Mel? Up to the challenge?' he asked, only half joking.

She looked back at him eagerly. 'I don't *think* so, I *know* so,' she replied, glancing up at the big clock on the wall. 'But—

first things first—I'd better go to bed, stock up on my energy reserves for the morning!'

'Good thinking,' he said. 'When I've locked up at midnight I'll hit the sack, too. But the dogs will need their last walk in a few minutes.'

Melody picked up her holdall from the chair and went to open the door, turning briefly. 'By the way—thanks again for taking me to the seaside,' she said. 'It's been a…a good day….'

He grinned down at her. 'Even if it has ended rather unexpectedly,' he said. Then his expression clouded. 'I hope they've stabilised Fee,' he said. 'If she does lose this baby, I don't know what words we can use to comfort her.'

'Well, as far as we know, the worst has not happened,' Melody said firmly. 'And the best thing we can do is to keep the wheels turning here and put their minds at rest on that score, at least.' She stifled a yawn, leaning against the wall for a second. 'But if I don't lie down soon, I'll fall down! I'm starting to ache in every limb since that swim!'

Adam opened the door for her at once, and as she brushed past him he held her arm gently for a moment.

'Callum is sure to ring me. To let me know how things are,' he said, 'and also when he's likely to be coming back.' He hesitated. 'I won't disturb you to tell you, but I'll slip a note under your door—for you to see when you wake in the morning.'

'I'll set my alarm to go off early,' Melody said, yawning properly this time.

Adam moved away from her, then had a sudden thought. 'Would you like a cup of tea?' he asked. 'Or something stronger?'

She glanced up at him quickly. 'How did you guess? A cup of tea would be fantastic,' she said. 'No sugar, and just a dash of milk, thanks.'

'I'll bring it up in a few minutes,' he said, adding, 'You do look all-in, Mel.'

Upstairs, Melody spent as few minutes as possible in the bathroom, then set her travel alarm clock for half past six before sinking down onto the bed gratefully, not even bothering to get beneath the duvet. This had been one long day, she thought. Brilliant in many ways—too many ways!—but ending un-thinkably with Fee being rushed off like that. Even in her near sleeping state, Melody frowned in sympathy. The signs were not good, she realised, despite her forced optimism when she and Adam had been discussing it.

Adam…. In her mind's eye, she saw how the seawater had glistened and run down his body as they'd walked across the sand, the muscles in his suntanned thighs rippling and tighten-ing as he'd held her closely, supporting her over the pebbles. With sleep now almost upon her, Melody shifted slightly on the bed. This had to stop, she thought. It *must* stop! She seemed to have been thrust into a whirlpool since the moment she'd pur-chased Gatehouse Cottage. The property seemed to have come complete with a resident male who just happened to be tall, dark, handsome—and horribly desirable! Desire? *Desire?* That had become a defunct word in her life—or she'd thought so! Go away—go *away*! she implored whoever was listening. Don't want it, don't need it… Her eyes flickered open for a second. 'That's not true,' she whispered to herself. 'The truth is—I'm *frightened* of it!' Then, utterly exhausted, sleep finally claimed her.

Presently there came a discreet tap on her door, and Adam's low voice saying her name. He failed to rouse her, and he turned the handle gently and went inside, closing the door behind him.

Going over to the bed, he looked down on Melody's inert form, saw her slender body barely covered by the simple night-dress she was wearing. She'd released her ponytail so that her hair was spread out in a luxurious fan of honey-coloured waves across the pillow, and her eyelashes, resting gently on the curve of her cheek, must be the longest he'd ever seen on a woman.

He swallowed, putting the mug of tea down quietly on the bedside table. The picture she presented had sent his senses rocketing, and he turned away. His natural instinct was to slip in alongside her—hold her, caress her… But he knew he'd be wasting his time. Not because she was frigid—she was far from that; she was warm and utterly appealing, in a certain way irresistible! But she was definitely not the sort of woman to engage in temporary relationships—there'd be no such thing as a quick fling in *her* life! And anyway, he thought, irritated again at the way his mind was working, he had no wish—or intention—to ever commit himself again to anything permanent. So he might as well accept this no-win situation and take the whole business of this woman crossing his path at face value. And stop allowing his thoughts to give him all this aggro!

Melody woke even before the alarm went off. She'd slept well, and now, feeling refreshed and ready for anything the day might bring, she slid out of bed and went over to the door. A note lay on the floor, and she picked it up, going over to the window-sill and pulling the curtains aside. A ray of sunlight shafted across Adam's strong, purposeful writing on the paper.

> One a.m. It looks like action stations, Mel. Callum was advised to stay with Fee for the moment—at least until they've seen the consultant together, which they hope will be today. I've told him we're taking over until he gets back, and he's over the moon about that. But the best news is that Fee hasn't lost the baby—yet. See you later!

Melody's heart lifted—all was not lost! she thought. The worst had not happened. And, meanwhile, there was a guesthouse to run!

She showered and pulled on fresh jeans and a white T-shirt, dragging her hair back in a formal knot on top, to keep it well out of the way. Then, going quickly downstairs, she met Adam at the kitchen door as he came in with the dogs.

'You've had a good rest,' he said approvingly, noting her bright eyes and wide-awake manner.

'Slept like a log,' she replied. 'Thank you for the tea, by the way,' she added, not bothering to admit that she'd not tasted it because she hadn't seen it until she woke up.

'You didn't answer my knock so I just left it,' he said.

'Yes, thanks,' she murmured, hoping that she hadn't been exposing too much of herself at the time… Well, not enough to interest his perceptive gaze, she thought. But she didn't really care one way or the other.

In the kitchen, the dogs immediately went over to their water bowls and lapped furiously. 'I've already checked the dining room,' Adam said. 'All the tables are set for breakfast, and all we have to do at the moment is put the cereals out—they're stacked in the tall cupboard over there. The juices and fruits are obviously in the fridge—to go in those glass bowls on the shelf.' He paused. 'Everyone helps themselves to all that, of course…' he added.

'Yes. That's the easy bit,' Melody said. 'Now, let's see if I can get the bacon just as everyone wants it—and fry the eggs without damaging the yolks!'

Adam put the kettle on, looking across at her. 'I think the cook should be fed first,' he said. 'Tea and toast do you, Mel?'

'Perfect,' she said, adding, 'And I can always cook for you later on, if you like…'

'Oh, I seldom eat fried breakfasts,' Adam said, reaching for two mugs for their tea. 'But you never know—I might be tempted.'

They smiled across at each other as the kettle began to hum, and Melody felt a ridiculous sense of anticipation. She'd never been in the catering business before—this was going to be a whole new experience! But her greatest sense was one of genuine pleasure in helping out Adam's friends—to at least do something to minimise their present crisis. Because, although she tried hard to push it from her mind, she could not stop feeling guilty about the purchase of the cottage—the cottage they had wanted so badly. For her, it had been an unbelievable bolt from the blue, and somehow it didn't seem quite fair that it was hers.

Together, they did everything they could before the guests started arriving for breakfast, and soon the delicious aroma of percolating coffee—which Adam took charge of—seemed to bring several of them down at once. By half past eight, Melody had grilled a couple of dozen sausages, large numbers of delectable rashers of back bacon—all put aside to keep warm— while lining up dishes of mushrooms and slices of black pudding ready to be fried. The boxes of eggs stood on the kitchen table, to be done last. Turning briefly from her task, she wiped her brow with the back of her hand. Even this early, the sun was hot as it streamed through the open window.

Adam came in from the dining room to fetch more milk, pouring it into a huge glass jug. 'So far, so good,' he said. 'They're all munching away on their cereals at the moment.'

'How many full English breakfasts did you say you'd be needing?' Melody asked, not looking at him as she lifted hot slices of fried bread from the pan.

'Six—almost due,' he said. 'When you're ready, Mel.'

'Just the eggs, then,' Melody said, turning to crack them open. 'Fingers crossed that the yolks don't break and I can present them just like Fee does,' she said, glancing up at him.

He touched her shoulder briefly. 'You're doing Fee proud,' he said—and meant it. Because Melody had entered willingly into the whole episode—in the middle of her holiday, after all, he reminded himself. He'd observed the precise way she'd organised all the food, her deft handling of Fee's pans and utensils. She was certainly no slouch, he thought, fascinated to see how her small hands slid the eggs into the hot fat, with not a single one broken in the process. Well, she'd informed him that she could rise to any occasion, and now she was proving it!

'I'll clear away the dirty dishes,' he said over his shoulder as he went out, 'and then come back for the breakfasts. If you're sure you're ready?' he added.

'I'm ready,' Melody said, lining up warm plates in a row, and placing all the items of cooked food onto them. 'One without black pudding, and three with double eggs,' she chanted aloud. 'One without black pudding, and three with double eggs…' She kept repeating the mantra, hoping that she'd got it the right way around, and added the slices of fried bread that everyone had asked for. Then she carefully wiped the edges of the plates with a clean teatowel, and stood back. They looked good, she congratulated herself.

Adam came back almost at once, and immediately started to load the dishwasher. 'Four more have just come down,' he said. 'Two want full English, one without sausage. And one wants scrambled eggs, and one poached. Those last two on toast, please, one of which must be gluten-free.'

'Okay—that special bread is over there,' Melody said. 'I'll remember.'

Adam loaded two large trays with the food already prepared, and looked at Melody. 'This all looks fantastic, Mel,' he said. 'You're doing a great job!'

'You, too,' she replied, looking up at him, her face flushed from the heat of the cooker.

At nine-thirty, the last guest arrived for his breakfast. By now the dining room was almost deserted, and Melody couldn't help feeling relieved that the end was in sight. She plonked herself down on one of the kitchen chairs for a moment, staring at the hard-worked toaster in front of her. She'd lost count of the number of slices she'd sent into the dining room, and was thinking that if none of the guests had another crumb to eat that day they'd hardly starve! But everyone had been very co-operative and pleasant when Adam had briefly explained that the owners had been called away unexpectedly.

'Well, we've got nothing to complain about,' someone said. 'The owners are lucky to have such efficient stand-ins!'

In a few moments Adam came back in, looking slightly rueful. 'Sorry, Mel—our last guest has requested poached eggs on haddock. He's chomping away on a big bowl of muesli at the moment…'

'Where's the haddock?' Melody asked anxiously. 'I haven't seen any, or given fish a thought. It's certainly not in the fridge—I know everything that's there off by heart…'

'Try the freezer, then,' Adam said. 'It must be in there.'

It was, and it was frozen solid. Muttering under her breath, cross that she hadn't spotted it on the menu, Melody split open the pack and put a fillet into the microwave to defrost. Then she filled the kettle for boiling water.

'This is going to take a few minutes,' she said, looking up at Adam. 'Go and keep him talking—or give him some more cereal!'

Adam grinned at her as he left the room, while Melody concentrated on the job in hand. Why couldn't this guest have asked for bacon and eggs, like everyone else? she thought. But presently, with the fillet of sunshine-yellow haddock and two perfectly poached eggs sitting proudly on top, she felt quite pleased with herself. Well, if she was asked for that again she'd be ready, she thought.

Eventually, fully satisfied, the man left the dining room. Adam and Melody immediately cleared the tables, setting them all again with crockery and cutlery for the following day, and presently, in the kitchen, with the fully laden dishwasher gurgling and gushing away in the corner, Adam sat astride one of the chairs, draping his arms over the back of it in mock fatigue.

'Blimey,' he said quietly. 'That was all go. Well done, Mel. You did a fantastic job.'

'It was a joint effort,' she acknowledged, sitting down as well, and leaning her arms on the table. 'And once I got into the swing of it I rather enjoyed myself,' she said. 'I might even consider a new career!' She paused. 'How much help does Fee have normally?' she asked.

'Only one part-time girl for breakfasts,' he replied. 'But Callum's always on hand. And don't forget they've been doing this a long time. They're experienced. We're not!'

After a few minutes Melody stood up and began clearing everything away, replacing the pots and pans she'd used back in their rightful place. Adam still sat, watching her. 'I have an imminent appointment with my shower,' she said, 'and I may be gone some time!'

He waited before answering. Then, 'Why don't you leave that until later…when we've finished?'

Melody frowned. 'But we have, haven't we?' she said.

'We've fed everyone, certainly,' he agreed. 'But as soon as they've all disappeared for the day there are the rooms to service…'

Melody clapped her hand over her mouth. 'Oh, what an *idiot*! I haven't given the rooms a single thought.' She paused. 'Is no one coming in to help?'

'Unlikely,' Adam said casually. 'I had another call from Callum early this morning—no change in Fee, by the way—and he said that the girl who usually helps with the rooms is still not well enough… She'll turn up if she feels like it, apparently. But I don't think we should count on it. Anyway,' he added, 'we've got all day. It's not as if we have to provide evening meals as well!'

Melody sat back down on her chair for a second, then immediately got up again. 'Right. Well, then. Come on,' she said, looking across at him. 'Where do we begin?'

'There's a trolley in the utility room always set up with everything necessary,' Adam said, getting up as well.

Just then there was a discreet tap on the door. The guests who were leaving wanted to settle their bill, and Adam ushered them over to the desk in the hall, making pleasantries as he went. In the kitchen, Melody looked around her. Well, everything was neat and tidy here, she thought. Now for the next stage in the proceedings!

As Adam was finally wishing the departing guests a safe journey onwards, he heard a short, sharp scream, and Melody's voice ringing out.

'Oh…damn you—*damn* you!' he heard. 'You swine!'

'*What* the—?' he said under his breath, and he burst open the kitchen door, seeing Melody over by the window, rubbing furiously at her arm, clearly very agitated. 'What ever is it?' he demanded, reaching her side in a couple of strides.

'A wasp! It just flew in through the window and pitched on my arm and stung me! The wretched thing!' she cried. 'I did nothing to deserve that…I didn't even see it! Not until I felt it!' She kept rubbing. 'I *hate* wasps! What are they *for*, anyway? What purpose do they serve?'

Although slightly concerned, Adam made himself keep a straight face as he took her arm and examined it closely. He didn't bother to mention that they often had swarms of the things at this time of year—or that when the fruit-picking began down at her cottage she was likely to encounter one or two more!

'I can see the sting,' he murmured. 'Hold still a minute.' Then he took her arm to his mouth and sucked at it firmly.

'Ow—ow!' Melody said pathetically. 'It really hurts! I've only ever been stung once before in my life, and I didn't appreciate it then, either! Wretched spiteful creature!'

For a few moments neither of them spoke, while Adam continued tugging at her skin with his lips and tongue, peering at it every now and then. Then, satisfied, he looked down at Melody. 'It's out now,' he said soothingly. 'Just dab some vinegar on the sore spot—you'll soon be good as new.'

But he didn't let go of her arm. He just brought it once more to his lips…only this time he kissed it—once, twice, three times—gently. With her eyes open, Melody looked up at him. And suddenly, without any warning, their lips met, tentatively at first, then with increasing passion as he wrapped his arms around her, drawing her in close to him as if he never wanted to let her go. To his enormous pleasure and delight, she didn't resist, but entered into it with him…allowed herself to desire…and to be desired.

Melody felt her senses swimming as they stayed locked together in a state of heightened excitement, then she eased herself away—gently but firmly.

'Thank you,' she said shakily. 'For removing the wasp sting, I mean,' she added.

He smiled down, his body painfully taut with his sensual need of her. 'I enjoyed every second of it,' he murmured softly.

For a few moments neither of them said anything in the rather tense atmosphere, then Melody's commonsense took over—and brought her back to earth with a bang! What was going on? she asked herself. Was she in the middle of a dream? A dream in which she'd just cooked breakfast for everyone at the guesthouse that she was *paying* to stay in…and in which, thanks to a wasp sting, she'd just allowed Adam Carlisle to kiss her in the sort of way she'd never expected to experience ever again? Worst of all—she'd wanted him to!

'I'm sorry,' she said, glancing quickly up at him. 'That…that must have been the effect of the wasp stinging me.' She swallowed. 'It…sort of took me by surprise.'

He didn't attempt to touch her again, but let his eyes do the talking…and they were talking volumes! 'Don't apologise,' he said softly. 'I like surprises. Especially ones like that.'

# CHAPTER EIGHT

THE rest of the day passed in a blur of activity as, between them, Adam and Melody went into each of the rooms. Melody automatically took charge of the order in which everything should be done, but it was Adam who knew which cupboards held the fresh linen, where all Fee's equipment was kept, and it was he who insisted on wielding the heavy vacuum cleaner—which he did with ferocious energy—while charging up and down the stairs to answer the phone or fetch something they needed from the ground floor.

'Fee has a thing about disinfecting everything,' Adam said as he reached for a bottle of detergent, and Melody nodded.

During her short stay, she'd been gratefully aware of how spotless her room and bathroom were kept, but today was even more aware that her own mother would have spent years doing what *she* was doing now. And as she'd dusted the windowsills and picture frames she'd had the weirdest sense that Frances was there, too, helping her. Stop imagining things, she scolded herself, more than once. Anyway, Callum and Fee had done so much renovating her mother would have hardly recognised the place. But Melody couldn't avoid the feeling that the very walls seemed to speak of the past, and of the people who'd lived in it. And that had the distinct advantage of making what they were doing actually pleasurable—it became a surprisingly happy chance, rather than a chore. Together with all the cleaning they'd done at the cottage, her holiday was indeed turning into a sort of activity break, but one which not many people would ever sign up for! she thought.

Plunging herself so enthusiastically into what she was doing also provided Melody with an emotional shield against the turmoil that was threatening to engulf her. Because the atmosphere between her and Adam had perceptibly changed—and she knew he felt it, too. Their eyes had barely met since he'd kissed her—yet it was the thing starkly uppermost in her mind. The feeling of his arms wrapped around her so comfortingly, so protectively. Her head against his chest, hearing the thudding of his heart… Then the fusing of their lips, which had caused her emotions to rocket off into outer space, making her knees almost give way.

But along with all the other good things she'd been taught, Melody had more than her fair share of common sense, and she recognised the fleeting passion she was experiencing as just that—fleeting. A holiday infatuation. That was it, she told herself. A pointless, temporary attraction to someone she'd met during a time away when neither of them had the distraction of more important, essential matters. Oh, they'd no doubt promise to keep in touch—he'd ring, she'd ring, they'd meet up, make plans. Except they wouldn't, of course. With the link of sun and summer and relaxation gone, their association would melt away like ice in the sunshine, and that would be that.

And that would suit him very well, thank you, she thought. Where women and sex were concerned, he wore his *modus operandi* for all to see: take what you can, when you can, with no expectations of anything more. He was certainly no chauvinist—she freely admitted that—but he fitted the type of male she'd met many times before. The sort who took what he could get, but didn't expect to part with any more of himself than he wanted to give. And that was fine by her! That was exactly what she wanted—no more ties, no more tears, *ever*. That morning they'd already taken a dangerous step too far, but no harm— no real harm—had been done, and that was how it must stay. And the marked coolness between them now proved to her that those were his sentiments, too.

Just then he ran up the stairs two at a time, after having gone to answer the phone, and Melody said, 'I want everything to look as good as when Fee's here.' She glanced up at him as she sprayed polish on the curved mahogany banister, and rubbed at it briskly.

He shook his head briefly as he coiled up the flex of the vacuum cleaner. 'Well, if you put any more effort into that,' he observed dryly, 'it'll disappear—and so will you. Give yourself a break, Mel. You're not a carthorse.'

That evening Callum returned for a flying visit, and was overwhelmed by how Adam and Melody had been handling everything.

'I can't thank you both enough,' he said, kneeling down on the kitchen floor to make a fuss of the dogs. 'All I can say is that when you're up against it, you really find out who your true friends are.'

Adam shot a quick glance at Melody, and although she'd deliberately tried to avoid making anything that could be described as meaningful eye contact with him since their intimate coupling, he managed to fix his gaze to hers. His conspiratorial wink dented her reserve for a second, then, smiling briefly, she looked away.

'Oh, I've carried out all Mel's commands to the letter,' he said. 'She's a hard task-master! But truthfully, Callum, it's a pleasure to be of some use at a time like this. Don't worry about it.'

'I'll be honest, Adam, knowing that you were here set my mind at rest—not to mention Fee's. We've hardly given a thought to Poplars…'

'I should hope not!' Melody said. 'Now, Callum, tell us the latest…tell us the important bit.'

Callum sat down heavily on one of the comfortable, well-worn chairs and looked up at them. 'Well, as you already know, our baby is still holding his/her own…' he began.

Melody felt a curious pang of something she found hard to explain. The man had referred to 'our' baby—even though the scrap of humanity had such a long way to go before it finally emerged into the world.

'And although we've been this way before,' Callum went on, 'we're pinning our hopes on an eminent specialist who's visiting the hospital tomorrow or the day after—they're not sure which. He's apparently a leading light in this field, and there's a new drug available which might help Fee to go full-term. But we both need to talk to him—so I'll have to go back to the hospital, I'm afraid. And just wait for him to turn up. As always, there are issues which will need to be discussed, and we must both be there.' He made an apologetic face. 'I'm really sorry to take advantage of you like this, but I'm between a rock and a hard place, and—'

'Shut up, Callum,' Adam said. 'You don't need to apologise to *me*, for heaven's sake! About anything!'

'No, I know that.' Callum turned to Melody. 'This guy comes under the heading of "Super Mate",' he said, with a detectable break in his voice. 'Nothing is ever too much for him. He's helped us out so much over the years… I can heartily recommend him—in all respects!'

A cushion came flying across the room and landed squarely on Callum's head as Adam hurled it. 'I repeat—*shut up*,' he said. 'What the hell else are friends for?'

'But you, Mel,' Callum said, turning to her. 'Fee and I can't begin to thank you. We've heard all about how you've stepped so magnificently into the breach…as if you'd been born to it! And I mean you're on *holiday*, for Pete's sake!'

Melody smiled. 'You know, Callum, I've come to the conclusion that I'm not very good at prolonged periods of inactivity,' she said. 'I've already had a good break…pleasing myself, relaxing…and I think Adam might have been feeling the same. He was determined to help me clean my cottage—as if he needed that on *his* holiday!' She paused. 'You just make sure that Fee stays safely where she is until they're satisfied she and the baby are okay.'

'Well, as I said, we're pinning our hopes on this new man and his new drug,' Callum said, getting up from the chair. 'But now what I need is a shower and a fresh change of clothes—and Fee's asked me to take some stuff back for her.' He turned to Adam. 'The room which became vacant today—' he began, and Adam interrupted.

'Is vacant no longer,' he said. 'I could have let it three times over.'

'Great,' Callum said. 'But we're expecting other vacancies before the end of the week, aren't we? If I remember rightly?'

'Then that'll be very convenient,' Melody said. 'Three friends of mine are coming to visit at the weekend, and have asked me to fix them up. They'll love it here.' She didn't look at Adam as she spoke.

'Ah, yes, your friends from the big city,' he said lazily. 'We must take special care that all *their* needs are supplied.'

Now she *did* look at him. The expression on his face was as blank as hers, and told her nothing. But just thinking about Eve and Jon—and Jason—went some way towards helping Melody adjust her thinking. Their presence here would dilute the situation, would help her to shake off the 'Adam effect' and remind her that in the very near future she would be out of here and back to normality. Because she hadn't felt normal since she'd set foot in the area. Hadn't felt normal since she'd parted with all that money and become a two-home owner. And she hadn't felt normal since she'd met Adam Carlisle. She had allowed him to unfasten—so easily, it seemed to her—the protective cloak she'd wrapped around her emotions ever since Crispin had been taken from her.

Two days later, both part-time girls had returned to work—which did lessen the load dramatically, although privately Melody couldn't help thinking that she and Adam had managed more efficiently without them. Then, by arrangement with Callum, they were joined by the mother of one of the girls, who apparently sometimes worked for Fee. Which released Adam and Melody to resume their own plans.

That morning, Melody had driven away early—not even stopping to have breakfast before she went, in order to prevent bumping into Adam—determined to spend time by herself and to explore some of the area new to her. It was true that since Callum's departure they had spent less time together, and it didn't please Melody to realise that she missed Adam's presence—that even in the short time they'd known each other she'd come to depend on his company. This made her even more certain that she should put some space between them.

The following morning, the day before her friends were due to arrive, Melody wandered down Poplars' long drive towards Gatehouse Cottage, realising that she'd barely thought about it over the last few days. Of course at the moment there was nothing for her to do there—other than go inside and admire it all over again, and form mental pictures as to how she was going to furnish it. She'd already decided that the walls were to be washed throughout in a mellow buttermilk shade, with white gloss paint on all the woodwork. That would give her wonderful scope to fill the place with colourful furnishings and bright paintings, she decided.

Opening the front door, she stepped inside, aware again of the sense of awe she felt at owning this modest but desirable dwelling. Because this was not just *any* dwelling—something she might have just stumbled across. She had unwittingly come home—to the home she'd been told about so often that it felt familiar and warmly embracing. She smiled briefly as she looked around her. It smelt and looked clean and sweet and wholesome—thanks to the hard work she and Adam had put in the other day. How long ago that seemed now! she thought. And once the decorators had come and gone—she'd sort that out as soon as she got back to London—the cottage would be ready to welcome her as its new owner.

Despite the rather snide comments Adam had made about her not having the time or opportunity to come down here very often, she'd prove him wrong! She'd mark up her calendar with possible dates, and make sure that nothing prevented her from keeping them!

Going up the narrow staircase, she peeped into the spotless bathroom, and shivered again as she remembered how that spider had dropped down inside her T-shirt, and how she'd screamed like an idiot! And how Adam had rushed to her side and held her close. Standing quite still for a second, she realised that she'd never, ever go inside this room again without remembering the incident…without remembering Adam. Because it had been a turning point in her life. A point at which she'd had to face up to a need she'd thought she'd conquered. And which she'd thought she would never feel again.

Striding across the fields, calling brusquely to the dogs to keep up, Adam's expression was dark. He was annoyed and angry with himself. Despite everything that had happened since, he still couldn't believe that he'd allowed himself to get carried away the other morning and actually kiss Mel…even if it *was* something which had featured in a number of his dreams!

She was proving to be so much more than just a female who'd titillated his male instincts. Seeing the way she'd responded so readily to Callum and Fee's present dilemma had taken him by surprise. Of course he'd already witnessed her enthusiasm for cleaning up her own precious acquisition—but that was different. That was only to be expected. Putting in time and effort on your own behalf was not particularly laudable—anyone would do it. But to be deeply concerned about others—and to be ready to do something about it as she had—was a different matter entirely.

And the embarrassing part of it was he felt she resented the liberty he'd taken. There had been a deliberate coolness in her attitude ever since—as he should have known there would be. She was not a run-of-the-mill woman who'd enjoy a light relationship and treat it for what it was: a pleasurable but temporary phase. He frowned as his thoughts ran on. For a highly desirable woman like her, keeping unwelcome suitors at bay must be an ongoing problem, he thought—especially in the City, full of sharp-suited, superficial men with loaded wallets. Yet, he reminded himself, it couldn't be denied that she'd *enjoyed* their encounter, brief though it had been. For those few precious seconds she'd been his—it was only afterwards that she'd appeared to regret it.

He shrugged. If she was saying thanks, but no thanks, well, he'd comply—for his own good as well as hers. He'd made up his mind that there would not be a woman alive on this earth who'd ever leave him feeling so betrayed again. Because how could he know who to trust? He'd thought Lucy was the woman of his dreams, that they'd have a long and happy life together, hopefully here in the village, among all that he knew and loved. But the unthinkable thing which had happened had been so much more than the break-up of a couple…it had been a shattering, devastating experience, and had touched too many other lives as well as his own.

Bringing all these thoughts to the front of his mind had creased the handsome brow, set the uncompromising mouth in a formidable line. Enough was enough. It was time for him to pack up and go back to work—a long way from all this. Distance had its merits, and he was going to put some between himself and the new owner of Gatehouse Cottage as soon as possible.

The end of his walk had brought him to the back of the cottage, and without really wondering why he was doing it, he went around the front and up the path to look in at the window—and then saw the front door was open. Automatically he pushed it wider and went inside—just as Melody was coming down the stairs.

'Oh…hi,' she said, as she came down to stand in front of him.

'Hi,' he said casually, not bothering to give any explanation as to why he was there—because he had none. Then, 'I've been walking the dogs—saw the door open…'

She smiled briefly. 'I've just been daydreaming,' she said. 'Picturing where I'm going to put everything. After I've bought it all!'

For a second Adam experienced a wave of something approaching dislike of her and all her enthusiasm, remembering all too clearly how she'd breezed in and spoiled the plans of his best friends. And then he stared down at her. She was simply dressed, in a short above-the-knee denim skirt, her feet barely covered in dainty narrow-strapped white sandals, and her white blouse was trimmed with a tiny edging of lace at the neck and cap sleeves. As usual, her hair was shining as golden as a buttercup, held back from her face by a white scrunchie. Adam swallowed, feeling the familiar rush of adrenalin hit him. He cleared his throat.

'I've had a call from Callum. He's due home tonight—and Fee is coming back early next week,' he said.

Melody's eyes lit up. 'Oh—that's fantastic. What have they said about the baby?' she asked, going into the sitting room and turning to face him as he followed her.

'Well…so far, so good. Of course no one's committing themselves, but the specialist seems to think that there's more than a glimmer of hope this time,' he said. 'Fee apparently has a very particular genetic condition that the drug they propose using might overcome. She's been instructed to rest up for the next few weeks.'

Melody clapped her hands in delight. 'Oh, Adam—that… that's really great!' she exclaimed. 'They must both be thrilled…because there *is* real hope, isn't there?'

'It looks like it,' he said guardedly. 'Naturally they're terrified to tempt fate by being too optimistic, too soon. But I could tell by Callum's voice how excited they already are.'

'Well, *I'm* excited, too!' Melody said. 'Just imagine—one of those guest rooms being turned into a nursery!' She paused. 'I know which one I'd choose—the one that looks over that big horse chestnut tree, that gets the sun in the morning.'

'Steady on,' Adam said easily. 'There'll be plenty of time for all that in due course. When Miss or Master Brown puts in an appearance.'

Together they went outside, and the dogs—who'd been lying on the front lawn—got up to greet them. Melody's mobile rang, and she turned away to answer it. Adam crouched down to fondle the dogs, unavoidably hearing what was being said.

'Oh—hello, Jason…' Melody said. 'How's things?' There was a few moments' silence as she listened. Then, 'Oh, dear—no. Oh, what a shame… Well, let's make it another time, then, shall we?

I mean… Sorry? Are you sure you want to do that? Won't it be more…well, fun, when the others are able to come as well?'

There was another silence, and Adam, glancing up at her, saw Melody's expression change.

'Well, of course. If you really think you want to… Yes, I've fixed you a room. I'll just cancel the one I've booked for Eve and Jon.' There was another long pause. 'Well, give them my love—I'll be back in just over a week, in any case. And I'll see you tomorrow night sometime. You've got the directions I sent to Eve? I think you'll find them straightforward enough. Okay…okay. See you tomorrow. Bye… Bye, Jason.'

Melody snapped her phone shut and glanced down at Adam. 'Well, that's a shame,' she said. 'My friends—Eve and Jon— have both gone down with a really bad dose of something horrible, so they won't be coming tomorrow after all.' She sighed. 'But Jason—Jason is driving down by himself.'

'Well—that'll be cosy, won't it?' Adam said laconically. 'Just the two of you. He'll have you all to himself.'

Melody shot him a direct glance—and remembered why she'd invited Jason to come down in the first place! To stop Adam getting to her emotionally and also to send out a message to *him*. But even as she thought about it she wanted to curl up inside. The thought of having to entertain Jason by herself for forty-eight hours wasn't something she was looking forward to. She had tried, as tactfully as possible, to put him off, but he wasn't having any of it. The tables had been neatly turned on her and she was going to have to be an unwilling participant in a game of pretend. She desperately hoped that Jason wasn't coming with the wrong idea…that she had a special reason for inviting him… She groaned inwardly. What had she let herself in for?

# CHAPTER NINE

'CALLUM—I really feel that I should be helping out in the kitchen,' Melody said next morning, as she took her seat in the dining room, glancing up at him as he came towards her.

He grinned, and Melody couldn't help thinking how young and boyish he looked—compared to how he'd appeared the other night. Then he'd seemed so tired and careworn, but this morning it was different—now that he had sound reasons to be optimistic.

'I am so, *so* pleased that Fee is okay—is *going* to be to okay!' she amended. 'It's such good news, Callum.'

'It is—but fingers crossed,' he said carefully. 'For my part, I feel I should be serving *you* smoked salmon and champagne! Fee and I will never be able to thank you enough for all you did while I was with her at the hospital, Mel.'

'Oh, I won't be needing anything like that, thank you.' Melody smiled. 'Just some of your lovely scrambled eggs, please, Callum.' She paused. 'I didn't see you come home last night,' she added. 'Were you very late getting back?'

'No—not too bad. But you'd obviously already gone to bed, Mel.'

'Yes—I was rather tired,' Melody said.

In fact, she had purposely gone to her room early, so as not to give Adam the chance to invite her somewhere for supper. In any case, she'd been to the village during the day and bought a packet of sandwiches from the post office, which she'd had with the cup of tea she'd been able to make with the things available by her bedside.

'Well, Adam and I did sit up for a bit—talking,' Callum said. 'And opened a bottle or two to keep our throats lubricated!'

Melody smiled as he left the room, then got up to help herself to some juice. There were only two other people left eating their meal—certainly there was no sign of Adam. *Good*, she thought. Let's hope he makes himself scarce—at least while Jason is here. She frowned as she returned to her table. Jason was going to leave London as early as he could, and would ring her at some point to let her know when he expected to arrive. Melody bit her lip. She'd be feeling so different if Eve and Jon had been able to come, she thought. Having Jason here by himself was going to be a bit too 'cosy'—as Adam had dryly pointed out. Still, it was too late to change anything, so she'd have to make the best of it, she thought philosophically.

Presently Callum came in with her eggs, and she glanced up at him. 'I've a favour to ask, Callum,' she said.

'Name it,' the man said. 'It's yours!'

'Could I borrow something suitable to put fruit in?' she said. 'I've decided to go down to the cottage and pick some of my gooseberries—they're practically falling off the branches, they're so ripe.'

'Of course—we've some plastic boxes that we keep specially for the purpose,' Callum said. He paused. 'Adam was saying that he was going to help you with all that,' he went on. 'It's a very time-consuming job.'

'Oh, I'll be fine on my own,' Melody said quickly. 'I've no other plans for today anyway—my friend won't be here until this evening… Oh, by the way—one of the rooms I booked isn't needed now, Callum…'

'No—I know that. It's okay, Mel—Adam told me about it last night.'

Melody looked at him quickly. No doubt she—and her business—had been one of the topics of conversation, she thought, when the two men had been chatting. Perhaps the main one! She'd have loved to be a fly on the wall!

Callum hesitated, as if he wanted to say something important—then thought better of it and turned to go. 'By the way,' he said over his shoulder as an afterthought, 'this dry spell is coming to an end. Rain is forecast for tomorrow—so you'd better get that fruit in asap!'

'Maybe it's time for me to go back to London, then,' Melody answered. 'Everything has to come to an end some time.'

Presently, she popped into the kitchen to pick up the boxes she'd need. The breakfast girl had already left, and Callum was sitting at the table doing his accounts. Without looking up, he said casually, 'Adam's gone visiting friends this morning—but he'll be back later. Shall I tell him where you are…what you're doing?'

Melody shrugged. 'If you like,' she replied, equally casually. Well, what else could she say? She couldn't say, *No, don't tell him anything. I don't want him to get close.* That would give him more importance than he deserved—or more importance than she wanted to give him. So she left without another word, and made her way down the drive to the cottage.

Callum had been right. It was taking ages to strip the gooseberry bushes. The stems were spiky and uncomfortable, and the sun was baking on the back of Melody's head and neck as she stooped and reached for the fruit. But by late lunchtime she'd filled two large boxes and felt it was time for a short break and a drink—because this was thirsty work.

Going into the cottage, she cupped her hands under the cold water tap in the kitchen and gulped one or two mouthfuls—there was nothing suitable to drink from. Then she wandered into her sitting room and sat down on one of the boxes which Adam had so thoughtfully provided the other day. Somehow she wasn't feeling good this morning, she acknowledged. The euphoria she'd felt ever since she'd purchased the cottage seemed to be edging away from her. Ever practical, Melody tried to take stock of what was going on in her head. Was she getting cold feet, doubting her own wisdom in buying an expensive property in an out-of-the-way area? she asked herself. Or was there something else going on to ruffle her happiness? She clicked her tongue, annoyed with herself at feeling momentarily downbeat. What had changed to knock her off that dizzy perch of delight? Maybe, she thought, it was the same thing that she'd heard people say about childbirth…after the thrill of producing the offspring came the baby blues!

Sitting there with the afternoon sunlight lapping around her, Melody leaned her head against the wall for a second and closed her eyes. She knew that if Eve and Jon had been coming today she wouldn't be feeling like this. They would have been excited for her, enthusiastic at her unusual recklessness, and they would have cheered her up…because they were like that. But Jason was something else. As far as Melody could remember he'd never expressed the slightest interest in buying property—in fact, she didn't know much about him at all. She'd told Adam that he was a 'sort of' boyfriend, but that had been a deliberate lie. They'd never been close—he was just another member of her team—and that was why she'd been surprised when he'd insisted that he'd be coming down here alone today.

A sudden footstep by her side brought Melody back from having almost fallen asleep. She nearly fell off the box she was sitting on, and, looking up quickly, saw Adam standing there.

'Don't get up on my account,' he said smoothly. He pushed the other box to one side and sat down, facing her. 'Callum told me you were fruit-picking—d'you want some help?'

Melody stared at him for a moment, realisation hitting her like a crack on the head. Why had she been trying to find excuses for her present state of mind? she asked herself. Because the reason was sitting there beside her, gazing at her now with those bewitchingly dark eyes, his faintly cynical, murderously seductive expression melting any defence she could muster to protect herself from him. To protect herself from wanting him.

She hadn't answered him, so he repeated the question, but in a slightly different way. 'Shall we go and pick some more gooseberries?' he asked gently, tuning in to her vulnerability. 'I noticed that there are lots more on the bushes.'

'In a minute,' Melody said listlessly. 'I got rather hot out there—though Callum informs me that rain is on its way, so I suppose we'd better make the most of this sun while we've got it.'

'Have you had any lunch?' he asked suddenly, thinking how washed-out she looked, and that she might even be suffering from a mild touch of the sun.

'Not yet,' she replied. 'I…I didn't think about it…'

'Then that's the next thing we're going to do,' he said firmly, taking her hand and pulling her to her feet. 'We'll go to the Rose & Crown for a light snack—it'll be cool in there… Oh, and by the way, I've printed off the photographs to show you. I think you'll like them. They'll be a good set to take back and show all your friends and other interested parties.'

Feeling distinctly light-headed, Melody was glad to be taken charge of. And although she didn't feel like anything to eat, Adam insisted that she nibbled at a little bit of his ploughman's platter at the pub—which she did, washing it down with a whole bottle of still water. Then they went back to Poplars.

'I'll bring the prints up to show you in a minute,' Adam said, as Melody went up the stairs to her room.

Languidly, she washed her hands and face, wishing that Adam wasn't so obviously going to be part of her afternoon—but she realised that there was still all that fruit to pick, and it was kind of him to offer his help. Presently he knocked on her door, and came in with a folder under his arm.

'Have a look at these,' he said, darting a quick glance at her and thinking how white-faced she still was. He laid the prints out side by side in two rows on her bed, and Melody was surprised at how attractive they were. Even devoid of any of the usual trappings of glamorous lighting and expensive furniture, the cottage looked a desirable place to live in. The angles of the rooms Adam had chosen to take showed a pretty, slightly ancient dwelling, with huge potential as a comfortable place to live. Even the bathroom looked inviting enough!

'Adam—it all looks so good!' she exclaimed. 'And so much bigger!'

'Well, the sitting room is actually quite large for that type of place,' he said. 'And of course there's plenty of space outside for future extension—if you want it. Callum always envisaged a conservatory to open out on to the garden…if he'd ever owned it,' he added, not looking at her.

Melody swallowed, then stood back. 'Well, these are a fantastic representation of it for me to show everyone,' she said. She paused. 'I suppose we'd better get back to the gooseberry bushes…'

'You're going nowhere,' Adam said. 'You need to lie down, Mel, and have a sleep. Leave the bushes to me.'

She sat down weakly on the edge of the bed. 'D'you really mean it? D'you mind? It seems a bit off for me to relax while you sweat it out.' But the fact was she felt that if she never saw another gooseberry it would be too soon!

'Well, there you go,' he said cheerfully. 'I'll be your willing slave. But I'll expect my wages.'

Melody couldn't be bothered to think of a quick, slick reply to that—or even to wonder if there was any significance in his remark. Because her priority now was to lie down and chill out…

'Mel—your friend's arrived. He's waiting for you downstairs.'

Callum's voice outside her door woke Melody from the deepest sleep she could ever remember having, and with a start she jumped off the bed. 'Thanks, Callum. I'll be down in five minutes.'

She washed rapidly and slipped into a cream cotton sundress—then had to spend several minutes trying to brush the tangles from her hair. Pausing briefly, she recalled how Adam had done this exercise for her on the beach, and she shivered as she remembered the feel of his fingers threading their way gently but firmly through the thickness of the strands. Then, thrusting her feet into her loafers, she went quickly down the stairs.

Jason was standing by the front door, staring out, and he turned to see her.

'Hi, Mel! You look good enough to eat!' He automatically hugged her to him, and Melody lifted her cheek for the customary kiss of greeting which he obviously expected—feeling distinctly awkward as she did it. The man was nothing special to her, and she soon pulled away.

'Jason—you made it!' she said. 'But I didn't get a call from you to let me know when you'd be arriving…'

'I texted you—twice,' he said. 'Didn't you get my messages? To tell you I was being held up?'

Melody realised that she'd been so deeply asleep she'd not been aware of a thing!

Jason ran his hand through his hair. 'God—what a journey! I thought I was never going to get here.'

'Oh—was it that bad? Poor you…' Melody said soothingly, thinking how pathetic he sounded, almost petulant.

'There were two sets of roadworks on the motorway,' he went on complainingly, 'which meant all the traffic had to be diverted off—and when I eventually got away and into the countryside I felt as if I was taking part in an orienteering exercise!' He looked down at her. 'Did you deliberately try to find the most inaccessible holiday destination known to man?

Melody stared back at him, thinking how different he seemed. Casual wear didn't improve his appearance, she thought instinctively. He looked far better in a smart suit and tie. And where had his good humour gone?

She shrugged. 'Well, you're here now—' she began.

'Yes—and it's a good thing I was able to leave London earlier than I'd thought,' he said. 'Otherwise who knows what time it'd have been?'

Melody glanced at her watch. 'I take it you've checked in?' he said. 'Is your room okay?'

'Yes it's…okay,' he said, non-committally. 'But I haven't eaten since breakfast. I hope there's somewhere decent for supper?'

Melody sighed inwardly. This was going to be even worse than she'd thought. 'There is quite a nice pub,' she said. 'But wouldn't you like to see my cottage first, before we eat?'

He hesitated. 'All right—is it far from here?'

She smiled. 'Just a stroll. Takes about three minutes.'

Together they went down the drive, with Jason looking round him, taking it all in. 'This is an extremely isolated spot,' he said doubtfully.

'Yes—isn't it wonderful?' Melody countered. 'So blissfully peaceful.'

They arrived at the cottage, and Melody stood by the gate, spreading her arms. 'Behold!' she exclaimed. 'My holiday retreat…my rural castle!'

'Um…very nice,' Jason said unconvincingly. 'Smaller than I'd imagined, from what you said to Eve on the phone.'

'Well, there is only me,' Melody pointed out. 'And there's plenty of space for an extension—if I ever decide I need one.'

Inside, she took him around with as much enthusiasm as she could muster—because the vibes she was getting were distinctly unfavourable, and it was putting her off.

'Well, at least it's nice and clean,' he said, as they went from room to room.

'That's because it's been thoroughly scrubbed from end to end!' Melody exclaimed.

Upstairs, she pointed out at the garden. 'Just look at all those apples and pears!' she said. 'I'll be able to have my very own Harvest Festival! There's nothing like fruit really fresh straight from the tree…'

'Yes, but what are you going to *do* with it all?' Jason said. 'There's masses of everything, and it'll take ages to pick—and who's going to eat it? Of course it would be fine for a family with a few kids, but there's far too much for one person.'

Melody looked at him, genuinely disliking him at that moment. It was all too clear that the man was no country-lover, and now that she thought about it, all his interests seemed to be city-based. She bit her lip. His reason for wanting to come down this weekend had to be more to do with seeing *her*, she thought with a sinking heart, and she cursed herself for having suggested he come along.

She could see at once that Adam had practically stripped the gooseberry bushes, but he'd obviously long gone.

After a few more minutes looking around—during which Jason seemed determined to point out every disadvantage he could think of—she said lightly, 'Well, perhaps it's time to go to the pub.'

'I'll second that,' Jason replied. 'I hope I'm going to be able to buy you something other than the ubiquitous pie and chips'.

He encircled her waist with his arm, and for a horrible moment Melody thought he was going to kiss her—properly. She pulled away neatly. He obviously didn't think much of her cottage, and she was beginning to think even less of him!

In the Rose & Crown she immediately saw Adam and Callum, sitting in the corner having a meal. Thinking it only polite, she went over and introduced Jason to Adam—he'd obviously already met Callum on his arrival—before making her way to another table a little way away.

'Who's the guy?' Jason asked, nodding briefly in Adam's direction.

'I told you. He's called Adam,' Melody said casually.

'Yes, but who is he? A local?'

'No. He's here on holiday. Like me.' She paused. 'He's been very kind—helping me with stuff, picking some of those gooseberries.'

'How very thoughtful of him,' Jason said cynically. The way Adam had looked at Melody just now had told its own story, and Jason deliberately made a fuss of pulling out Melody's hair for her, whispering something in her ear as he did it.

Melody tried very hard to enjoy the evening. She knew Adam was watching them out of the corner of his eye throughout the meal, sizing the situation up. Remembering why she'd asked Jason here in the first place, she had no option but to pretend she was having a good time. So now and then she leaned forward animatedly, feigning interest in all Jason was saying, and laughing occasionally at one of his 'jokes'—which were getting less funny with every glass of wine he was consuming. But she did manage to eat her prawn salad and half of a jacket potato—though Jason didn't seem to enjoy his food at all, complaining that the steak was overdone and tasteless.

By the time they got back to Poplars it was late, and she turned to look up at Jason. 'I hope you find your room comfortable, Jason, and that you have a good rest after your night-mare journey here—' she began lightly. But he caught hold of her, almost roughly.

'Oh, come on,' he said. 'Surely you don't expect me to sleep all alone in a big old strange house—not after having driven several hundred miles for the privilege.' He brushed the top of her head with his lips. 'You're looking so gorgeous, Melody,' he murmured. 'It would be such a waste for you to be unaccompanied tonight.'

Melody wrenched herself away from his grasp. 'I'm sorry, Jason, if you got the wrong idea about coming down—' she began, but he interrupted again.

'It was your suggestion,' he reminded her testily.

'Yes, because I thought you—and the others—would be interested in seeing what I'd been up to on my holiday…and in sharing in my excitement. But it's obvious that you are not. And *I* am certainly not interested in sharing my bed with you—or anyone else. Not tonight. Not ever!'

# CHAPTER TEN

MELODY was feeling the same unutterable loneliness that she'd felt in the days and weeks after losing first her mother and then Crispin. Once again she was by herself, not knowing which way to go or what to do.

Since she'd shut her door very firmly on Jason earlier, and heard him stomp crossly downstairs to his own room, she'd just stood by her window staring out across the orchard.

When she'd bought Gatehouse Cottage she'd felt without any doubt at all that she'd done the right thing—felt that an unseen hand had guided her to do it. But tonight she felt almost overwhelmed by negative thoughts.

She tried to reason with herself. She had invested in something which would never devalue—that was obvious. Property wasn't like expensive cars or holidays. Property lasted—and while people lived and breathed, the demand for it would never cease. So at least all that money she'd spent was intact. But investment had not been her first thought when she'd bought it. What had filled her heart and soul was the thought of being the owner of that very particular cottage, with all its associations, and the feeling that she belonged there, even though she had no memory of it. But now Jason—a man she knew so little of outside work—had made her confidence crumble, made her wonder whether her long sunny holiday had knocked her off balance. Had made her act impulsively and out of character by spending all that money.

And whether it was because she hadn't felt well all day, or because of the evening she'd spent with Jason during which he'd spelt out all his numerous reservations about what she'd done, Melody felt herself disintegrate inside. Without any warning her eyes misted over and filled with tears, and she sank down onto her bed and sobbed quietly, her shoulders shaking. As if in harmony with her mood, she heard the rain which had been forecast starting to patter against her windowpane.

A light tap on her door made her freeze for a second, and she leaned across to the bedside table and grabbed several tissues, rubbing fiercely at her eyes and nose.

'Yes?' she said. 'Who is it?' It had to be Jason, trying his luck a second time, she thought. Well, she would not open her door. But she went across and stood there for a moment. 'Who's there?' she asked tremulously.

'It's me—Adam.' His voice was low, and with a gasp of something that could only be described as relief Melody opened the door.

He came in quietly, closing it behind him. Then stood looking down at her for a few seconds. 'What's the matter, Mel?' he asked.

That did it. Melody started sobbing all over again.

After a minute or two, when he sensed that she was becoming calmer, he said, 'Now, are you going to tell me what this is all about?'

She went across to the bed and slumped down heavily. 'Oh, it's just…it's just Jason,' she said, her voice muffled into another tissue.

Adam stiffened—he'd thought as much! 'Why—what's he done? He hasn't tried anything on, has he? Something you didn't appreciate?' he said.

'No—no, it's nothing like that.' Melody sniffed.

Adam thought, 'Well, *I'm* surprised he's not here in your bed…you seemed to be having a pretty good time this evening!'

'Oh, I don't know, Adam,' Melody went on. 'He arrived here in a foul mood today, but the things he said about the cottage…about me choosing to have a place down here…'

'Well, what *did* he say?' Adam demanded.

'How long have you got?' Melody said, the trace of a watery smile on her lips. 'Firstly that it's in the back of beyond, and that even without undue traffic problems it's always going to take for ever to get here.'

'That's why we like it,' Adam retorted. 'To keep people like him away.'

'Also that I'd have to arrange for someone to look after the place for ninety per cent of the time because our work does tie us to London more or less permanently.' She reached for another tissue. 'And I must accept that there's some truth in that.'

'Go on,' Adam said.

'And he doesn't think much of the design of the place—thinks it's plain and uninspiring. Nothing to get so excited about.' She blew her nose and looked up. 'And he reckons I'll have to find someone—an agent, I suppose—to keep going in and out, especially in bad weather, to make sure everything's okay. Looking out for burst pipes, or squatters seizing the chance of taking up residence in unoccupied premises.'

Now that she'd started Melody couldn't stop, letting all the words pour out in a litany of misery.

'And he thinks there's far too much ground—too labour-intensive, according to him,' she went on. 'And that I'll have to employ a gardener more or less full time—certainly in the spring and summer—and that all the fruit trees are far too much for me to deal with, and that in any case I'll never be able to eat all the produce—which is obviously not meant for one person.'

'Anything else?' Adam asked dryly. 'Any more astute observations?'

'Just that he thinks there are far more suitable properties nearer town—more up-market, more "with-it", to use his expression. He thinks Gatehouse Cottage is in a sort of time-warp. In fact to him it's spooky. That's what he thinks.' She turned her face and looked up into Adam's eyes. 'I know I shouldn't take any notice of him, but I'm afraid all his remarks have left me feeling shattered.' She paused. '*You* think I was right to buy, don't you?' she pleaded.

Adam waited for a moment, longing to place his lips over her long wet eyelashes, thinking that in all the times they'd been together he'd never seen her look so lovely. So desirable. Then he pulled himself together sharply. She and Jason were obviously very close, judging by their tactile behaviour earlier, and Jason undoubtedly expected his opinion to be requested—and valued. Too bad if she didn't like what he said, Adam thought, trying not to remember the ridiculous tremor of jealousy he'd felt when he'd seen the man's hand cover Mel's. And then he suddenly thought of Fee, lying so hopefully in her hospital bed, and Callum, whose ambitions to own Gatehouse Cottage had been thwarted by this complete stranger.

He paused before answering Melody's question. 'Well, it's not for me to say, Mel,' he said coolly. 'That's something only you can decide in the end. But I suppose some of Jason's remarks do have the ring of truth.' He shot her a quick glance. 'There are always going to be problems with any venture, and you just have to accept that.' He paused. 'It's true that when we were chatting in the pub—you know, on the day of the auction—I did wonder whether you'd be able to make full use of your investment. Whether you'd ever be able to spend quality time down here…'

He didn't want to look at her as he spoke, feeling like an exe cutioner. But after all, he consoled himself, it wasn't he who'd thrown cold water all over her tonight, it was her outspoken friend who'd done that. He turned away, his hands in his pockets. Could this after all turn things around for Fee and Callum? It meant so much more to them than it could possibly do for Mel… She'd obviously acted on the spur of the moment when she'd bid for the place—she'd soon find something else to take her fancy. The village didn't mean a thing to her. She didn't belong. Not like they all did.

He cleared his throat. 'I suppose your…bloke…*might* have appreciated being let in on your rather dramatic decision to cough up so much money—you know, before you actually did it?' he suggested. He paused. 'But—hey—don't get so upset, Mel,' he said cheerfully. 'If you do decide to change your mind, I'll take the cottage off your hands! After all, you only beat me at the auction by a whisker, didn't you? But you're a woman of firm convictions. I'm sure you'll make the right decision in the end.'

Slowly Melody got up, and went over to stand by his side. 'You're right—I will!' she said harshly. 'And thanks a bunch for the ringing endorsement! So you're clearly of the same opinion as Jason—but why should I be surprised? Men don't like being beaten at anything—not by a woman. I outbid you, and you didn't like it! Well, you and Jason can both go and take a flying leap! Gatehouse Cottage is mine, *mine*—whatever anyone else thinks! And I'll make it work—don't you worry about that! When I make up my mind about something—anything—I never change it!'

She stood away, glaring up at him. Gone was the pale face and watery eyes. Her cheeks were glowing with emotion.

'As far as my money is concerned, that's as safe as houses—ha-ha! And as for the "drawback" of this location—I'll deal with that! Yes, I may be dominated by my work calendar, but everyone can expect time off at regular intervals, and I shall treat my breaks in exactly the same way as I do my business commitments. Virtually unbreakable.' She paused for breath, but didn't give him a chance to interrupt. 'And have you ever noticed,' she went on, 'how any journey becomes less of a problem once it's familiar? I'll get to know every bend and twist in the road like the back of my own hand! And to know that my little house in the woods is here, waiting for me—well, the wheels won't turn fast enough!'

Adam stared down into her face, marvelling at her transformation over the last few minutes. This was one determined woman!

'As for finding someone to look after the cottage while I'm away… Well…I'll ask Callum to be janitor. And if he agrees I'll make it more than worth his while. If he's too busy, I'm sure someone in the village will oblige.' She tossed her head. 'Money talks,' she added. 'And the same goes for the garden and the trees. I'll be bringing friends down every summer to help with some of the fruit-picking—they'll think it's a real laugh, something away from the norm—and what we can't do ourselves I'll *pay* someone to do!' She held Adam's gaze defiantly. 'I can't think what came over me earlier,' she said. 'In my line of business we don't have problems—we only have opportunities! And that's what this is going to be! An opportunity for change—for me to have another life away from work and the pressures of living in London.' She turned on her heel. 'Now I need to get to bed. So goodnight, Adam!'

By now, it was gone midnight, and Adam went down the stairs to his own room on the ground floor. Going over to the window he stared out across the garden—which was by now sparkling with the teeming rain—his mind going over the last hour. He'd only offered to go up to the second floor to save Callum doing it—who always made a point of checking outside all the rooms to make certain that all was well for the night before retiring himself—and then he'd heard Mel crying. He'd hated hearing it… Not that it had been any of his business, whatever it was.

Going into the bathroom, he undressed quickly and switched on the shower, glancing at his appearance in the mirror, which was rapidly starting to steam up. Looking objectively at his own face for a moment, he felt that he was trying to tell himself something… Shrugging, he stepped into the shower, letting the hot jets strike his tanned, athletic body harshly, making him tingle all over, making him feel alert and alive as he soaped himself vigorously. In his mind's eye he could still see Mel's tear-stained cheeks, and he wished that she was there now, as naked as he was. The anger and resentment which had flared up in her so unbelievably quickly had only added to her seductive charm, enflaming his own passion, making him want to press her soft curves to his hard, muscular body and lie with her in the soft folds of his bed. And make love to her.

His lip curled at the thought. That was about as unlikely to happen as the sea losing its salt!

With a huge white towel slung carelessly across his shoulders, he suddenly stopped what he was doing and stood quite still for a second. What was going on here? Had he *completely* lost the plot? After everything he'd vowed to himself—and confided to Callum—he'd never let another woman make a fool of him. But he knew he wanted to do more than just take Mel to his bed. He wanted to take care of her. Of course he'd wanted her from the first moment they'd met—that was merely par for the course in his life, the invariable rule when he met a beautiful woman. But that superficial, transitory sensation was turning into something far more dangerously fundamental and life-affirming. He *liked* her—big-time. And he still wanted her. How could it have happened with someone he'd known for such a short time? What about the expression 'once bitten, twice shy'?

Dropping the towel, he reached for his dressing gown,

padding barefooted into his bedroom. Naked, he threw himself down on the bed and stretched out his hands behind his head. He felt annoyed with everything—annoyed with himself. He'd lost the cottage, he'd lost his determination to resist the lure of the female sex, and now he'd lost the camaraderie which had existed between him and Mel. She'd seemed as furious with him as she was with Jason, seeing his remarks as a total lack of support. And, highly perceptive as she was, she would have easily recognised the whiff of opportunism when he'd said he'd take the cottage off her hands. He was left with nothing. Why hadn't he kept his big mouth shut?

Turning over, he thumped his pillow irritably. It was time to get away from here. His holiday was at an end.

Melody lay quite still in her bed, the duvet pulled up around her neck and shoulders like a cosy cocoon. Although she was still half asleep, a thousand thoughts and emotions wove themselves in and out of her head. Then suddenly her eyes flew open and alarm bells rang out in her head. She had spent the night in a dream world— and *what* a world! A world full of a heart-stabbing mix of tangled accusations and recriminations, where she had faced Adam like a prize fighter squaring up for the battle of her life!

They had each been holding the end of a thick rope and pulling, tugging, *tugging*… She'd actually felt her hands burning as she'd clung on desperately as it threatened to slip from her grasp. But he'd been far stronger than her, and little by little he had gained ground until, after what had seemed like hours of frustrated effort, she'd been pulled towards him fiercely—and she'd thought he was going to strangle her! To wind the length of vicious, knotted string around her neck. She'd gasped out loud. He had won! He was the victor! He had captured her, and his black eyes had stared down at her danger-ously, his low, overpoweringly sexy voice whispering in her ear.

'The cottage will not be yours for much longer,' he'd hissed. 'You'll never live there. It's mine now, Mel, and so are *you*! There's no escape—we both know it—so why don't you just accept the inevitable and give in? Give in to me, and what *I* want!'

And suddenly the rope had vanished, and all she'd been able to feel was his arms around her, crushing every last breath from her body as their lips met in a frenzy of passion.

She sat up now, trembling all over. Trembling with the knowledge that she had not wanted to wake up, that she had wanted to go on and on dreaming… But she knew that this was all wrong, *wrong*! What had happened to her since she'd met Adam Carlisle to make her feel so emotionally captured and vulnerable? she asked herself. Because she was horribly aware that, in spite of all her determination to go solo for the rest of her life, she seemed to have slipped so easily within his inescapable radius.

Drawing her legs up, she rested her head on her knees. She was convinced that he had no significant interest in her—and why would he? With his looks and heart-throbbing sensuality he could flit from flower to flower as he liked—and fly off again. No problem! And anyway, during much of their time together they'd been engaged in housework, which had hardly set a peal of sexual bells ringing!

Yet during the passing of the night she had entered a forbidden world with Adam. They had lain together, and the first tentative touch of his hands on her bare skin had made her long for the unexplored, unimaginable excitement of what was to come. He was with her still, clearly… Her dream had not filtered away and been lost, but was still real, tangible.

His face, with the expansive brow, achingly seductive eyes and that faintly cynical half-smile which always filled her with a breathless intensity, had looked down at her as she'd lain beneath him. And when he'd told her that he would never let her go from his life, she'd known that she would have given herself to him freely. And when he'd declared that they were meant to be together always she had looked up at him, drinking in his every word, longing to believe that everything he was saying was true. And her lips had parted, moist and inviting, as he'd bent to cover them with his own, the hardness of his body against her sending a terrifying thrill of anticipation right through her, which even now refused to go away, leaving her with a desperate longing for it to have been true.

It was the memory of that all-defining moment of acute desire which now made Melody throw back her duvet and climb quickly out of bed. It wasn't too late, she thought, no real harm had been done. If she took action now, today, she could put a stop to this madness and get her life back on track.

It must have been raining all night, because as she drew back the curtains the dripping leaves and branches presented a rather dismal sight, totally different from the one she'd been so used to. Gone was the soft mellowness of warm, dry foliage. Everything looked sodden, cool and uninviting, and Melody heaved a sigh. What on earth were she and Jason going to do with themselves today? she thought. This was the first time on her holiday that the weather had presented a problem. She frowned, remembering the evening they'd spent together. They'd parted company very tight-lipped, but had agreed— rather frostily—to meet for breakfast at nine o'clock. She sincerely hoped that he was in a better mood today… Maybe he *had* been overtired, she thought, trying to find excuses for him, which would have been the reason why he'd been so negative about the cottage and everything else. Still, she thought, he had behaved very childishly, and had shown a side to him she'd found totally unpleasant.

She showered and dressed, feeling downbeat and faintly disoriented. Perhaps she'd suggest they'd go for a drive into the country, find a pub to have lunch. She stopped what she was doing for a moment, thinking of Adam, and how he'd added his own unwelcome comments when he'd found her crying. Well, she didn't want to see him today. Especially with Jason there. She knew he always breakfasted early, so hopefully they wouldn't bump into each other. She knew she'd find it horribly embarrassing for them all to come face to face.

But, taking everything into consideration, her mind was clear about one thing. She was leaving here as soon as possible. It was time to give up and move on. She would leave her beloved little cottage to its own devices, just for a few weeks— a cooling-off period she'd call it—and let her heart settle back into its normal passive state. Of course she couldn't go until Jason had left, but she'd pack most of her things now, in readiness. She needed to get back to London, where work was the only thing that absorbed her mind. Kept her sane and in control.

She emptied the wardrobe of her clothes, packing all her suitcases neatly, and cleared the chest of drawers. She could leave at a moment's notice, she thought.

Downstairs, Jason was already sitting at her usual table, and Melody could see that he was still rattled. He didn't bother to make a pretence of getting to his feet, or move her chair for her to sit down, but somehow Melody managed a weak smile of greeting.

'Hi,' she said, looking across at him quickly.

'Oh—hi,' he said casually.

'Did you sleep okay?'

'Not bad. Thunder woke me a couple of times.'

'Really? I didn't hear it,' Melody said, picking up her menu.

'Fantastic day,' Jason said sarcastically, glancing out of the window. 'What does anyone *do* in weather like this? Can we go to the gym for the morning, and then have a swim in the Olympic-size pool?'

Melody didn't bother to rise to that. 'I could show you a bit of the countryside—' she began, and he cut in.

'No, thanks. I saw quite enough of that yesterday.'

Just then Callum arrived to take their order, and Melody was so pleased to see his smiling face she could have hugged him. He grinned down, throwing her a mildly conspiratorial look that lifted Melody's spirits briefly.

After they'd finished their meal, Jason sat back, throwing his crumpled napkin down in front of him. 'Well, the breakfast wasn't bad,' he said grudgingly. 'And very generous.'

Melody looked across at him blankly. 'Do you know, Jason, that's the first positive remark you've made since you arrived here,' she said quietly.

He returned her look unblinkingly. 'What d'you expect?' he said. 'I didn't drive all that way to admire nature—or unremarkable boxes for living in—it was another side of creation that dominated my mind.'

He paused, and Melody thought, Why did I ever like you? Why did I ever think you were a nice guy, and fun to work with? She feigned innocence at his remark. 'Perhaps you'd explain?' she said.

'Come off it,' he snapped, still staring across at her. 'I know you've got a reputation for being a mysterious sort of woman, but I didn't think you were a tease.'

'A tease?' Melody frowned, mystified.

'Oh, I know all about women like you,' he went on coolly, as if they were discussing a cure for the common cold. 'Give out the signals, then do the disappearing trick. Offer the apple—whip it away. Naughty, naughty!'

Melody's jaw dropped in disbelief as he went on.

'You asked me here for the weekend, and I naturally thought we were going to have a good time together…'

She had had enough. 'What you "naturally thought" is your

problem!' she said heatedly, the blood rushing to her cheeks. 'I invited Eve and Jon down because I knew *they'd* be interested, and it occurred to me that maybe you might be, too!'

Melody crossed her fingers as she said that, knowing that she *had* had a certain agenda in including him—but not the one he was talking about!

She leaned forward so that her face was close to his. 'Watch my lips, Jason,' she said tersely. 'The idea that you and I might ever, *ever* share a bed was further from my mind than the idea of taking a walk to the North Pole in my nightie!' She sat back. 'And I consider it highly presumptuous of you to think so!' Thoroughly upset, she got up, pushing back her chair. 'I don't think it's a good idea for us to spend any more time together,' she said. 'And—'

'On that point we agree,' he replied, lounging back. 'I've already settled my bill—I'll be driving home this morning. It might not be too late to salvage something of the weekend.' He paused. 'And by the way—I forgot to tell you. I'll be handing in my notice at the office. I've decided that life's too short to work in a madhouse.'

Back in her room, Melody finished packing methodically, her hands still trembling slightly at the run-in she'd just had with Jason. What a loser, she thought angrily—and what a nerve, thinking he had a fling lined up for himself! Well, he knew the score now, and thank goodness they wouldn't have to see each other any more. In their line, when staff gave notice the parting of the ways usually happened overnight—to the advantage of everyone concerned. He'd been a very weak member of the team, in any case, she thought. He wouldn't be missed.

To her great relief there'd been no sign of Adam, and now, feeling upset and distracted, she went downstairs to find Callum. He was in the kitchen, and he looked up as she came in.

'Mel! Come and sit down.' He pulled out a chair, glancing at her quickly. 'Your…friend has checked out. I hope everything was okay for him…?'

''Oh, he found no fault with you and Poplars,' Melody said at once. 'The fault was all mine, Callum!' She paused. 'I'm glad he's gone,' she said firmly. 'The proverbial wet blanket, and a creep to boot.'

Callum looked away. 'Yes…I think that Adam was a bit concerned about you last night—you know, in the pub. He wondered…'

Melody shook her head briefly. 'It's okay, Callum—I can take care of myself. But it was kind of Adam to be bothered on my account.'

Callum looked at her steadily. 'I think he's a bit more than just bothered about you, Mel,' he began, and she cut in—she didn't want to hear any more.

'I'm really sorry—but I'm leaving later as well, Callum,' she said slowly. She took the cottage keys from her pocket. 'Would you do me a tremendous favour?' she asked. 'Would you keep these, and just look in at the cottage now and then? I'm not exactly sure when I'll be coming back—probably not until next month.'

'No problem.' Callum grinned. 'We've taken care of the place for so long now—all the time it's been empty—it'll make no difference. Leave it to us.' He looked down at her soberly. 'D'you really have to go?'

'Afraid so—there's a panic on at work, and I'm needed,' she lied.

'We'll miss you, Mel—really,' he said. 'Can't you wait until Adam gets back? He's having lunch with the de Wintons over at the big house—the Manor—across the valley, but he'll be home later, and I know he'd want to see you before you go.'

Melody stood up. 'No—I'm sorry to have to depart, but…it

can't be helped.' She hesitated. 'I'll leave Adam a note, explaining.' She slipped her bag from her shoulder. 'Now, let me settle my bill—and I've *loved* staying here, Callum. It's been like a home from home.'

'And we've loved having you,' Callum said. He waited before going on. 'I'm fetching Fee back from hospital on Monday—it's a shame she won't see you to say goodbye.'

Melody felt as if she was being pulled painfully in two directions—desperately wanting to stay, but knowing that she mustn't. Spending any more time with Adam was not the way forward. Not the way it had to be. 'I'm sorry,' she said quietly. 'Now—would you help me with my cases?'

Presently, driving back to London in the pouring rain, Melody found her mind going over and over everything that had happened during her holiday, and why she'd decided, at this particular time of her life, to go there at all. Of course it had been a personal mission, hoping to find answers to a mysterious part of her mother's life, but she'd learned nothing—nothing of significance had happened at all. Except the purchase of a cottage! *The* cottage! But she still didn't know why Frances had been so secretive about the man who was Melody's father.

It had been an idyllic few weeks, marred only by Jason's arrival on the scene—self-inflicted though that had been, she had to admit—but she still felt unsure of the wisdom of setting up a home for herself so far away from everything. It had seemed so right during her post-purchase honeymoon, but now all Jason's comments seemed to make some sense.

She pulled in to the side of the road for a moment, and reached for her bottle of water, drinking freely. Well, she had plenty of sustenance readily available if she needed it, she thought, smiling briefly and glancing down to the floor of the car at all the bags containing the gooseberries they'd picked.

She'd share those out as soon as she got back to work. She leaned her head back, taking another drink, and looking with unseeing eyes through the drenched windscreen. She'd have to arrange for all those apples, pears and plums to be gathered at some point. Not just this year, but every year from now on. In her position, the garden *was* a drawback—delightful though it had first seemed. And she'd confirm the date for the decorators to begin as soon as possible, and arrange for someone to sort out the windows... Blinds, or curtains, or both? she wondered.

She sighed, knowing that all this would have to be fitted in with her other life. And how much of that other life would release her to come down to her cottage? To relax, to chill out, to do all those things that were supposed to be good for you?

She put the cap back onto the bottle, squeezing it tightly. In spite of all these practical issues, she knew only too well what her real problem was. She couldn't risk letting Adam Carlisle penetrate her life, her sensibilities, any more than he had already done. He was the problem, not the cottage, because she admitted to herself that he had become more to her than she'd have thought possible, and she didn't want it. She didn't want him or any man. And, so far she'd succeeded perfectly well in that aim, ever since Crispin had been killed.

She switched on the engine decisively. She had been right to escape this morning, before seeing him. And although she realised that he would always be a visitor to the area, and that they would be bound to come across each other from time to time, it would never be the same as this had been. The novelty of everything that had happened over the last week or so would have worn off, died. And with it—hopefully—the unsettling thought that she was not as emotionally unassailable as she'd thought.

# CHAPTER ELEVEN

DESPITE the fact that she'd still had another week due to her, Melody returned to work on the following Monday. Anyway, it was quite nice to think she had some time in hand she could use up later in the year.

Eve and Jon were at their desks, desperate to hear about her holiday—and the cottage! Melody looked across at them both as she booted up her computer.

'The holiday was fantastic,' she said. 'The weather was perfect—right up until the very last day—and look: I've got some photographs of the cottage to show you.' She fished out from her briefcase all the prints Adam had prepared for her, passing them across. The others examined them closely—and were wildly enthusiastic, as Melody had known they would be.

'Mel—it's gorgeous! So quaint!' Eve said. 'Oh, look—*look*, Jon—look at the garden! It's a little paradise!'

'Yes, and the little paradise is full of gooseberries—among other things,' Melody said. 'I've got a load of them for you in my fridge. Enough for about fifty pies!'

Eve spread all the prints out on the desk in front of them. 'It looks just like the sort of place a small child would draw. Absolutely charming,' she said slowly.

'It's not all that big—' Melody began, and Eve interrupted.

'Who wants a mansion as a holiday retreat, for goodness' sake? Just so long as there's room for *us*—when we keep invading you!' She turned to Jon. 'Maybe *we* could look around for something down there?' she said eagerly.

'Maybe,' he agreed non-committally. *They* didn't have the financial resources that Mel seemed to have, he thought.

'I was desperately disappointed that you couldn't come down at the weekend,' Melody said, thinking how pale her friends were looking—or perhaps that was in contrast to *her* deep suntan!

'So were we,' Jon said at once. 'But we were not a pretty sight, Mel. We really succumbed to the wretched sickness bug that's swept the office. You were better off out of it, I can tell you.'

'Umm—pity Jason hadn't caught it as well,' Melody said enigmatically, and they both looked at her quickly.

'Yes—we were wondering about that,' Eve said. 'He insisted on going on with the plan.' She paused. 'You've heard that he's gone, by the way, rather suddenly?' she asked. 'Though he never really fitted in, did he? It wasn't a surprise when he made the big announcement.'

Melody made a face. 'He thought—wrongly—that he and I were going to enjoy a passionate weekend together,' she said, putting all the prints away carefully. 'And it gave me great pleasure to disabuse him on the point.'

The others burst out laughing. 'You're joking! What—you and *him*?' Jon exclaimed. 'Why on earth did he imagine that he would succeed where all others have failed? He must have been kidding himself if he thought he'd found the Holy Grail!'

Melody looked away. She remembered Jason's remark about her being 'mysterious', and she supposed that her unwillingness to engage in any romantic attachments would attract some criticism from the people she mixed with. Well, so be it, she thought. Her life was her own, to live as she liked, whatever anybody else thought.

Work had built up in her absence, as she'd known it would, and there wasn't time for much gossiping about her holiday. But that pleased Melody. She wanted to forget it all—temporarily at least—and use her brain for the thing it had been trained for. So it was late before she'd finished what she had to do, and everyone else had packed up and gone home by the time she left the building.

By now, she'd realised how tiring the day had proved, and decided to hail a cab rather than bother with the tube and the considerable walk to her flat.

Presently, after paying the driver, she was just inserting the key into her door when a low voice behind her made her jump anxiously. She turned quickly.

'Hello, Mel. I was beginning to think you weren't coming home tonight.'

'Adam!' Melody was genuinely amazed to see him standing there. 'What are you doing here? And how did you know—? I mean…'

'How did I know where you live? From all the details you gave to Callum when you checked in to Poplars, of course,' he said. He came to stand right beside her, and looked down into her upturned face. 'I have to go back to Malaysia tomorrow. But I had a meeting in London this afternoon and couldn't turn down the opportunity to look you up.' He paused. 'I hope I'm…I hope I'm not taking liberties,' he added slowly.

Melody thought desperately, Please don't touch me, Adam… Keep your distance, please! She shrugged. 'Of course not. Come in.' Her voice shook slightly. Well, she was tired— and she needed a drink and something to eat.

He followed her up the thickly carpeted stairs to her first-floor flat, which was spacious and luxurious, and looked around appreciatively as Melody switched on all the lamps. She threw her bag and briefcase down on to one of the huge sofas, and looked up at him.

'Drink?' she asked casually. 'There's some whisky.' Crispin's whisky, she thought. Still there, untouched.

'Whisky would be great, thanks,' he said. He'd barely taken his eyes off her, admiring her as he'd done so many times before. She looked trim and businesslike in her fine-quality black suit and ivory silk shirt, her black high heels making her look slightly taller than usual.

She paused. 'Everything's over there on the table,' she said. 'Help yourself. I must change into something I can relax in.' She turned away. 'It's been a long day.'

'I hope you were able to get the "panic" sorted out,' he said archly. 'You know—the thing that made you shoot off in such a hurry?' And Melody found herself blushing as she remembered what she'd written in the note she'd left him.

'Yes—I did get the…problem sorted, thank you,' she said flatly.

There was a distinct coolness in the atmosphere, and they both felt it. Well, after all, the last words they'd exchanged had hardly been the most friendly! But she did pause for a moment to look back at him, her face expressionless.

'I'm sorry I had to dash off like that—' she began.

'Not as sorry as I was,' he said, going over to pour himself some whisky, and Melody stared after him, wondering what was coming next.

He looked so stunning, she thought, swallowing, with his height, powerful frame and broad shoulders throwing huge shadows across the walls of the room. It was the first time she'd seen him formally dressed, she realised, and it added even more to his dynamic sex appeal. But what was he doing here, in the sanctity of her flat? she asked herself. She'd left Poplars early to get away from him. She'd never expected him to turn up here, uninvited.

He turned to look at her, his glass in his hand. 'I thought you were out of order to leave so abruptly,' he said coolly. 'Surely whatever it was that was so urgent could have waited another couple of hours?' He drank from his glass. 'Or perhaps it was something else? Callum indicated that you and Jason had not been exactly—'

'It was nothing to do with Jason,' Melody interrupted coldly. 'I told you, I had to come back earlier than expected.'

'Well, I still think it was a rather off-hand way for you—for anyone—to behave,' he said shortly.

Suddenly Melody felt trapped—and annoyed. And she didn't like being spoken to like a child, either. 'I'm sorry if it didn't please you,' she said shortly, 'or if you took it the wrong way. But what's done is done.' She turned abruptly. 'I shan't be long. Make yourself at home.'

In her bedroom, feeling completely dazed—not to say shattered—at Adam turning up, Melody slipped out of her office clothes and shrugged into her navy tracksuit. Then she undid her hair from its knot, running her brush through it briefly and leaving it loose around her shoulders. She didn't bother to find her mules, but walked barefoot across the thick pile of her carpet to open the door, pausing for a moment. How was she going to get rid of him? she wondered—and then felt guilty. He hadn't behaved badly towards her, after all—not really, if you didn't count his unhelpful remarks about her purchase of the cottage, and his seeming to side with Jason. And if you didn't count him telling her off just now for her quick get-away from Poplars. Could she ever forget how he'd helped her scrub the cottage from end to end? There'd been no need for him to do that. Still, she hadn't got over the shock of finding him on her doorstep when she'd come home… He *could* have rung to warn her of his impending visit, she thought. That would have shown some consideration.

Biting her lip, she went across the dimly lit hallway and into the sitting room, where Adam was studying Crispin's huge globe of the world on its imposing mahogany stand. He glanced up as she came over to join him, and he caught his breath. Why did everything the woman wore glamourise her? he asked himself. There was nothing exceptional about the thing she had on—except that it had the effect of making him want to gather her up in his arms and mould her to him.

'What a beautiful object,' he said, turning back to the globe, revolving it slowly.

'Yes. It was my present to Crispin on his last birthday,' she said soberly.

He gave her a quick glance, feeling the need to lighten the mood. 'Would you like to see where I spend most of my working life?'

She looked down as he traced his finger over the smooth surface.

'See…there it is. Malaysia. A very long way away…' He recognised the faint drift of her perfume as she peered down to see where he was pointing.

'I've never been that far away from home,' she said. 'In fact, I've not travelled very much at all—except skiing in France and Switzerland with our friends. When I was young, my mother and I liked holidays nearer home—when we could afford to go at all,' she added simply.

So it was obviously her husband's money that had bought all this, Adam thought briefly. Though their combined salaries must have been considerable.

'Oh, you'd like Malaysia,' he said easily 'The people are lovely. Who knows? I may have the chance to extend your knowledge of the world some day, and take you there.'

Melody looked up at him. That'll never happen, she thought.

'But before that,' he said smoothly, 'I'd like to take you somewhere for a meal.' He hesitated. 'You were so late getting home, I was afraid I was going to be dining alone this evening.'

Melody shook her head. 'Sorry—no. It's already gone nine, and I only eat very light meals in the week.' She hesitated. 'But I'd be happy to make us some omelettes. Cheese—or I think there are some prawns, if you prefer.' Her eyes twinkled for a second. 'I could even knock you up a full English. I come highly recommended!' she added.

'I'm fully aware of that,' he replied, and their eyes locked together, and somehow, suddenly, they were back to where they had been on those few hectic mornings in the kitchen at Poplars. They had shared a curious experience, and they'd both enjoyed it. And were enjoying the memory of it. 'I'll pass on the full English—though a cheese omelette sounds fantastic. Thanks.'

Melody went over and switched on the huge flat-screen television. 'Take your pick,' she said, handing Adam the remote control and going out in the direction of the kitchen.

'Can't I help?' he called after her.

'No, not this time,' she replied.

Going through the hall, she glanced into her dining room—it was not quite as large as the sitting room, but was an ample size to entertain ten or twelve guests at one go. But the room would not be used tonight. They'd eat from trays on their laps, she decided.

Melody knew exactly how to prepare a good omelette. It had always been one of her masterpieces! She cooked in butter, using two frying pans, and the eggs were soon ready for her to carefully lift them over and on to warm plates. She'd already cut thin slices of wholemeal bread to accompany them. Then she opened a bottle of white wine and selected two glasses from the shelf, before taking everything in.

Immediately Adam stood up and switched off the television, pulling a small table nearer to them for the trays, and presently, sitting side by side on the sofa, they made short work of their supper.

Adam was impressed as he swallowed the last morsel. 'Mmm, delicious,' he said. 'Funny that none of the guests ever asked for omelettes.'

Melody put down her own knife and fork, and sat forward to remove the two trays, but he put a hand briefly on her arm.

'Let me at least do the clearing away,' he said, getting up. He looked down at her. 'And am I allowed to make coffee? You know I do it so well!'

Melody smiled. 'Oh, go on, then,' she said. 'You'll find everything you need by the kettle.'

She watched as he made his own way to the kitchen—well, the geography of the place was hardly complex—suddenly realising how good it felt for someone else to be there, sharing in the task of even a simple thing like preparing the after-supper drinks, and remembering, with a pang, that that had always been Crispin's job. She heard Adam fill the kettle, take mugs from the shelf, open the fridge door for milk, and wondered again, how this could be happening. How had the man managed to thread himself into *this* part of her life as well?

In a few minutes he returned, with the cafetière and everything else on a tray, which he put down in front of them. 'This is a fabulous apartment, Mel,' he said casually. 'And so beautifully furnished.' He paused. 'I can easily see why Jason took such a dim view of the cottage. I'm sure he'd rather be staying here than there.'

'Well, it won't matter what he thinks,' Melody said, leaning her head back against the cushions. 'Because I won't be inviting him anywhere, ever again.'

Adam raised one quizzical eyebrow. 'Oh,' was all he said. But of course Callum had tipped him off about Mel's describing the man as a 'creep'. Clearly he'd put more than one foot wrong, Adam thought wryly.

'Finish the wine, Adam,' Melody said lazily. 'It'd be a shame to waste that last drop.'

He lifted the bottle, judging the contents. 'Oh, I think there's enough for us both to have half a glass,' he said.

Melody was slightly shocked to realise just how much she'd drunk—quite a lot more than her usual quota! But she allowed him to top up her glass before he emptied the rest into his own.

'Do these places come on the market very often?' he asked, without looking at her, and Melody thought, I hope you're not thinking of buying one yourself!

'Oh, now and then,' she said casually. 'They are at the top end of the market for this kind of place, but it seems there's no shortage of money, because as soon as one becomes vacant it's snapped up.' She looked across at him, her eyelids threatening to droop from the effect of the alcohol—and her fatigue after the long day. And, unusually for her, she felt her natural reserve slip. 'I never expected to be able to afford something like this,' she confided honestly. 'When I think of the little house I spent my childhood in…'

'I'm sure your husband left you well provided for,' he suggested gently.

'Yes,' she replied, feeling sad all over again. 'He was well insured.'

But surely, Adam thought, that would not explain how she'd been able to buy Gatehouse Cottage—she'd hinted at one point during a conversation that she hadn't had to borrow for it.

And as if reading his mind, she said, 'The cottage… I bought the cottage with a legacy left to me by the cousin of my mother's we used to live with. I had no idea she had any money—not that kind of money, anyway. We were always quite poor.' There—now she'd told him, Melody thought. So what?

Sitting close—but not too close to her on that enormous

sofa—Adam wished that he hadn't decided to come here tonight. She had reawakened that irrepressible desire in him that he knew would never be satisfied. Would never be fulfilled. Why hadn't he just left things as they were, gone back to the Far East tomorrow and tried to forget her? Time not only healed, sometimes it dealt with a problem, he thought. Let water run under the bridge. That way things often evened themselves out. But it was too late. He *was* here.

He tore his gaze away from her. 'I'm sure you want to know about Fee....' he began, and Melody sat forward with a jolt.

'Oh, of *course*!' she exclaimed. 'Dear Fee! How is she? Is she home?'

'Yes. I waited until Callum brought her back—waited to see how things were. They have high hopes this time.' He paused. 'I only hope they're right.'

Melody felt really bad for a second. She'd hardly given Fee a thought over the last two days, but it wasn't because she didn't care—she *did* care! It was just that she had so much stuff going on in her own life...

Adam leaned forward to pick up the cafetière and filled the two mugs, passing her one. 'I seem to remember you like cream?' he murmured, picking up the small jug he'd put on the tray. Without answering, she held her mug forward. For a while, there was silence between them as they sipped the delicious brew. Then Melody said, 'When do you go tomorrow?'

'I fly from Heathrow at eleven p.m.,' he said. 'For a twelve-hour haul to Kuala Lumpur.'

Melody frowned. 'That sounds an ordeal.'

'Not really,' Adam said. 'I use a superb airline. And the cabin staff—who always look beautiful in Malaysian national dress—are among the best in the world.'

Melody closed her eyes, feeling sleepy and relaxed. 'I suppose it's a very hot climate?' she said.

'Yes, it always is,' he replied. 'But there are things to compensate. You can go to Penang from Kuala Lumpur, to the Cameron Highlands, where it's much cooler—and where, incidentally, you can get delicious strawberry teas.' He turned to look at her again, noting that somehow they'd moved slightly closer together, so that he could smell the warmth of her skin, smell that particular fragrance in her hair which he'd recognise blindfold anywhere. 'It's an idyllic setting,' he went on softly. 'You'd love it. And there's an amazing butterfly population…' There was a long, uncomplicated silence before he whispered, 'Are you asleep, Mel?'

'No, of course not. I'm listening to you.' Listening to that voice which makes me want to curl up inside, she thought. She opened one eye and looked at him. 'Are the hotels any good?'

'The hotels are superb. I'd take you to a sumptuous hotel where you'd be treated like a princess… The food's amazing— mostly home-grown produce—and the national dish is satay— chicken or beef kebabs marinated in lime juice… The fruit, of course, is exotic—pineapples, papaya, bananas…'

Melody smiled faintly. 'You sound like an employee of the Malaysian Tourist Board,' she said.

He shrugged. 'It really is a great place,' he replied.

They both sat there, almost wallowing in the comfortable atmosphere which enveloped them. Then he said, 'So…have you any idea when you'll be going back to your "little house in the woods"?' he asked.

'Oh—not exactly,' she replied. 'But it'll be in the reasonably near future. There's all that fruit to be taken care of, isn't there?' She paused, needing to ask him roughly the same question. 'And you…when do you expect to be visiting Poplars again?' she said.

He shrugged. 'Not too sure at the moment. There's…there's a lot going on with the firm. So I really can't say.'

Presently, Melody said, 'Where are you staying tonight?'

Adam hesitated. 'I'm booked in at my father's club,' he said. 'That's where I've left my cases. I suppose I ought to be going…d'you have a taxi number handy?'

There was a moment's pregnant silence. Then, 'Stay here,' Melody said quietly, without looking at him. 'You do realise what the time is, don't you?'

'I know it's late,' he replied cautiously. He looked at her, an expression of disbelief crossing his features. He was being invited—*she* had invited him—to spend the night with her! His mouth dried at the prospect.

'Well, then—stay,' she repeated, her eyes still closed.

He put his hand gently over hers, and it excited him to feel her turn her palm and curl her fingers in response. Until a few moments ago he might have expected her to push him away! 'Are you…sure, Mel?' he asked softly. 'I mean—I could easily get a cab.'

'Oh, don't bother to do that,' she replied. 'It seems pointless at this time of night.' She gazed down at his strong brown hand where it covered hers. She and Crispin had always held hands as they'd watched television. Now she looked up at him, her lips slightly parted, her eyelashes bewitchingly moist. 'But you do understand that I'll be disturbing you in the morning? I'll have to leave before you've even surfaced…' she murmured.

Don't count on it, he thought to himself. He didn't think they'd be spending much of the night asleep in any case!

With a dainty yawn Melody got up, stretching her arms above her head languidly, and together they took the coffee things back into the kitchen, before switching off the lights and going across to the hallway. Melody put her hand on his arm briefly.

'You'll find the spare room very comfortable,' she murmured. 'Just look around you for anything you need.' She paused. 'I moved all Crispin's belongings into that room, because I haven't

decided yet what to do with them. Feel free to help yourself—
and there are plenty of toiletries in the bathroom.'

She reached up and planted the lightest of kisses on his
cheek. Her lips were cool.

'Goodnight, Adam—sleep well,' she whispered. And with
that she opened her bedroom door and went inside, closing it
firmly behind her.

# CHAPTER TWELVE

'MEL? *Hello*, Mel! It's Fee here!'

Melody's face creased into smiles as she heard the woman's voice. 'Fee—how great to hear from you!' she said.

It was a Saturday morning in mid-September, and Melody, still in her dressing gown, was idly reading the daily paper as she sipped her first coffee for the day. 'How are you, Fee? Not overdoing things at Poplars, I hope?'

Fee chucked. 'Oh, I'm being treated like a queen, Mel. I'm following doctor's orders to the letter, and am glad to say that I've not had any recurrence of the symptoms I've had in the past.'

'That's fantastic!'

'Of course Callum would wrap me in cotton wool if he could,' Fee went on, 'but I know exactly how much I can do, and it's obviously good to keep active—within limits.'

'You must both be feeling very excited,' Melody said.

'Cautiously excited is how I'd describe it,' Fee replied. 'But listen, Mel…I never had a chance to thank you so, *so* much for what you did for us here, when I had to make that hasty trip to hospital,' she went on. 'We've never been caught out like that before, and Callum and I agree that if you and Adam hadn't stepped in to help us we'd just have had to apologise profusely to the guests and send them all on their way. An unthinkable prospect!'

Melody smiled. 'You know, Fee, we really enjoyed ourselves,' she said. 'Preparing breakfast for a crowd is never likely to faze me in the future!'

'Well, we'll always be grateful to you,' Fee said. She paused. 'You know, Adam described you as an unusual woman when he met you on that first day—and he was right. I can't think of many guests who'd be ready to put on an apron and get stuck in in an emergency!'

They chatted on for a few minutes, and Melody thought how good it was to hear Fee's warm and friendly voice again. It filled her with a rush of pleasurable homesickness. Why wasn't she there in the village now?

As if reading her thoughts, Fee said, 'But I've also rung to know about you, Mel, and when you're coming back to visit. We didn't even have a chance to say cheerio in the summer, did we?'

Melody made a wry face to herself. 'No—I'm sorry about that…sorry I had to dash off, Fee,' she said. 'But I *had* had a very long break, and all good things must come to an end—though the end was a bit sudden.'

'Well, of course we realise your work is important…we quite understood.'

That made Melody feel worse than ever!

'Now then,' Fee went on, 'is it possible you could come down for the last weekend of this month? That's when we have the Harvest Fair.'

'Oh—I remember you talking about that,' Melody said, getting up and wandering over to the window.

'It's one of *the* occasions in the village,' Fee said enthusiastically. 'It's always fun—and of course makes good profits for our various local charities. But more than that, Mel, it brings the community together in a wonderful spirit of goodwill… which has to be a good thing.'

'Of course,' Mel agreed, feeling slightly guilty at Fee's words. What had she, Melody Forester, done for the village so far? Precisely nothing, she thought. But that was going to change—she would be returning there as often as possible.

'There is something else,' Fee said. 'All the fruit in your garden is ready—especially the plums, which are absolutely gorgeous this year, thanks to our summer. Would you allow us to pick some of it to sell at the Fair?'

'Of course I would!' Melody said. 'It's been on my mind, as a matter of fact.'

'A few of the Boy Scouts from the local troupe would be happy to do it,' Fee said. 'If you like, they could pick everything for you, and we'd just keep a few basketfuls for the Fair. Would that be okay?'

'Sounds perfect,' Melody said, and without another thought, added, 'And I *will* come down on that weekend, Fee. I'll look forward to it.' She hesitated. 'Will you reserve me a room at Poplars, please—for three nights?'

Later, as she went around the flat tidying up, Melody realised that Fee had only mentioned Adam once… Well, he was probably sitting under a tree with a dusky Malaysian maiden, his mind a long way away from England, she thought.

She stopped what she was doing for a second. It seemed such a long time ago that he'd turned up here, totally unexpectedly. When she'd emerged from her bedroom the following morning he'd already been up and dressed. And the looks they'd exchanged had spoken volumes, with Adam's slightly raised eyebrow and quizzical expression making Melody's heart quicken—as usual. Yet there had been not a hint of awkwardness between them as they'd consumed coffee and toast in the kitchen, and he'd thanked her politely for a very comfortable night's sleep as they'd parted company in the street.

Two weeks later Melody found herself once more making the long drive south. She'd left work early, hoping to be at Poplars in time to take Fee and Callum out to supper. She had actually asked Eve and Jon to come with her, thinking that they'd enjoy the whole event, and the chance to see the cottage, but they were committed to attending a family wedding—much to Eve's dismay.

'When are we *ever* going to see it?' she'd grumbled.

'Don't worry,' Melody had said, 'there'll be plenty of other occasions. And I promise to bring you back loads of fruit!'

Now, with her favourite CDs playing, the late-afternoon sun shining—and good weather forecast for the weekend—Melody felt her spirits soar as she sped along the motorway. Although there *were* one or two traffic hold-ups—as Jason had so cynically predicted there always would be—it was just seven-thirty as she once again drove up the long drive of Poplars…to see Adam's red Porsche already parked! As soon as she saw it colour flooded Melody's cheeks. She'd not given a thought to the possibility that he might be here this weekend as well!

She pulled in alongside, and even before she could collect her things together Adam's strong footsteps crunched across the gravel towards her. He opened her door, smiling down at her darkly.

'Hello, Mel,' he said casually, as if she shouldn't be at all surprised at seeing him.

Was there a conspiracy going on here? Melody asked herself. But anyway, did it matter? They both had equal interests in the area, and it was a free world. She returned his smile.

'Well, hello, Adam,' she said. 'I didn't realise that…'

'Oh, didn't Fee tell you I was coming for a few days?' he asked lightly. He paused. 'I hope it isn't a nasty surprise, Mel?'

'Of course not. Don't be silly,' she replied quickly—with a

hint of *why should it matter to me whether you're here or not* in her voice.

He took her case from the boot, and together they went across to the entrance. Fee came out almost at once, automatically giving Melody a hug.

'Fee—you're looking absolutely blooming!' Melody said.

'Thank you,' Fee said. 'And if you actually mean that I'm looking plump—then say so! The pounds seem to be piling on!'

Together they went into the kitchen, where Callum was giving the dogs their supper. He immediately came over to Melody, his hand outstretched in greeting. Presently, the four sat around chatting, the dogs nudging Melody's legs for some attention.

'The fruit's all been taken care of,' Callum said. 'There was plenty for the Fair and more than enough for you, Mel!'

'Thanks for that,' she said gratefully. 'That's one thing sorted, at least.' She shot a quick glance at Adam. 'I didn't know that Adam would be here, too,' she said.

'Oh, didn't I mention that on the phone?' Fee said innocently. 'Adam usually tries to come back for this particular occasion—and this weekend is a very special one this year, in any case. More special than usual,' she added.

Melody raised her eyebrows. 'How so?'

'My parents are celebrating their Golden Wedding Anniversary,' Adam said. 'And they decided that here, among old sights and old friends, was where they wanted to spend it. At Poplars—their old home.'

'We've all known each other for such a long time,' Fee said. 'It's going to be like a big family get-together.'

Melody felt a sudden tightening in her chest. It seemed that she was probably going to meet people who would have known her mother, and the thought made her slightly panicky... But wasn't this what she wanted? she asked herself. Perhaps something, some little hint, might at last explain why Frances had never wanted to return here. And *she* could still keep the secret…because Melody's connection with the place was still not known by anyone. And it would stay like that for ever, if she wanted it to. No one need ever know that she was Frances's illegitimate daughter.

She smiled quickly. 'After I've unpacked my few belongings,' she said, 'I hope you'll allow me to take you to the Rose & Crown for supper.'

'Sorry, Mel, no can do,' Callum said, getting up. 'There are a few last-minute things I've got to sort out up at the village hall for tomorrow.' He paused. 'And I'm hoping that my wife will agree to have an early night. We've all been rather busy lately. But thanks for the offer.'

'I understand,' Melody said at once. 'And, judging by the cars, you're still pretty full.'

'Eight guests are due to check out in the morning,' Callum said. 'Then it'll be just Adam and his parents and you staying, Mel. And we can all relax.'

Adam stood and glanced down at Melody. 'I've picked up your key—allow me to show you to your room, madam.' He took her case from her. 'At least *I* can join you for supper— I'm not having an early night,' he added. 'My parents are visiting friends this evening,' he explained, as they went up the stairs. 'But they'll be very interested to meet the new owner of Gatehouse Cottage.'

Melody couldn't help feeling slightly bewildered. She'd come here in good faith, to take part in an annual ritual in the life of this village, but somehow Adam had stepped in from nowhere and was filtering himself into her life—again.

He opened her door and put her case down inside. 'I'm hungry,' he announced. 'See you downstairs in half an hour.'

In less than that time Melody ran quickly back downstairs. She'd not bothered to change out of the black jeans and pale grey shirt she'd travelled in, but had undone her hair, leaving it loose. Adam was waiting by the door, and looked up as she joined him. As always, her appearance, her femininity, stirred him, and without thinking what he was doing he took her hand lightly in his.

Melody looked up at him. 'Now,' she said firmly, 'this time supper really is on me. I shall insist.'

'Okay,' he replied easily. 'But at least let me drive us.'

As they made their way down the drive, Melody suddenly turned to him. 'Do—do you mind if we don't go to the Rose & Crown?' she asked tentatively, thinking of the evening she'd had to endure there with Jason. 'I'd rather go somewhere different.'

He glanced back at her. 'Suits me,' he said. He paused. 'Let's go to the pub we went to on our first day.'

Melody couldn't help being aware of the possessive pronoun. *Our* first day suggested something familiar and intimate, something to be continued—and although at one time it would have put her on the defensive, for some reason it didn't. Because she had to admit to being totally at ease with Adam—an ease mixed with a definite feeling that she was once more on home ground. That she was actually *at* home.

How weird was that? she thought. She hadn't even taken possession of her cottage yet—not really. It was still an empty shell. But she had already made plans for the decorators to begin work next month, and soon after that the rooms would be furnished and she could begin to start thinking of her future—and how much of it would be spent there.

At the pub, the same corner table was empty, and Adam grinned at her as they sat down. 'I think this is how it all started,' he murmured.

They both decided on the seared sea bass and salad for their meal, and Melody realised just how hungry she'd been as she put down her knife and fork.

'That was fantastic,' she said. 'Though probably not to be compared with the exotic stuff you've been eating recently. How was Malaysia, by the way?'

His eyes glinted across at her. 'Still there,' he replied, 'and just as lovely.'

But not as lovely as you, Mrs Forester, he could have added, admitting to himself for the first time that he was head over heels in love with this woman. He had not stopped thinking about her since that evening in her flat. And, worryingly, what he'd inter-preted then as lust was now something far, far deeper. More reliable, more lasting. But could it be trusted? Could this new gut feeling of his be trusted? And what chance did he have with her, in any case? She'd hardly thrown herself at him, he thought wryly.

He realised that he was going to have to use all his powers of persuasion to make any headway with her. But now that he'd come to terms with his own feelings—now that he'd accepted the inevitable—there was no going back. In spite of all that had happened in the past, he was going to marry Mel. However long it took.

Suddenly she sensed that something was going on in his head, and she stood up quickly, feeling uneasy. She needed to get away, to be by herself, she thought. 'I'd like to go now, Adam,' she said. 'I do feel a bit tired after the journey.'

Before he could go over to the bar she'd edged past him neatly, settling their bill with the landlord, and as she rejoined him he looked down at her. 'Thank you very much for my supper,' he said solemnly, thinking, That's the last time you'll do that for me, Mel Forester. From now on *I'm* the captain of the ship!

It was getting late as he parked the car at Poplars, but the lights were still on in the kitchen. Adam glanced in at the lighted windows as they approached the building.

'Ah, good. My parents are still up,' he said. He paused. 'Come in for a minute, Mel. I'd like you to meet them.'

Melody caught her breath for a moment as she followed Adam. His mother, Isabel, would have known Frances very well…

'Mother—Dad—' Adam began. 'I'd like to introduce you to Mel…'

'Mel…? *Melody!* It *is* Melody, isn't it? It *must* be! My dear little girl, I would know you anywhere! You are the image of your mother!' Isabel Carlisle went straight over and caught hold of Melody's hand. 'But the last time I saw you, you were just a week old! I never expected to see you ever again! What a lovely anniversary present!' The woman held Melody away from her, looking at her searchingly as a shy smile crossed the girl's face and she nodded her head in amazement. 'Robert— isn't she *exactly* like Frances?'

Robert Carlisle looked across and smiled genially. 'Yes—a beautiful replica,' he agreed.

For a few seconds after that there was complete silence, during which Adam's face was a picture of puzzlement. He looked at his mother, utterly confused.

'What's going on?' he demanded. 'And Mel is short for *Melody*? You're not Melanie, then, as we all supposed?'

'No. Melody is an unusual name,' she said, 'so I always intro- duce myself as Mel—which is simpler for most people to accept.'

Isabel brought her over to sit beside her. 'And… Frances…?' she began.

'My mother died six years ago,' Melody said quietly.

'Well, I'm sorry to hear that.' She paused. 'Now, tell me all about yourself, my dear.'

'Yes—*do*,' Adam said tartly, wondering how on earth his mother had any idea who Mel was.

The girl looked up at him, her face flushed. 'My mother— Frances—was housekeeper here for many years,' she began. 'You probably knew her yourself, in your early childhood.'

'And a marvellous one she was, too,' Isabel said.

'Gatehouse Cottage was where she lived all that time,' Melody went on, realising that there was no point any more in keeping up the pretence. 'And it was where I was born,' she added quietly.

Adam's face was dark, his expansive brow creased in confused annoyance. 'Were you indeed?' he said flatly. 'So why the big mystery? Why have you never mentioned any of this before?' he demanded.

Melody found difficulty in answering him. How could she tell him that she wasn't keeping her own secret, but a secret that belonged solely to her mother. It must seem very deceitful to Adam, she realised, that in the considerable time they'd spent together she'd deliberately kept him in the dark. 'It was…difficult…' was all she said.

'Why difficult? *What* was difficult? Nothing to be ashamed of, surely? I don't get it,' he said harshly.

'I…just…don't know…' Melody began miserably, wishing with all her heart that she *had* told him before this. She turned to Isabel. 'Although my mother frequently spoke of the village—of the people, and Poplars, and the cottage—she was adamant that she would never set foot here again. And she would never tell me why.' She paused, and Isabel took her hand, holding it gently in hers.

'I think I can explain—if you want me to,' she said.

Melody nodded. 'Please…' she whispered. 'I must know…' She didn't look at Adam, conscious that her heart was thumping uncomfortably. What was she going to hear?

'Thirty years ago,' Isabel said, 'the Forsythe family owned the Manor—the place across the valley from here—as well as most of the village and outlying area. It was a tremendously wealthy dynasty. The Lord of the Manor at the time was Barnaby Forsythe, who inherited it rather early in his life—still in his twenties, in fact—but rose to the task magnificently. He and his young wife Elizabeth were wonderful—popular with the whole community, and so generous to poorer families who might have sometimes found it difficult to pay the very reasonable rents on their cottages.' She paused. 'Of course times have moved on, and most of those properties are privately owned now.'

She seemed lost in thought for a moment, before continuing. 'Then, one day, a terrible tragedy occurred. Two years into their marriage Elizabeth was thrown from her horse, and overnight she became paraplegic. It was a horrible thing… They were such a glamorous couple, so much in love. Life for them, in its fullest sense, was over.' She took a tissue from her bag. 'Of course money was never a problem, and Barnaby saw that she met the top specialists, had the best of care—but what solace is money in a situation like that? I know that they would have given away every last penny just to be able to live a normal life.' She wiped a tear away from her cheek. 'We'd always been firm friends of the family, and we mourned with them. As the whole village did.'

Melody swallowed a lump in her own throat as the story unfolded. But what was this to do with *her*?

'Elizabeth and your mother knew each other, of course, and were of a similar age,' Isabel went on. 'Some years after the tragedy Elizabeth was taught to paint, holding the brush between her teeth, and Frances used to sit and paint with her for hours and hours on end. They became very close, naturally.' She glanced at Melody. 'Your mother was very artistic—an accomplished artist, wasn't she, Melody?'

Melody's mouth had begun to dry as all these facts became known, her brain desperately trying to see where she fitted in to all this.

'One summer evening, after one of their normal sessions, Elizabeth insisted that Barnaby should escort Frances back home across the fields. They'd gone on rather later than usual, it was a particularly dark night, and…'

'And Barnaby made love to Frances,' Adam said shrewdly. 'At Gatehouse Cottage.'

'Yes. He did,' Isabel said, without a trace of embarrassment. 'And the few of us who ever knew about it had every sympathy. For fifteen years—fifteen youthful years—Barnaby had lived a celibate life, tending and supporting the wife he loved with such dedication and loyalty. He was an inspiration. And on that one evening he fell into a few hours of passion with a woman he admired, respected and loved—your mother, Melody.' She held Melody's hand again. 'Frances and I were always honest with each other,' she said, 'and I believed her implicitly when she told me that she and Barnaby had been lovers for just one night and that one night only. Could anyone with a heart find fault with that?'

No one spoke for a few moments as Isabel's words began to sink in. Then the woman met Melody's gaze unfalteringly.

'I believe—I sincerely believe,' she said quietly, 'that a man is capable of loving two women equally—in exceptional circumstances, as these most certainly were. But…' She smiled briefly. 'In our culture, only one wife is allowed at one time. You were conceived in love, Melody. Never have any doubt about that. And that liaison was enough to bring into the world the only child either of them would ever have.' She paused. 'I take it that Frances never had other children?'

Melody shook her head. 'Sadly—no,' she replied quietly.

'Well, you were a true love-child, Melody,' Isabel said. She sighed. 'In the same month that Barnaby and Frances were lovers, Barnaby took Elizabeth to Australia. They stayed for a year with a branch of the family over there.' She shook her head. 'The really sad part is that it could not have had a happier ending for the three of them.'

Melody found herself floating in a sea of disbelief—and sympathetic dismay at her mother's predicament—while Adam had been stunned into silence at everything he'd heard.

'Is there more?' he asked flatly.

'Well, Frances wanted it kept secret…only a small handful of us ever knew the truth. Don't believe it when it's said that people can't be trusted to keep their mouths shut,' she added. 'Her secret was safe with us.' She paused. 'A week after your birth, Melody, you and your mother moved away, and were literally never seen here again. Until tonight, of course, when I thought you were a vision as you walked in.' She smiled.

Melody swallowed, trying hard to come to terms with all that Isabel had told her. 'And did my…father…' her *father*—she was anonymous no more! '…did my father know about me?' she asked simply.

'Not until a year later, when I took it upon myself to tell him,' Isabel replied. 'I felt it right that he should know he had a child. They were still abroad when I spoke to him about it.'

'And what was his reaction?' Adam asked, by this time as transfixed as Melody.

'He was overwhelmed. With joy,' Isabel said. 'I don't suppose he ever told Elizabeth, because her well-being was his sole concern, and he'd never have wanted to hurt her. But do you know…?' She paused for a moment. 'I believe that Elizabeth might have had a deeper reason for insisting that Barnaby should escort Frances home that night…might have hoped that what happened, would happen.' She looked up at the others. 'It's our right, as human beings, to be as one,' she said quietly, 'and I'm sure that Elizabeth felt that, too. And that she should offer—and sanction—the one precious gift she was incapable of giving.'

Robert got up from his chair. 'Yes, it was a very sad story,' he said. 'Made more so by the fact that five years later they were both killed in a road accident out there in Australia where they eventually moved after selling the Manor to the de Wintons.'

'Added to which, of course, he never ever saw his

daughter—of whom he would have been immensely proud,'
Isabel said, smiling at Melody. 'Because Frances was determined not to bring the Forsythe family's name—a well-re-
spected name in the locality—into disrepute. Their reputation
should never be sullied by *her*. He tried valiantly, through me,
to send maintenance for his child, but Frances was stubborn and
refused. She'd gone away for good—severed all links with the
village—and wanted no handouts from anyone. But in the end
she reluctantly agreed to invest a very generous one-off sum
for their daughter—to be given to you, Melody, on your
mother's death.' She paused. '*She* wanted none of it. I tried to
keep in touch with Frances, and did so for many years, but
gradually we began to lose touch.' She shrugged. 'Time passes.
People move on,' she said quietly.

Dazed by all this revelation, Melody felt her senses
swimming. No wonder she felt so much part of the place, she
thought. She was a daughter of this soil! She had come back
to her roots…in every sense. And of *course*! In a blinding flash
she realised where her legacy had really come from! Not from
her aunt at all—of course not! There'd been no money there to
speak of. That gift was her father's gift…a gift which had
enabled her to buy Gatehouse Cottage. And which had brought
her life full-circle!

# CHAPTER THIRTEEN

SLOWLY, Melody got up from her chair, wondering whether she had the strength to go up the stairs to her room. She was both exhilarated and exhausted by the unbelievable news she'd just been given. Looking quickly at Adam, she was rewarded with a stony-faced expression that sent her heart plummeting. He was annoyed—of course he was! And she had some explaining to do!

The older couple stood up, too. 'I think it's time for bed,' Isabel said. 'It'll be a long day tomorrow—and then on Sunday we're having a celebration lunch here at Poplars, Melody. We've arranged for people in the village to do the catering, because we don't want Fee to have anything else to do at the moment—we do hope you'll join us for that.' She smiled. 'In fact, it will make our day to have Frances and Barnaby's daughter to share it with us.' She dropped a light kiss on Melody's cheek, then hugged Adam before going towards the door. 'Goodnight, my dears—and sleep well.'

After they'd gone, Melody faced Adam, trying not to look as guilty as she felt. He stared back at her.

'Well, what a complete fool you've made of me,' he said harshly, and his meltingly sexy tones suddenly held a distinct air of menace. 'You must have been having a good laugh at my expense.' He snorted derisively. 'I do hope you've enjoyed the joke!' He paused. 'But what a curious game you've been playing, Mrs Forester.'

'I haven't been playing a game,' Melody replied quietly, trying to stop herself from trembling. She had just been given the most amazing news about herself, about her own life, and she was finding it difficult to take it in all at once. But now she had to try and appease Adam—he did, after all, deserve some sort of apology.

'Well, what do *you* call it, then? Am I allowed an explanation?' He almost spat out the words.

'Please, Adam. I'll do my best to get you to understand.'

He shoved a chair to one side and sat down, leaning back and looking at her coldly. 'Go on, then,' he said. 'Why the big mystery? What on earth was *that* all about?'

Melody didn't sit, but stayed where she was, one hand gripping the side of the table for support. 'It wasn't something I felt I could talk about—to anyone,' she said. 'Because I had no idea why my mother had refused to come back here—though it's much clearer now! There was obviously a secret, but she would never talk to me about it, maintaining that the past should be the past.'

'Not dwelling on the past is one thing,' Adam said shortly. 'Ignoring it, pretending it hasn't happened, is another. Far better to confront it, deal with it—and move on.'

'And that is exactly what I think I was trying to do,' Melody said quietly. 'Enough time had passed since my mother's death for me to feel that I should come here and just…well, just *be*… Though I had no real expectation that I would discover anything.'

'But all the times we've been together—especially at the cottage—and you never volunteered a single thing!' Adam said. 'And being so secretive about your connection here—I mean, you *knew* you'd been born here, at least! It smacks of dishonesty, deceit, Mel.' He ran a hand through his hair. 'I feel as if I've been taken for a very long ride!'

Melody was stung to respond to that. She'd never been accused of dishonesty before!

'Dishonesty by omission, perhaps,' she retorted. 'But let's not forget what we're actually talking about here, Adam. We're talking about *my* life, *my* past, *my* history! Surely what I wish to reveal is *my* business?' She paused, conscious that her knees were shaking. 'What I felt I had to do was keep faith with my mother's wishes, and I still don't know if she'd be pleased that I've come here or not. But I am so relieved to know, at last, what I was not allowed to know before. And after hearing the truth— after hearing all that your parents told me—I *understand*. For the first time I can understand…and…strangely…I can start to feel—well, complete.'

Neither of them spoke for a moment, then Adam said, 'Well, I congratulate you on being able to keep things close to your chest! It must take practice to be that devious. I mean, how have you managed to keep it up? How have you managed not to let one tiny word slip that might have told us where you were born, who you really were….'

'Because I didn't *know* who I was!' Melody shot back. 'I knew I'd been born here. That was all. In coming here on holiday I had the vaguest hope that something might explain my mother's determination to stay away for ever.'

Melody sat down now, filled with such a strange mixture of emotions she didn't know whether to laugh or cry. But her overwhelming sense was one of gratitude—gratitude for her mother's obvious integrity, and gratitude at knowing, at last, who her father was. She had to admit to an intense feeling of pride in belonging to Barnaby Forsythe, in sharing the blood-line of a man who had loved so deeply—not just the woman he'd married, and to whom he'd been devoted, but also the woman he'd come to love as well: her mother. *Whatever* Adam Carlisle said, families were the ultimate tie—the ultimate strength of human bonding, she thought. To be loyal, to love and be loved—there was nothing more important in the whole world. What else did anyone need?

The unusual, uncomfortable silence between them told Melody that Adam was not won over by her explanation of her position in all this. He stood up.

'Well, I think that one day you should try your luck in politics,' he said unkindly. 'The only qualification you need is to be a convincing actress—and you're certainly that, Mel. Acting mixed with a little cunning might even get you the position of prime minister!'

Melody gave him a long, measured look, her lips set. 'Your opinion is of very little interest to me,' she said coldly. 'My conscience is clear—even if you don't see it that way. All I can do is apologise that I didn't feel able to tell you what you now know about me. I've explained my reasons.' She picked up her bag. 'Goodnight, Adam.'

She went to go past him, but he thrust himself up from the chair, pulling her to him, pinning her arms to her sides—and then his mouth came down on to hers in an angry movement. She felt his tongue probing her lips and she gasped—in surprise and shock at the suddenness of what he was doing. Then in a moment of unbelievable surrender she collapsed into his arms. This evening's revelations had been too much for her to cope with—she needed support, and she wanted someone to rejoice with, she thought desperately. She needed Adam!

Almost at once the ferocity of his kiss changed into the sort of breathtaking passion that she'd missed so much over the last year, and she clung to him. For a few timeless moments they stayed locked together, each lost in their own thoughts, each wallowing in their sudden intimacy, until Melody pulled right away, looking up at him, her eyes glowing with desire—and disillusionment!

Hadn't he just called her deceitful—and *cunning*? Horrible, hurtful words! But her problem was, she realised, that he did have a point. To him she must seem unnecessarily secretive— yet if she'd told him that she'd been born in Gatehouse Cottage what a can of worms that would have opened! Questions would have followed—most of which, until half an hour ago, she'd had no answer to. But he'd never understand, she thought. He was not in the frame of mind to even try.

After a moment she turned away and left the room without another word.

He just stood there, motionless, listening to her light footsteps tread softly up the stairs. Then he pushed his chair back, scraping it harshly on the tiled floor. He still felt totally staggered at what he'd heard about Melody's past—how she had transmuted from casual tourist to direct descendent of the Forsythe clan! She'd turned up here from nowhere when, amazingly, Gatehouse Cottage had been up for auction, and she, a complete stranger, had won it. But of course she was no stranger after all. He thrust his hands in his pockets. To think that if fate had handled things differently she might have ended up as Lady of the Manor in her own right! A slow smile spread briefly across his handsome features. Fate could be an unpredictable mistress!

It was nearly one o'clock in the morning, and he remembered that he'd promised Callum to do the last rounds tonight, before turning in himself. So, with the dogs safely asleep in front of the Aga, he switched off the lights and left the room, locking the heavy front door securely, before making his way noise- lessly through the building. It was quiet everywhere, but he stood outside Mel's room for a few moments, listening, remem- bering all too clearly that other night when she'd been so upset.

Presently, back in his own room, he sat on the edge of his bed for a moment. A couple of months ago he'd known nothing of this woman's existence—but he knew about it now! And he admitted to himself again that he had fallen for her—completely. Nothing could change that now. Come what may, Melody Forester was going to be Mrs Adam Carlisle—whatever the cost! But would he ever really be able to trust her? Oh, he didn't mean in the accepted sense—he was certain that she was not the sort to play around with other men—but her ability to keep so quiet about herself over all these weeks had to say something about her, surely? If she could deceive on that level what else was she capable of? And if he couldn't trust her, what chance would a serious relationship have?

He gritted his teeth—he'd risk it! He'd somehow make this come right. Despite all his preconceptions about marriage, he'd put his head in the noose once again—and risk being throttled! he thought. Because, quite simply, he couldn't help himself. She had bewitched him totally, and he wanted to spend the rest of his life with her. Loving her, protecting her, sharing himself with her. All he had to do now was convince her to see his point of view…

The next morning Melody arrived down for breakfast rather late—all the other paying guests had already gone. But Isabel and Robert were there, drinking their coffee, and they looked up as she came in, greeting her warmly.

She helped herself to rolls and fruit juice, but declined a cooked meal from the girl who was serving breakfasts that morning.

'Another wonderfully warm day,' Robert observed, smiling over at Melody.

'Oh, they always manage to have it just right for this event,' Isabel said cheerfully. 'And practically everyone gets involved…it's a real community affair. Adam always tries to get home in time for it—likes making himself useful in whatever way he can,' she added fondly. 'He usually gets roped in to take his turn in the stocks, for the children to throw wet sponges at him!'

Melody smiled inwardly. After all the names he'd called her last night, she'd queue up to hurl a few, she thought.

There was silence for a few moments, then Isabel said, 'Melody, I do hope that everything I told you—you know, about your mother—didn't upset you too much, my dear. We did think afterwards that it would have come as something of a shock, perhaps…'

Melody smiled. 'I wasn't upset,' she said carefully. Well, not about that, anyway, she thought. 'I'm grateful to you for telling me. Not that it will make any significant difference to my life in a practical sense, but speaking emotionally it has made all the difference in the world. I feel a…whole person, now, rather than half a one.' She hesitated. 'It would have been so good to have had a sister—or a brother.'

'Well, it certainly *can* be…' Isabel began, glancing at her husband, who was pouring himself more coffee. 'But sadly for us our two—Adam and Rupert, our twins—have never got on. It's such a shame.'

Melody caught her breath. Was she going to be told what she wanted to know? She threw discretion to the winds. 'Why?' she asked softly. 'What went wrong?'

'It was not Adam's fault,' Robert cut in. 'I'm afraid Rupert has a very jealous streak—sorry though we are to say it—and try as we did, we can do nothing about it.' He paused. 'Regrettable though it is, people are as they are, and that's all there is to it. The boys were never treated any differently—we love them both equally. But it's always seemed to be Adam who finds it so easy to succeed in everything—academically, in sports—and he was always very popular with women, who seem drawn to him like bees to a honey pot. Whereas Rupert has always found that side of things very difficult. Always had a chip on his shoulder about something or other. Silly chap. His own worst enemy.' He drank from his cup. 'But we have to hand it to Adam—he always tried valiantly to pour oil on troubled waters, because he knew how upset we were, as he was himself.' He paused. 'But now our boys have not spoken for two whole years.'

The emptiness in their hearts was palpable as Melody listened.

Isabel went on, 'Then, of course, the unbelievable—the worst thing of all happened—'

Robert cut in. 'Oh, don't spoil the day by bringing all that up, Isabel,' he said. 'Keep it for another time. This is our celebration weekend, remember!'

They all stood up, then, to leave, and Melody said quietly, 'Maybe it will all come right one day?' she suggested. 'Old sores can sometimes heal…'

Isabel sighed. 'I'd love to think so, Melody. But the damage is done, I'm afraid. And there's no undoing it.'

So, Melody thought, as they went their separate ways, Adam had a secret of his own! Whatever could it be?

Later, wearing a cream cotton sundress, Melody made her way up to the field and the village hall. Even before she got there she could hear music, raised voices and laughter. The place was packed with people enjoying all the sideshows, and children darted around excitedly. She decided to go straight to the hall, where she knew Fee would be.

'Hi, Mel,' Fee said, as she came up. 'See—your fruit has been snapped up!'

'Well, I hope there's something left for me to buy—' Melody began, but Fee cut in.

'There's certainly no need for you to buy fruit! We've packed the rest of it, all ready for you to take back with you.' She glanced up briefly. 'Adam's up at the other end of the field, doing sterling duty at the carousel—which, would you believe, has packed up. Something to do with the generator. He's offered to work the thing by hand so as not to disappoint the children.

Good job it's confined to the under-sevens,' she added, 'or he'd be doing himself a mischief!'

Melody was surprised. She hadn't thought Adam was a child-lover—not enough to put himself out, anyway. But later on, as she made her way along the field, she could see the gaudy carousel moving rapidly around—and Adam standing in the centre, his hands stretched above his head as he grasped and pushed the metal rods so that the six little cars could circulate to the obvious delight of the small occupants. He was so engrossed in the task that he didn't see her for several minutes. But suddenly their eyes met, and despite all the heated feelings of last night, they both smiled at each other.

Melody's heart missed a beat. He was so unutterably gorgeous, she thought, his suntanned skin shining with perspiration, his hair glistening blackly in the hot sunshine. And when he smiled at her like that she felt a rush of such passionate excitement that she felt ashamed at the longing in her heart. What had this man done to her? Had he completely robbed her of her common sense?

'If you're waiting for a turn,' he called over affably, 'I'm afraid you don't qualify.'

'Then there's no point in waiting in the queue,' she called back with a smile in her voice, thinking that the collective weight of those tinies must be considerable.

Presently, after she'd spent some money on the various stalls, and bought several raffle tickets, Melody made her way back to the hall, where she and Fee were going to have lunch together. Fee was already there, sitting at a table, and Melody went across to join her.

'Everything's going well out there,' Melody said, sitting down. 'All the tins are rattling with money!'

'You're not bored, are you, Mel?' Fee said. 'I mean, this isn't really your sort of thing, is it?'

'I'm not bored at all!' Melody said. 'I love the atmosphere. Everyone's so friendly.'

There was a lull in the conversation, then Fee said, 'I want you to know that Isabel told us—Callum and me—everything she told you last night, Mel. And it came as a rather wonderful surprise,' she added. 'We none of us had any idea that Barnaby Forsythe had fathered a child. Of course we were only children ourselves at the time. It's an amazing story, isn't it? And amazing that you should turn up, after all this time, and buy Gatehouse Cottage.'

'I wonder if I shall ever feel *unamazed* ever again!'

Fee touched Melody's hand briefly. 'We shall love knowing you're down at the cottage,' she said earnestly. 'Even if it isn't very often.'

'I shall make it as often as I possibly can!' Melody exclaimed.

Much later, after she'd watched the races, and the tug-of-war—where, naturally, Adam and Callum were on the winning side—Melody wandered back to Poplars. The Carlisles had insisted on booking a table for the six of them at the Rose & Crown for supper, but now Melody decided that she wanted to be by herself for a while. To come to terms with her new identity. Even though she knew it would not make a scrap of difference to her future life, it entirely changed her perception of her past. She decided that she'd go for that lovely walk across the fields, where she'd picked the flowers.

It was a beautiful early autumn evening, the sun still warm as she trod the now familiar route. Her personal jigsaw was complete, she thought—so why wasn't she feeling as euphoric as she should be?

Twenty minutes later she came to the field which led to the stream she'd bathed her feet in—which subsequent rainfall had added to considerably. The water now gurgled and chuckled along, and Melody dropped to her knees, scooping up a handful to put to her lips. She didn't know whether she was doing a wise thing or not, but it tasted wonderfully sweet on her tongue as she took another generous gulp. Adam's voice interrupted.

'What a charming picture,' he said.

Melody leaned back on her heels and looked up. He crouched down beside her, so that their faces were close, his white teeth glistening as he gave her that slow, incredible smile.

'Can you ever forgive me?' he said softly. 'After all the things I said last night?'

'Adam,' Melody said, 'when I really thought about it afterwards, I realised how deeply hurt you must have felt at my…deviousness…'

He put a finger on her lips gently. 'Please, Mel—please don't go on,' he said. 'What you actually proved, and what I didn't see then, was your total loyalty. That you would always keep your word. I had no right to speak as I did. But…but I thought I might lose you.'

'Lose me?'

'I was afraid that I would lose my trust in you…that you might be capable of…' He was finding it difficult to find the right words. 'Of betraying me,' he added.

'But how would I do that?' Melody frowned.

'I was afraid that in future I might not always feel absolutely sure of you, Mel…'

Melody shook her head slowly. 'You've lost me, Adam.'

He took both her hands in his. 'I want you, Mel. I want you to marry me. I want us to be together for all time, with no secrets between us—ever.'

Melody refrained from gasping out loud at this unexpected proposal of marriage—and at the heat that rushed right through the length of her body at his words.

She returned his penetrating gaze with her own steady, patently honest green eyes. She knew that his own troubled past was somehow etched into his words, and she said, 'First can I be allowed to learn your own secret, Adam? About Rupert? Your parents were explaining that your brother can be difficult…'

Still holding her hands tightly, he said, 'I was once engaged to be married. To Lucy. The wedding was planned, arrangements made—and I thought she was the one for me. Then one day Rupert made the surprise announcement that he'd had a fling with my intended wife, and that she was expecting his baby.'

Melody was horrified. No wonder Adam was cynical about relationships!

'It was bad enough for me,' he went on, 'but in a way worse for my parents, who felt that Rupert had betrayed us all. Betrayed the whole family.' He shrugged. 'As it happened, Lucy lost the baby early on, and their affair ground to a halt. He was never serious about her,' he added grimly. 'My brother only wanted to prove that he could get one over me. Take what was mine.' He took a deep breath. 'We haven't spoken since. So…' He paused. 'That's my secret, Mel. And that's all there is.'

Melody looked at him with such an overpowering need to hold him in her arms that she whispered softly, 'Make love to me, Adam.'

He gazed down at her for a long, tense moment, and then without another word he put his arms around her and lowered her to the ground slowly. Carefully he undressed her, touching her half-closed eyes, the tip of her nose, the smooth skin at the base of her neck and then her firm, aching breasts with his mouth and tongue, heightening her unashamed passion to such an excited level that she thought she was going to cry out.

'I love you, Mel,' he said softly. 'And I want you.'

Then, effortlessly, he undressed himself and knelt up, raising himself above her. And under the mellowing sky, with nature all around them, they made unhurried, tender, sensuous love—until, exhausted, they lay back on the soft turf.

After a few silent moments, Adam turned his head to look at her. 'You'll have to marry me now,' he murmured.

Suddenly the impact of his words stabbed at her painfully. Hadn't she vowed never to truly love again? Hadn't she vowed never again to risk loss and the emptiness of being alone? But how could she resist Adam's powerful masculinity? How could she resist the thought of lying in his arms night after night for the rest of her life?

Without looking at him, she said, 'So—what would happen? Where would we live?'

He waited before answering. 'At the Manor, of course,' he replied. 'Your rightful home. The de Wintons have sold it to me—we've been in negotiations all the summer.'

'But what about Malaysia?' she asked.

'Oh, did I forget to say? We're selling up—selling the business. My parents are well into their seventies. I shall have my share of the proceeds, to make what I will of my life. I knew I'd always intended coming back here eventually, and the Manor coming up for sale seemed too good a chance to miss.' He looked down at her. 'And what more appropriate wife could I possibly ask for?'

A thousand thoughts invaded Melody's brain—tormenting her, warning her.

'I want to say yes, Adam, I really do,' she whispered. 'But I'm *afraid*.'

'Afraid? What of? Not of me, surely?' he said, bringing her close to him.

'No. I'm afraid of losing again—afraid of losing you,' she said simply. 'I'm afraid to trust fate, that's all.'

He understood what she was saying. 'Don't you think we're in the same boat?' he said gently. 'I'm afraid of betrayal; you're afraid of loss. But that's not the way to live a life, and you know it, Mel. We *have* to trust—trust our love, trust each other.' His mouth came down onto hers again. 'We have to trust in *hope*. And keep our fingers crossed,' he added, smiling faintly.

Around the long table in the kitchen of Poplars the next day, the atmosphere was electrically charged—to such an extent that, not for the first time, Melody thought she was going to burst with excitement and anticipation. The Golden Wedding Anniversary had been given due attention and congratulation— but it was Melody and Adam who were now the centre of the celebrations.

Fee and Callum were all smiles, and Adam's parents were ecstatic.

'We were afraid that Adam would never find anyone else,' Isabel confided to Melody, as yet more wine was being passed around. 'We are both so happy about it, Melody. It just seems so...*right*, somehow.'

Melody hugged her affectionately. 'On the scale of happiness,' she said simply, 'my own is off the top!'

The main meal—deliciously presented by the caterers— had come to an end, and presently Fee said, 'Now there's just one more thing to be sorted...shan't be a sec.'

Adam, sitting close to Melody, his hand holding hers tightly, said quietly, 'We mustn't forget the dogs. They deserve a walk after all the noise we've been making.'

'Let's go, then,' she whispered. 'I need some fresh air!'

Then the door opened, and Fee came in bearing an iced celebration cake, alive with lighted candles—followed by a rather spare man with tousled brown hair.

There was a moment's stunned silence, then Isabel rose quickly to her feet.

'*Rupert!*' she exclaimed. 'My dear Rupert—we didn't think for a moment that...'

Callum got up. 'This is all down to my wife,' he explained,

shooting a quick glance at Adam. 'She thought it was right to remind Rupert what a special weekend this was for you, Mr and Mrs Carlisle. So we got in touch, and—and, well, here he is.'

The next few moments passed in a haze for Melody, as Isabel and Robert embraced Rupert—whom she could see did not much resemble his brother in any way. He looked tired and unsure of himself—unsure of the reception he'd get, at least from Adam.

Adam went over and held out his hand. 'Hi, bro,' he said quietly. 'Long time, no see.'

The two men shook hands, and for a moment nothing was said by anyone. But Isabel was crying silently, and Robert suddenly needed a handkerchief to blow his nose loudly.

'I need to say something,' Rupert said, his voice a little unsteady. 'I've needed to say it for some time, but I've only just found the courage.' He hesitated. 'I've come to wish my parents another fifty happy years together—but most of all I've come to ask your forgiveness. All of you. But especially you, Adam.' He turned away, gathering his courage to go on. 'I've thought of this moment so many times in the last two years—wondered whether you'd ever speak to me again. But I hope you will. Because I've missed you. I've missed all of you. I've had a rotten couple of years since I left the firm—since I ruined your plans, Adam. I thought I could do much better by myself—doing my own thing, no ties, no shackles, that kind of thing. I was wrong. I need you. I need all of you. But will you ever want me, ever again?'

Without a word Adam put his arms around his brother's neck and held him tightly. 'Don't go on, Rupert,' he said huskily. 'Because I want to thank you—from the bottom of my heart.'

'Thank me?'

Adam turned and held out his hand to Melody, who came across at once. 'Meet the girl of my dreams,' he said softly. 'This is Melody, who is going to be my wife. And if you hadn't taken Lucy off my hands—well, I wouldn't be free, would I? You saved me for another day, Rupert—and it will be the best day of my whole life.'

Four months later Adam and Melody sat either side of Fee's hospital bed, with Melody cradling Master Toby Adam Brown in her arms.

'Now we know how it's done,' Callum joked, 'this is only the beginning! We've warned the entire village to expect an influx of small Brown kids, running wild about the place.'

'I still can't really believe it,' Fee said, looking wan but deliriously happy. 'Our luck seems to have changed with your arrival, Melody.' She glanced at Adam. 'Everything seems to have come right. For all of us.'

'Amen to that,' Adam said. 'But I suppose your work on Gatehouse Cottage will have to wait for a while now, Callum?'

'Oh, it'll all happen—in its own time,' Callum said good-naturedly. 'We've got our baby, we've got the cottage, and we've got the rest of our lives. We don't need another thing.'

Fee took the baby from Melody and looked up at her. 'Thank you for postponing the wedding so that I can be behind you on the day, Mel,' she said. 'I've never been bridesmaid to anyone before. I can't wait!'

'*You* can't wait!' Adam exclaimed, putting his arm firmly around Melody's waist. 'How d'you think *I'm* feeling?'

*A sneaky peek at next month...*

# By Request

**RELIVE THE ROMANCE WITH THE BEST OF THE BEST**

*My wish list for next month's titles...*

In stores from 21st December 2012:

*3 stories in each book - only £5.99!*

☐ Swept Away! – Lucy Gordon, Daphne Clair & Joanna Neil

☐ Her Amazing Boss! – Barbara McMahon, Nikki Logan & Anna Cleary

In stores from 4th January 2013:

☐ The Saxon Brides – Tessa Radley

Available at WHSmith, Tesco, Asda, Eason, Amazon and Apple

*Just can't wait?*

*Visit us Online*

You can buy our books online a month before they hit the shops! **www.millsandboon.co.uk**

1212/05

# Special Offers

Every month we put together collections and longer reads written by your favourite authors.

Here are some of next month's highlights— and don't miss our fabulous discount online!

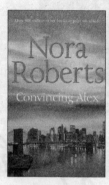

On sale 21st December    On sale 4th January    On sale 4th January

## Mills & Boon® Online

Discover more romance at
**www.millsandboon.co.uk**

 **FREE** online reads

 **Books** up to one
month before shops

 **Browse our books**
before you buy

*...and much more!*

**For exclusive competitions and instant updates:**

 Like us on **facebook.com/romancehq**

Follow us on **twitter.com/millsandboonuk**

Join us on **community.millsandboon.co.uk**

*Visit us Online* | Sign up for our FREE eNewsletter at
**www.millsandboon.co.uk**

# Have Your Say

*You've just finished your book.*
*So what did you think?*

We'd love to hear your thoughts on our
'Have your say' online panel
**www.millsandboon.co.uk/haveyoursay**

- Easy to use
- Short questionnaire
- Chance to win Mills & Boon® goodies

*Visit us Online*

Tell us what you thought of this book now at
**www.millsandboon.co.uk/haveyoursay**

YOUR_SAY